FROM THE
NANCY DREW FILES

THE CASE: A computer hacker is tampering with school records, destroying evidence, and extorting money from students at Brewster Academy.

CONTACT: The daughter of a local banker has been threatened with academic disgrace—or worse—if she doesn't participate in the scheme.

SUSPECTS: Victor Paredes—*Brewster's computer whiz brags that he could penetrate the confidential school files with the flick of a PC switch.*

Walter Friedbinder—*the new headmaster has a sterling academic record, which may not be as bright as it appears.*

Phyllis Hathaway—*the assistant headmaster, who helped design the school's advanced computer system, is bitter that Friedbinder was hired for the top job instead of her.*

COMPLICATIONS: Victor Paredes has fallen for his new tutor, Nancy Drew, and now she's fallen under suspicion—and under fire—in the computer conspiracy!

Books in The Nancy Drew Files® Series

Available from ARCHWAY Paperbacks

THE
NANCY DREW
FILES™

Case 62
EASY MARKS

CAROLYN KEENE

AN ARCHWAY PAPERBACK
Published by POCKET BOOKS
New York   London   Toronto   Sydney   Tokyo   Singapore

AN ARCHWAY PAPERBACK *Original*

An Archway Paperback published by
POCKET BOOKS, a division of Simon & Schuster Inc.
1230 Avenue of the Americas, New York, NY 10020

Copyright © 1991 Simon & Schuster Inc.
Produced by Mega-Books of New York, Inc.

ISBN: 0-671-73066-5

First Archway Paperback printing August 1991

10 9 8 7 6 5 4 3 2 1

NANCY DREW, AN ARCHWAY PAPERBACK and colophon
are registered trademarks of Simon & Schuster Inc.

THE NANCY DREW FILES is a trademark
of Simon & Schuster Inc.

Cover art by Tom Galasinski

Printed in the U.S.A.

IL 6+

Chapter

One

NANCY DREW STUDIED the heavyset, balding man seated behind his wide mahogany desk. Harrison Lane was president of People's Federal Bank, one of the largest banks in the River Heights area. As he spoke—his voice confident and self-important—Nancy knew one thing for certain. He was lying.

"As a trustee of Brewster Academy, I'm very concerned that this scandal not become public," he droned on. "That's why I've asked you here today. I've heard of your detective work, and I want you to find out who is running this transcript-changing racket and stop it before the school's reputation is damaged beyond repair."

Nancy's blue eyes focused on the man's wed-

1

ding ring, which he'd begun twisting. His hazel eyes also gave him away as not telling the whole truth. They were darting around his office, not focusing on any one thing.

As a successful amateur detective, Nancy had learned to trust her instincts about people. And Lane's body language—the darting eyes and fidgeting movements—was practically shouting to her that he was insincere. At the very least, he was withholding an important piece of information.

Nancy uncrossed her long legs and leaned forward in her chair. "I don't want to be rude, Mr. Lane," she broke in, "but I don't think you're being entirely straight with me. Is there something you're not telling me?"

Lane's eyes widened in surprise. This was obviously the last thing he'd expected to hear. "I'm afraid you'll have to be satisfied with the information I can give you, Ms. Drew," he sputtered.

Pulling her bag onto her shoulder, Nancy stood up and headed for the door. "I'm sorry, Mr. Lane. I just can't work that way. Without all the facts, I'd be wasting my time. Goodbye, and good luck with the case."

Nancy had already opened the door when he called, "Wait! You're right. I haven't been completely candid with you."

She closed the door and turned back to him. Now maybe she could find out what was really going on.

"The real reason I'm so worried about this is that—well, it involves my daughter Sally," Lane went on in a lowered voice. He stopped fiddling with his ring and gazed squarely at Nancy. "Yesterday I discovered that she paid one thousand dollars to have her marks from last year electronically altered on the school's computer. Our culprit is getting money from these kids.

"I was making a deposit to her college fund and I saw that a thousand dollars had been withdrawn," he explained. "When I went to use my bank card, I noticed that it wasn't in its usual spot in my wallet. Sally and my wife are the only ones who would have the opportunity to take the card, withdraw the money, and then return the card to my wallet. I confronted Sally, and she admitted she had used the money to pay someone to change her grades on the school's computer. Naturally, as her father, and as a trustee of Brewster, I'm alarmed."

"Of course," Nancy told him. "Do you know who she paid?"

"She swears she doesn't know," said Lane, shaking his head.

Nancy raised a skeptical eyebrow.

"I know it sounds unbelievable," he went on.

"It has something to do with an unsigned message on a computer—something like that. Maybe you'd better get the story from her."

"Maybe I should," Nancy agreed.

Nancy turned up the collar of her denim jacket as she went down the wide front steps of the bank, heading for her blue Mustang in the bank's parking lot. It was late September, and all around her the maples rustled in brilliant shades of red, orange, and yellow.

Soon Nancy was steering her car away from downtown River Heights. As she followed the directions Harrison Lane had given her, she noticed that the houses became larger, the lawns more perfectly kept. She pulled onto Evergreen Road and stopped in front of a huge, white clapboard house with a long, glassed-in porch on the left.

Nancy walked to the door and rang the bell. She half expected a maid to answer, but instead a tall blond girl wearing a black miniskirt pulled open the door. She had the same hazel eyes as Harrison Lane. "Hi. I'm Sally. And you must be Nancy Drew. Daddy called to say you were coming," the girl said in a high, breathy voice. "Come on in."

"Thanks," Nancy said, smiling politely. She followed Sally through an elegantly furnished living room and out onto the glassed-in porch. Well-tended tropical plants grew in pots all around them. "So what do you need to know?" Sally asked as they settled down on a flowered couch.

"Why don't you just tell me the whole story, from the beginning?" Nancy suggested.

Sally nodded. "I don't know if Daddy told you this, but I'm not exactly a brain in school. Daddy has this dream of sending me to Washburn University—that's where he and Mom went. Anyway, with my grades, there's no way I'll ever be accepted there. So, when I found this message in my E-mail, I couldn't say no."

"In your what?" Nancy asked, confused.

"E-mail," Sally repeated. "My computer mailbox. Brewster has this awesome new computer system. Everybody in school has their own E-mail box. We can send messages back and forth, and get school notices and home-work assignments—you name it. I can even access it from here, with my personal computer, but during the day I just use the terminals at school."

"I see," Nancy said. "So this message turned up in your computer mailbox offering to alter your grades for a thousand dollars," she sur-mised, remembering what Sally's father had told her.

Sally nodded. "That's right. It was last Tuesday, a week ago."

Nancy's eyebrows drew together in a slight frown as she said, "I don't get it. How did you know it wasn't a joke?"

"Because whoever sent it already knew everything there was to know about my transcript," Sally replied. "My grade-point average, term by term, ever since ninth grade. My PSAT scores. Even the marks I got in particular courses. How could he know that much, unless he had a way of breaking into the school records? And if he could do that, I figured he could probably change the records, too."

"Hmm. I'd like to see that message," said Nancy. "Is it still in your E-mail?"

"Are you crazy?" Sally scoffed, laughing bitterly. "And take the chance that someone might see it? I copied down what I needed to know, then I deleted the whole file."

Too bad, thought Nancy. Now there was no way to examine the message for clues Sally might have overlooked. "How did you pass on the money?" she asked aloud. "Was that in the message, too?"

"Sure. All I had to do was deposit it in the person's account. I used the quick-deposit box at Daddy's bank. Simple!"

Nancy sat up straighter. "What about your

copy of the deposit slip?" she asked. "You didn't throw that away, did you?"

"I don't think so," Sally said slowly. "It's probably still in my jacket pocket." She jumped up and ran out of the room, reappearing soon after with the pink carbon in her hands. "One thirty-four, dash fifty-two, seventy-two, nine," she read from the paper. "That's the account number."

As Sally spoke, Nancy pulled a small notebook from her bag, flipped it open to a fresh page, and copied down the number. Then she jotted down some of the information Sally had just given her. It was certainly a lucky break that the account was at Sally's father's bank. Harrison Lane could help her trace the owner of the account.

When Nancy looked up from her notebook, Sally was staring at her, a troubled look in her eyes. "You must think I'm a real creep, huh?" she said.

Nancy wasn't sure how to respond. "I'm sure you're sorry for what you did—" she began, but Sally cut her off.

"Come here," she said, pulling Nancy back through the living room and into a study. Black-and-white photographs hung on all the study walls. "Dad on the Washburn football team," Sally said, pointing to one of the pictures. "And here's Dad graduating from Washburn. Mom graduating from Washburn. Mom and Dad at the Washburn University Senior Formal. Ever since I was little, all I ever heard was, 'Someday when you go to Washburn . . .' I just couldn't let my parents down." Tears brimmed in Sally's large eyes.

"Hey," said Nancy sympathetically. "I'm not here to judge you. I'm here to figure this thing out."

Quickly Sally brushed away a tear. "I hope you find out who's doing this. I bet I'm not the only one who's been approached. If there's anything I can do to help, just tell me."

"Well, there *is* something," said Nancy. "You mentioned that you can get your E-mail from Brewster on your home computer. Would you show me how it works?"

Sally nodded. "Sure, come on. The computer's in my room."

Nancy followed Sally upstairs to her bedroom. A yellow floral spread and matching canopy adorned the bed in the middle of the room. Over by the window was a computer desk with a PC on top of it.

Nancy watched as Sally turned on her computer, plugged the telephone into the modem, dialed the Brewster Academy number, and finally logged onto the school's system. "There's another message in my box," Sally told her, stiffening.

"That's funny. I checked my E-mail when I left school today and there weren't any messages. This must have come in after three."

"See what it says," Nancy urged her.

Sally tapped a couple of keys and the screen cleared. Then lines of writing began to scroll upward from the bottom. Nancy leaned over Sally's shoulder to read them:

Your record has been corrected. Keep your mouth shut about this. What goes up can come down. And little girls who play with fire sometimes get burned.

Chapter

Two

"THAT'S A THREAT!" Sally cried, a small quiver in her high-pitched voice. "This person is turning out to be a major creep!"

"That's for sure," agreed Nancy, frowning. She did some quick mental arithmetic. If more students were involved, each paying a thousand dollars, then a lot of money was at stake. No wonder the grade changer was so nasty—he wanted to make sure no one threatened his operation.

"Would you print that out for me?" Nancy asked.

"Sure." Sally hit the Print Screen button on her keyboard. The printer began to chatter, and a moment later Sally tore off the page and handed it to Nancy.

"Hmm," Nancy said as she studied the paper. "What are these numbers across the top? I recognize today's date, but what are the rest?"

Sally glanced at the page. "That's the time of transmission. And see this—09.176? The 09 refers to the E-mail facility, and 176 is my box number. And that IW443 is the sender's password. The first two letters are usually initials. I don't know anyone with those initials, though."

Nancy made notes next to each number as Sally explained. "How could I find out which terminal this was sent from?" she asked.

"I'm not sure. I'll ask around and see if anyone knows," Sally volunteered.

"Good," Nancy said. "You were right that this message was sent after school hours. It says 4:09 here. Do you know which parts of the school stay open after three?"

Sally shook her head. "Not really. I'm not big on after-school activities. Some of the classrooms must be open, though," she said. "There are all sorts of clubs and meetings after three."

Still gazing at the paper, Nancy went to sit on the edge of Sally's bed to think. After a moment she looked back up at the blonde and said, "Okay, here's what we're going to do. First I'm going to try to trace the bank account number. If we're lucky, that information will lead us right to the grade-changer and the case will be wrapped up.

"If that doesn't work," she continued, "I'll have to go undercover at Brewster."

"Wow," said Sally in an admiring tone. "Sounds like a great plan."

"Let's just hope it works," Nancy told her. "In the meantime I need you to try to find out if there are other kids who've been contacted by this anonymous grade-hiker. Try not to be obvious about it, though. Whoever it is could be dangerous if he senses you're trying to find out his identity."

Sally nodded. "You can count on me."

Nancy smiled at her. "Good." She flipped her notebook shut and tucked it in her purse, then stood up. "That's about it, except for one last thing. Is there anyone you suspect?"

Sally ran a hand through her blond hair. "Well . . . there is one person, but—" she began hesitantly.

"But what?"

"But he's a real sweet guy," Sally replied. "The only reason I thought of him is that he's a computer whiz. His name's Victor Paredes. If anyone could break into that computer, it would be him. He's a senior."

Nancy nodded, making a mental note of the name. The two girls went downstairs just as Harrison Lane was coming in the front door. After greeting him, Nancy made arrangements with him to check out the account number. Then, after saying goodbye to Sally and her father, she left.

Twenty minutes later, as she pulled into her driveway, Nancy saw Hannah Gruen, the Drews' long-time housekeeper, rushing out the door. "What's the matter, Hannah?" Nancy called from her car.

"Nothing, dear," said Hannah, smiling warmly. "I'm spending the evening with a friend, that's all. Oh—here comes my taxi now." Hannah waved and headed down the driveway toward the cab that had pulled up. "Dinner's warming in the oven," Hannah called over her shoulder. "Eat it before it gets dried out."

"'Bye, Hannah," Nancy told her. "Have fun."

Going inside, Nancy saw that there was mail on the low table in the entrance hall. Most of it was for her father. But Nancy felt her heart skip a beat when she came to a letter with familiar handwriting. A letter from Ned!

A tingle ran through her as she took it up to her room to read it.

Ned Nickerson, Nancy's boyfriend, was away at Emerson College. This was the first letter she'd received from him since he'd returned to school from summer break. It wasn't a very long letter —just news about classes and his friends. But the part at the end about how much he missed her made Nancy resolve to visit him soon.

She settled back against the pillows on her bed to write him back. By the time she was done, her father had come home and it was time for dinner.

Over baked chicken with chestnut stuffing, Nancy told her father about her case. Carson Drew had a respected law practice in River Heights and was often a help to her.

"I'm not sure if other kids are involved, or if Sally was singled out. And what makes it especially tricky is that changing a grade in a computer file doesn't leave any trace," she concluded, spooning a second serving of stuffing onto her plate. "You can't examine a floppy disk for erasure marks or analyze how old the ink is, the way you can with something on paper."

Her father smiled. A distinguished-looking man in his forties, he had dark hair that was flecked with gray at the temples. "Don't I know it! A few years ago, people were talking about the 'paperless office' that computers were supposed to create. But I probably use more paper in my practice now than I did before we computerized. We print out every version of every document we draft, so that if any problems come up we can pull the file and put our finger on the exact bug. I'm surprised that Brewster Academy doesn't do something of the sort as well."

"Maybe they do," Nancy said. "But I don't know about it. I hope I don't wind up having to go over a ton of paperwork to check which grades have been changed," she added, sighing. "But if that's what it takes, I'll do it. I'd rather catch this hacker by checking the bank's information."

"Hacker," Carson Drew repeated. "What a funny word that is! I remember the first time I heard it. It was six or seven years ago. A high-school girl here in River Heights managed to figure out how to monkey with the billing on the telephone company's computer."

"Uh-oh, I think I see what's coming," Nancy guessed. "She had a boyfriend in Tokyo, right?"

Her father smiled. "Not exactly, but you aren't far from wrong. At summer camp she had gotten to be very close friends with her counselor, who was also from River Heights. But in September the counselor went off to college on the West Coast. The girl was having some emotional problems, I gather. She got into the habit of calling her former counselor two or three times a week and talking to her for an hour or more at a time."

"Sounds like a pretty expensive habit," Nancy remarked. She scooped up the last of the chicken with her fork and popped it into her mouth.

"Eventually it was," Carson replied. "But for several months, she managed to, ah, hack the telephone company computer and erase the calls from her parents' bills. Apparently she was very clever about it, too. The telephone company had quite a job catching up with her."

"And when they did?" Nancy asked.

Her father leaned back in his chair. "Her parents asked me to step in and deal with the telephone company. I talked them into settling for the amount they were owed on the calls, plus a detailed explanation from the girl of how she had broken into their system and altered the bills. They needed that even more than the money, you see. Otherwise, someone else might have come along and found the same weak point in their security. I understand their computer experts were very impressed by the girl's skills."

"So she didn't end up with a police record or anything like that?" Nancy said with a laugh. "She was lucky to have you for a lawyer!" She stood up and collected the plates from the table. "Hannah left fruit salad in the fridge. Want some?"

"I think I'll pass." Her father stacked the serving dishes and followed Nancy into the kitchen with them.

"Whatever happened to the girl?" Nancy

asked. "Did she go on to be a computer crook or a computer genius?"

"Genius, I think," her father answered, laughing. "I remember hearing that she started her own computer company right here in town."

Nancy paused with a plate in midair between the sink and the dishwasher. An idea had occurred to her. "You know, I might need to consult someone like her if I get in over my head in terms of computer know-how. What's the woman's name?"

"Can't tell you. Sorry, honey," replied her father as they stacked the dishwasher together. "That's privileged client-lawyer info."

"Dad!" Nancy moaned. "I can just go to the library and look it up in a newspaper."

Carson Drew grinned. "I was able to keep the story out of the papers. You could try, but it wouldn't do much good."

"You're a great lawyer, Dad," Nancy told him, laughing. "Too good!"

There was a teasing glint in his eyes as he said, "I am, aren't I?"

Nancy checked her watch as she approached the front door of People's Federal Bank—ten minutes to nine. The bank wasn't open yet, but Nancy saw through the heavy glass doors that

Harrison Lane had spotted her. Holding a large ring of keys, he opened the door from the inside and let her in.

"I have some information for you," Lane said in a low voice. Behind him, tellers and bank officials were getting ready to start the day. Some of them glanced at Nancy with mild curiosity, but returned to their business right away. "That account you asked about—it's in the name of I. Wynn."

"I. Wynn?" Nancy repeated, breaking into a laugh. "Get it? I Win—You Lose," she explained when she saw Lane's questioning look. "It's obviously a fake name, don't you think?"

Lane shook his head. "It's real. We checked it against the Social Security number the person gave."

Suddenly Nancy remembered the initials in Sally's message-sender's password: I.W.! "Can I speak with the bank official who opened the account?"

"Certainly." Lane ushered her over to one of the customer service desks, to the left of the long tellers' counter. A slender African-American woman in her thirties sat behind the desk. She smiled at Nancy as Harrison Lane introduced Nancy and explained what she wanted.

"Mrs. Tillman here opened the account. I'll let

her tell you the rest," said Lane, leaving them.

"Do you remember what I. Wynn looked like?" Nancy asked as she settled into the chair beside the desk.

"I certainly do. It was about ten days ago. She was a strange-looking little thing—"

"She?" Nancy interrupted.

Mrs. Tillman nodded. "Oh, yes. A dark-haired girl, about your age, maybe a little younger. Her skin was very pale and her hair was jet black. It looked dyed. Perhaps it was a wig."

"And you say she was small?" Nancy prompted.

"Yes, very petite, and nervous. But, you know, I figured she was just a kid. It's easy to be nervous in a big bank like this. Her information checked out—at first, anyway."

"What do you mean?"

Mrs. Tillman opened the desk's file drawer and flipped through the manila folders, pulling one out. Nancy could see the name I. Wynn written across the top. "Well, like this, for instance," Mrs. Tillman told her. "The previous bank reference she gave was for a savings and loan company in Texas. There is such a place, but it folded a few months ago."

After consulting the file again, Mrs. Tillman added, "She used her Brewster Academy student ID for signature verification."

Nancy nodded. "Do you have an address for I. Wynn?" she asked.

Mrs. Tillman punched some numbers into the computer terminal on her desk. "Fourteen twenty-one Sycamore," she read off the amber writing on the screen. "She opened the account with one hundred dollars. Ninety-five of it was withdrawn from a machine two days later. A few days after that a thousand dollars was deposited in cash. That was all withdrawn the day after that."

Nancy looked over Mrs. Tillman's shoulder to check the dates. The thousand dollars had been deposited the previous Tuesday—exactly when Sally said she'd made her deposit. There were three other similar deposits and withdrawals. It seemed as if Sally was not the only student the grade-changer had contacted.

"Were all these transactions done at a cash machine?" Nancy wanted to know.

"Two different cash machines—one located at Archer Avenue, the other at Ivy Avenue," Mrs. Tillman confirmed.

Both those branches were quite close to Brewster Avenue, where Brewster Academy was located, Nancy noted. "Thanks very much," she told Mrs. Tillman.

* * *

Ten minutes later Nancy turned her car onto Sycamore Street and began looking for number 1421. The neighborhood was run-down and deserted. Most of the houses were faded and sagging, as if they were simply waiting for a good excuse to collapse. Scraps of paper and debris littered the branches of the scraggly bushes lining the cracked sidewalk. There were only a few cars parked along the curb, but Nancy had a feeling that few, if any, people actually lived there.

She parked in front of the address Mrs. Tillman had given, then took a long look at the place. If the other houses on the block were neglected, this one looked flat-out abandoned. She was tempted to leave. Still, it *was* possible that the house held some clue to the identity of I. Wynn. She had to check it out. After taking a flashlight from the glove compartment, she got out of her car and walked up to the front door to ring the bell. No one answered.

Nancy's blue eyes focused on the door's heavy padlock. Maybe she'd find an easier way in around back. Before going, she grabbed the padlock and gave it a yank, to make sure that it was locked. To her surprise, the screws that held the hasp to the doorframe pulled right out of the rotted wood. The door swung slowly in, as if inviting her to enter.

Glancing over her shoulder to reassure herself that the street was deserted, Nancy took a quick step inside and pushed the door closed behind her. Then, fumbling with the switch on her flashlight, she started forward in the gloomy hallway.

Suddenly, with a loud crack, the floor under her feet gave way. Nancy let out a gasp as she felt herself falling through space!

Chapter
Three

INSTINCTIVELY, Nancy flung her arms out to the side. She let out a cry of pain as her hands and forearms slammed against the floorboards an instant later.

Her arms felt as if they were about to snap in two, and the splintery edges of the broken boards were digging painfully into them through the denim of her jacket. Her legs flailed uselessly below her, but the worst pain was in her shoulders. Nancy felt as if her weight were about to pull her arms from their sockets.

Gritting her teeth, she moved her legs carefully in every direction, groping for anything that might give her extra support, but there was nothing. If her arms slipped, she was bound to fall!

Okay, Drew, think. What if you let yourself down and hang full length by your arms, then drop to the basement below? She glanced nervously down into the murky darkness, imagining the jumble of sharp-edged pieces of machinery or nail-studded boards she might land on. No, the only sensible way out was upward.

Nancy tried using her arms to push herself up out of the hole, but after half a minute, she gave up. She didn't have enough leverage.

Looks as if I'll have to come up with plan B, she thought. Taking a deep breath, she let it out slowly and began to pull her right knee up toward the floor. Her aching arms felt as if they couldn't hold on much longer, but soon the toes on Nancy's right foot were touching the underside of the floorboards. With one last effort, she turned her foot to one side and pulled it toward her. It just barely cleared the far edge of the hole.

With a loud sigh of relief, Nancy extended her leg onto the floor and let it take some of the strain off her arms and shoulders. She rested that way for a few moments, then pulled her other leg up and rolled cautiously to one side. If there was one weak spot in the floorboards, there might be others.

Just above her head, a little daylight filtered in

through the dusty windows on either side of the front door. Nancy spotted her flashlight in a corner next to the door. She crawled over and retrieved it, then got carefully to her feet.

Beyond the yawning hole, the floor of the hall was thick with dust. A few pieces of old furniture kept the place from being completely empty. Nancy decided it was too dangerous to investigate the house. She'd have to find out about I. Wynn some other way.

Nancy squinted in the sunlight as she stepped out onto the rickety front porch. For the first time she noticed a small nameplate on the side of the doorframe opposite the bell. On it, the name *Ignatz Wynn* was written in small, shaky handwriting. Ignatz, huh? thought Nancy. That was hardly a girl's name. What was the story here?

She checked the mailbox that was nailed to the porch railing, and discovered a letter. It was from the People's Federal Bank, a bank statement from the look of it. It had been mailed only a few days earlier. Nancy put it back into the box. There was no need to read it; she'd already seen the transaction records of the account.

A movement in the house across the street caught her eye. Someone had parted the venetian blinds and was peering at her through the slats. In the next instant the person was gone.

Crossing the street, Nancy knocked on the

door of the house. No one answered, so she rapped harder. Slowly the door opened, just enough for Nancy to see a short, gray-haired woman in a worn housedress. "What?" the old woman snapped, gazing up at Nancy suspiciously.

"Excuse me, but I was wondering if you could tell me something about Mr. Wynn?" Nancy asked.

The woman's blue eyes narrowed. "Who wants to know?"

"I'm his niece," Nancy told her, mentally crossing her fingers.

The woman's face softened a bit, and she opened the front door wider. "Well, I hate to tell you this, honey, but your Uncle Iggy passed on. He just lay down one night and didn't wake up. It was a peaceful death, I guess."

Nancy's mouth fell open. "You mean, he's—dead?" *That* was news!

"Has anyone—I mean, anyone *else*—in his family been by?" she inquired after a moment.

"I didn't know he had any family," the woman told her. "I saw a woman come by one day. And a man the next. But I don't know who they were."

"Was the woman small?" Nancy asked. "That would be my cousin, Marie," she added quickly.

"This was someone else, then. She was kind of

fat. The man was on the tall side. I didn't get a good look at them. I mind my own business."

Nancy smiled to herself at this last remark. "Do you know what's going to happen to the house?" she asked.

The old woman snorted with laughter. "Sure I do. The government is taking over ownership. Iggy owed so much on back taxes that the state owns that house for sure. They were trying to blast him out of there for years, but he wouldn't go. Bless that stubborn old wino. He wasn't budging."

Nancy nodded.

"How long ago did—uh, Uncle Iggy die?" she asked.

After thinking a moment, the woman replied, "Two weeks ago. It was in the paper and all—just a single line crammed in with all the other unimportant dead folks' lines. Wasn't like they put his picture in or anything."

"That would explain it," murmured Nancy, thinking out loud.

"Explain what?" asked the woman, raising an eyebrow.

"Huh? Oh—nothing. Thank you very much for talking to me," Nancy said hastily. "I've got to be going."

The woman nodded and shut the door.

Nancy's mind was racing as she headed back to her car and slipped behind the wheel. The real I. Wynn didn't have anything to do with this scam, she realized. The culprit must have picked the name from the obituary column. It was perfect. Ignatz Wynn had no relatives, according to the woman across the street, and his house was empty. How had the culprit learned Wynn's Social Security number, though? That was a mystery for now.

Nancy drummed her fingers against the steering wheel as she pondered another question. Who were the man and woman? They could be in on the grade-changing scheme. Or they could be real estate people or officials from the state. The only thing she knew for sure was that neither of them was the petite girl who had opened the account as I. Wynn.

Starting up the engine, Nancy headed for home. The muscles in her arms were throbbing. She was sure she had some cuts and bruises that should be taken care of, too. She let out a sigh. This case wasn't going to be as easy to solve as she had hoped. Her culprit was very clever.

Time to go undercover, she decided. It looked as if she wasn't going to visit Ned at Emerson this weekend.

* * *

By four o'clock that afternoon, Nancy had taken a long, hot bath and rubbed ointment on the scratches on her arms. Still wrapped in her bathrobe, she picked up the phone on her bedside table and called Sally Lane at home. After saying hello, she asked, "Can you think of a believable reason for me to be hanging around the school, asking questions?"

After a brief pause, Sally's high-pitched voice came back over the line. "What about the new tutoring program? That could work. One of the tutors just dropped out, and they're looking for a replacement."

"That'd be perfect," said Nancy. "The kids who need tutoring are likely to be the same ones who'd want their grades changed. Do you think your father can get me into the program?"

"No problem. I'll talk to him tonight."

"Okay, call me back when you've spoken to him. Thanks for your help, Sally," Nancy told her. "And remember, don't talk about this with anyone."

"My lips are sealed," Sally assured her.

The next morning Nancy parked her Mustang in a visitor's slot in the Brewster Academy parking lot and got out. She smoothed her red, black, and white plaid skirt and straightened the collar of her white blouse, then retrieved her attaché case from the back seat. She wasn't sure what a tutor might wear, but she hoped she looked the part.

Brewster Academy was a two-story gray stone building, with slate-colored shingles and two massive chimneys on either side of the roof. It looked as if it had escaped from a print of a New England town. The school was beautiful, but that didn't change the fact that something very ugly was going on there.

One of the front doors opened, and Harrison Lane stepped out on the top step. He'd called her the night before to tell her that everything was set, and she'd brought him up to date on what she'd learned about I. Wynn. Now, spotting Nancy, he waved.

"There you are," he said as she walked up to him. "I've been waiting for you. I just had a word with Walter Friedbinder, our new headmaster. He's arranged everything."

Lane led her inside and down an echoing hallway to a door with Administration painted in gold on the frosted glass pane in its upper half. Inside was a small anteroom with a desk, a waiting area, and a couple of file cabinets. Through a doorway to one side, Nancy caught a glimpse of an elaborate-looking computer setup.

The woman at the desk raised her head and

said, "Please go right in, Mr. Lane. The headmaster is expecting you." Nancy noted her nameplate: Ms. Arletti.

Nancy had been expecting the headmaster to be a gray-haired man, perhaps with a trim mustache, but Walter Friedbinder was young and athletic looking, with short-cropped, reddish hair and intense blue eyes. He sprang up from his desk as they entered his office.

"Welcome to Brewster Academy, Ms. Drew," he said, offering his hand. "It's nice to have you with us."

"Thank you. And please call me Nancy," she said. "But maybe I'd better use the name Nancy Stevens around here. My name has been in the papers, and it might be best if no one knows I'm a detective."

"Of course," said Friedbinder, the smile fading from his face. "I hope you can help us. As I'm sure Harrison told you, this is my first year at Brewster. I accepted the position as headmaster because I admire Brewster's progressive educational system. The thought that the school might be ruined by a scandal makes me sick."

"I'll do what I can, Mr. Friedbinder," Nancy told him.

His smile returned. "Please call me Walter. We try to keep things informal around here."

He returned to his desk and picked up a file

folder. "I think you'll find whatever you need to know about the tutoring program in here," he said, handing it to Nancy. "Now, why don't we go next door and I'll introduce you to my assistant head, Phyllis Hathaway. She can take you down to the learning lab and get you settled in."

"I've got to be off," Lane told them, checking his watch.

Just as they left the headmaster's office, the door across the anteroom swung open. An attractive woman with dark hair pulled back in a French braid came out. She was about thirty years old and stylishly dressed in a black linen dress.

"Why, hello," Lane said. "It's been a long time. How are you?"

The woman gave him a surprised look, then smiled politely and said only, "Fine."

There was an awkward pause, then the banker said, "Well, goodbye, everyone," and left.

Walter urged Nancy across the room.

"Phyllis," he said, "this is Nancy Stevens, who is joining the tutorial program. I said you'd help get her squared away."

Nancy was glad that he'd remembered to use her alias. The fewer people who knew her true identity, the better.

"Hi, Nancy," the woman said. "I'm Phyllis Hathaway. Come into my office. I'll tell you a little about the program, then we can go down to check out the classroom where you'll be working. Have you done much of this sort of work before?"

Walter rushed to answer before Nancy could reply. "Nancy has excellent qualifications," he said, his voice harsh and impatient.

Phyllis's expression hardened. "I'm sure she does," she said in a clipped tone that clearly said, Mind your own business.

The headmaster's face reddened, but he didn't say anything more. Instead, after another awkward pause, he said, "Well, I'll leave you to it. Nancy, if you need anything, just let me know."

He disappeared into his office, and Nancy followed Phyllis into hers.

"I hope that didn't make you uncomfortable," the woman said apologetically after they were seated. "I've been at Brewster for a number of years, ever since I finished college out in California. But Mr. Friedbinder is new to the place. We're still learning to work with each other. I guess we're experiencing what's called a personality conflict."

"That happens, I suppose," Nancy murmured. She glanced around the office. Half of Phyllis's desk was taken up by the high-powered computer work station Nancy had glimpsed before. The bookcase behind Phyllis's chair seemed to be filled mostly with software manuals and books on computer programming.

"I've heard that the school has a very advanced computer system," Nancy remarked.

Phyllis beamed. "It certainly does—the most powerful of any high school in the state. We're very proud of it, and I'm especially proud because I was able to help design it. I'm sure you'll enjoy using the system, too, once you get the hang of it. Now, here's what we hope to accomplish with the new tutoring program. . . ."

As Phyllis spoke, Nancy realized that this case was going to be a challenge in more ways than one. In addition to unmasking the grade-changer, she was going to have to help students with their English, history, and social sciences. It sounded as if she was going to have to do a lot of homework herself!

"That's the plan in a nutshell," Phyllis concluded. "Now, why don't I give you a quick tour of the place?"

They were getting to their feet when the telephone rang. "Excuse me a moment," Phyllis said, reaching for the receiver.

Nancy stepped just outside Phyllis's office and waited. She was reading her notes and thinking over her approach to the investigation, when suddenly a phrase caught her attention.

"—too dangerous," Phyllis was telling the

caller. "Listen, Dana, I don't like him any more than you do. I'd love to see the conceited nitwit squirm, but I'm not sure I want to go any further with this. Yes . . . okay . . . maybe I *am* getting cold feet. But this could really hurt Brewster. I know . . . I know . . . the financial rewards are compelling. And I really do need the money. Let's just take it more slowly. This plan has the potential to end in disaster."

Chapter

Four

Nᴀɴᴄʏ ᴇᴅɢᴇᴅ ᴀᴡᴀʏ from the office door. She didn't want Phyllis to guess that she'd overheard any of her conversation.

It looked as if Nancy had another suspect. Phyllis had a motive—apparently she needed money, though Nancy didn't know why. And who was it she wanted to see squirm? Maybe Friedbinder, considering their strained relationship. A grade-changing scam would accomplish both things. Phyllis had the opportunity, too. Who would have better access to the school's computer than she?

There was only one catch. Phyllis was tall and elegant. Even in a disguise she wouldn't fit the description of the petite I. Wynn—or of the woman who'd been seen at I. Wynn's Sycamore Avenue address. But maybe that was where this Dana person came in.

"Sorry to keep you waiting," Phyllis said, coming out into the anteroom. "Now let me show you the learning lab."

Nancy and Phyllis took the stairs up to the second floor. Using a key, Phyllis unlocked the door and ushered Nancy into a small room with a teacher's desk, four student desks, and a folding table that held a telephone, computer terminal, and a small printer.

"Once in a while you may have to share this room with Mickey Randolph—he's the other tutor," Phyllis told Nancy. "His specialty is science and math. Unfortunately he's out of town for the next few days, though. A relative passed away."

"I'm sorry to hear that," Nancy said. In more ways than one, she added to herself. Randolph might have information that would help her.

"Yes, well, here is some background on each of your students," Phyllis continued, handing Nancy a manila folder she took from the teacher's desk. A schedule was taped to the top of the folder. "Let me give you a password so that you can use the computer, too."

Phyllis found a scrap of paper on a desk and wrote out a code.

"NS four forty-four," Nancy read when Phyllis handed her the paper. "What does that stand for?"

"Nancy Stevens, four hundred and forty-fourth password," replied Phyllis. "I'll load it into the system when I get back to my office. You'll be able to use it right away."

"Thanks," said Nancy as Phyllis left. She sat back down in a student's seat and thought. Sally Lane's message had been sent by IW443. Four forty-three was the last password entered into the system before Nancy's. That could mean that the grade-changer was someone who hadn't been at the school a long time. Or it might mean that the person had two passwords and had assigned himself or herself the I. Wynn password without the school's knowledge.

Yet Phyllis was aware of the number of the last assigned password. It must be in her records. Did she know who was using it? Was Phyllis, herself, using it?

Nancy's thoughts were interrupted when her first student arrived. He was a tall, awkward boy named Dan. "I don't see why we have to learn this stuff," Dan mumbled as Nancy opened the history book. "These geeks are dead, man."

Nancy could see that she had her work cut out for her.

Her next two students weren't much easier.

One was a girl with short red hair who needed help in English. Apparently, she had never bothered learning much spelling or grammar because she had Spellcheck and Grammarcheck on her home computer.

The other one was a girl who was failing history. She admitted to Nancy that she'd been caught writing her reports from miniseries on TV.

To each of the three students, Nancy asked the same leading question: "Wouldn't it be great if you could somehow change your old grades now that you're going to start doing better?" She asked it casually, with a smile, but her blue eyes scrutinized their faces for any trace of reaction. All three students agreed it would be wonderful, but Nancy didn't note any signs of guilt or nervousness.

Nancy glanced at the name of her fourth and final student before lunch. Victor Paredes. He was the guy Sally had named as the computer whiz, she recalled. Apparently he needed tutoring in English.

There was a tap on the open door. Nancy looked up and saw a guy standing there, grinning at her. He was very good-looking, tall and broad shouldered, with light brown, almost amber eyes, and dark brown hair.

"Hi, Teach," he said.

"Hi, Stu," she retorted. "Come on in."

Nancy looked over the sheet that detailed what he was supposed to work on, then got down to it. Victor was very quick, but it was obvious he had never bothered to spend more than two minutes on English grammar before. Now that he *was* bothering, he caught on easily.

"If any of my teachers were as pretty as you, maybe I would have paid more attention to this stuff," said Victor, gazing into Nancy's eyes.

"With lines like that I'm surprised you *didn't* get better grades." Nancy laughed, trying to deflect his flirtation.

At the end of one of the exercises, Nancy said, "Now, that wasn't hard, was it? It's too bad you can't go back and change last year's grade in English, now that you know how to do the work."

"Who says you can't?" Victor replied. "I could, if I wanted to."

Nancy started, then caught herself and said lightly, "Don't be ridiculous. Your grades are in your permanent file."

"Sure," said Victor, flashing her a dazzling grin. "And my permanent file is in the school computer, along with everybody else's."

Nancy fought to keep cool as she said, "Yes, I know. But you need special access codes to get to them, don't you? Otherwise, people would go around giving themselves whatever grades they wanted." She held her breath and waited to hear what he would say.

"There are ways to access those codes," Victor replied. "You'd have to be really smart to figure out how. But I could."

Nancy laughed. "You're not big on modesty, are you?"

Pink spots bloomed on Victor's cheeks. "Well, I don't want you thinking I'm dumb just because I bombed out in English," he told her. "I mean, being smart is sort of attractive, isn't it? And I want you to see my good side."

Again, Nancy tried to ignore his flirting, though she couldn't help being charmed by it a little, too. "You mean, you've figured out how to get into the locked files in the school computer?" she asked, trying to get the conversation back on track. "That's pretty amazing—if it's true."

"It's true, all right. Here, I'll prove it to you." He went over to the terminal and turned it on. "Let's see, what would light a fire under the honchos in the big office? Hey, I know!"

Nancy looked over his shoulder. His fingers were moving over the keyboard too quickly for her to follow, but on the screen she saw a demand for a password, then a directory of files. Apparently, Victor had somehow figured out how to get

41

past the security codes and break into the system.
The glowing cursor moved down the list of files
and stopped at one named HEADMAST.BIO.

Victor pressed a couple of keys. The screen
cleared, then filled up with Walter Friedbinder's
biography.

"Now, what should we do with him?" Victor
started typing again. Every now and then he gave
a little snort of amusement. Finally, he turned on
the printer, printed out the document, and
handed it to Nancy. She started reading.

Walter "Twinkletoes" Friedbinder, the new
headmaster of Brewster Academy, has one
of the largest collections of soda bottle caps
in the United States. He has earned degrees
in both Fahrenheit and Celsius and is a
founding member of River Heights's Flat
Earth Society. Dr. Friedbinder's research
into loose-leaf notebooks and the effects of
heating them in oil led to his famous discov-
ery of the fried-binder. . . .

Nancy laughed. "Victor, what have you done?"
she cried, trying unsuccessfully to scold him.
"This is terrible!"

He pretended to be hurt. "I thought it was
pretty good for the spur of the moment."

"But—but what if somebody sent this out,

without noticing the changes you made? Mr. Friedbinder would probably fire them!"

"No problem, Nancy." Turning to the keyboard, he entered a couple of commands. "There, I've restored the original version. I'll show you."

The printer began chattering again. When it stopped, Victor ripped off the page and handed it to Nancy. Scanning it quickly, she saw it was a straightforward, unaltered press release about Walter Friedbinder. She folded the two pages and put them in her shoulder bag.

"Very impressive. Can you really get into any file in the school computer?" she asked. "Even stuff like student records?"

"Just about," Victor boasted. "Figuring out the access codes is my hobby, the same way some guys customize cars, or play video games, or collect weird road signs."

Nancy shook her head. "Aren't you running a big risk, though? Changing people's grades is really asking for trouble."

"Wait a minute," he said, holding up a hand. "I never said I *was* changing grades, just that it wouldn't be that hard to do." He pointed toward the file folder on the desk. "If I was into changing grades, do you think I'd still have that D from last year's English class on my record?"

"That's a point," Nancy conceded. She was

about to ask Victor more questions, but the bell in the hallway started to ring.

"Wow! I can't believe it's lunchtime already." Victor turned off the terminal and gathered his books. At the door, he looked back. "Thanks for the English lesson," he said. "I actually understood some of it. Hey, could I interest you in getting a burger after school? With me, I mean. My treat."

Nancy thought quickly. Victor might well be behind the grade-changing scheme. Even if he wasn't, he seemed to know more about the computer system than anyone else around. "Okay."

"All right! I'll meet you in the parking lot around three." He flashed her a quick grin, and then he was gone.

Nancy found herself smiling. She couldn't help liking Victor, so far. In the past she'd learned the hard way that—well, even bad guys could have charming smiles.

All the students were probably down in the lunchroom by now. This would be a good time to check out some of the other classrooms.

Nancy shut the door to the learning lab behind her. Checking each classroom, she made her way down the second-floor hallway.

Half the school was on the first lunch shift, so

many of the classrooms were empty. Nancy was looking for rooms with computers, places where the mysterious E-mail message might have been sent from, and also a place where the hacker—if it turned out to be a student—could sit, undisturbed, to work his or her grade changes.

Suddenly she stopped. Alone in a classroom with three computers was a short, petite girl with shoulder-length dark hair held back with a headband. She sat working on one of the computers. When Nancy's shoe scuffed the floor, the girl jumped and turned around anxiously.

"Oh! You scared me!" she cried, seeing Nancy in the doorway. The girl wore an oversize purple sweatshirt over loose-fitting corduroy pants. Her surprised expression quickly changed to one of annoyance as she asked, "Are you looking for something?"

"Just checking out the building," Nancy told her. She introduced herself as Nancy Stevens and explained that she was the new tutor at Brewster. As Nancy spoke, the girl hit a few computer buttons and closed out the file she'd been working on. Was she finished, Nancy wondered, or was she hiding what she had been writing?

"Catching up on homework?" Nancy asked pleasantly.

"Not quite," the girl said curtly. "My name's

Randi Peters. I'm the editor of the *Academician.*" She was clearly impressed with her title. "I'm working on an article for the paper. Hey, how about being interviewed?"

Nancy blinked. Had her cover been blown already? "Interview me?" she said cautiously. "About what?"

"About the tutoring program, of course," Randi said. "I haven't done a story on it yet. I think it's a natural, don't you?"

"Sure," Nancy agreed quickly. It was perfect —only Nancy hoped *she* would be the one getting useful information. "But I don't have my schedule on me. I don't know when I'll be free. I'll have to call you."

Randi smiled. "Okay. See you soon, then."

Nancy said goodbye and returned to the learning lab for her afternoon tutorials. After her last student, she met Victor in the parking lot and followed his battered old green sedan to the Roost, a hangout a few blocks from Brewster Academy.

The place was just beginning to fill up. Nancy nodded to Sally Lane, who was sitting with friends in a nearby booth. With a quick tilt of her chin, Sally quietly acknowledged the greeting. Nancy looked around, admiring the dozens of high-school pennants hanging from the ceiling and the motorcycle fixed high on the back wall.

"There's a table over there," Victor said, pointing to the far side of the room.

"Great," said Nancy. "I'll just wash my hands and be right back."

As Nancy passed Sally's booth, one of the girls sitting with her—she had short, wavy blond hair and pale blue eyes—looked up. Nancy was surprised when she saw the expression of hatred on the girl's face. She tried to think if she had crossed paths with the girl somewhere, but nothing came to her.

Nancy was drying her hands when the bathroom door flew open. Startled, Nancy glanced over her shoulder. The girl from Sally's booth was standing with her back against the door and her hands in the pockets of her leather motorcycle jacket. Her expression was even more hostile than before. There was no mistaking it now—Nancy was definitely the target of her anger.

The girl was short and delicate, but the fury on her face made Nancy cautious. She knew that rage often made people stronger than they seemed.

"I know who you are and what you're up to," the girl snarled.

Who was this girl? What *did* she know? Right now the most important thing was to get away from her. "If you'll please move, I'd like to leave," said Nancy, advancing toward the door.

With shocking strength, the girl pushed Nancy back. "You're not going anywhere," she said in a voice full of menace. "Not until I'm through with you."

Chapter

Five

Nancy staggered back, almost losing her footing. This girl was out of control. Nancy would have to deal with her carefully.

"I'm telling you, you're mistaken," Nancy said. "I don't know you."

"Maybe not," the girl countered. "But I'm going to make sure you remember me for a long time."

The girl pulled her right hand back, as if to rake her nails across Nancy's face. As her arm started to move, Nancy reached up and caught her wrist. Her thumb pressed on a spot where the nerves that control the hand run close to the surface. The girl turned pale, and her hand opened.

"Let me go," she muttered through clenched teeth.

"Kim!" a high-pitched voice called. "What's going on in there?"

Nancy took a quick step to the left and put her back to the wall, ready to take on two attackers if she had to. But the newcomer was Sally, her hazel eyes filled with concern.

"Nothing," Nancy's opponent said, almost spitting out the word. A moment later she stormed out of the rest room.

"Who was that, and what is her problem?" Nancy asked Sally.

"Her name's Kim Forster," Sally replied. "When she saw you walk in with Victor, it kind of lit her fuse, if you know what I mean."

"You mean, she and Victor—" Nancy leaned back against the wall. "I thought maybe she found out I was investigating this case and she was involved somehow."

"I doubt it," said Sally. "She's got this intense thing for Victor. They dated for a while. Kim didn't seem that upset when it ended, but for the past couple of weeks all she can talk about is what a rat he is."

"That's odd," Nancy remarked. "I wonder what set her off?" With a shake of her head, she added, "Well, I've got other things to worry about. Have you discovered if any other kids have been approached by the grade-changer?"

"No luck so far. How about you?"

"Nothing yet," Nancy told her. "Listen, I'd better get back to Victor. He's probably wondering what happened to me."

"And I'd better get back to Kim," Sally replied. "Now that she's cooled off a little, I'd better make sure she stays that way."

As Nancy walked back to her table she could almost feel Kim's glare boring into her back. If that was the way Kim was after cooling off, it was a good thing that she hadn't stayed heated up!

Victor looked up as Nancy sat down. "You were gone so long that I went ahead and ordered for you. A cheeseburger and french fries—okay?"

"Fine. I just ran into a friend of yours." Nancy made a slight motion of her head in the direction of Sally and Kim's booth.

Victor glanced across the room, then shifted uneasily. "Oh. Did you have any, uh, problems?"

"Sort of. Kim seems to be pretty hot-tempered and impulsive."

"You could say that," he replied with an empty little laugh. "Did she try to show you her deed? The one that says she owns me?"

"No," Nancy said, chuckling.

"Good. It's a forgery, anyway." He paused and studied the top of the table. "We had a few dates, that's all. No big deal. And we stopped dating, because it wasn't working for either of us. We were both okay with that—I thought. But now she looks at me like I'm a worm she's planning to dissect for her biology project."

Nancy leaned back to let the waiter set their food on the table. She wanted to get off the topic of Kim and back to investigating the case. "How long have you been interested in computers?"

"Since I was fourteen," he said. "I was in a car accident. I got banged up pretty bad—missed a whole year of school. I should have graduated last year, but I had to make up the year I lost. Anyway, while I was laid up, I started hacking around with my dad's home PC. I couldn't do much else that year." Victor leaned back in his chair and smiled. "And *that* is how I became the computer genius you see before you today."

"I bet I can guess what you're going to study in college," said Nancy, taking a bite of her burger.

His smile disappeared, and he became serious. "The big question isn't what, it's where. The places that have really good Information Sciences programs cost a fortune. I don't have that kind of money. I'm at Brewster on a full scholarship. So either I get a college scholarship or I settle for a second- or third-rate school. That's where you come in."

"It is?" Nancy asked cautiously.

"For sure. You're going to help me raise my grades. I'm counting on it." He gave her another of his charming grins.

Nancy couldn't help smiling back, but as she did, she studied Victor's face. He seemed to be open and uncomplicated, but could she really tell? Did his remark have a double meaning, or was he simply talking about the tutoring program?

"How about a movie tonight?" Victor asked boldly as he wolfed down the last of the fries.

Time to tell him about Ned, said Nancy to herself. She told Victor all about her relationship with her boyfriend. To her surprise, Victor began searching for something under the table, then the chair. "What are you looking for?" she asked.

"Ned," he said with a smile.

"Well, he's sure not here." Nancy laughed.

"Exactly," said Victor, gazing meaningfully into her eyes. "I am. So let's forget about Ned."

"I can't," said Nancy. "Anyway, I'm your tutor—I don't think I can go out with students."

"It's not like you're a real teacher. Come on, why not?" Victor replied.

Nancy felt herself melt a little in the warmth of

his gaze, but all she said was "I have a couple of errands to run. Let's get the check."

"I should get home, too," said Victor. "My computer must be starting to wonder what happened to me." He signaled the waiter and paid for their burgers, and then they left.

As she drove home, Nancy reviewed the case. Even though she liked him, Victor Paredes definitely had to be a suspect. He had bragged to her that he could do whatever he wanted with the computer system. He hadn't made a secret of his poor grades in English or about his need for money to go to college. What if he had first cracked the school records access code while trying to change his own transcript, then realized that he had a very profitable product to sell? He was no dope—he might have decided to leave his own grades unchanged for the time being, just in case suspicion fell on him. Hadn't he been awfully quick to bring up just that point?

Nancy laughed. That was like saying that because a criminal might try to look innocent, anyone who looked innocent must be guilty!

Pushing Victor out of her thoughts for the moment, Nancy started to think about Kim. Had her attack on Nancy really been caused by jealousy? Or was she somehow connected to the case? But Nancy didn't see how Kim would know that she was a detective, or that there was a grade-changing scheme.

And what about Randi, the newspaper reporter? Was she as straight as she seemed? She obviously knew how to use the computer very well, and she had seemed anxious to clear her computer screen when Nancy showed up. In addition, she was petite and a brunette, just as Mrs. Tillman had described I. Wynn. So far, she was the only one who fit that description.

And, of course, there was Phyllis Hathaway. She was still Nancy's number-one suspect. Nancy resolved to find out more about her and her mysterious friend Dana the next day.

The next morning Nancy had a break after her third student. It wasn't long enough to do any investigating, but it did give her time to go to the faculty lounge and fix herself a cup of tea. As she was carrying it back to the learning lab, she ran into Victor. He was standing in the hall talking to a heavyset young woman with curly dark hair and green eyes. She was wearing a navy blue business suit and had a still-damp raincoat draped over her arm. It had poured all morning.

"Hey, Nancy," Victor called. "Come here, I want you to meet someone." When Nancy joined them, he continued, "You were asking questions about the school computer system? Here's someone who knows it inside out. Meet Ms. MacCauley, president of PointTech Computers and queen of the River Heights hackers."

"Victor!" the woman said in mock outrage. "I've told you before, you don't call people hackers these days. It's like—oh, I don't know what, but don't do it."

Victor saluted. "Yes, ma'am!" Then he turned back to Nancy. "Ms. MacCauley heads up PointTech, the company that designed the system here at Brewster. Whenever it goes down, she's the one who catches the flak and puts it back on line."

"Does the system go down often?" asked Nancy.

"No," Ms. MacCauley answered.

"Yes," said Victor at the same moment.

"Let's put it this way," Ms. MacCauley said, smiling. "It's a complex system that's had a lot of different demands put on it. It's designed to handle them, but sometimes the pressure makes it a little ornery. That's when I step in, to give it lots of strokes and a few well-placed strategic kicks."

Nancy returned the woman's smile. "I can easily imagine kicking a computer," said Nancy. "But how do you go about stroking it?" Maybe this was her chance to learn something helpful about the computer system at Brewster. "Do you have a few minutes to show me a little more about the system?"

Ms. MacCauley glanced at her wristwatch, then said, "I guess I do."

"There's a terminal in the learning lab, where I'm working," Nancy added.

Victor gave a snort and said, "Thanks to Ms. MacCauley, there's a terminal in practically every space in this school, except the broom closet!"

The woman turned to him and said with a straight face, "What happened to that one? Did someone steal it?" Then, laughing, they all went up to the learning lab.

A few moments later Nancy found herself seated at the terminal with an expert leaning over each of her shoulders. She turned on the power, typed in her password at the log-on prompt, and hit the Enter button.

A list of menus appeared on the screen. "Is there anything in particular you'd like to know how to do?" Ms. MacCauley asked her.

Nancy hesitated a moment. She had to be careful what she asked. If Victor was the grade-changer, she didn't want him to suspect she was on his trail.

"I was wondering," she said lightly, "if someone sent you a message, would there be any way of finding out what terminal it came from?"

"You could," Ms. MacCauley replied with a nod. "If you refuse the message, the computer will tell you that it's returning the message to its place of origin. It will say: 'Returning refused message to terminal twelve,' or whatever terminal it is."

"And how could you find out where terminal twelve is located?" asked Nancy.

"You couldn't," Ms. MacCauley replied. "You'd have to have access to a set of computer files that the regular student user couldn't get to."

She'd have to ask Walter to look at the file, thought Nancy. "Why can't students have that information?" she asked Ms. MacCauley. "Is it for security reasons?"

"Not really. We simply didn't want to overload the active systems with files students don't need. By storing this information in a separate reference directory, we freed up some space for active use. No one but authorized personnel can get into that file."

"Authorized personnel and me," Victor piped up.

Ms. MacCauley shot him an exasperated look. "Victor," she said, covering her ears, "I'm not hearing this. Don't tell me these things."

Disregarding the playful warning, Victor leaned in closer to Nancy—closer than he had to. "Watch this," he said as his fingers flew across the keyboard. "Ta da!" he crowed finally.

There it was! A complete listing of all the terminals in the school next to their code reference numbers. Nancy's heart skipped a beat. Maybe she could just get a copy of the list now without bothering the headmaster. But she couldn't ask for it without making Victor suspicious.

"Oh, no!" Nancy exclaimed suddenly, glancing at her watch. "A student's due to arrive any minute, and I'm not prepared yet!"

Nancy jumped up from her seat and pretended to twist her ankle. She pitched forward, bringing her hand down on the keyboard—making sure to hit only one button: Print Screen.

Noisily, the printer sprang into action. "Oh, my gosh!" she cried, feigning surprise.

"Are you okay?" asked Victor.

"It's just my ankle," she moaned. "I hope it doesn't swell up."

"I'm going to get a cold, wet towel," Ms. MacCauley volunteered. "That might keep it from swelling."

"Let's take a look at that," said Victor as Ms. MacCauley left the room. He knelt down in front of her and propped her foot up on his leg.

Slipping off her loafer, he gently rotated the ankle. "Does that hurt?" he asked, his amber eyes meeting hers.

They were startled by a strangled cry from the doorway. Nancy looked over and saw Kim standing there, her face crimson with anger.

"You'll be sorry," she cried. "You two will wish you were never born when I'm through with you!"

Chapter

Six

KIM TURNED AND FLED down the hall.

"I'd better try to talk to her," Victor said, dashing out of the room.

Nancy hit the Advance button on the printer, and the paper moved up enough so that she could tear off the three sheets of the printout and slip them into her bag.

"What was that about?" a voice spoke up behind her.

Nancy whirled around to find Ms. MacCauley standing in the doorway. For a moment she thought the woman had been talking about the printout. Then Nancy realized she was watching Kim and Victor.

"Just some kind of misunderstanding," said Nancy.

Ms. MacCauley turned her attention back to Nancy. "How's your ankle?" she asked, offering her a few cool, wet paper towels.

"Huh—oh, it'll be okay." Nancy took the towel and pressed it to her ankle. "Do you know what else? I feel so stupid. My student isn't even due to arrive for another half-hour. I was mistaken. I'm not used to my schedule yet."

"Terrific," said Ms. MacCauley, settling herself at the terminal. "We can continue while Victor sorts out his love life." With nimble fingers, she closed out the directory of computer terminals. She chuckled and shook her head as she worked. "That Victor! He'd better watch his step or he'll land in big trouble someday. Once you know how to break into a system it's very tempting to make mischief. Believe me, I know."

There was something in the way she said "I know" that jolted Nancy's memory. Nancy gave Ms. MacCauley a probing look. She was obviously in her early twenties, only a few years older than Nancy. Nancy tried to remember what her father had told her about the girl who had gotten in trouble for using her computer to alter her parents' telephone bills. Ms. MacCauley seemed to be about the right age. She had her own computer company in River Heights, too. And the remark she'd just made indicated that she had gotten into computer-related trouble. Nancy would be willing to bet that Ms. MacCauley was the girl her father had defended!

Trying to remain calm, Nancy said, "I suppose a person could tamper with all sorts of things, like bank records, government files—even telephone bills."

Ms. MacCauley looked so sharply at Nancy that Nancy knew her hunch was right.

"Well, uh, let me show you how the E-mail works," Ms. MacCauley said, her attention on the computer once again. "See these menus on the screen?" Nancy nodded, and Ms. MacCauley went on, "You see the word MAIL? That allows you to send and receive electronic mail. Do you have a mailbox yet?"

"Phyllis Hathaway gave me a password," Nancy replied. "But I don't know if I have an E-mail box."

"That's easily fixed," said Ms. MacCauley. She tapped in some commands. "There. From now on, whenever you log onto the system, it will tell you if there's any E-mail in your box. I've just sent you today's student mailings. Try it. Log off, then log back on."

Obediently, Nancy exited from the system,

then reentered and typed in her password. When she hit Return, a blinking message flashed on the screen: You have three E-mail messages. Do you want to read them now? Y/N.

Nancy pressed Y. A school calendar appeared on the screen, followed by a list of weekly club meetings and an announcement of tryouts for the next Drama Society play.

Ms. MacCauley then showed Nancy how to send a message and how to refuse one.

Nancy kept her eyes on Ms. MacCauley's face as she said, "This system is really impressive. When I met Phyllis yesterday, I got the impression that she had designed it. But didn't Victor just say that you had?"

Ms. MacCauley stiffened. "Ms. Hathaway and I have both worked on it," she said in a tight voice. "She has a solid background in computers and a thorough understanding of the school's needs."

Why was she suddenly so cool? Nancy wondered. Had Nancy hit on something when she mentioned Ms. Hathaway?

"Well, however it happened," Nancy said lightly, "the computer system seems to be a big plus at Brewster. You should be proud of yourselves."

"We are," Ms. MacCauley replied. "Too bad

the trustees didn't feel that way when they chose the new head for the school. Phyllis would have been the perfect choice." Abruptly, she got to her feet, saying, "I have to get back to my office."

"I'll walk you outside," Nancy volunteered. She stretched a little as she got to her feet. "I could use some exercise." Besides, there was more she wanted to learn from Ms. MacCauley.

"I have one more question," said Nancy, grabbing her raincoat. "Could I read a message and still find out where it was sent from?"

"This is one of the few systems on which you can," Ms. MacCauley said proudly as they went downstairs to exit. "If you save the message after reading it and *then* refuse it, you'll see the terminal code come up as it's returned to its origin."

The sun was beginning to peek out through the heavy gray cloud cover. But the parking lot was still awash, and Nancy and Ms. MacCauley had to sidestep large puddles in the parking lot.

Ms. MacCauley stopped next to a blue compact car that was several years old. "Nice to meet you, Nancy," she said, offering her hand. "Good luck with the tutoring."

"Thanks," Nancy replied.

Ms. MacCauley got behind the wheel and drove off, giving Nancy a quick wave. Nancy waved back, then turned to go inside. The head-master was standing a dozen feet away, watching her, his hands jammed into the pockets of his raincoat.

"Hi, Mr. Friedbinder," Nancy said as she walked up to him. "Walter, I mean."

"Hello, Nancy," he replied. "I just went to check on my car windows. Kind of late now that the rain has stopped, I guess. Oh, by the way, how's your work going?"

Nancy glanced around to be sure they couldn't be overheard, then said, "I'm beginning to get a few leads. But I should warn you—I'm pretty sure this is going to turn out to be bigger than just one incident."

"That's bad," said Walter, shaking his head slowly. "I hope we can control the damage. By the way, I'd be careful about getting too friendly with Dana MacCauley."

Nancy blinked. *Dana* MacCauley? She must be the Dana that Phyllis Hathaway had been talking to on the telephone the day before!

"Why do you say that?" Nancy asked.

He hesitated before answering, "In my opin-ion, MacCauley took Brewster Academy to the cleaners. She talked the school into buying a system that's much more complicated and ex-pensive than was needed. I wasn't here when it was bought and installed. If I had been, I would have made a real stink. I could have designed a better one in my sleep!"

"Are you suggesting that she's a crook?" Nancy asked.

"I didn't say that," Walter said quickly. "There's nothing illegal about selling someone something he doesn't need. But it's not very principled, either. I may as well tell you that I'm interviewing other people who can keep the computer system going. As soon as I've found someone, Dana MacCauley is going to be out in the cold."

Nancy frowned. "Do you think she has any idea of the way you feel?"

"I'm sure she does," he said. "I haven't made any secret of my dissatisfaction."

As she and the headmaster moved along the walk to the door, Nancy's thoughts raced. Dana must know more about the computer system than anyone. If she knew that her company was about to run into serious financial trouble, she might be frantic to accumulate extra cash.

Could she and Phyllis have dreamt up the grade-changing racket together? That would explain Dana's touchiness concerning Phyllis's involvement in setting up the computer system. Maybe their motive wasn't just the money. Maybe they hoped to involve Walter Friedbinder in a scandal, a scandal that would cost him his job. Both women had made it clear that they thought Phyllis should have been chosen as the new head. Did they also think she might be chosen as Walter's replacement, if he were out of the way?

"I'll leave you now, Nancy," said Walter, breaking into her thoughts. "Good luck with your work."

The headmaster continued down the hall toward his office, and Nancy went up to the second floor. Victor was waiting outside the learning lab, leaning against the wall with his hands in his pockets.

"Hi, Teach," he said, straightening up. He flashed his handsome smile.

Nancy rolled her eyes. "Were you able to calm Kim down?" she asked. "I'm beginning to think it's not safe to be seen with you."

"Forgive me, O exalted one!" he wailed. "I have offended you!"

Nancy couldn't help but laugh. "I do hope you explained what really happened."

"Oh, I explained," he told Nancy. "I don't think she heard a word I said, though. She just kept saying she was going to get even with us for everything."

Nancy was puzzled. Kim had seen her and Victor together only twice, for a total of about twenty minutes. Why was she so upset? "Everything? Like what?" Nancy asked.

"Beats me," Victor said with a shrug. "All I can say is, Kim is getting to be a very big drag. I wouldn't be surprised if she—"

The bell down the hall started to ring and drowned out the rest of his sentence. When it stopped, he said, "I'd better run. I am enrolled in school here, and I don't want to get kicked out. I'll look for you after school. Maybe we can go back to the Roost for a hot fudge sundae."

He walked away quickly, leaving Nancy staring thoughtfully after him. Was Victor getting a little too fond of her? Keeping an eye on him because he was one of her chief suspects was one thing, but playing with his emotions was something else. She *had* told him about Ned, but he didn't seem to care.

She would just have to watch her step with Victor. For a start, she was *not* going to be around after school for him to find. And the next time they met, she was going to be sure to find a way to work Ned's name into the conversation.

Nancy unlocked the learning lab, turned on the lights, and checked her watch. She still had three or four minutes before her next student. The computer terminal caught her eye, and she walked over to it, switched it on, and typed in her password. She had a message in her mailbox.

She called it to the screen, expecting an announcement of an upcoming Glee Club concert or a raffle to raise money for the volleyball team.

Instead, these words appeared: Snoops and spies get hurt, Nancy Drew. Go home before you get erased—for good.

Chapter

Seven

H<small>ER HEART POUNDING,</small> Nancy stared at the monitor screen. She wasn't imagining the message. It was still there. She leaned closer to study the transmission information at the top of the E-mail message. She knew that password—IW443!

And the time of transmission was— Startled, Nancy rechecked her watch. The message had been entered only minutes before. Recalling what Dana MacCauley had shown her, she saved the message, then refused it. Returning message to terminal 29, came the message on the screen.

In a flash Nancy took her printout from her bag. "Twenty-nine, twenty-nine," she muttered, running her finger down the list. "There it is!" The message had been sent from the terminal in the newspaper office. If she hurried, she might catch its sender.

At the door, she bumped into the girl who was arriving for her tutoring session. "Sorry," Nancy gasped. "Have a seat, I'll be right back!"

As she dashed down the corridor, everyone turned to stare at her. When she reached the *Academician* office, she found it locked and the frosted glass in the upper half of the door dark. Nancy shook the knob a few times.

"Are you looking for someone?" a voice asked.

Startled, Nancy whirled around to find Randi, the girl she had met the day before.

"Oh, yes," Nancy replied, thinking fast. "A student I'm supposed to tutor asked me to meet her in this room, and she hasn't shown up. Has anyone been here that you know of?"

"She wanted to meet you at the *Academician* office?" Randi repeated in a dubious tone. She unlocked the office door, flipped on the lights, and motioned Nancy in.

Nancy quickly took in the whole office. Crowded as it was with furniture, there wouldn't be anyplace for anyone to hide, she saw at once.

"I was in the office myself until ten minutes ago, and there wasn't anyone else here," Randi told her. "Are you sure you're not mistaken?"

Before Nancy could answer, Randi continued, "I know I've seen you before. You look so familiar. I know! I've seen your picture in the newspaper! Who are you? What are you doing here?"

Nancy felt her heart sink. She couldn't let her cover be broken—not now! "As I told you yesterday, I just started working in the tutoring program," she replied in a rush. "You might have seen my picture because I just won the River Heights art contest. Second prize."

"Maybe that was it," said Randi suspiciously. Then she shrugged. "Hey, why don't I interview you about the program now?"

As the girl reached for a pad and pencil, Nancy hastily said, "I'm not the one you want. I just started, I'm only temporary, and I don't know that much about it. Why don't you interview Ms. Hathaway or Mr. Friedbinder?"

Randi wrinkled her nose. "They're not actually working in the tutoring program; you are. I want to get a ground-level view of it."

"Then the people you ought to talk to—" Suddenly Nancy clapped her hand over her mouth. "Uh-oh, I just remembered, I left someone in the learning lab waiting for a tutoring session!"

Randi was staring at her as if she *had* lost her mind. Too late Nancy remembered that she'd just told Randi she was meeting a student there at the newspaper office. Luckily, all Randi said was, "Okay, but I still want that interview with you, Nancy Drew."

Shooting Randi an apologetic smile, Nancy hurried back down the hall.

Suddenly she gasped and stopped short so quickly a guy with a big stack of books under one arm, obviously late to class, walked straight into her. She helped him pick up his books, thinking about what Randi had said.

Randi had called her Nancy Drew—not Nancy Stevens. Somehow she'd uncovered Nancy's real identity. Randi wasn't the only one who had addressed her by her full name in the last hour, either. The author of that threatening message had done the same. Walter Friedbinder and Sally Lane were supposed to be the only ones who knew her real name, but if Randi knew, others might, too.

Nancy groaned. It was going to be even more difficult to track down the grade-changer now.

When she reached the learning lab, it was empty. The girl must have gotten impatient and left. Nancy turned on the computer and checked her E-mail. No new messages had come in for her.

"Hey, there," a familiar voice called from the doorway. "Sharpening your computer skills?"

Nancy turned to see Victor stroll into the room. "Something like that," Nancy answered him. "Listen, will you excuse me? I have to make a phone call."

Victor's face fell, but all he said was, "Sure. I just sneaked out of class to say hi. Catch you later."

Once he was gone, Nancy dialed the number of the People's Federal Bank. Harrison Lane came on the line at once.

"Nancy!" he said. "I was just going to call you. Eight hundred dollars that was deposited yesterday in I. Wynn's account was withdrawn from the Archer Avenue bank machine at eight-thirty this morning."

"Before school hours," Nancy noted. "Mr. Lane, is there any way you can program the bank's computer to alert you the next time somebody tries to make a withdrawal or deposit from that account?"

"That shouldn't be too hard," the banker said. "We'll just put a flag on the account number, with instructions to telephone me when it pops up. We can also tell the computer to take extra time to process any transaction for that account. That way, we'll have enough time to react to the alarm."

"Great," said Nancy. "Can you set it up right away? I don't want our crook to decide to pull out of this scheme before we have a chance to catch whoever it is."

"Neither do I," Lane agreed. "I'll flag that account the moment we get off the phone."

"Thanks." As she hung up, Nancy's stomach growled, reminding her that it was almost time for lunch.

Nancy's heart sank when she entered the anteroom separating Phyllis Hathaway's and Walter's offices. She'd rushed there after grabbing a quick bowl of soup in the cafeteria, hoping to find Phyllis out to lunch, but apparently the assistant head was eating in that day and was hunched over some papers on her desk. As Nancy watched, Phyllis took a bite from a sandwich, then turned her attention back to her work.

Stepping out of Phyllis's sight, Nancy leaned against Ms. Arletti's empty desk to think. She had to get the woman out of there so she could search her office.

As she thought, Nancy became aware of Walter Friedbinder's voice from inside his office. "Sure, Mel. We'll talk about it at the staff meeting before the board arrives. . . . Fine. See you then."

Nancy stood up straight as an idea came to her. A second later she sneaked inside Walter's office and closed the door behind her.

"What—?" he began when he saw her, but she silenced him by putting a finger to her lips. His gaze was openly dubious, but he waited while Nancy explained in a whisper what she wanted to do.

"So I call Phyllis in here for an emergency meeting, giving you a chance to search her office?" Walter's intense blue eyes took on a pleased glint. "I'm sure I can handle that."

"Great," said Nancy, smiling at him. "I'll wait out in the hallway until I hear her go into your office. If you can keep her here for ten minutes, that ought to be long enough."

A few minutes later Nancy slipped into the assistant head's office and stood with her back to the closed door. In a flash she scanned the room—two filing cabinets, desk, the computer station, a bookcase, and a coatrack with a raincoat on it. She decided to start with Phyllis's desk, which was against the wall to the left of the door.

Sitting in the desk chair, Nancy glanced through the papers on the desktop, next to the half-eaten tunafish sandwich. They were nothing but notes on an upcoming parents' visiting day. Next she pulled open the top desk drawer and sifted through a jumble of paper clips, rubber bands, and pens.

Nancy saw nothing that would link Phyllis to I. Wynn or the scam. Nor did she find any clues as to what "plan" Phyllis had meant during her phone conversation with Dana that Nancy had overheard.

A few times Nancy paused to listen but heard only the distant hum of Phyllis and Walter talking in the other office.

Next she tried the file. It was locked, but she easily jimmied it open using the lock-picking kit she always kept in her purse. What is this? she thought, her gaze lighting on a binder that was tucked in among the files. The spine was labeled "Computer Password Logbook."

Great! Snatching up the binder, she opened it to the first page. It was a chronological listing of the computer passwords. Next to each password was the name of the student to whom it was assigned and the date the password was issued. All of the entries on the page were made in a neat, flowing script, probably Phyllis's.

Nancy's head snapped up as she heard a door open and then Phyllis's voice, loud and clear. "Nonsense, Walter, I have the file in my office. It'll just take a second to grab it."

Nancy's breath caught in her throat, and she slammed the book shut. She could hear Walter objecting, but Phyllis wasn't paying any attention. Her heels clicked on the floor as she crossed the wooden anteroom.

Nancy checked frantically for somewhere to hide, but there was nothing—no closet, no enclosed space. Unless she could suddenly disappear, Phyllis was going to catch her red-handed!

Chapter

Eight

NANCY DIDN'T HAVE TIME to think about what to do. Holding the binder to her chest, she slid the file drawer shut, then rushed over to squat in the corner behind the door, on the far side of the desk. A split second later Phyllis's clicking heels stopped outside the door and the knob was turned.

Nancy held her breath as the door swung in toward her. She stayed low so Phyllis wouldn't see her silhouette through the frosted glass in the top half of the door. Please leave the door open, Nancy begged silently, and stay on the other side of the room!

She heard a drawer being opened and some

papers being rustled over by the desk. Would Phyllis notice the unlocked file drawer or the missing binder?

Every muscle in Nancy's body tensed as Phyllis's shoes clacked back toward Nancy. The assistant head paused at the door a moment, then the door was closed and she was gone.

Nancy's knees went weak, and she let out a long breath. Phew! I'd better work fast and get out of here in case she comes back again! she thought. Reopening the binder, Nancy flipped excitedly to the last page of entries.

There at the end was her own password, NS-444. Just above it was the listing for IW443. The name listed was— Nancy squinted, trying to make out the letters. The initials *I* and *W* were clear, but the rest of the name was scrawled illegibly.

Hmm. She compared the handwriting of the IW443 entry to the others. It seemed to be not as distinct but similar otherwise. Had Phyllis tried to disguise her writing so that no one could link her to the fake entry? Or was someone else trying, not quite successfully, to imitate her handwriting so that Phyllis *would* be implicated in the scam?

Nancy shook her head. She needed concrete evidence. Flipping back to the first page, Nancy ran her finger down the listings until she found Phyllis's and Victor's passwords and copied them down. As an afterthought, she wrote down Randi's password, too. Then she replaced the binder in the drawer and began looking through the other files.

It seemed to be dull stuff for the most part— budget information, personnel files, minutes from staff meetings, curriculum files. There was a fat computer file and a manual for the school's system, but Nancy didn't see how reading that would help solve her case.

She glanced at her watch. She'd been there for almost ten minutes now! Phyllis had to be returning any second. Shutting the drawer, Nancy moved quickly over to the filing cabinets, opening them one by one. There was no time to examine them thoroughly, but she didn't see anything unusual or incriminating at first glance.

With a sigh, Nancy closed the last drawer of the file cabinets and scrutinized the office to make sure everything was the same as when she'd entered. Then, after cracking open the door to check the common waiting room to make sure it was empty, Nancy slipped back through the empty anteroom and into the hall.

Well, she hadn't hit the jackpot, as she'd hoped, but at least she had those passwords now.

Maybe they would lead to some valuable discoveries.

Nancy sat at her bedroom desk and pounded on the papers in front of her. "I need a break here!" she muttered into the air.

It was Sunday evening. She'd spent all of Saturday afternoon at Sally Lane's, using her computer. After Sally had shown her how to access the Brewster computer with her PC, Nancy had gone to work. Using the passwords she'd copied from Phyllis's log, she accessed first Phyllis's, then Victor's, then Randi's files.

She'd called up each and every file, checking for anything that would point to any of them as her suspect. By the time she was done, she'd read enough administrative memos, computer programs, and newspaper stories to last a lifetime! But she hadn't found a single thing to incriminate any of the three.

That day she'd given herself a break and had gone shopping at the River Heights Mall with her best friends, George Fayne and Bess Marvin. But her mind was not on shopping. She kept trying to make sense of the evidence she had so far: the threatening message that had been sent from the newspaper room; Randi's knowledge of her real name; Phyllis's hush-hush phone call with Dana;

Victor's abilities to doctor off-limits files; the use of her real name on the threatening message. . . .

Depending on how she read the clues, any one of her suspects could be guilty. Nancy had laid out all her notes and papers on her desk, waiting for something to strike her, some pattern she'd overlooked.

A sheet of paper drifted to the floor and caught her eye. Bending to retrieve it, Nancy saw that it was the funny version of Walter Friedbinder's biography that Victor had concocted. She picked up the original biography and compared the two. It was amazing how easily he had turned a serious press release into a joke.

As her eyes flicked from one version to the other, it occurred to her that Friedbinder's real biography was pretty amazing in itself. He had received both a master's degree and a doctorate in his first five years after college and taught at the same time.

"Wow!" Nancy said softly. "That's pretty impressive."

After getting his doctorate, Friedbinder had become dean of students at a small private school. While there he had increased both the percentage of graduates going on to four-year colleges and the number of acceptances at highly prestigious colleges.

No wonder Lane and the other trustees decided to offer Friedbinder the job of headmaster at Brewster. Many people thought the best indication of a school's success was the list of colleges its graduates attended. A private school that wasn't seen as successful would stop attracting students and eventually go broke. So Friedbinder's obvious skill in that area must have been an important plus, at least in the eyes of the board.

Nancy noticed the title of Friedbinder's Ph.D. dissertation: "The Development of Creative Problem-Solving Skills." The press release said he'd gotten it published. The dissertation sounded as if it might help Nancy in her work, so she decided to ask him about borrowing a copy.

Nancy saw Friedbinder at eight-thirty on Monday morning in the school hallway. His manner was brusque and businesslike. "I need to speak to you privately, Ms. Stevens. Right away," he said.

As she followed him into his office, Nancy wondered why she had become Ms. Stevens, instead of Nancy. She soon found out.

"When I came in this morning," said the headmaster, rustling through the papers on his desk, "I found this note in my mailbox." He held it up.

"What does it say?" asked Nancy.

"I'll read it to you, word for word,"

Friedbinder replied. He took a pair of glasses from his coat pocket, adjusted them on his nose, and read:

"Good grades are big business at Brewster. And the people raking in the dough let a computer do their dirty work. Want your grade changed? Talk to Victor Paredes and Nancy Stevens."

Chapter

Nine

THE FIRST THING Nancy noted was the use of her alias: Nancy Stevens. Whoever wrote the note probably wasn't the same person who had sent her the threatening message on Friday.

The next thing that struck her was that the note concerned grade changing. Its author knew about the scam.

"That's very interesting," Nancy said, taking a seat. "Do you mind if I have a look at it?"

Walter Friedbinder passed it to her. The accusing message was printed in blue felt-tip ink on ordinary lined loose-leaf paper. The large block letters indicated to Nancy that the writer had apparently tried to disguise his or her handwriting. Nancy noticed one peculiarity, though. The small letter *k* had a closed loop for the upper arm, so that it looked like a small capital *R* with a line sticking up from it. Nancy was sure she would recognize it if she came across it again.

"Well?" Friedbinder said. "I thought you were going to solve this case! Now you're being accused of the crime. What's going on?"

Nancy looked up. "Hmm? Oh—I have a pretty good idea who wrote this and why. The interesting part is that Victor and I are accused of grade changing, and not of, say, writing graffiti in the halls or selling test answers."

"What do you mean?" asked the headmaster.

"This person knows about the grade-changing scam," she explained. "Maybe he or she has been approached by the culprit."

"What about Victor Paredes?"

"I'm watching him," said Nancy. "But I don't have enough evidence to accuse him. I don't think the person who wrote this does, either. This is the work of a jealous girlfriend."

Friedbinder seemed to accept this, and his manner relaxed somewhat.

The nine o'clock bell sounded in the corridor outside. Nancy stood up. "I have a student in a few minutes," she said. "Will you excuse me?"

"Of course," Friedbinder replied. "And please forgive me. This whole business has made me tense."

She was in the doorway when she remembered to ask him for a copy of his published dissertation.

"I'm sorry," he replied. "I have only one copy of it, and it must be in one of the cartons of books I haven't unpacked yet. In any case, it's pretty dry stuff."

As she walked upstairs to the learning lab, Nancy had a lot to think about. Why had he been so worried about the letter? The idea of her being involved was ridiculous—he had to know that. He was probably so worried about the effects of a scandal that he wasn't thinking clearly.

As for the note's author, Nancy knew of only one person who would want to make trouble for her and Victor, and that was Kim. But why had Kim—assuming she was the one—accused them of grade changing? She must know that someone at Brewster really was changing people's grades for money.

Kim didn't seem to have the computer know-how to be in on the scheme, but had she received an E-mail message from the grade-changer? Or heard rumors from students who had? And what about the fact that the note accused Victor? Was that pure spite or a shrewd guess? Victor was, after all, one of Nancy's suspects. Did Kim know that he was involved? And if so, how?

Nancy shook her head. Too many questions

and no answers. She unlocked the learning lab and checked her watch. There were still a few minutes before her student was to arrive. After dumping her things on a chair, she went to her desk to make a phone call. "Mr. Lane?" she said, when she was put through.

"Nancy! I was just going to call you," the banker said. "A deposit of five hundred dollars was made to the account after four on Friday afternoon. My immediate staff had gone home, so I wasn't told about it until this morning."

Nancy whistled. "So if I. Wynn hasn't already withdrawn his money, he should start withdrawing the cash today. Can you arrange for me to be notified here at school as soon as there's any activity in the account?"

"I imagine I can," Lane replied. "You'll have to move quickly, though. I'll buy you as much time as possible by placing a special hold and recheck command on the account number, as well as the slowdown we've already put in place."

"Thanks," said Nancy. "If I'm lucky he or she will go to the Ivy Avenue branch, which is the one closest to the school."

There was a tap on the door. Nancy finished her call and went to answer it. Victor was standing there, looking glum.

"Hi, partner," he said. "How do you like a life of crime?"

"What are you talking about?" Nancy asked. "And what are you doing here?"

"I switched appointments with Margie Adams," he said. "And if you don't know what I'm talking about, you will as soon as Dr. F. gets hold of you. I just came from a grilling in his office."

"I thought I explained everything to him. That letter really shook him up. I can't believe he called you to his office! You'd better come in," she said to Victor, pulling him into the learning lab.

Victor sprawled in the chair next to the computer terminal as Nancy sat at the desk. He gave her a shrewd look. "So you do know about it," he said. "I thought so."

"You're talking about the anonymous letter, right?" Nancy asked.

"Anonymous!" he said with a loud snort. "Kim did everything but staple her photo to the top and put her thumbprint in the lower corner!"

"I figured it had to be her," Nancy said, nodding.

"Listen, I've known Kim since eighth grade, and I've never met anyone else who makes those funny *k*'s. Isn't that proof?"

"That depends," Nancy replied. "Not if lots of people know she writes that way."

Victor stared at her, then laughed. "Hey," he said, "you'd make a great detective!"

Nancy studied his face. Had that been an innocent remark? Or had Victor somehow penetrated her cover? Did he know her name was really Nancy Drew?

She decided not to respond directly to his comment. "Why should Kim—or anyone else, for that matter—accuse us of changing people's grades for money?" she asked.

"Well," he answered in an embarrassed voice, "I guess it's my fault. One time, when Kim and I were going out together, we were talking about how broke we both were. I said I knew how to make a lot of money by offering to change people's school transcripts."

"Victor, you didn't!" Nancy exclaimed.

His cheeks turned pink. "I was just goofing around," he protested. "I could have said, 'Let's hold up a bank or something,' instead. I didn't mean it, but I guess Kim didn't know that."

"No, I guess not." Nancy fell silent. Could she believe Victor? He *was* acting uncomfortable. Was it simply because he knew his comment might be misunderstood? Or was this a sort of double-whammy, in which he gave away something embarrassing but harmless in order to convince her that he was being completely open?

"I just told this to Mr. Friedbinder," Victor added. "But I couldn't tell if he believed me. I hope he did. I hear colleges pay a lot of attention to your headmaster's letter of recommendation, and if he shoots me down, I'm dead."

Nancy realized the conversation was starting to get a little too personal. She was supposed to be tutoring Victor, after all. "Why don't we see about bringing up your marks in English," she said brusquely, reaching for her stack of books, "and let Mr. Friedbinder worry about what he says in his letter? Okay, Stu?"

Victor grinned. "Sure thing, Teach!"

After twenty minutes of solid work, Nancy said, "Nice going. Keep this up and I don't think you'll have any more problems."

Victor stretched his arms and yawned. "Thanks," he replied. "But I can't help thinking that a lot of what you're doing could be done by a computer. Not the really creative part, of course, but all those drills."

"You should talk to Mr. Friedbinder about that," Nancy told him. "He wrote a doctoral dissertation on creative problem solving. It was even published. I wanted to read it, but his only copy is packed away."

"Really?" asked Victor. "I bet I could find you another copy somewhere. Let's see."

He leaned over and switched on the terminal, then entered a series of commands, separated by pauses. "I'm logging onto an interactive database," he explained. "One of the things it has is a directory of published dissertations in different university libraries. Do you remember the title and the name of the school?"

Nancy told him, and he typed in the information. After a short while he entered some more commands, then still others. Finally he sat back. "Nope," he said. "No good. There is one dissertation that sounds kind of similar, but it's by someone else at a different school. I guess you'll have to wait until Friedbinder unpacks his copy of it."

Suddenly the phone rang. Harrison Lane was on the other end. "Right now, at the Ivy Avenue branch. You'd better—"

"Thanks, so long," said Nancy, not waiting for him to finish.

Grabbing her coat, she ran for the door.

"What's the matter, Nancy?" Victor called after her.

"Uh—nothing, Victor. Tell anyone after you that I had an emergency. Had to go." Without another word, Nancy tore down the hallway and out to her car in the parking lot.

Nancy reached the bank in a record-breaking five minutes. She parked right in front and jumped out of the car. Her heart thumped hard in her chest. There, coming out of the bank, was a petite teenage girl with long, almost black hair. She fit the description of I. Wynn exactly.

The girl raised her head, and her face went white when she made eye contact with Nancy. That gave Nancy a good look at her face.

It was Kim! She was wearing a wig, but Nancy recognized her anyway.

"Stop!" Nancy cried as Kim bolted for a red car parked down the street.

Chapter

Ten

SPRINTING TO HER CAR, Kim jumped in and turned the key to rev the engine. With a squeal of rubber, the red car roared away from the curb and tore down the street.

Nancy didn't hesitate. She jumped into her Mustang and broke her own personal record for getting under way. Soon she spotted the car several blocks ahead. It was turning left onto a side street. Nancy followed as fast as the law allowed.

At the side street, she made a racing turn and sped down the winding, tree-lined avenue, the red car still far ahead of her.

Nancy pressed down on the accelerator. Her blue Mustang responded instantly, and the gap began to narrow. They were heading into Sally Lane's posh neighborhood. The street went down a little hill and curved to the left before straightening out. As Nancy came out of the curve, she muttered, "Oh, rats!"

The street was empty as far as she could see. Somehow Kim had given her the slip.

Nancy braked to a screeching halt. The car couldn't have gotten that far ahead in the few seconds it was out of sight. It must have turned into one of the driveways.

She began to move again, at little more than walking pace, pausing to peer up each driveway. At the fifth one she got lucky. She could just see the back fender of a red car, sticking out from behind a trellis of vines. She pulled over and parked just beyond the driveway.

The redbrick house was very large, with white shutters, and was set well back from the street. Matching oak trees flanked the brick walk that led to the front door. Nancy walked up to the door. The name engraved on the brass door knocker was Archibald. Hadn't Sally told her Kim's last name was Foster, or—Forster, yes, that was it.

Nancy pressed the mother-of-pearl bell to the right of the door. After a few moments a middle-aged woman with gray hair, wearing a navy blue dress and two strings of pearls, opened the door.

"If it's the Junior League raffle," she began, "I'm afraid I've already—"

Nancy smiled politely and said, "No, ma'am. I'm looking for Kim."

The woman raised her eyebrows. "Kim? Oh, yes, of course. You must be one of her school friends. It's around the back, dear. Over the garage."

Nancy thanked her and went in the direction the woman had indicated. At the back of the house, separated from it by a high hedge, was a two-story brick garage with spaces for four cars. A wooden staircase led up to a second-story door on one side. Nancy climbed the stairs and knocked.

No one answered, but Nancy was sure she heard someone stirring inside. She knocked again, louder, then called out, "Kim? I have to talk to you."

There were more rustling sounds, then the door swung open. Kim stood there obviously defeated, the black wig in her hands. "Come on in," she said, "before Mrs. Archibald hears you."

Nancy followed her into a small but comfortable living room. On a table between two windows was a large photo in a silver frame. The picture showed a younger and happier Kim seated between a man in a dark suit and a woman in a black dress. Apparently her parents were the housekeepers for the Archibalds.

Seeing where Nancy's attention was focused, Kim rushed over and turned the photo facedown on the table. "Why don't you stay out of my life?" she cried.

"I'm afraid I can't," Nancy told her. "Kim, what were you doing at the bank?"

"Just what you said," Kim shot back hotly. "Why can't you leave me alone?"

"What I said?" Nancy echoed, very confused.

"I haven't kept a single penny of it for myself, and you both know it," Kim continued.

Nancy simply stared at the girl. What was she talking about?

"Kim, listen to me," Nancy said. "I'm a detective. Whoever you think I am, you're wrong. My real name is Nancy Drew. The reason I'm at Brewster is that someone on the board of trustees asked me to find out who is responsible for the grade-changing racket. And I'm pretty sure you can help me."

"Oh, su-u-re," Kim replied, rolling her eyes. "This is a test, right? To see if I can be trusted? Don't worry. I'll live up to my end of the bargain." With that, she collapsed into a chair and began crying bitterly.

Nancy waited until Kim calmed down and

straightened in the chair, wiping the back of her hand across her cheeks. "I guess that's it, huh?" Kim told her. "Now you'll lower my grade-point average, just the way you said you would if anything went wrong. I can kiss college good-bye."

Nancy went over and held Kim by the shoulders. "Listen to me! I am *not* the person responsible for this. I swear! You've got to tell me what's going on, Kim. It's the only way I can help you."

Kim stared up into Nancy's eyes. "Are you for real?" she finally asked.

Nancy nodded.

"I was so sure you had to be involved. I just couldn't see Victor running this on his own," Kim continued. "He loves fooling around with the school computer and getting it to do weird tricks, but once he's figured something out, he gets bored and goes on to something else. He couldn't be bothered to do the same thing over and over, not even for money. So I figured he had to have a partner. Then you showed up, and I was sure."

"If Victor *did* have a partner, it would be someone at the school," Nancy pointed out, perching on the edge of the sofa. "But I've only just started there, and this grade-changer has been operating for almost two weeks. Besides, what makes you so sure Victor's involved?"

Kim stared down at her lap and said so softly that Nancy had to lean in closer to hear, "He told me so. He said that he'd changed someone's grades. He pretended to feel really bad about it, but now I can see that was just a put-on. If he'd meant it, he wouldn't have kept doing it, and he wouldn't have forced me to get involved."

Nancy's breath caught in her throat. "Why did you write that note to the headmaster?" she asked after a pause. "It was you, wasn't it?"

"Sure. I was furious at you and Victor for what you were doing to me," Kim replied, her pale blue eyes flashing. "I wanted to get you in as much trouble as I could without getting myself in hot water. It didn't work, did it?"

"It might have," Nancy told her, "except that Mr. Friedbinder knows who I am and why I'm at Brewster. How did you get involved in this racket?"

"There was a message in my E-mail," Kim explained. "Whoever sent it knew I couldn't afford to pay to have my grades changed, but he said I could improve my transcript if I ran a few errands. He also said that if I didn't agree, my transcript could end up looking a lot worse than it really is. So I opened the account wearing this dumb wig. And he tells me when to pick up the money."

"Why didn't you go straight to the headmaster and tell him about it?" Nancy asked.

Kim shook her head sharply. "I couldn't bring myself to turn Victor in. I'm really hung up on the guy."

"Victor's not the only one who could be responsible," Nancy told Kim. "If I'm going to catch the culprit, I need to know how the money transfer works. I know you have a bank card for that account, but how do you know when to use it, and what happens to the cash?"

"I get an E-mail message," Kim replied. "In code. If it says M five, I know I should withdraw five hundred dollars on Monday. T ten means one thousand dollars on Tuesday, and so on. It's usually after or before school, but today the message said to go at lunchtime. I'm missing math right now."

"How do you deliver the money?" Nancy asked.

"I put the bills in a brown envelope and leave it in one of the faculty mailboxes before school."

"What?" Nancy exclaimed, straightening up. "Which one?"

Kim shrugged. "It's not labeled. It's on the bottom row, on the side near the door."

Nancy frowned and stared into space. Then she said, "I'm going to need your help to put the person behind this out of business. How about it?"

Kim nodded hesitantly.

"Great," Nancy continued. "Now, here's what I have in mind. I want you to deliver the money you picked up today."

"You do?" said Kim incredulously.

"Yes, I do," Nancy replied. "And then I want you to stay home from school for the next two days. Think you can play sick for that long?"

"No problem," Kim said. "No problem at all."

At eight forty-five the next morning Nancy was standing near the coffee urn in the faculty lounge, paging through a news magazine. She glanced up just as Kim came in, stuck a brown envelope into a mailbox on the bottom row, and scurried out.

More and more teachers were drifting in, checking their mailboxes, and getting coffee. Each time one of them blocked Nancy's view of the mailboxes, her anxiety level soared. She longed to move closer, but she didn't dare. The person behind the racket knew Nancy's real reason for being at Brewster—the threatening message in her E-mail proved that. If she was seen too near the mailboxes, the culprit would sense a trap and leave the envelope with the money where it was.

Nancy straightened up and felt her pulse beat faster. Dana has just walked into the room and paused near the mailboxes. Was this the pickup?

But then she turned and headed straight for the coffee urn. The envelope was still in place. "Hi, Nancy," Dana greeted her. "How are you getting along with the computer system?"

"So far, so good," Nancy replied. "You're here early. Is there a problem?"

Dana smiled. "No, no. Not this time. I have an appointment near here in a little while, and I thought I'd stop by to make sure the computer beast is behaving itself."

Nancy smiled back distractedly. She was very aware that Dana was blocking her view of the mailboxes. She made a half-step to the right, but Dana moved in the same direction and began asking her about tutoring. She wanted to know if Nancy had thought of using the computer system.

If she could have, Nancy would have pushed Dana aside. She *had* to see that mailbox.

Slowly Nancy angled to the left. Again, Dana adjusted her position so that she was blocking Nancy's view. This is unbelievable! Nancy said to herself. Was Dana moving on purpose? It didn't seem so because she kept talking excitedly about the applications of the computer in tutoring.

Nancy was about to explain that she wasn't in charge of the program, when Friedbinder entered and paused to survey the room. When he saw Dana and Nancy together, he scowled and turned his back on them. A moment later Phyllis came in. She, too, noticed Dana and Nancy. She gave Nancy a quick nod, then turned to Victor, who had appeared at the door to speak with her.

Dana, her back to the door, missed all this. As the nine o'clock bell rang, she said, "Oh dear, I'd better run. We'll talk again about coming up with an interactive approach to tutoring. I really think it's the way to go."

Heading for the door, Nancy looked at the mailboxes and drew in a quick breath. The brown envelope was gone!

Chapter

Eleven

NANCY CONTINUED in the direction of the door, fighting down an impulse to break into a run. How could she have let someone make off with the envelope, right under her nose!

Pausing outside the door, Nancy peered up and down the hall. To her left she saw a girl in jeans and a T-shirt, with books under her arm. To her right was Phyllis Hathaway, just going into the administration offices. She was too far away to see if she had anything in her hand.

The trap had failed, that was obvious. The question was, why? Was it an accident that Dana had blocked Nancy's view at the crucial moment, or had she done it on purpose?

If it had been a coincidence, then it was just a

piece of bad luck. If not, it meant that Dana and Phyllis were guilty *and* that they knew Nancy was trying to trap them. The only way they could have known that was if Kim had told them.

Nancy shook her head. Stop jumping to conclusions, Drew, she told herself. Walter Friedbinder and Victor had also been near the mailboxes. Either of them could have made off with the envelope, too. She would simply have to come up with a new plan for trapping the guilty party.

"Hi, there," someone called. Nancy turned and saw Randi coming down the hall toward her.

"I looked for you yesterday," Randi continued. "I still want to do that interview. Are you free at noon?"

Nancy decided it was time to be direct. "Randi, yesterday you called me Nancy Drew. How did you know my name?" She watched Randi's face carefully. The threatening message had been sent from one of the terminals in the newspaper office after all. That fact alone put Randi in a very select group of potential suspects.

Randi rolled her eyes. "Oh, come on! It's not such a big deal. I was just goofing on you yesterday. Can you blame me, after that art show story you gave me? Of course I know who you are. I'm a journalist, right? I read the River Heights papers every day. I've seen your name and picture."

"Have you told this to anyone else?" asked Nancy.

"No," replied Randi. "A good journalist doesn't go around blabbing about her biggest story before she's even written it. So tell me, what are you *really* doing here?"

"I can't tell you. But I will when it's over," Nancy promised. "As long as you keep quiet about it now."

"Deal," Randi agreed.

Nancy groaned inwardly as she walked away. A reporter on the trail of a hot scoop was the last thing she needed. She just hoped Randi kept her word.

For the next couple of hours Nancy was too busy helping bewildered sophomores understand the mysteries of past participles to give any thought to her case. When she ushered her last student out the door, she returned to her desk to do some quiet thinking.

Could she eliminate Randi as a suspect? She was inclined to say yes. Yet one thing still bothered her. Randi had been the only one near the newspaper office when the threatening message was sent.

"Hey, I can practically see the wheels going

around!" Victor said, interrupting her thoughts. He was standing in the doorway, grinning at her. "Do you know you have steam coming out of your ears?"

Nancy gave a laugh. "Hi, Victor," she said, in a tone of resignation.

"Wow, what enthusiasm!" he replied, falling into the chair across from her. "You looked a lot more lively when I saw you down in the faculty lounge. Maybe you need to drink more coffee."

"Maybe I need to do less tutoring," retorted Nancy. "By the way, what were you doing in the faculty lounge?"

"Uh-oh, she's starting to pull rank on me," he teased. "I had a right to be there. I was picking up something for one of my teachers."

Nancy sat up straighter. "Oh? What? For whom?"

He opened his eyes wide. " 'For whom,' " he repeated. "Golly, if I keep hanging around with you, can I learn to talk like that? Or am I a hopeless case?"

"You're the one who said it, not me," Nancy replied, with mock sternness. "But seriously, how about answering my question?"

"About the package? Sure. Mr. Farley, my physics teacher, ordered some reprints of an article, and he asked me to get them from his mailbox and bring them to the lab for him. Why?"

Victor's story could easily be checked, so easily that Nancy doubted he would have told it if it weren't true. Still, that didn't mean that the reprints were the only thing he had picked up in the mailroom.

"You didn't notice a brown envelope, about this big, did you?" she asked, indicating the size with her hands. "Someone was supposed to leave it for me, but it hasn't turned up."

"Nope," he replied, shaking his head. "But I wasn't really paying attention. I was too busy plotting my next exploit."

Nancy raised an eyebrow. "And what's that?"

"Just imagine," he said, leaning closer. "Tomorrow morning, at the beginning of first period, a cartoon of the headmaster's face appears on the screen of every terminal in the school."

"Victor—" Nancy began.

He held up his hand. "Wait, I'm not done. The eyes look one way, then the other. Then, just when everybody is getting spooked, he puts his thumbs in his ears, wiggles his fingers, sticks out his tongue, and makes a really rude noise!"

Nancy laughed in spite of herself. "You won't really do it, will you?" she asked. "You'd get yourself expelled!"

"I know," he said with a sigh. "I have to face it—I'm chicken."

Nancy sat back and studied him a moment. She couldn't think of anyone who made her laugh as often as Victor did. She was growing to like him and had to admit that she found him very attractive. But if he was guilty, Nancy couldn't afford to be blinded by his charm.

She'd been hoping not to have to wade through stacks of paper records. But now she could see she'd have to do it. Obviously, she couldn't cross-check everyone's records. With four hundred students at Brewster, each taking five courses a year and being graded four times in each course, that would make—eight thousand data points to check. But she could start by cross-checking Victor's and Kim's grades, those of her tutoring students, and then a few other students at random.

Making an excuse to Victor, Nancy went downstairs to the school office.

"Hi, Ms. Arletti," she said to the secretary. "Is the headmaster free?"

In response, Walter Friedbinder appeared in his office door and said, "Hello, Nancy. What can I do for you?"

Nancy explained that she wanted to check the school records of some students against their teachers' grade rosters. "I'd like the files on Victor Paredes, Kim Forster, and a few others."

"Victor Paredes, huh?" said Friedbinder. "His name keeps coming up, doesn't it? His record and Kim's are on the computer. You can use the one here in the corner. But digging out the grade rosters is another matter. They should be in the file room, shouldn't they, Ms. Arletti?" He gestured to a door behind the secretary's desk.

"That's right," Ms. Arletti replied. "But they're in a locked file cabinet, along with other confidential papers. It might take me a while to hunt up the key."

"Why don't you come back after lunch?" the headmaster suggested. "I'll make sure we're ready for you by then."

"Here's a key to the outer door, in case I'm out," Ms. Arletti added. "I'll put the file cabinet key in an envelope with your name on it and leave it here on my desk."

"Thanks," Nancy told her. As she turned to go, she noticed the door to Phyllis Hathaway's office was slightly ajar. Was she inside, listening?

Nancy went back to the learning lab and worked for twenty minutes, but soon her impatience got the better of her. Surely Ms. Arletti must have found the file cabinet key by now. Nancy didn't want to wait until after lunch.

Downstairs, the office door was locked. Nancy found the key she had been given and went in. The envelope with her name was right where Ms. Arletti had said it would be. Nancy took it, went into the file room, and turned on the overhead light.

The room was lined with a dozen gray, four-drawer file cabinets and some shelves piled high with papers. Nancy realized that she had no idea which one she wanted. Was she going to have to try the key in each of them, one by one?

Then she gave a little snort of laughter. There was no point in trying the key unless the cabinet was locked! She tried the top drawer of the nearest cabinet. It opened easily. She shut it and tried the next, which also opened. She kept going until, on the fifth try, she found one that didn't open. Maybe this was the one.

She tore open the envelope and took out the little key. She was about to fit it in the lock when a noise caught her attention—the sound of footsteps retreating down the hall outside the office. Someone was running away from the office. Then came a *whoof!* A yellow glare suddenly filled the room.

Nancy whirled and gasped in terror. Flames were shooting up from all around the open doorway, charring the paint on the doorframe. In a flash the flames swooped across the floor, setting stacks of papers on fire.

Already the doorway was completely blocked, and the flames were advancing toward Nancy. Her body tensed as she frantically searched the small, windowless room.

She was trapped!

Chapter

Twelve

THE TINY ROOM was filling with black, acrid smoke. Nancy's eyes were stinging, and when she tried to take in a breath, the overheated air seared her lungs.

Struggling to remain calm, she buried her nose and mouth in the crook of her elbow and got down on the floor. The air was a little cooler and less smoky down there, but she knew that wouldn't last. If she didn't find a way out, and very quickly, she was going to die.

Somewhere outside, a fire bell was clamoring. Help was probably on its way by now, but she doubted it could arrive in time to save her. Should she try to run *through* the flames? She shivered with horror at the idea. There was no way to do that without being burned, but at least she would have a chance. By staying in the file room, she had no chance at all.

Why wasn't the sprinkler system working? Nancy raised her eyes to the ceiling and spotted the manual turn-on valve. She didn't hesitate or even take a moment to think or plan. Drawing in a deep breath, Nancy held it, and sprang to her feet.

Under the turn-on valve was a tall steel bookcase. Nancy hurled some of the books onto the floor.

Her chest felt as though a loop of barbed wire were tightening around it. She began climbing the bookcase. The hot metal of the shelves seared her hands, but she ignored the pain. It was happening to someone else, in a distant place.

The higher she got, the thicker the suffocating smoke became. Finally, teetering on the top of the case, her foot braced against a lower shelf, Nancy reached up to the sprinkler valve.

Come on! Come on! she thought desperately as the stubborn valve refused to move. A glob of purple darkness floated in front of Nancy's eyes. A deep nausea rose up inside her. Nancy, you can't pass out, she urged herself. Hang in there!

With a last, desperate twist, Nancy gave the valve all she had. Suddenly bursts of water sprayed down from the small sprinkler heads mounted in the ceiling.

In minutes the flames were dying and Nancy could see the doorway clearly. Coughing and feeling sick, she staggered across the smoky office, collapsing into the arms of a helmeted firefighter, who was just arriving.

When Nancy opened her eyes, the first thing she saw was a clear sky dotted with fluffy white clouds. She blinked, then turned her head. She was lying on a stretcher in the school parking lot, just outside the open door of an ambulance. On one side of her was an alert paramedic with an oxygen tank in his hand. On the other was Victor, more serious than she had ever seen him.

"Am I okay?" she croaked in a husky voice that surprised her. "The fire's out?"

"I was going to ask you that," Victor replied. "And don't worry about the fire. You had it out so fast they're going to make us go back to class soon."

Nancy sent questioning messages to various parts of her body. Once she had received the answers she told him, "My hands hurt. And it aches when I breathe. Everything else seems to be all right."

"We'll be taking you to the hospital in a few

THE NANCY DREW FILES

minutes for examination and treatment," the
paramedic said. "Do you feel up to answering a
few questions from the fire marshal before we
go?"

"Sure." Nancy started to sit up, then thought
better of it when the parking lot started swirling
around her. She would have to stay lying down
for now.

The fire marshal was a man of about fifty with
a deeply lined face and kind brown eyes. He
squatted down next to the stretcher and asked
her to tell him what had happened. "Then it was
you who turned on the sprinklers. That was
quick thinking, young lady. That probably saved
your life, as well as kept the fire from doing
serious damage. We're not sure yet why the heat
sensors in the sprinkler system failed. Brewster
may be in for some heavy fines for having faulty
safety equipment."

"It was arson, wasn't it?" Nancy said in a low
voice.

"What makes you say that?" the fire official
asked her, frowning.

"The way it started, all at once, and spread
across the floor," Nancy replied. "It seemed to
flow, and to me that sounds like some kind of
liquid was burning, not just a bunch of old
papers."

"We don't know what else may have been

stored in that room," the fire marshal said. "We're looking into that now. Thanks for your help, Ms. Stevens. If I have any more questions, I'll be in touch with you.

"Okay, Bill," he added, straightening up and turning to one of the paramedics. A few moments later Nancy's stretcher was secured inside the ambulance, and the vehicle sped away.

Her father was already at the hospital when Nancy arrived. So was Harrison Lane. They joined her in her examining room. After she and the paramedic assured them that she was basically in good shape, Lane said, "Sally called and told me what happened. I called your father. Nancy, I feel terrible that I put you in such danger. I never expected anything like this. I want you to drop this investigation."

"Not yet," Nancy told him, shaking her head.

"I beg you," the banker continued. "If there has to be a scandal at Brewster, so be it. We'll live it down somehow. At least we won't be putting you in further jeopardy."

Nancy shook her head again.

"I told you you were wasting your time," Carson Drew said to Lane. "Once she's made up her mind, it's impossible to talk her out of it."

"I can't give up now," Nancy insisted. She paused while a doctor examined the burns on her hands and put a soothing ointment on them. As he began to wrap them loosely with gauze, Nancy continued.

"The reason the file room was torched is that I'm getting close to a solution to the case—too close for somebody. But I don't think that I was meant to be trapped like that. If I had gone to the file room when I said I was going to, I would have found the fire department on the scene and the file room already gutted. But I was impatient to check something, so I went early."

Her father gave her a sharp look. "Then you think the person who set the fire is someone who knew when you were planning to go to the file room. There can't be too many people like that."

Nancy thought a moment. Who *did* know she would be there? There was Friedbinder and Ms. Arletti. Phyllis Hathaway might have been in her office and overheard Nancy asking to check the files. It was possible a student had been in the office with her at the time. And, she recalled, she had suggested to Victor that someone might think to check the grade rosters.

"That's a strong possibility," she said. "Of course, the fire's timing could have been a coincidence. The fire could even have been an accident."

"You can rule out that possibility," Lane told her, frowning. "I spoke to the fire marshal a few minutes ago, and he told me unofficially that he's planning to list it as arson. There's also strong evidence that someone tampered with the sprinkler system so it wouldn't go off as it should have. Isn't there anything I can say to persuade you to give up this case, Nancy?"

Nancy managed a grin. "You could tell me you've found the grade-changer. Other than that, I can't think of a thing that would make me quit now."

Forty-five minutes later Nancy was released from the hospital. She talked her father into driving her back to Brewster. "I *have* to get back there, Dad," she coaxed. "The grade-changer is getting scared. The arson proves that. Who knows what he or she is up to at this very moment—probably scrambling like crazy to cover up this scam in any way possible. I. Wynn could disappear altogether if I don't get to him soon."

"Okay, okay," Carson gave in. "Let's hear what you've got so far."

As they drove toward Brewster, Nancy laid the case out for her father. "I haven't decided that Phyllis and Dana are guilty yet," she said, after listing all the clues that pointed to the pair. "And I have to admit, I'm wondering more and more about the headmaster now. Walter knew that I was planning to check some of the records, *and* he knew when.

"By the way, Dad," she added with a grin. "I've figured out that Dana was your client."

"I had a feeling you would," her father told her, a proud gleam in his eyes.

A few minutes later he pulled into the Brewster parking lot. Nancy thanked him for the ride and the emotional support and promised that she'd call him to drive her home later.

As she walked into the school, the smell of smoke made Nancy's stomach turn. It was almost three o'clock, but the halls hadn't filled up yet with crowds of students going home. She went straight to the office, where Ms. Arletti clucked over Nancy's burns, her narrow escape, and the mess the fire had made of her office.

It *was* a mess. Much of the furniture had been scorched, and the carpet was soaked with chemicals from the fire extinguishers. Nancy swallowed twice and looked into the file room. The walls and ceiling were dark with soot, and a thick layer of charred, water-soaked papers and books covered the floor. But the file cabinet appeared to have suffered little more than scorched paint.

"One of the maintenance staff will be in to clean out all that rubbish," Ms. Arletti explained. "With any luck, we'll be back to normal by tomorrow. Thank goodness the computer system wasn't damaged. If we lose that, we might as well close the school."

"I hate to bother you," said Nancy, "but it doesn't seem as if the grade rosters were burned. Could I look through them?"

Ms. Arletti sighed. "You're a determined young woman, aren't you? Go ahead."

Nancy opened one of the cabinet drawers and found Kim, Victor, and Sally's files. She winced from the pain as she grabbed them, balancing them gingerly in her arms. Then she took another small stack of student files at random. "Thanks," she told Ms. Arletti as she left the office. "I'll return this stuff tomorrow."

Wanting a place to sit down and go over her materials, Nancy went upstairs to the learning lab. Before opening the files, she decided to check her E-mail.

Three messages were waiting for her. All of them amounted to get-well notes, one each from Walter Friedbinder and Phyllis Hathaway, and the third from Victor, who added an invitation to join him for a hot fudge sundae at the Roost.

Nancy smiled to herself and started to compose an answer. Then she noticed a flashing box appear in the upper corner of the screen. Another piece of E-mail was arriving for her. The password of the sender was IW443!

Chapter

Thirteen

Nancy instructed the system to print the message on the screen.

You got away this time. Next time you won't be so lucky. Get out of here while you still can. This is your last warning!

Controlling her reaction of shock and rage, Nancy quickly saved the message, then told the computer to refuse it. *Returning message to terminal 29* appeared on the screen. The message had come from the newspaper office again. It had been entered on the system only seconds before.

Nancy whirled around and dashed out the door. The person who had sent the threat would have no way of guessing that Nancy would read it instantly, and not minutes or even hours later. The chances were that he or she was still at the terminal.

Nancy stopped running just before she reached the corridor that led to the office of the *Academician* and began to walk softly. She wanted to catch the guilty person in the act. If he or she tried to leave the office before Nancy got there, it didn't matter. She would still see the culprit at close enough range to identify him or her, and that was almost as good.

Her heart pounding, Nancy tiptoed up to the door. It was standing ajar. This was it—the moment of truth. She cautiously peeked in. Randi! She was seated at the same terminal where Nancy had seen her the week before. Her back was to the door, and she was typing something on the keyboard.

Stepping into the room, Nancy said, "More threats, Randi? You might as well save computer time and make them in person. I'm here now."

"Nancy!" Randi jumped up from her chair so quickly that it fell over backward as she spun around to face the doorway.

"You startled me," the student reporter continued. "What are you doing here?"

"Catching you red-handed," Nancy replied.

Randi gave her a puzzled look. It was almost

convincing. "I don't know what you're talking about," she said. "But I don't think I like your attitude."

"What were you writing just now?" Nancy demanded. She pushed past Randi and approached the terminal.

"A story for the paper, about the girls' soccer team," Randi replied. "Not that it's any of your business."

Nancy looked at the monitor and read: "Paced by star forward Lisa Mongiello, the team rolled over the Deerfield Falcons, 10–2, last Thursday, clinching their first pre-season game."

"I want to know what's going on here," Randi insisted. "Either tell me right now or get out of my office."

"About two minutes ago someone sent me a threatening message, from this terminal," Nancy said. "Do you have anything to say about that?"

Randi's face turned red. "That's a dirty lie! I don't know what kind of game you're playing, but I've been right here, working on the paper, for the last half-hour. And no one—*no one*—has been anywhere near this terminal except me!"

Randi seemed completely sincere. But what about the message that had come from this room? Since she was the only one there both times Nancy had received messages, she was clearly implicated in the scheme.

Or was she? Nancy suddenly thought of another possibility. "You say you've been using this terminal steadily for the last half-hour?" she asked in a softer tone. "Did anything unusual happen during that time?"

Randi frowned. "Unusual? No. Well—the computer locked up on me for a few seconds at one point, but that's not so unusual. It happens every day or so. I keep meaning to ask someone about it."

"What do you mean, 'locked up'?" Nancy asked eagerly, a tingle of excitement spreading through her.

"It quits working, sort of," Randi explained, shrugging. "The screen blanks out, the keyboard goes dead, and then a few seconds later, everything is back to normal. Listen, what's going on? What's all this about threats? What kind of case are you working on?"

"I can't tell you now," Nancy replied, "but I think I'm beginning to see some of the answers. I promise I'll tell you everything I can, when the time comes. Right now, I'd better get moving. I need to find Victor Paredes."

"Why don't you see if he's logged onto the system?" Randi suggested. She bent to set her chair upright again. "Knowing Victor, he probably is, unless he's asleep or in the shower."

Sitting down in front of the terminal, Randi

pressed some keys. "I was right," she said after a moment. "He's in the computer room. Do you want to use my terminal to talk to him?"

Nancy didn't want her conversation with Victor to be open to everyone who happened to be using the computer system. "No thanks. I'll go down there in person."

"Suit yourself," Randi told her. "I'll tell him you're coming. And remember, I'm expecting to hear what this is all about. Otherwise, I'll have to start an investigation of my own."

Just as Randi had said, Victor was at one of the computer room terminals. "You look pretty good for someone who just got back from the hospital," he commented. "How do you feel?"

"I've been too busy to tell," Nancy said. "Listen, I have an important question for you. Is it possible to send a message from one terminal in the system to another, but make the system say that it came from a different terminal?"

"Hmm." Victor leaned back in his chair and stared into space as he considered this. "I don't see why not," he answered at last. "It shouldn't be that hard to program the computer to accept a message for retransmission from a different origin. But you'd leave a trail, of course."

"You mean, a record of where the message really came from?" Nancy demanded, her blue eyes widening. "Do you know how to find a record like that?"

Victor studied her face for a moment, then nodded. "Probably. A message *to whom*, received when?"

Nancy smiled at his half-joking use of *whom* and then gave him the information he needed. He busied himself at the terminal, humming the refrain from a hard-rock tune under his breath. Finally, just when Nancy was sure she couldn't stand to wait a second longer, he pushed his chair back and said, "Okay, I got it. The message was actually entered a couple of minutes earlier than it said, and the real place of origin was the work station in Ms. Hathaway's office."

"You're sure?" Nancy exclaimed.

"Not a hundred percent sure," he admitted. "There might be a second layer of tricks. Call it eighty percent."

"Good enough!" Nancy started for the door, then paused to look over her shoulder. "Thanks, Victor," she added. "You've been super."

"You're welcome. And don't forget that hot fudge sundae."

Ms. Arletti's office was almost back to normal, except for the lingering smell of burnt and wet wood. She looked up from some work on her desk as Nancy came in. "Ms. Hathaway?" she replied to Nancy's question. "Oh, what a shame, she just walked out this second. She had an urgent phone call a few minutes ago and told me she had to leave. You can probably catch her in the parking lot if you hurry."

"Thanks," Nancy called, jogging out the door.

Nancy's car was in the visitors' parking lot because she hadn't been assigned a permanent teacher space yet. She climbed in, wincing as her hands touched the wheel, and drove around the back of the building, where faculty members parked. A red sedan that looked like Phyllis's was just pulling out into the street. Nancy waited a few seconds, then followed.

The car turned right at the next corner, then left a couple of blocks later. Nancy followed, far enough back to stay unnoticed, she hoped. She was beginning to think she knew where Phyllis was going.

A few minutes later her hunch was confirmed. As Phyllis's car approached Archer Street, the right turn signal started to blink. Sure enough, Phyllis's car slowed as she reached the bank branch, about halfway down the street. Nancy slowed, too, then pulled in behind a van parked on the street. Its bulk would help hide her car from anyone in the bank.

Nancy watched as Phyllis parked in the lot and

headed for the bank. While she observed her, Nancy's attention was drawn to a dusty blue car that she knew was Dana MacCauley's. Nancy ducked down in her seat until it, too, pulled into the bank lot, then slid over to the passenger seat and removed a small pair of binoculars from the glove compartment. From there she could just see around the bulk of the van.

Dana was pulling into a spot near Phyllis's car. It was obvious that they had a prearranged meeting. Dana's must have been the urgent phone call Ms. Arletti had referred to.

Dana called to Phyllis, who was waiting for her at the entrance. Together they continued toward the bank. Dana put her bank card in the door slot and the two women entered the twenty-four-hour lobby. Nancy longed to get out of her car and move closer. But she didn't dare. The glass walls of the lobby made it too easy for the women to notice her.

Nancy picked up her binoculars and peered into the window. With a happy, almost triumphant look on her face, Phyllis handed Dana something.

It was a wad of cash!

Chapter

Fourteen

NANCY HELD HER BREATH and adjusted the focus on the binoculars. That money had come from Phyllis's purse, not the machine. She couldn't tell the denomination of the bills, but even if they were twenties, the amount would be large. Dana studied the wad a moment, then smiled and shook Phyllis's hand. Dana wrote out a deposit slip, put the cash and the slip in an envelope, and deposited the envelope in the automated teller machine.

Nancy watched the women a while longer. They seemed happy when they left the bank, got into their respective cars, and drove off. Nancy's mind was racing. Normally two people didn't meet at a bank just to make a deposit. Obviously they were up to something. Was Phyllis giving Dana her cut of the illegal money?

When both cars were out of sight, Nancy got out of her car and went to a phone booth near the bank.

Luckily she was able to reach Harrison Lane in his office. After Nancy explained what she wanted to know, he took the number of the telephone she was calling from and promised to call her right back. In fact, it was almost ten minutes before the telephone rang.

"I'm sorry to have taken so long," the banker told her, "but I wanted to be absolutely sure of my facts."

"What did you find?" Nancy asked. "Was I right? Was a big deposit just made into the I. Wynn account?" She held her breath and waited for his response.

"I'm afraid not," said Lane.

Nancy's mouth fell open. "There wasn't?"

"No," he replied. "I'm sorry, but the only recent activity in that account was that withdrawal yesterday afternoon. By the way, I gather your little trap was a success."

"Yes and no," said Nancy. "I got answers to some questions, but the big one is still a mystery. If anything, it's more of a mystery now than ever. You're positive that no one put money into that account from the Archer Street cash machine in the last fifteen minutes? Maybe your records are running a few minutes behind?"

"No, I'm afraid not," Lane said once more. "The only activity at that cash machine in the last quarter-hour was a deposit of two thousand dollars into the account of PointTech Computers. Hmm—I think that's the company that installed the system at the school."

"PointTech?" she repeated. Suddenly an idea occurred to her. "Thanks, Mr. Lane. I'll let you know if I get any closer to a solution." Then Nancy said goodbye and hung up.

As she walked back to her car, she tried to make sense of what she had just learned. Of course! she thought. I should have realized right away! The I. Wynn account was just a cover-up account. It was only for drop-off and pick-up purposes. The money was actually going into the PointTech account. It was the perfect cover. Yet there had been no activity in the I. Wynn account at all. Maybe the two thousand dollars represented most of the cash students had paid till then.

Nancy was distracted from her thoughts as she felt her hands throbbing. It was time to put more anesthetic cream on them, so she started up her car and drove home, hoping her dad wasn't mad because she hadn't called him.

* * *

"Hannah, that pot roast was delicious," said Nancy, pushing her empty plate away from her. It turned out that Carson Drew had had to work late anyway, so Nancy and Hannah ate a dinner of pot roast, potatoes, and broccoli alone. "I couldn't eat another bite."

The housekeeper raised her eyebrows, a teasing glint in her eyes as she said, "I guess that means you won't be having any of my chocolate-chip cookies."

"Bite your tongue!" Nancy exclaimed. "You know I can always find room for a cookie, Hannah."

She got up and began helping Hannah clear the table, but the housekeeper waved her away. "I'll get it, dear. You need to give those poor hands a rest."

"Thanks, Hannah." She gave Hannah a quick hug after grabbing a couple of cookies, and went up to her room. Stretching out on her bed, Nancy simply let her mind wander. In the past she'd discovered that sometimes confusing clues made sense when she did this. She began to drift off to sleep, images from the case swimming through her mind.

One face continued to reappear—that of Walter Friedbinder. Walter Friedbinder standing next to the faculty mailboxes. Walter Friedbinder making plans to check the filing cabinets. Walter Friedbinder reacting to the note Kim had left him. And, Nancy thought, he knew her real last name.

She'd noted his odd behavior on several occasions, but she'd been so busy concentrating on Dana and Phyllis and Victor that she hadn't actively investigated the headmaster.

Nancy suddenly came fully awake and sat up in her bed. She got up and went to her desk for Friedbinder's biography. Then she began dialing the universities that he said he'd attended. It was late, though, and she wasn't able to get through to any of the offices. She'd have to wait until the morning to check on Friedbinder's background story.

Propping her elbows on her desk, Nancy rested her chin in her palms. She could be wrong about Friedbinder. After all, Kim was the only suspect she'd ruled out so far.

She headed downstairs, her mind still on the case, but the sound of the doorbell interrupted her thoughts. Nancy opened the door to find herself face-to-face with Victor.

"Hi," he said a little nervously. "I hope you don't mind, but I looked up your address in the phone book."

An alarm went off in Nancy's brain. In order to look up her address, Victor had to know her last name—her real last name. "Is that so?" she asked. "How did you know where to look?"

"Kim told me who you really are." Victor's tone was flat. The sparkle in his amber eyes and his easy grin were gone. He was pale and seemed anxious. "I'd like to talk to you," he said. "Want to take a drive? It's kind of important."

"Okay," Nancy agreed, grabbing her denim jacket from the hall closet. She called to Hannah to let her know where she was going. "Come on," she said, pulling the door closed behind them.

They climbed into Victor's beat-up car and began to drive. The night had grown foggy, and the streetlights gave only a hazy, dim glow. Occasionally Victor flipped on his wipers to brush the mist from the windshield. For five full minutes neither of them said a word. Then, pulling to a stop at the curb of a residential street, Victor turned to her.

"So you're the famous Nancy Drew," he said. "I guess I'm the guy you're after, huh?"

Nancy shot Victor a quick look. What was he saying? Was this an admission that he was the grade-changer? "I don't know," she hedged. "Are you?"

"Don't play games with me," Victor said, a rough edge in his voice. "I know changing Phil's grade wasn't right, but I'd do it again."

"Why don't you just tell me how it all started," she said carefully. Nancy didn't want to reveal that she didn't know about Phil or even who he was. I'll just hear Victor out, she decided.

"That's simple," Victor replied. "About a year ago, a guy who's been a close friend of mine since we were kids told me he was in big trouble. He's an ace basketball player, and a couple of good universities had their eye on him, but he had flubbed one of his courses during fall semester. He was afraid that they were about to put him on academic probation, right before basketball season started. He'd be bumped from the varsity and lose his chance at a scholarship."

"So he asked you to change his grade?" Nancy suggested.

Victor shook his head. "Not a chance! He never even knew. It was all my idea. I did a good job, too. I didn't dare change that D he'd gotten. It would have been too easy to spot. So instead, I eased his other grades up, just enough to bring his average above the danger line."

"I see," Nancy said. "And once you found out how easy it was, you decided to keep doing it, only for money."

Victor stared at her blankly for a moment before asking, "Is that what's going on?" His amber eyes grew wide with surprise. "I figured you were trying to find out who changed my pal's grades. I thought Friedbinder had noticed it and put you on the case. Boy, do I feel dumb! What you're investigating is much bigger, isn't it? Well, I can tell you for sure that it's not me. I don't care if you believe me or not, it's the truth. I fiddled with my friend's record—one time. Afterward I swore I'd never do anything like that again. And I haven't."

Nancy didn't know what to think. Victor's manner was very convincing, but all good liars could be convincing. She measured Victor against what she knew about the true criminal. Victor could be made to fit the profile, but only by making a number of unlikely assumptions.

She didn't see why he'd tell her about his friend Phil if he really was changing grades for money. Then there was the fact that Nancy's threatening messages had come from Phyllis Hathaway's computer. It would probably be pretty hard, if not impossible, for Victor to gain access to her office. And why would he bother when he had easy access to so many other terminals?

Besides, Nancy had better candidates already, ones who fit the pattern of facts almost perfectly.

"I guess I blurted out my little secret when I didn't really need to," Victor noted. "Are you going to tell Friedbinder?"

Nancy was silent for a long moment. Then she

said, "Why don't you confess to him yourself, Victor? That would probably help things go more in your favor. I don't think it would be fair to penalize someone too harshly for one mistake. And I suspect the people in charge at Brewster will end up feeling the same way—once they understand the circumstances."

"I hope you're right," Victor said in a gloomy voice. He turned around and started the engine, then added, "It's weird, but I feel better now that you know. Thanks for listening. I'd better get you home."

"One more thing," said Nancy. "Don't confess right away. Wait a day or so."

"Why?" he asked.

"You may be confessing to a whole new set of people," she told him. "That's all I can tell you right now."

Victor whistled softly. "Sounds like big-time stuff."

On the drive back, Nancy settled into her seat and closed her eyes, starting to plan her next move. When she opened them, she saw that they were just passing Brewster Academy.

"I just saw lights in the school office," she said urgently, grabbing Victor's arm. "It's nearly nine. Who'd be there at this time?"

Victor pulled over to the curb. "Cleaning people?" he suggested, following her gaze. "Maybe they brought somebody in to work on the fire damage."

"Maybe," Nancy replied. "But I'd like to check it out. Do you mind?"

His answer was to drive into the school parking lot. They got out of the car and walked quietly up to the front door. To Nancy's surprise, it was open.

"I don't like this," Nancy muttered. "Come on."

Down the hallway, a fan of light spilled out from the open door to the administration offices. Nancy led the way, creeping on tiptoe, and peeked inside. Dana MacCauley and Phyllis Hathaway were standing in the far corner of Phyllis's office, staring down at the screen of the computer terminal. Dana was shaking her head, a puzzled expression on her face.

Suddenly Phyllis let out a cry of alarm. "Dana, do something, quick!" she shouted. "It's starting to reformat the hard disk. If we can't save the file, our entire plan will be ruined!"

Chapter

Fifteen

Nᴀɴᴄʏ's ʜᴇᴀʀᴛ ᴡᴀs ᴘᴏᴜɴᴅɪɴɢ. She was tempted to rush in and catch the two women off guard, but there was one thing she had to check first.

Victor tapped Nancy's arm, then whispered, "I could probably help them out."

That gave Nancy an idea. "Yeah, go ahead," she said quietly. "Do what you can, and keep them in there for as long as possible."

Victor nodded, giving her the thumbs-up sign. Nancy stepped back as Victor sauntered into Phyllis's office. "Hey, ladies, what's the problem?" she heard him say in his most upbeat voice. "I saw lights and came to investigate. Don't want anyone burglarizing my school."

"Boy, am I glad you're here!" Dana exclaimed. "Sit down and see what you can do with this."

From the hallway, Nancy watched as Victor sat in front of the computer and began to work. She waited until they were all staring at the computer screen and then stole silently through the anteroom and into Friedbinder's office. She didn't dare turn on the light. Outside the security lights glistened through the foggy mist. It would have to be enough light.

Nancy tugged at the middle drawer of Friedbinder's desk. It was locked. Taking a letter opener off his desk, she used it to work at the lock. Open, she silently urged it.

With a satisfying click the lock finally gave, and Nancy pulled open the drawer.

"Jackpot!" she murmured softly. In the dim light she saw all she needed. Eagerly she sorted through papers. There was a bit of ripped newspaper—the obituary of Ignatz Wynn. The name and address were highlighted in yellow. There was also an opened letter addressed to the deceased Mr. Wynn. Inside was a Social Security check with Wynn's Social Security number written on it. Nancy recalled the old woman telling her that a man had come by the house. It must have been Friedbinder. He'd been snooping around for the Social Security number, and he'd found it.

Nancy continued to sort through the papers. On a yellow legal pad she found names and Friedbinder's notes to himself scrawled casually across the paper. "Sally Lane—$1,000," read one line. Altogether, Nancy counted six more students' names with numbers scribbled beside them. On the top of the pad he'd written a note to himself. "Kim Forster—eager to go to college. Needs scholarship. Can't afford payment. Any use?"

"You found a use for her, didn't you," said Nancy, completely disgusted. She tore the sheet off the pad of paper and stuck it in her jacket pocket. Then she continued to search through the drawer. The next thing she found was a small notepad. Opening it, Nancy saw computer notes. Most of them were unintelligible to Nancy, but she recognized the dots, squiggles, asterisks, and letters as being computer commands. They were definitely in Friedbinder's handwriting. Here was good proof that Friedbinder had a very sophisticated knowledge of computers!

Suddenly the sound of raised voices made Nancy jerk up her head. "Mr. Friedbinder!" Victor nearly shouted, warning Nancy. "What are you doing here?"

"I might ask you the same," Nancy heard Friedbinder reply, his voice full of accusation. "As if I didn't know."

Shoving the notepad into her jacket pocket, Nancy moved quickly to the door but not quickly enough. She was momentarily blinded as Friedbinder entered his office and snapped on the light. He stopped short when he saw her. "And what are you doing here?" he growled.

"My job," she said coolly.

Friedbinder seemed to relax. "And you've done a good job, too," he said. "I see you've witnessed all three of them. I should have guessed they were all in it together."

He was trying to pin the whole scam on Phyllis, Dana, and Victor, but Nancy already had the proof she needed. "Why are *you* here?" she asked, trying to keep her voice neutral.

"Forgot some papers," he said. "It was just a lucky coincidence I got here in time to see them trying to finish the job they started by setting today's fire."

"What job is that?" asked Nancy.

"Isn't it obvious? Trying to destroy evidence of their little grade-changing racket. I guess they realized you were getting close."

Friedbinder walked to his desk, picked up the phone, and dialed a number. "Harrison? Walter here. Listen, Nancy Drew and I have our grade-changer," he said into the receiver. "Can you get down here? Good."

At that moment Phyllis Hathaway appeared in

the doorway, her face livid with anger. Apparently she'd overheard part of the conversation. "What are you up to now, you—you worm?" she cried.

"Nice try, Phyllis, but it won't work," said Friedbinder, glowering at the assistant headmaster. "I think you can kiss your career as an educator goodbye."

"Is that so?" Phyllis replied. "Well, for your information that's exactly what I intend to do. I've just given Dana the last payment making me half owner of PointTech Computers. I'm giving you my notice."

That certainly explains a lot, thought Nancy— the money changing hands, the phone calls, the meetings.

"Why would the records being destroyed spoil your plan?" Nancy asked, recalling what she'd heard Phyllis say when they came in.

"Because I couldn't resign with Brewster in the middle of a total computer breakdown. That would be pretty irresponsible. It would look as if I'd done it to make work for PointTech—which is not true," Phyllis said emphatically. "A major computer problem would delay my leaving by months."

"That's almost convincing," Friedbinder sneered. "You and your partners don't fool me. First Dana saddled Brewster with an overelaborate and faulty computer system. That was bad enough. But now this grade-changing plan . . . Is your greed limitless?"

Nancy observed Friedbinder carefully. He was as tense as a tiger ready to spring. His icy blue eyes were fixed menacingly on Phyllis. He was hardly the controlled headmaster one would expect.

Dana and Victor walked into the room. "We haven't done anything wrong," Dana insisted. "I sold Brewster a fine computer at a fair price. Anyone in the business will say the same. And if you are implying that we are involved in some grade-changing—which I just overheard—you're insane!"

"Then what are you doing here now, after school hours?" Friedbinder asked.

Phyllis stepped forward. "There was a message on my answering machine, saying that someone was going to sabotage the computer system this evening. I thought it was probably a crank call, but I couldn't take the chance that it wasn't on the level. I collected Dana, and we came right over."

"Just in time to see the hard disk erase itself," said Nancy. "Mr. Friedbinder, I think *you* have some explaining to do."

"What!" he cried. "I—I—you're in on this, too!" he sputtered.

"You know that's a lie," said Nancy, facing Friedbinder squarely.

Just then, a breathless Harrison Lane rushed into the office. "What on earth is happening here?" he asked.

"Ms. Drew seems to have lost her mind completely," said Friedbinder. "Either that, or these three have induced her to join their sordid scheme."

Turning to Nancy, Lane asked, "What is he saying?"

"He's upset because I've accused him of being the phantom grade-changer," Nancy told him, her eyes still on the headmaster. "Which he is."

"What!" cried Harrison Lane.

"You can't prove anything," Friedbinder said at the same time. "Those records are completely lost. Erased."

"No, not really," said Dana. "At the end of each workday, the contents of the computer's hard disk are automatically copied into a high-capacity tape cartridge. That way, no matter what happens, you can't lose more than one day's work. I'm surprised at you, Walter. Obviously you didn't finish reading the user's manual I provided."

"Would those include a record of when and from where the command to erase the hard disk was entered?" Nancy asked.

Dana smiled. "Yes, they would."

"I bet I can access those files right now," said Victor, leaving the room.

"I find this hard to believe," Lane put in. "Why would a man in Walter's position do such a thing?"

"Greed," Nancy suggested.

"I'll sue you!" Friedbinder shouted. "You'd better watch your step, Ms. Drew!"

Victor returned to the office. "I won't be able to get those records tonight. It'll take too long."

"That's because there's nothing to get," said Friedbinder. "You have nothing on me."

"I wouldn't call these nothing," said Nancy, pulling the yellow sheet of paper, the newspaper clipping, and the pad of computer notes from her pocket. "'Sally Lane, one thousand dollars . . .'"

All the color drained from Walter Friedbinder's face as Nancy read the list of students and the amounts he'd gotten from each of them. "Where did you get that?" he sputtered, his face purple. Without waiting for an answer, he lunged toward Nancy.

Nancy was ready for him, but before he reached her, Victor butted his shoulder into the headmaster's chest. Friedbinder went flying backward and landed on the floor.

Harrison Lane examined Nancy's evidence. "I don't think we'll be needing computer records," he said. "You'll be hearing from the board's lawyer in the morning."

"This is an outrage!" cried Friedbinder, climbing to his feet.

"No. Fraud, arson, extortion—those are outrages," replied Lane.

Friedbinder flashed a furious gaze at Nancy. "I was on easy street," he said, puffing his chest out arrogantly. "I had those kids so scared I knew they'd never tell anyone what was going on. And who would they blab to, anyway? Me, that's who." He let out a short, disdainful laugh. "Everything was going great—until you came along."

His face red, he sneered, "If I'd had my way, you would have died in that fire, Nancy Drew! I planned to set it before you showed up. When I heard you go in early, I figured I might as well get you, and the evidence, out of the way at once. It was easy to pour that gasoline around the door without your hearing—you were so involved."

"You mean, you were trying to kill Nancy?" Victor gasped. Grabbing the headmaster's right arm, he twisted it behind his back, as if to ensure he wouldn't try to make a run for it.

"Don't worry, Victor," Nancy told him. "Friedbinder's not going anywhere for a long, long time."

Chapter

Sixteen

AT LUNCHTIME the next day Nancy walked into Phyllis Hathaway's office. Phyllis, Dana, and Victor had been working there all morning, trying to retrieve the school's erased files.

"Here she is now, our heroine!" cried Phyllis. Nancy had dropped her tutorial look and was wearing jeans and a large, soft cowl-neck sweater of deep blue.

Nancy laughed. "I'm just here to wrap up a couple of loose ends—and to say goodbye."

"You should be proud of us, Teach," said Victor. "We managed to save all the computer files."

"While we were at it, we did some investigating of our own. Guess what we've discovered," Dana added. "Walter was transmitting messages from his terminal, routing them to a midpoint terminal, sometimes two midpoint terminals, and then sending them to their final destination."

"So I was right. That's why the messages seemed to be coming from the newspaper room," said Nancy.

"Well, guess what *I* found out this morning," Nancy told them, leaning against Phyllis's desk. "I called all three colleges mentioned in his résumé. Not one of them has ever heard of Walter Friedbinder! He's a complete fraud; never even graduated from college. Then I called the last school where he was headmaster. I told the new headmaster what had been going on, and he began going through *their* files. Guess why he had such a great reputation for bringing up the school's academic performance?"

"He electronically doctored students' records?" Phyllis guessed.

"Yep," Nancy replied. "Apparently, the one thing he didn't make up was his ability with computers, though we may never know how he got to be such a whiz."

"Harrison Lane told me that he's organizing a class-action suit against Friedbinder to get all the students reimbursed," said Phyllis. "The board of trustees is suing him for fraud. Plus, he'll probably be indicted for arson and attempted murder. I'd say he's in for a whole lot of trouble."

Dana chuckled softly. "Couldn't happen to a nicer guy." She patted her computer, adding, "All the students' grades are back to what they were, thanks to PointTech's brilliant back-up system."

"Speaking of PointTech," Nancy said to Phyllis, "are you still joining the company? You know, Brewster will probably ask you to be their head now."

"They'll have to ask someone else," Phyllis told her. "It was a big step for me, but now that I've made it, I can't go back. I'm leaving Brewster at the end of the month."

Nancy got up. "Well, good luck. I have to go now. I just wanted to say goodbye."

Victor's eyes locked with hers. "I'll walk you to your car," he said, getting to his feet and grabbing his jacket.

They walked out the front door of the school. It was a warm day. The thermometer had climbed into the low sixties, and a warm breeze rustled the vividly colored leaves on Brewster's campus. "Did you tell Phyllis what you told me last night about changing your friend's grade?" Nancy asked him as they walked.

"I did, this morning," Victor replied, grimacing slightly. "She said it wasn't fair to punish Phil for something he knew nothing about. Then she gave me a long lecture about ethics and technology, which I deserved, I guess. My punishment is to stay after school and work on getting those files back together until it's done."

Nancy gave him a sympathetic smile. "That's tedious work, isn't it?"

"Major tedious," he agreed.

They walked on in silence for a little while longer, until they reached Nancy's car. Opening the driver's door, Nancy threw her bag onto the passenger seat and climbed in behind the wheel.

Victor leaned down, resting his elbows on the open car window. "I hope you didn't come to say goodbye to me, too, Nancy," he said seriously. "I really want to see you again."

Nancy took in his handsome face, broad shoulders, and beautiful eyes. Then she sighed. "Victor, I told you about Ned. I like you, but—"

Victor stopped her words with a warm, tender kiss on the lips. "Victor, I can't," she said. "If it wasn't for Ned—"

Suddenly Victor looked under her car, then checked the back seat. He walked to the front of the car and checked under the hood. "What are you doing?" Nancy asked with an exasperated laugh.

"Looking for Ned," he answered, flashing her his disarming grin.

Nancy couldn't help playing along. "Ned isn't here," she told him.

Victor's grin grew even wider. "That's right," he said. "So I'm going to keep trying for you, Nancy Drew."

Nancy's next case:

Nancy has joined Ned on campus for Emerson College's homecoming weekend, and that means pep rallies, parades, and of course the annual gridiron clash with archrival Russell University. But when danger takes the field, the cheers turn to tears—because winning is academic when a player's life is on the line.

Bad grades have sidelined the first-string quarterback, and now the pressure's squarely on the shoulder pads of backup Randy Simpson. But a series of anonymous threats leave Randy running scared—and Nancy running out of time. She has to find out who's calling the shots before the game reaches sudden death . . . in *MIXED SIGNALS*, Case #63 in The Nancy Drew Files™.

"Who are you?"

Amelia fought against the urge to demand to know why he held her daughter in his arms. Reece didn't warm easily to anyone. Strangers terrified her.

The man cradled Reece's head in a tender way that made Amelia's heart dip. Child in arms, he rose on powerful legs and approached. As a priceless jewel set in precious metal, he placed Reece beside Amelia on the hospital bed.

"My name's Ben Dillinger. Your daughter found me in the parking lot of the mall where you fainted." Questions sparked deep in his brown eyes. "Why *did* you faint?"

"That isn't any of your business," she whispered.

"When I see a life in jeopardy, it *becomes* my business. You were driving when you passed out, and your car crashed into a pole. You nearly died today."

Amelia had always faced life head-on without backing down. But suddenly, the pressure threatened to do her in. "What am I gonna do?"

"Let me help you, Amelia."

"But why?"

"Because I care."

Books by Cheryl Wyatt

Love Inspired

*A Soldier's Promise
*A Soldier's Family
*Ready-Made Family

* Wings of Refuge

CHERYL WYATT

An RN turned stay-at-home mom and wife, Cheryl delights in the stolen moments God gives her to write action and faith-driven romance. She stays active in her church and in her laundry room. She's convinced that having been born on a naval base on Valentine's Day destined her to write military romance. A native of San Diego, California, Cheryl currently resides in beautiful, rustic Southern Illinois, but has also enjoyed living in New Mexico and Oklahoma. Cheryl loves hearing from readers. You are invited to contact her at Cheryl@CherylWyatt.com or P.O. Box 2955, Carbondale, IL 62902-2955. Visit her on the Web at www.CherylWyatt.com and sign up for her newsletter if you'd like updates on new releases, events and other fun stuff. Hang out with her in the blogosphere at www.Scrollsquirrel.blogspot.com or on the message boards at www.SteepleHill.com.

Ready-Made Family
Cheryl Wyatt

Steeple Hill®

Published by Steeple Hill Books™

STEEPLE HILL BOOKS

Steeple
Hill®

Recycling programs
for this product may
not exist in your area.

ISBN-13: 978-0-373-87526-9
ISBN-10:   0-373-87526-6

READY-MADE FAMILY

www.SteepleHill.com

Printed in U.S.A.

I led them with cords of human kindness,
with ties of love; I lifted the yoke from
their neck and bent down to feed them.
—*Hosea* 11:4

To my church family at The Vine in Carbondale, Illinois. I've fashioned Refuge Community Church after everything you are. Thank you for teaching me how to love God and live out my faith. Thank you for embracing ethnicity, and for stretching wings of refuge across every socioeconomic barrier to serve the community without agenda. Thank you for being a place where people can come as they are and be loved.

Dear Jesus, this one's for You.
Help me always write as worship.

Melissa Endlich, every reader touched by these stories is because you and the Steeple Hill Books team took a chance on an unknown, unpublished, unproven author. Thank you from the depths of my heart.

Acknowledgments

Thank-you to Gretchen Reynolds for help with research for Carolina's outer banks.

Huge thank-you to to Donna Fleisher for all your Air Force assistance. Thank you also to Amn Nolan, Pennock and "BH," as well as Nancy Barnes, her squadron commander husband and the PJ community at Hurlburt Field who input ideas and answered my gazillion research questions. I appreciate your help with all things pararescue! May God watch over you and keep you safe while you do these things, "So others may live."

Congratulations to Connie Kuykendall, who won the opportunity to name a character in my book. Gus Johnson is the perfect name for Refuge's lovable hillbilly mechanic!

Chapter One

Chapter One

"**M**ister! Mommy needs help!"

The child's cry spun U.S.A.F. Pararescue Jumper Ben-li Dillinger on his toes to face its source. Purchases clunked beside his car, Ben's feet propelled him toward the youngster.

Tears falling from two teddy-bear-big eyes brought Ben, heart and body, to his knees. Speaking of bears, she clutched a tattered brown one.

"What's wrong, princess?"

Ben scanned Refuge Mall's parking lot for the mother. Maybe she had car trouble. But it wouldn't make sense for a parent to send a child this young for help. No vehicle with its hood propped, either. In fact, his was only one of the few remaining since closing time minutes ago. Not only that, the child's duress surpassed a stranded-car scenario.

A tiny hand tugged him up. "C'mon! Mommy's over here. Something bad happened!"

Urgency speared Ben. Hand in hand they loped around the building. Near a pharmacy across the deserted lot, a compact car that had seen better days sat, trunk open. Steam billows hissed from a gaping hood accordioned by impact. A dented front bumper hugged a light pole. A motionless human form plastered to the dash spiked Ben's pulse.

He loosened his hand from the girl's and ran at a dead run toward the car, then stopped. Kid couldn't be more than six, seven years old. Too short for an SUV to see if it sped across the lot. Ben circled back, swept her up and sprinted to the fractured vehicle. Primer, faded red paint and rust coated the exterior. The child panted, either from ninety-degree heat or fear.

Closer now, Ben wished for more light from the low-slung southern Illinois sunset and peered through the driver's side window. A young woman lay slumped over the steering wheel.

Wavy, light brown hair spilled over her cheeks and dusted the dash. Fog misted the inside glass, prohibiting him from assessing her further. At least the haze indicated she had to have been breathing recently. Child still hoisted with one arm, Ben yanked the driver's side door handle with his free hand.

Locked. And hot.

"Ma'am?" He pressed his face to the front glass. Palm flat against it, he pounded on it, then the side window. Nothing. Hand fisted, he banged harder, called louder. "Ma'am!"

He set the little girl down on the curb and gave her shoulders a comforting squeeze. "Stay put, princess. I'm a paramedic. I'll help your mom."

If it's not already too late.

Ben hustled down the length of the car. Jerked the back door handle. Resistance met his effort. Hands cupped against the glass, he peered, called and pounded.

Other than music wafting like a dirge from within, eerie, dead silence entombed the interior. He imagined ovenworthy temperatures inside the car could fry eggs on the dash.

Was she even still breathing? He squinted.

Patches of deathly pale skin peeked through her mass of curls, identical to the little child's in color and texture. What part of her arms he could see below her T-shirt hinted at pink. Good. Not mottled or cyanotic. His own breathing slowed.

Rushing to the passenger side, Ben flipped open his phone, dialed 911 with one hand, tried the doors with his other.

All locked.

He reported his name, credentials, findings and location to the dispatcher then remained on the line. Car couldn't be as old as he'd thought. Otherwise, it wouldn't have those child safety locks. He'd kick a window out if he had to.

"*Jesus, please.*" Ben ran moist palms over his shorts and looked around for something besides himself to break in with.

Trunk.

Yes! He dived in, shoved a plastic bag aside and crawled through. Scrambled over the folded-down backseat, entering the car as the child had probably exited. Smart kid. How long had they sat here before she'd gone for help?

Car was definitely DOA but the radio was still running. Weird. He recognized the song as one he'd learned chords to during worship practice at Refuge Community Church this morning.

Ben climbed in and turned the radio down. "Miss?"

No answer.

Hand on her sweat-drenched shoulder, he leaned bare knees to sit and counted her breaths. He pressed two fingers to that spot on her neck and hoped to feel life pulse beneath his fingers. Her shoulders rose and fell with the sweet breath of life. With respirations present, she *had* to have a heartbeat.

What was the deal?

Ben increased the pressure of his fingers in tiny increments. There. Yes. *Thank You.* His own heart rate slowed.

Moist hair clung to the victim's face. Ben brushed it away and updated the dispatcher. "Other than a mask of pallor, she looks peaceful in slumber." Except a young mother wouldn't sneak a Sunday afternoon snooze in a scalding parking lot.

"I have an inkling something's up with her heart." Translucent gray lips blended into her face. Same starkly pale color. Not a hint of pink. Mauve-blue circles ringed her eyes.

"Caucasian female, early twenties, small build. Pulse weak and erratic. Respiratory rate normal but shallow. She's overheated, though not dangerously." Phone to ear, Ben informed her there was an unattended child with the unconscious driver.

"Sir, we have a unit en route but they have a long detour due to a broken-down train blocking the tracks across Main. It may take longer than normal for them to arrive."

"Ten-four. If her stats change, I'll contact you."

Hands beneath the woman, he lifted her torso off the steering column and leaned her against the seat. Palming a lever on the side, he tilted it back. Careful with her neck in case she'd injured it, he lifted her chin, opening her airway. The movement elicited a weak moan but other than that, no response.

Probably she'd become incapacitated prior to running into the block. Hard to tell since she didn't have her seat belt on.

Ben dipped his head out the passenger door and gave the child a reassuring smile. "Ambulance is on its way."

Hopefully it'd get here soon, but the ambulance service sat blocks from Refuge's lone hospital, located clear across town.

Wrist tilted, he peered at his watch. Needed to meet his younger brother Hutton at the airport in…a short hour.

Hutton's frequent panic attacks and Mosaic Down Syndrome made it difficult for him to travel by air to begin with, much less fly alone as he'd done today. Ben not being there to pick Hutton up could propel him over the edge and bomb to bits any bridge of progress Ben had made with Hutton's trust.

The little girl inched from the curb to the door. Big brown eyes grew wider with each shuffling step. "What's a matter with her?" She chewed the end of her finger and her chin quivered as she peered beneath long eyelashes at her mother.

Heart caught, Ben wanted to scoop her up and hug her, but didn't suppose he should, being a stranger.

"Not sure. Help's coming, though." The faded seat creaked when he pivoted into a better position to face the youngster.

Huge tears bubbled, then dripped from a pair of eyes struggling to be more brave than scared as they glistened at him. When she stepped toward Ben and reached up tiny hands, he couldn't help it. He opened his arms to her. The waif of a girl moved like a minimissile. He lifted. She scrambled up in his lap then burrowed beneath his chin. Tucked herself into his chest like she belonged there.

Rivulets of sweat trailed down his back. Pink ribbons affixed like fluffy tiaras atop her head tickled his neck as he leaned over the mother and rolled down the driver's window. The little girl's hair felt squeaky clean. Groomed and cared for. A warm breeze lifted the strands, bringing hints of strawberry.

He transferred weight from knees to rump in the seat to monitor the mother and hold her trembling child simultaneously.

With featherlike motions, the little girl rubbed her mom's arm with one hand and clenched her stuffed animal tighter with the other. "Did she die?" Small whimpers puffed out heart-shaped lips resembling the mother's. "Because my guinea pig died and never came back to life again and I'd miss Mommy so, so bad if she never came back to life again." Tears spilled over the rims of her eyes and raced down rosy cheeks.

Ben hugged her closer, wishing he'd anticipated the scope of her fear. "No, princess. Your mommy's not dead." Being a U.S. Special Operations airman had trained him to notice every intricate detail about everything. His senses took it in automatically no matter the situation. He regretted not picking up on her fright and distortion about her mother's condition.

"B-but she won't wake up. L-like my guinea pig. I tried and tried to wake Mommy. But I couldn't." She shuddered.

"She only passed out," Ben explained. "Honest."

"P-passed out what?"

"No, I mean she fainted. It's like a deep sleep is all. Can

you remember what happened?" He placed a soothing hand
on her back, moving his thumb side to side much the same
way he strummed his guitar strings during worship. He prayed
silent songs for God to comfort her and chase away fear.

She shrugged one shoulder. "We was in the store to buy
some, um, um, I can't tell ya that part." She dropped her
voice to whispers and fiddled with the buttons on her denim
overall dress.

"That's okay. Tell the part after you left the store," Ben
whispered back.

"We got in the car and Mommy told me to buckle up. Only
she didn't buckle in Bearby like usual."

Panic surged Ben's heart rate. "Bearby?" *Dear God, don't
let there have been another child in this car who wandered
off.* Ben scanned the parking lot and started to scoot from the
seat when scraps of tattered yarn thrust in his face.

"Bearby's my...well, it was *supposed* to be a baby but
Mommy's only learning how to sew. He looks lots like a bear
and a little like a baby so I named him Bearby." The girl suspended the toy in front of Ben's face.

"Ah. Got it." He peeked around the bear-baby thing. "So,
there weren't other children in your car?"

She shook her head and rubbed a frayed loop of Bearby's
worn string hair. One blink later a faraway expression
embraced her features and she veered Bearby back in front
of Ben's nose. "He doesn't like to be ignored."

"Oh. My bad." Ben took Bearby's paw-hand between his
two fingers and shook gently. "Nice to meet you, Bearby. I'm
Ben." He raised his vision to the girl. "What's your name?"

"Not s'pose to tell ya since you're strange. But if you asked
Bearby, he'd say I was Reece North."

Ben reassessed the mother. Nothing had changed. She
didn't look worse, but she didn't look better either. A prayer
song worked its way into his mind. *Giver of life...* He whis-

pered it over the woman. When he looked up, he caught the child watching him curiously.

"What's your mom's name?"

"Amelia Grace North, and you can recognize her because one of her eyes goes crooked and she hates that."

No idea what that meant. Lazy eye, maybe? But the child's chatter seemed to keep her from fretting about her mother.

"What happened after she forgot to buckle Bearby?"

"She kept breathing long. You know, like you're going off the diving board. She blinked fast and said she needed to drink and sit but she was in the seat. I tried to get her water. She yelled to get in the car. Mommy never yells, and I cried."

"I understand." He leaned down and ran his hand around the floorboard. Bingo. He lifted the worn wallet and located Amelia's ID. Pretty girl. Organ donor. Twenty-four. Two years younger than him. Must have dropped weight since this photo.

Other than a North Carolina driver's license, the wallet contained seven dollars in bills, pictures of what looked to be Reece, a few coins and a red construction paper heart engraved with "I love Mommy." No credit or debit cards. No checkbook. No emergency contact list. Very odd.

He faced Reece. "Then what happened?"

The child rubbed her mother's cheek with Bearby's fluff. "She said sorry and we'd get some water at a drive-through. Then she started the car and took off. Her words turned silly and she went asleep when she was driving and we bumped the light."

"So, she fell asleep before she hit the pole?"

"Yes, sir." Her head bobbled up at a siren's whine.

In the distance, blinking red LED lights strobed through a row of white-dotted dogwood trees planted in the median on the far side of the mall.

He rechecked Amelia's vitals and returned his attention to Reece. "Was she feeling all right earlier today?"

Reece sighed. "I think she was feeling kinda sad today. Grandma and Grandpa are nice to me but mean to Mommy. Yell, yell, yell. That's all Grandpa does to her. We was living with them, and now we don't live nowhere."

The whine of more approaching sirens widened the little girl's eyes. "Blinkin' panda cars! The cops are comin' too?"

Ben chuckled. "Seems that way. They'll take care of your sick car while the ambulance crew takes care of your mom." Maybe he should call a family member. "Where is your father?"

"Who knows? He left my mom when I was in her belly." She dropped her chin to her chest and scooted off his lap.

Gripped with the inexplicable urge to tug her back, Ben resisted. He exited the car, whistled and flagged paramedics over. An echoing whistle sounded beside him.

Arms shot above her head, Reece waved them in crisscross motions too, mimicking Ben's stance. She watched him instead of the approaching responders. "Met my dad but a judge said he can't be around me because he's unfit. Took me to bars where he works and forgot me a few times when I was only a kid."

Ben stifled a laugh. Seemed to him the girl was still a kid, but in her mind she must not be. Gusts of compassion moved him. "I'm sorry to hear that. It's his loss, you know?"

Defiant chin tilted skyward, a scowl pinched her freckle-dotted face. "Don't matter, 'cause we don't need a man or anyone else around to help us."

Kid come up with that on her own? Or from something the mother said? Suddenly, uniformed men and women flocked to the scene.

Stepping back, Ben studied Reece, the mother and then their sparse possessions in the seat. Thick emotion settled deep for this young unconscious woman and her daughter.

Clearly they'd fallen on tough times as evidenced by the lone white, lumpy trash bag. Well-worn clothes, toys and holey socks sprigged out its top. A large, black lawn bag resided in the trunk. When he'd moved it aside to enter the vehicle, old pillows and thin blankets had spilled out.

The economy car was clean inside save scattered crayons and coloring pages. High mileage. By the looks of that crinkled hood and inverted bumper, it'd have to go in for significant work. Repairs could cost more than the car's worth.

Police and EMTs buzzed around the car. Ben relayed information as they tended Amelia. Reece stayed on his heels. Her darting eyes and feet proved her skittish of everyone.

Everyone except him.

Stallings, a local officer who skydived at Refuge Drop Zone, listened to Ben's report. He rifled through the wallet Ben provided. He clicked his police radio and recited data.

"What are they doing to Mommy?" Drawn near to Ben's side, Reece monitored the paramedics with distrust as they poked and prodded on Amelia, now flat on a stretcher.

"Helping her." Ben knelt to eye level. "Everyone needs a little help sometimes. It's okay to need help, you know?"

Her pert nose squished up at him. "Did you ever need help?" Her voice softened to thoughtful whispers, as though she longed to connect with someone who understood the plight of hard times.

Ben studied her tiny, pearl-smooth hands cradled in his large, work-roughened ones and thought a moment. He honestly couldn't recall a time in his adult life when he'd been in a situation to need help. Other than dangerous missions with his seven-man PJ team in which everyone's survival depended on teamwork. His childhood had been a different story.

He was sure the rest of life wouldn't pass him by without thrusting him into the throes of need again.

Knowing chitchat distracted her from the interventions being carried out on her mother, Ben smiled at Reece and tapped her arm. "When I was about your age, our house burned down. We lost everything except our lives."

She sucked in a breath. "Everything?"

"Yep. Everything. And we needed lots of help. Even though we were new in town, the Christian churches helped us with food, shelter, clothing and even new toys for me and my brother."

Though Ben meant his words to sooth, a cynical scowl that made the girl look much older, pulled her eyebrows down below a curtain of thick bangs. "All's I know's when we needed help, everyone turned their back. Especially that guy who is supposed to be my dad and his no-good family and the church."

"I'm sorry. Not every guy is like your dad. And not every church is like that one."

Her shoulders dipped in an upside-down shrug. "I know. But, try to convince Mommy of that."

"Your grandparents from North Carolina, too?"

"Yep. The beach. Said if I stay with them, they'd take me swimming all the time. But I want to stay with Mom. She acts tough but she'd get lonely without me." Reece's grin gave Ben a glimpse of empty gum space where two teeth were MIA.

A blue sedan pulled up. Miss Harker, the local Department of Children and Family Services caseworker whom he knew from church, exited her vehicle and approached with a smile. Relief lifted weight from Ben's shoulders. Officer Stallings must have notified her. Ben eyed his watch. He needed to get to the airport stat but felt torn. Reece close stuck to him.

Standing, he gestured toward the caseworker. "Reece, this is Miss Harker. She's from the Department of Child and Family Services. She'll watch you while the doctors help your mom."

Reece's grip squeezed blood from his hand, turning fingers white. Not the reaction he expected. Miss Harker moved closer.

Panic pounced in Reece's eyes. She darted behind him, peeking around his leg. "Bearby wants you to watch over us,

Mr. Ben. Not her." She jabbed a finger at Harker before curving it back into her mouth. Then Reece shot perturbed expressions at Harker. Visual declarations that stated she was up for a showdown of wills if necessary.

Miss Harker knelt and held out a gentle but firm hand to Reece. "Come on, honey. I'll take you and Bearby to get some food. I'll bet you're hungry. You like curly fries?"

She first ignored Harker's hand, then glared as if it held an immunization syringe. "No, thanks. Bearby don't want to eat."

Hands to shoulders, Ben guided Reece around. Pandemonium erupted. He needed to leave now to meet Hutton's plane. Silent pleading skipping across Reece's tortured eyes clawed at him. Arms twined tight around his, she strained with whale strength that belied her shrimp size.

Harker reached. Reece dived. Buried herself like a soldier under fire in a foxhole, deep in the crook of Ben's arm, as though trying to cement her place in his embrace. "I—I... Bearby wants Mr. Ben."

He took a step away.

Tears rushed from her fear-widened eyes, flooding his resolve, fumbling his feet, fencing his intent to leave this instant. But, he'd promised Hutton...

Miss Harker tried to woo and calmly tug the child from Ben. Would've been easier to pry himself from entanglement by a colossal octopus with twenty hyperactive tentacles.

Reece shrieked and clawed for his shirt, clearly heading into hysteria. "B-Bearby'll get scared without Mr. Ben! Please! Please!" Her wails drowned out those of the emergency vehicles.

He peeled her fingers loose. Betrayal in her eyes landed a mortar shell in his chest. Ben looked to Harker for what to do.

Miss Harker smiled at Reece, then eyed him. "Tell you what, Ben. I know and trust you. Seems the little one has taken quite a liking to you. Mind riding with us? Maybe

Bearby would feel safer that way." Miss Harker brushed a gentle hand along Bearby's misshapen head, careful not to touch Reece.

Visibly relaxed, Reece turned imploring eyes on Ben. "Please, Mr. Ben? Bearby *really* needs you."

Something in the girl's eyes and words sunk emotional hooks into him. By now, Ben figured out she projected onto the beloved toy. He recalled Reece mentioning Bearby doesn't like to be ignored. Her forlorn tone of voice and the lonely haunt in her eyes had suggested she was all too familiar with what that felt like. Sympathy ambushed him.

But, Hutton...

"Let me see what I can do." Phone out, Ben dialed his PJ team leader, Joel Montgomery, and asked him to meet Hutton at the airport. Refuge Drop Zone's skydiving facility, which Joel owned, sat minutes from the airport. Ben would have to trust God to be with Hutton if Joel was late. Hutton didn't cope well with change. Even altered minor plans became major stressors for him. Hopefully Hutton remembered and recognized Joel. If not, the situation could get sticky.

Satisfied Joel knew what Hutton looked like and would head to the airport ASAP, Ben ended the call and pocketed his phone.

Reece took his hand. "Thank you, Mr. Ben."

"No problem, princess." He retrieved her booster seat and art supplies, then walked with her around the dove-gray building to his red Chevy Malibu. He deposited his shopping bags in the trunk and locked it as Miss Harker pulled up. Reece scuttled closer to him and eyed Harker with deadly intent. Ben buckled in the booster, Reece, then Bearby, even though he felt silly. He picked up Reece's coloring pages as Miss Harker drove them around to follow the ambulance. Chatter would smooth things over.

"You draw these?" He spread pages across the seat.

"All except one." Reece pulled it from the bottom. A caricature drawing of Bearby holding Reece, both clad in the outfits they wore today.

Wow. "Where'd you have this done?" Outstanding artist.

"Mommy drew it. She draws all the time when she has paper. Isn't she good?" Reece's face lit.

"Real good. The best I've seen." He pulled up another paper. This one's tone seemed different than the rest, drawn in bright pastels. This drawing had a black face with a red frown and huge gray tears. "What's this one about?"

"For when I felt sad about being a mistake and I didn't have Bearby to love me." She grew quiet and solemn.

"You're not a mistake, princess. You're a child of God and a treasure to Him." Wanting to push back whatever dark cloud loomed, Ben slid the page under the seat and held up the caricature. "This really looks like cartoons of you and Bearby."

"Speaking of cartoons, what's your favorite?" Miss Harker asked from the driver's seat, probably to distract her and build rapport. The channel of conversation switched to cartoons, and Ben settled back to listen. And pray. While they talked, questions popped through his mind like automatic weapon fire.

What kind of person would ignore this beautiful gift from God and make her think she was a mistake? Didn't they know how many couples want children and can't have them?

Ben thought of his team leader, Joel Montgomery, in the process of adopting another child because of his wife Amber's infertility. And Ben's parents, who'd tried for years to have another child after him before conceiving his brother. Though Hutton had MDS, Ben's parents cherished him. Something Ben hadn't done until recently.

He'd always been embarrassed about his brother being different before. Now, he was ultraprotective of him, and he wanted to bring Hutton to Refuge so his parents could realize their dream of a year of world travel.

How could he have treated his brother like a sore thumb growing up?

Who in Reece's life would do something like that?

Ben stared through the ambulance windows, where IV fluids dripped through tubes he knew were attached to both of her emaciated arms. What kind of mom was Amelia North?

From the signs he'd noticed, a good one. Something had caused them to leave in a hurry. But what had led to her poor state of health today? Ben didn't know. For the struggling single mother's and little girl's sakes, he aimed to find out.

He didn't want any child to go through the hurt he'd put his brother through. Hurt he didn't know if Hutton had ever fully recovered from. He still didn't trust Ben fully, which was why Ben's insides twisted that he couldn't be at the airport for Hutton as he'd promised.

He prayed Joel would find Hutton before he wandered off somewhere in a state of confusion and panic. A personal code of duties wouldn't let him leave Reece until he made sure she was okay. Her mother's problems were life-threatening, sure, but hopefully only temporarily so.

Upon arriving at the hospital, Ben helped Reece out and handed her Bearby. "The police officer obtained your grandparents' phone number and will notify them about your mom."

Nothing could have prepared him for the horror striking Reece's face. "Oh, no! You didn't call them! They'll hate Mommy and for sure think she's bad now. If they take me, Mommy'll hate you for callin' the cops! Why did you? Grandpa and Grandma won't help her. They'll just yell and take me from her like they said!" Terror oozed from sodden eyes.

Why would they want to take Reece from her mother? Was she unfit? Or did the grandparents have issues not conducive to child rearing? What if they were cruel, and Ben telling Officer Stallings about them would cost Amelia custody?

Ben couldn't have felt worse if a bullet whizzed through his ribs. Tumultuous questions blew through him like three hundred MPH winds—threatening to bow him sideways.

Questions that demanded answers.

For Reece's sake, he would not rest or relent until he had them. He didn't walk away from something like this. Didn't turn his back on defenseless ones who cry out that something's wrong and they can't make it right. When someone couldn't fight for themselves, Ben would do it for them. Had always been that way, took up for those who couldn't take up for themselves.

Except his own brother.

But he had a second chance to make things right. Nothing could mess that up. He refused to let anything get in the way of taking over care of Hutton in his downtime. He'd figure out plans for what to do with Hutton during missions.

Wonderment stole over Ben as he studied Reece. So much like Hutton. Childlike. Dependent. Unconditionally loving. Reaching for normalcy. In need of security. Protection. Nurturing. His heart expanded then squeezed. This child had wiggled her way in it just that fast. When she'd burrowed beneath his arms and chosen to cling with trust that he had a feeling didn't come easy, she'd embedded herself deep into his heart.

Compassion dropped Ben to his knees to place steadying hands on her moping shoulders. "Reece, listen, we *had* to call someone. I didn't have a choice."

Hurt and betrayal spun like violent hurricanes in the gulf of angry eyes. Like lightning reaching to earth, it jabbed across the space separating them, leaving regret smoldering in the carnage.

"Reece…"

Dark clouds of accusation hovered. Any trace of vulnerability fled her face. Except her bottom lip, which quivered like palm trees in a high wind as it fought to form words. "I thought you were mine and Bearby's friend. If they come, they'll take me away. If they take me from Mommy, Bearby and me will never, ever like you again...

"And neither will Mommy."

Chapter Two

Amelia North awakened to the tallest Asian man she'd ever seen cradling her sleeping daughter. Fierce protectiveness roared to life and lifted Amelia's shoulders from the bed despite the lancing pain.

But the scene in the nearby chair stilled her. Reece, a portrait of serenity, slept soundly. Her head rested on the stranger's broad shoulder, a pillow of muscles on a pillar of strength. At least to her artist's eye.

Childhood memories of naptime with her dad strolled through Amelia's mind uninvited. Nostalgic father/daughter images stepped forward to hug her conscience. A hard lump formed in her throat. She stiffened her shoulders and swallowed, forcing it back down to that unfeeling place. Vaulted her heart shut against the emotional onslaught.

It hurt too much to feel. Hurt even worse to hope for restoration. She'd made too many mistakes, and forgiveness apparently didn't exist in her father's DNA.

Never mind that. What on earth was going on? Where was she? Amelia took in the room, feeling like she'd been dropped off in the twilight zone. The sterile environment, antiseptic smell and bland, generic room décor notified her that she'd obviously landed herself in a hospital or mental ward.

Then she remembered.

Parking lot. Wave upon wave of dizziness. Vision blurring. Hearing fading and returning, fading and returning. Quivering muscles. Failed motor function. Body sinking into the swirling deep, pulled by invisible undertows. Periphery closing in. Arms weak. Face numb. Hands fighting to steer to safety in a torrent of impending blindness. Reece's screams. Then total, terrifying blackness. Horrendous crunching. Desperately uttered prayers for Reece's protection and for God to send someone to help. Then nothing.

Then sketches of remembrance dawned of hazy words whispered in a cappella melodies to a song she'd never heard by a voice she didn't recognize.

Giver of life, oh Living Water, King of All Kings, Merciful Father, Lord of all Lords, Faithful and Righteous, Breathe on her Your Sweet Breath of life.

Maybe this man could fill in the missing pieces.

Amelia cleared her throat, bringing his attention from a newspaper. The strangest sensation drifted through her that he'd known the precise instant she'd awakened but waited for her to engage conversation.

"Who are you?" She gritted her teeth against the urge to demand her daughter back and to know why he held her in the first place. The weirdest thing was Reece didn't warm easily to anyone. Strangers terrified her.

The man cradled Reece's head in a tender way that made Amelia's heart dip with an old familiar ache. Without warning, it awoke a five-year-long yearning for Reece to have a father figure in her life.

Child in arms, he rose on powerful legs and approached. Sinewy with strength, arms the color of warm embers handled

Reece as one might an exquisite china doll. As a priceless jewel set in precious metal, he placed her beside Amelia in the bed.

Precision and control defined him as he took delicate care to position Reece's head in the bend of Amelia's elbow. The back of his hand brushed her forearm as he slid his hand out from between them. Amelia's skin tingled in the wake of his warmth.

She swallowed the want of human contact away. Not physical—she'd learned that lesson the hard way. It was emotional intimacy she craved.

Stop it. How dare you? You don't deserve it. Furthermore, you don't know him.

No doubt a brain injury had brought her here. Otherwise her mind and emotions wouldn't be rivaling for the ridiculous and vying for the absurd.

Calm, cool gaze rising to meet hers, he leaned near enough so that she caught whiffs of masculine soap. Creaks sounded as powerful fists closed around her side rail. She thought the thing might crack under his pressure. Guy had to be a body builder or some sort of Olympian.

"My name's Ben Dillinger. Your daughter found me in the parking lot of the mall where you apparently fainted from dehydration." Mouth flattened to a straight line. Muscles rippled along his chiseled cheek. Questions sparked deep in his brown eyes. His imposing height, commanding presence, and quiet yet unwavering confidence made her want to cringe and cover her head with the gauzy hospital blanket.

This was not the sort of guy you'd want to contend with as an enemy. Conversely, he struck her as the kind of person who, if on your side, would fight to the death for you if need be.

How she'd wished for that kind of friend all her life. The closest person to it was her cousin Nissa who was both her best friend and her biggest thorn. When Nissa was there, she was a rock. But when she got on her flighty, impulsive streaks, forget it. She couldn't be counted on. Of course, part of it

Nissa couldn't control due to her bipolarism. But still, when she went off her meds—look out.

Amelia cleared her throat and tried to insert bravado in her voice. "Well, thanks. You're free to go now."

But the man just stood there, looking at her as if he couldn't quite figure out what planet she'd orbited in from.

Then he narrowed his eyes but not in a judgmental way. "Why aren't you getting enough to eat?" He raked a hard gaze over shoulders and arms that she knew had grown too thin.

Self-consciousness jolted through her in waves. He couldn't possibly understand the circumstances that had brought her to this point. Or how fear kept her from eating. Fear that Reece wouldn't have enough. Fear she'd have to crawl on knees of humiliation and beg, only to be denied again. She resisted the urge to tuck loose sprigs of hair behind her ears. If it looked as mussed as it felt, no wonder he stared.

So what that she wasn't as attractive as other women? Wasn't like she could help being born with a lazy eye. It never bothered her unless she found herself in the presence of an extremely attractive man. Like right now.

Being a single mom took everything she had. As much as she longed to, she couldn't afford the time or money required to keep up with modern haircuts and clothing styles like her single and childless friends. Or at least the friends she used to have. When Reece came along, her friends vanished one by one.

"I'm not starving myself. This isn't your business, but I feed her plenty if that's what you're worried about," she whispered.

His brows rose. "Not my business? When I see a life in jeopardy, especially a child, it *becomes* my business." His voice lowered when Reece stirred.

And what a voice…like liquid velvet.

That he placed huge but gentle hands protectively over Reece's ears stirred emotions she'd thought had disappeared. Neither Reece's father nor her own cared who heard when they'd yelled at her. At least her father had never been physically violent like Reggie. Thankfully he was out of her and Reece's lives for good.

The darkening storm twisting Mr. Dillinger's face cautioned she might be about to get a serious verbal lashing. Something she'd grown accustomed to in life. Amelia tensed and steeled herself. After all, she deserved it.

She'd endangered her daughter's life today.

Shame crushed her under its weight and threatened to push long-held-back tears from her eyes. She blinked desperately. What if he saw to it that her daughter was taken from her? Would he?

Could he? Amelia seemed to remember bits and pieces of a DCFS caseworker being here. Had she dreamt that? Was the woman coming back for Reece? Amelia couldn't contain the violent trembling in her fingers.

His vision dropped to her hands before looking back up to her face. As if sensing her emotions, her fear, and noticing the acute tremors, his expression softened by detectable shades. His stance relaxed by fractions. Sharp guy. Didn't miss a stitch.

He leaned back. "But it just so happens I'm not that worried about her. It's *you* I'm concerned about. Your daughter told me you hardly eat. What food you have, you give to her. You nearly died today."

The truth exploded in her head. One by one, the words chased each other through her mind. *You nearly died today.* Then where would Reece be? Who would care for her? What kind of life would she have? No one would love her as much as Amelia. No one. Therefore, no one would care for Reece better. She'd almost ruined her daughter's life today by becoming absent from it.

Just as fast as the rebuke sliced through her, Amelia's brain reverted back to the "It's you I'm concerned about" part.

When was the last time anybody cared about her or showed

concern? Something melted in her toward Ben, but Reggie's vicious face surfaced in her mind like a mental taunt. She fought to refortify the boundaries around herself. Men were cruel and self-serving and not to be trusted. She'd do well to stay as far away from them as possible, physically and emotionally.

Yet Mr. Dillinger hadn't yelled. The tense bunch in her shoulders relaxed a measure.

A new layer of softness entered his eyes as his gaze washed over her. He didn't stare at her lazy eye like other men. Nor avoid her face out of pity. Nor did he seem to struggle with not knowing which eye to look in. He held his gaze like his stance, steady and strong and sure.

If she could attach a word to his expression, she knew what it would be. She also knew she didn't deserve it in the least.

Mercy.

Even her parents, two people who should love her more than anything no matter what, had told her so. Constantly reminded her of how she'd messed up her life with one wrong choice one indiscreet night her senior year, when Reece was conceived.

She'd naively thought Reggie would marry her when she'd told him she was carrying his child. Instead of banding her finger, he'd bruised her body. Beat her up when she refused to "get rid of it." He'd pummeled her stomach, nearly causing her to miscarry. Told her at the police station when she pressed charges that he wished she had lost it.

One year ago, he'd resurfaced, claiming he'd changed and convinced her he wanted to know his daughter. Come to find out, he only wanted to retaliate at Amelia for pressing charges for the assault during her pregnancy.

Subsequent astronomical hospital bills with no insurance thrust her into debt. Care and medication required to keep her pregnancy viable after the assault had cleared her bank accounts and eaten away her college fund. She'd spent the last five frugal years paying off her debts, starting with medical ones and ending with money owed her parents.

Saving her daughter's life had been worth it.

Tense seconds ticked by as Amelia and Ben stared at one another, communicating yet not. Clearly, he waited for an explanation and wasn't about to leave until he had one.

For once, Amelia was just too weak and tired to fight. And something in his eyes called to her. A flicker of caring?

What could she say but to be honest? She certainly didn't want her daughter to be taken away. They might as well bury her if that happened. Reece was her life.

Which was why she left her parents and their constant demeaning of her mothering. Worse, doing it in front of the daughter she tried her best to care for. But with her father, her best was never good enough. And her mom never stood up for her.

Amelia thought for sure God felt the same apathy and disdain toward her. Otherwise, He wouldn't churn the category-five winds and rip her sails every time she managed to surface from the last ocean of adversity life whipped her into.

Her entire existence had been one long, roiling storm of struggle, and Amelia could no longer envision a clear blue sky anywhere on the horizon. If she could just get out of this hospital and get to the new job that waited for her, she and Reece could get a fresh start.

Speaking of hospitals, how would she pay the bill? Tears threatened to overwhelm her. She couldn't catch up no matter how hard she tried.

Growing increasingly uncomfortable beneath the pressure of the stranger's scrutinizing gaze, she drew a much-needed breath and dropped her gaze to the blanket. Making sure Reece still slept, Amelia worked up courage to admit the truth.

Her fingers fiddled with fiber at the edge of the hem. "It's not because I don't want to eat. Times are hard." She cleared her throat to remove the clog in her voice.

"There are food banks."

It wasn't just his tone that told her he wasn't buying her story. The stubborn set to his jaw and determined glint in his eyes did.

Why would a complete stranger care when her own family and supposed friends didn't?

She glanced at his pressed khaki shorts and brown leather loafers. A black polo shirt was stretched tight across a well-developed chest. Obviously he appreciated nice things. His immaculate appearance made her all the more self-conscious. She tugged the hospital gown tighter. It could have wrapped around her twice. He seemed aware of every move she made.

Why did she care what he thought of her? What right did he have to stand here and stare? And interrogate her?

He saved your life.

Well, yeah, there was that. Maybe he was some kind of cop or something. Someone who had a right to know Reece was secure. Who was he? What did he do for a living? Something physical for sure. Military, maybe. Yeah, that had to be it. Or maybe his militant determination just made it seem so.

Another horrendous thought blew through her mind. "I remember a crash…"

"You were driving when you passed out. Your car crashed into a pole."

Crashed.

The room swam. She didn't want to know, couldn't face the question pounding her brain or dodge the dollar marks blowing into her mind like a thousand wayward leaves. She swallowed. She could barely afford to keep oil, gas and windshield wiper fluid in the car, much less pay for repairs. Or worse, another car.

A sigh escaped, challenging the grit she'd garnered within to make it no matter what, and do it without complaining.

She'd always faced whatever life brought her head-on without whining, breaking or backing down. For the first time in her life, the pressure threatened to do her in.

"What am I gonna do?" Had she said that aloud? For sure, she was on the verge of losing it. Folding under pressure. Just like her parents predicted she would.

"Let me help, Amelia."

Ben's soothing voice pulled her from the mental mire. She studied him. What she interpreted as deep concern emanated from his eyes.

Even if the remote possibility existed that he honestly cared... "You must have an ulterior motive."

"I care. Period."

If that were the case and she caved and accepted, that meant losing. And she wasn't about to let the naysayers win. It wasn't that she cared about losing as much as she feared losing Reece if her parents' predictions came true.

"I can't. Period."

Chapter Three

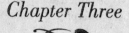

Ben held his tongue when Reece stirred. She rubbed her eyes and sat up, yawning. The transformation in Amelia mystified him.

Her face lit with an incalculable amount of love when she scooped up the girl as if she were a long-sought-after, newly found treasure. "Hey, Reece's Pieces. Have a good nap?"

Reece hugged her mom back, then scuttled beside her to eye the tubing in Amelia's arm. "Is that the medicine that fixed your electric lights, Mommy?"

Amelia blinked and eyed the IV, then Reece. Confusion crossed her features.

Fighting frustration at Amelia's reticence to his help, Ben picked Bearby off the floor where he'd fallen when Reece sat up. He set the toy in her lap. "Yes, that medicine is fixing your mom. Only they're called electrolytes. Something that when you get too dry, can cause your heart to go haywire."

Amelia's throat muscles constricted, letting him know he got his point across. Fear and remorse in her eyes told him he realized how life-threatening her lack of intake had become.

Silent, Reece watched the nonverbal exchange between her mother and Ben before wringing Bearby like a wet dishrag. No wonder the thing looked so tattered and misshapen. Kid never let it out of her sight. She clearly used it for comfort and apparently needed its remedy a lot.

God, please put some stability in this child's life.

Forcing a smile, Ben adapted a lighthearted tone. "But your mom's better now, so there's no need for you and Bearby to worry." Ben ruffled Reece's hair, then tickled Bearby beneath where he thought the chin might be.

Amelia's eyes went wild all of a sudden and darted over every surface in the room. "My wallet—"

"Is locked in the safe at the nurses' station along with all your money," Ben said.

"Did the doctor say when I could get out? I have to start my new job in another state—" her head tilted toward the wall clock "—a week from Tuesday."

Eyebrows up, Ben said, "You might want to call them. You're gonna be a few days late." Didn't the girl realize her car wasn't drivable? "The mechanic said two weeks minimum."

Amelia's face paled. "Two weeks?" She threw off the covers and let down the metal rail. "I can't wait that long. They might not hold the job." Snapping to her feet, she tried to reach for the IV stand but tottered sideways.

Arms snaked out, Ben lunged forward and steadied her. The contact startled them both. Frozen, they stood face-to-face, staring. Neither moved for the longest instant. Ben couldn't shake the thought that she felt so right in his arms.

Oh-kay. He definitely needed sleep.

"Take it easy. You're not leaving Refuge tonight. Certainly not in the next five minutes." He relaxed his grip on her arms, which were surprisingly more toned than he'd anticipated.

Expression dazed, she slid back to the bed. "But—I need to get to Missouri. We need time to get settled." Her eyes glazed with moisture but she turned away from Reece and bit her lip. Hands steepled, Amelia pivoted from Reece's line of sight and unleashed luminous eyes on Ben. "Did you bring me here?"

He shook his head. "Ambulance."

Her eyes widened. "How much will that cost without insurance?"

"Two or three grand."

She swallowed, shuttering her expression when she found Reece watching. "Okay, that's doable."

Tremors repossessing her hands told a different story. Able to assess body language with microprecision, Ben knew her weak smile was forced. He deducted that a couple grand would devastate their current financial situation. Not counting the cost of car repairs. Again, the urge to help seized him.

In Ben's experience, when thoughts grew this persistent, God was usually behind the nudging.

Amelia turned on cartoons for Reece then faced Ben. "I need to get something from my car."

"It's impounded."

Head dipped, her lips parted, letting loose a gasp. "Wha—"

Ben leaned in, keeping his voice low on account of Reece. "Registration isn't in your name. Nor is the insurance up to date." He'd discovered that while searching the glove compartment to find her parents' names, which he'd given to Officer Stallings.

"But I gave the money for insurance to my dad and he said he—" She drew a deep breath and fumbled for the call light. "I need to get out of here." Her thumb pressed the button numerous times as if firing a stream of torpedoes out of a submarine weapons hatch.

"Yes?" A voice broke through a speaker above her bed.

"I'm awake. I need to talk to my nurse, please."

Crackle. "I'll send her in." *Click.*

"Thank you."

Crackle. "Welcome." *Click.*

Ben checked his phone for a message from Joel, who'd promised to call after getting Hutton's prescriptions filled. Joel would read the labels and know Hutton had to take his meds with food. His own stomach rumbled at the thought.

Maybe if Stallings was still on duty, he'd let Ben retrieve the items Amelia sought from her car. Question was, would Amelia trust him with the task? His stomach growled audibly this time.

"Hungry?" Amelia stared at his midsection.

"A little."

She waved a dismissive hand toward the door. "Feel free to go get something to eat. I—I mean, not that I think you have to come back—"

He grinned. "Trying to get rid of me?"

Her eyes widened. Pretty color of brown, like Reece's. Far lighter than his.

"Of course not. I—I just meant—"

His hand circled her arm gently. "Kidding. Take it easy. I'm here because I want to be. That all right with you?"

She leveled Ben with a look. "Not sure yet."

He smiled. "Least you're honest." She'd gotten so flustered, she was downright adorable.

Her eyes rolled. "And you're pushy, not to mention bossy."

"Let's not forget nosy." By no means conceited, Ben was humbly confident. "And nice-looking." He kept a straight face.

Reece covered her chin and giggled.

Amelia dipped her head, but he caught the grin chasing the frown from her mouth. He got the feeling smiles were a rare commodity for her. He couldn't kick the urge to help her. At least offer. Who knew if she'd be a willing recipient? Only way to find out was test the waters and try to build rapport.

"And according to Reece, I'm strange." He poked a gentle finger into Reece's arm. She giggled again, and this time, her smile remained.

Amelia watched the interaction with what he interpreted

as guarded interest. "I teach her not to talk to strangers. She gets words mixed up sometimes."

His wink found Reece. "Happens to the best of us." He returned his attention to Amelia. "They brought a food tray a few minutes before you woke up. You should try to eat."

Shame darkened her features as she eyed the room until she found the tray. She started to stand.

Palm up, Ben stopped her. "Please, allow me."

He wheeled the creaky bedside tray over her knees in the bed. He hit the lever to adjust the table height but it caught. Too high for her to eat on. He fiddled with another lever. The table came down. Hard.

"Yow!"

Heat scorched his face and he lifted the tray off her knees. He cast his best sheepish grin. "Sorry. I never was any good at working those things."

She rubbed her knee and eyed him through long lashes, much the way Reece had at the mall. "Since you saved my life, I'll forgive you one little bruised knee."

He nodded, containing his reaction over seeing a quest for truce enter her eyes. And the hint of a captivating smile that he knew if turned up to full wattage would knock his jump boots off.

Amelia waved Reece close. "Here, try some of this." She offered what looked and smelled like a tuna salad croissant.

"My tummy's full, Mommy. Mr. Ben and Miss Harker got me something to eat at the big house. And see what else I got?" She lifted a plastic tiara. "This came with my chicken nuggets."

"What's the big house?" Amelia asked.

"Refuge Bed and Breakfast. To my estimation, it houses the best restaurant in town. Country dishes. Real eggs fried in bacon grease. Heart-attack-on-a-plate kind of meals. Though they do offer healthy alternatives."

Reece bounded on her knees in the bed. "Mommy, you *have* to go there. They have curly fries as long as your leg."

Amelia pulled Reece close. "Is that right? Who's Miss—?"

The door swished open. A nurse with a name tag bearing *Bailey, RN* scurried in. "Sorry about that. I was tied up with a new admit. Good to see you awake and coherent." Smiling, she switched out Amelia's IV fluid.

"You're hanging another bag?" Amelia eyed the wall clock.

"Yes, ma'am. You were severely depleted. You're fortunate. When you came in, the electrical conductivity of your heart wasn't firing well. We're playing catch-up. We'll draw blood in the morning. If your potassium's back on track, you could be discharged Tuesday to rest. The doctor will want to follow up with you Wednesday. Make sure nothing more ominous is going on."

"But I don't live here. We're just passing through town. I'm on my way to a secretarial job in Missouri. Waiting is out of the question." Panic piggybacked Amelia's words.

Nurse Bailey raised raven brows. "Tuesday would be the earliest you'd be released. We need to be sure you're able to keep liquids in and maintain normal potassium ranges on your own. Not only that, Doc Callahan has a strict policy to have hospitalized patients return to his office for a follow-up visit two days after discharge."

Silence blanketed the room. It was so heavy, Reece must have noticed. Her hand ceased coloring, and she regarded her mom carefully. Amelia's lazy eye started twitching. Nervous trait, maybe? Other than that, she didn't reflect the anxiety Ben knew blasted her the second those words left Bailey's lips.

Amelia brushed her hand down Reece's back. "We'll need to find a way around that." Her voice remained unruffled, but the pulse at her neck fluttered. "Maybe I could follow up with a doctor in Missouri."

Bailey regulated the IV drip rate. "Not sure that's an option. Besides, I gather your car's in worse shape than you."

Amelia's eyes sought Ben.

He pocketed his hands, mostly to keep from placing them on her shoulders in comfort. "When you crashed after fainting, your car didn't fare well." He paused to let her soak in the news.

Her enthralling eyes watered. She blinked and hid her face from Reece but one tear escaped.

His fingers ached to brush it, and her pain, away. "Once the police release it to a garage, it'll be in automobile ICU awhile, I'm guessing."

Bailey cast a kind smile. "And I'm afraid Dr. Callahan won't release you if he thinks you're gonna skip town. Maybe your man here can find you all a place to stay for a few nights."

Amelia's face flamed. "He's not, we're not—"

"I'm a friend," Ben finished for her, though they'd only just met and weren't friends. Yet. He wanted to spare her dignity.

The nurse halted and cut him a sour look. "But I assumed you were family, all the questions you were asking." She peered at Amelia. "You okay with him being in here?"

Properly scolded, Ben nibbled his lip. He felt oddly busted out even though it hadn't been his idea to stay. Miss Harker apparently had a "tense situation arise" with Amelia's parents that she didn't want to solve with Reece in earshot.

"He saved my life and possibly my daughter's. I think he just wants to make sure we're going to be okay."

Head lifted, Ben met and held Amelia's gaze. "Besides, I was watching Reece for Harker." He faced the nurse. "She must have gotten hung up." She'd gone downstairs to talk to Amelia's family by teleconference with the doctor. Maybe he ought to go investigate the holdup.

Nurse Bailey plumped Amelia's pillows. "All right, then. I assumed because he came in with you, and your little girl insisted on him staying, that he was family. My apologies for breaking any confidentiality. I'm usually rigorous about checking visitors, but we've been swamped this evening." She cast apologetic, motherly glances at Amelia. Then her smile vanished as she slashed another zesty look at Ben.

Uh-oh. Not even Amelia's endorsement had gotten him added to Bailey's friends list. No doubt if Amelia oracled the orders, Bailey'd bounce him right out of here.

"I haven't properly thanked him anyhow." Amelia eyed the phone, then Bailey. "Does it cost to use that?"

"Not for local calls. It won't let you call long distance unless you use a card or it's added to your bill."

Amelia's face fell. Ben spotted her attempt to hide it. He doubted Reece picked up on it since Amelia seemed ultra-mindful of choosing discreet words and controlling facial reactions. She lifted her arm as Bailey approached with a blood pressure cuff.

A beep sounded from the IV machine. Reece's eyes widened. "What's that?"

Ben pointed to the puffy cuff. "This gadget hushes flow for a second when it hugs your mom's arm. This alerts nurses. It's loud because it doesn't know when they're in the room."

Shards of respect sanded rough edges off Bailey's expression as she eyed him curiously and chuckled. "He's right. It hollers at us to find out what's clogged it from dripping."

"Hollers, huh? Hmm. Just like Grandpa. Only he's louder. You can definitely hear him from the other room."

"Reece, enough," Amelia warned. Swooshes sounded as the cuff released. Amelia eyed numbers Bailey scribbled on a clipboard. "About the bill. I don't have insurance. I'm self-pay. Will making payments be a problem?"

"Shouldn't. You can phone the billing department tomorrow during business hours and make arrangements."

After the nurse left, Ben tugged out his cell phone and offered it to Amelia. "Here, use this if you want."

She stared at it as if he'd presented a scorpion.

He flipped open the phone. "Dial, then press that green button to talk. Red hangs up. I have unlimited minutes. No sense paying for calls when you can use my phone for free."

The fight grew evident in her face as she eyed his phone then the one by her bed. He wished he could tell her he knew how hard it was to be the one needing help. But he wanted to spare her dignity and protect Reece from understanding the gravity of the dire situation she and her mom were in.

He set the phone on the table. "I've got to meet someone and grab a bite to eat. I'll be back tomorrow morning if that's okay. There's something I want to talk to you about."

Her eyes fluttered with apprehension. So vulnerable.

Maybe if he wasn't present, she'd feel better about using the phone. Besides, he needed, wanted to spend time with Hutton.

He handed her a note card with his alternate phone number, the Refuge Police Department's number and the number of the lone car garage in Refuge scribbled on it. "Here, in case you need to reach me, Refuge PD and the garage to check on your car. I pulled strings with law enforcement to get it worked on until you can prove ownership and get it out of impoundment."

Looking overwhelmed, she took the card. "How can I prove it's mine? I don't have a title. I bought it from my parents."

"Then they'll have to fax a title and vouch for you."

Though her eyebrows drew together into a discouraged frown, a determined glint entered her eyes. "Thank you."

Ben waved goodbye to Amelia, Reece and Bearby, then slipped out, leaving the phone without a backward glance. It was his personal cell anyway. He had his military phone on him. He'd call Joel, talk to Hutton. See where they planned to meet and buy them some grub.

He figured Amelia would find a way to be gone one blink after her doctor said the words, whether her car was ready or not. He'd do his best to be here before then. He at least wanted to say goodbye. At best, do more to help, which is what he intended to talk with her about.

At the door, Ben peered over his shoulder and found Amelia staring with half apprehension, half hope.

Trapped in the moment, his mind scrambled for words. "If you need anything before tomorrow, feel free to call."

Even if she were still here in the morning, would she let him help? He might have a fight on his hands. So be it. One thing he loved more than skydiving was chasing a challenge.

And something told him Amelia North fit the bill.

Chapter Four

Amelia wanted to crawl under the covers and die. Well, not die, exactly. Just disappear for a good five minutes. She hated handouts. Hated to be the one burdening people. But the guy was right. No need spending money she didn't have just because pride trumped common sense.

Speaking of common sense, what kind of crazy guy would leave his phone with a complete stranger? Definitely, this Ben character was cut from a different mold than any other guy she'd encountered.

And what on earth did he want to talk to her about tomorrow? Multiple scenarios hulked through her head, all confrontational. Dread settled in for what he would say when he saw her next. Probably found something else to scold her about.

Well, she could escape and evade all that if she could get out of here and get to her job.

Ugh! But then there was the problem of the doctor wanting her to follow up days after releasing her. If she went against medical advice, that would not only be unsafe healthwise, but an insurance company might decline her as a client once she got caught up enough to afford premiums for her and Reece.

Dialing Refuge's police department, Amelia asked what

she would need to verify ownership of the car. They repeated the information Ben told her and stated they'd given her the benefit of the doubt and towed it to the local garage.

Towed. That meant it wasn't drivable.

Amelia shook off discouragement and phoned the garage. No answer. She tried again. No answer. Maybe they weren't open on Sunday. Then how could police have dropped the car off?

She called a third time. After ten rings, a garbled answering machine sputtered on. She left a message after the closest thing resembling a beep. That no one answered, and that the garage answering machine sounded like it needed transmission fluid— or worse, a complete overhaul—didn't make her feel good.

A knock at the door broke into her thoughts. "Hello, Miss North. It's Doc Callahan. You decent?"

According to her dad, that was debatable. She adjusted her blankets. "Yes. Please come in." *And let me outta here!*

The room curtain parted and he entered. "Nurse Bailey notified me that you'd awakened."

Ben's phone rang. A number appeared on the face. "Excuse me a minute. That's the car garage."

He nodded and flipped through her chart.

Amelia pushed the button Ben showed her to answer. "Hello?"

"Thiz Eagle's Nest Vay-hicle Repair-a-returnin' yer call."

"Yes, I own the car that police escorted there after it was assaulted by a light pole today."

A hearty chuckle crossed the line. "Yessum. She's here. Perty banged up though."

"When do you anticipate it being ready to go?"

Amelia's gut clenched at the ensuing silence. Then weird chomping came across the line. Then a belch and more silence.

"We-ell. I don't rightly know if she'll ever be ready to go. If there's a possibilty of 'er a pullin' through a tall, I'd say yer lookin' at two weeks…minimum."

Maybe deep breaths would calm her racing heart and make it stop doing gymnastics in her chest. The feeling made her lightheaded again. And nauseous. She eyed her IV, hoping it would hurry and right her…whatever-those-things-were-called. "Then I'd best let you go so you can work on it." A little nudging couldn't hurt, right?

Another chuckle. "I don't work on Sundies," the hillbilly-sounding mechanic said. "Check back'n a day or two or three when I'll know more."

"Thank you." Heavyhearted and light-headed, Amelia hung up and faced the doctor.

He motioned to Reece, asleep in the recliner. "She down for the night?"

"Yes. Nurse Bailey brought blankets and pillows. When it's bedtime, she'll sleep anywhere. I can't count how many times I've intercepted her face heading for a dinner plate."

He chuckled, then his smile straightened as he pulled up a wooden chair and sat beside her bed. Uh-oh. Here it comes.

"Speaking of food, Miss North—"

"Please, call me Amelia."

"Okay, Amelia. Can we talk candidly a moment?"

She nodded. At least he didn't start out yelling. Still, tears sprang to her eyes. "Look, before you say anything, I know I've done wrong." She sniffed, hating that she couldn't make herself not cry. "I also know as a doctor you have to discuss this with me. But I want you to know up front I'm not anorexic."

He nodded. "I believe you. Your lab work and medical examinations don't show signs of long-term starvation. But as you know, you were dangerously dehydrated when you came in."

For the first time, Amelia noticed his name tag.

Oncologist?

Isn't that a cancer doctor?

Her heart nearly stopped. She sucked in a quick breath. He followed her gaze. "Oh, sorry I didn't explain before.

Refuge is a small town. We don't yet have a full-time ER doctor on staff. Until physician recruiters hire one, doctors in town take turns doing ER shifts whether they're in family practice or are specialists. I was on call when you came in. My background is in oncology but I am Refuge's trauma surgeon now. I think you're perfectly healthy other than an electrolyte imbalance secondary to flu and severe dehydration."

She sank back into the bed. "Oh, good."

Shuffling sounded as he adjusted papers. "But I want to make certain this won't happen again."

She sat up. "It won't. I promise. My life changed today. My baby, having to see me go down like that, then go for help—" Amelia shivered, shook her head, eyed Reece and swallowed. "I'll make sure I eat enough and keep myself healthy from now on."

"That's good. Your potassium is still borderline. You could use a couple more bags of fluid. I'm not comfortable releasing you tonight. I think the safest thing would be to see how you're doing tomorrow." He rose. "So I'll see you then, okay?"

"Thank you."

He gave her head an affectionate tap with his papers. "Finish your dinner and get some rest. And by all means, if you want a midnight snack, Nurse Bailey knows where the stash is." He waved and slipped out through the curtain.

Stuck. She wasn't going anywhere tonight. Maybe not even tomorrow or the next day or the day after.

But he was right. The safest route meant staying. Job or no job, making sure she was well and here to care for Reece took precedence. Amelia sighed and jabbed her fork prongs to the food, knowing this meal would be the first of a new leaf.

Like the romaine lettuce in her chicken caesar salad, Amelia felt crunched in a catch-22: to ensure eating, she had to have this job. It was her best hope. Having memorized the number of her boss-to-be, Amelia swallowed the last morsel, drew a deep breath and phoned his Missouri home with Ben's cell.

Four rings later, his gravelly voice answered. She explained her situation. In the wake of silence, she pressed her ear to the receiver. Maybe the call got disconnected. "Hello?"

"I'm here—"

Ominous gruffness hurled across the line with harsh expletives. "Get it together and be here a week from Tuesday or the job's gone."

Tuesday! That was nine days from now. The mechanic said two weeks minimum on her car, *if* it could be repaired.

Amelia took a deep breath and resisted the compulsion to beg, borrow and plead. "I just hope you understand how much I want, *need,* this job, sir. I'll do my best to be there."

Amelia hated that her voice and hands quivered.

"If you can't be here next Tuesday morning, your best isn't good enough. I need a secretary's behind in that office chair at eight that morning. Period." A *click,* then cold silence.

Heat flamed Amelia's face. Not embarrassment. Anger. The words went through her like a hot sword from her past.

Your best isn't good enough.

How many times had she heard that since she'd turned ten?

Doubt assailed her about this new boss. But Nissa had called in a favor, and Amelia needed a job.

She cradled Ben's phone in her palm and curled it close, enjoying that it smelled like him. She huffed and rolled over. Hopefully sleep would come swiftly. She drifted with one thing ticker-taping through her mind:

No matter how hard her new boss was to work for, no matter what she had to do to get to that job by next Tuesday, she would make sure it happened.

For the third morning in a row, Amelia watched the southern Illinois sunrise brighten her room but not her mood.

The flu virus had suddenly reared its fierce head two nights ago, rendering her unable to hold down food or water without the help of IV meds.

Amelia clutched her pocket planner as if staring at it would add days to the week.

She was running out of time.

Sharp knocks echoed off the door, pulling her attention from the calendar of doom and her nausea.

"Come in," Amelia called in a low voice, eyeing Reece as she slept.

Wiggling his fingers in what Amelia had come to know as his trademark wave, Ben, who'd been coming faithfully every morning, entered with a beautiful African-American woman. Envy pricked Amelia. She mentally chastised herself for having hoped he was unattached. His unwavering presence had been a bright spot in her days.

Watching Amelia watch Ben, a smile crept over the woman's mocha face. She stepped forth. "Hi, Miss North. I'm Glorietta Harker, the DCFS caseworker present when the ambulance brought you in. I'm also a friend of Ben's."

"Hi," Amelia said. The emphasis the woman put on *friend* caused Amelia's heart rhythm to beat erratically. As if the woman perceived Amelia's thoughts and wanted to reassure her she and Ben were not an item.

Not that Amelia had her sights on the guy or anything. It was completely normal to be attracted to him since he rescued her. Plus, he was tender and caring toward Reece. That, and his velvet voice, scored him points, too.

It wasn't fair that he looked better today than yesterday. A white T-shirt brought out his creamy complexion. Denim shorts doused him in a down-to-earth flair despite the potent energy in him that blared larger than life. This wasn't just any guy.

"Hey, Amelia. What's up?" His slow grin warmed to her toes.

"Not my potassium." She lifted her arm to show him her IV.

His smile faded. "Bummer. They'd had to restart it?"

"Yeah. My stomach isn't cooperating."

"Wow. You seem to be handling it okay though."

"Yeah. For now." *Only because you being here cheers me up.*

Amelia couldn't put her finger on what exactly it was that made Ben Dillinger one of a kind. But he was one of a few men in the world who stop all activity in a room when they walk in. Though a quietly content, almost shy demeanor orbited him, something in this man's core summoned respect. Precisely the kind of guy who made women's pulses trip.

Precisely the kind of guy who'd never notice Amelia in a million years.

Yet something in his eyes reached for her beyond a quest for friendship. Every time he looked at her, she felt tangibly embraced with sincere care.

Not that he'd even be remotely interested in her romantically, with all the problems and baggage she had. No guy in his right mind would pursue her.

But one of these days, her life would be different. She'd carve a good life out for her and Reece.

Then nothing would stop her.

Chapter Five

While a lab technician entered to draw Amelia's blood, Ben retreated near the door to absorb and process the shock of what Harker had told him on the way up here.

Amelia's parents had no interest in even checking on her, much less talking to Amelia or offering help. The kicker was they threatened to come get Reece. Ben thanked God Harker chose to be Amelia's advocate by insisting they not and had no grounds to.

On his way to bowl with Hutton last night, Ben had stopped by the Refuge PD to talk to Stallings about getting Amelia's car un-impounded. Stallings informed Ben that Amelia's father had said since she got herself in the mess, she'd have to get herself out.

At least he'd finally admitted Amelia had paid them for the car and did in fact own it. Maybe her old man wasn't completely coldhearted. Ben felt glad to be able to bear a bit of good news, especially after her flu relapse. One of her parents had faxed the car title and proof that Amelia held ownership.

Still, Ben could hardly contain his anger toward these people. Compassion churned in him for Amelia and what she must have had to endure up to now.

Any remnants of frustration he'd felt toward her that first day dissipated. He'd mistakenly thought she'd acted foolishly by endangering her and Reece's lives.

Maybe he'd judged her, and her situation, too harshly.

Footsteps sounded as Miss Harker came close to the bed and extended her hand. "My name is Glorietta Harker, but you can call me Glorietta. May I call you Amelia?"

Amelia stared at the hand, then the business logo on Harker's shirt and blinked rapidly. "You're the one from DCFS."

Retrieving her hand, Miss Harker nodded and sat on the side of Amelia's bed opposite of where Reece snuggled in a recliner asleep. "You remember me from before? I wondered, because you were pretty out of it that first day."

She eyed Harker as if undecided whether the woman was friend or foe. "I remember bits and pieces." She nailed Harker's gaze head on. "You gonna try to take my baby away?"

Harker's hand settled on Amelia's. "I lost a baby to a forced adoption at age fifteen that has haunted me just as long. Now, you tell me, do you think I hold even a remote interest in ripping a child from a capable mother's arms?"

A tense silence stretched between them. Amelia didn't speak.

"I am interested, however, in helping you get on your feet. I am a social worker of sorts. I have access to resources you may not be able to tap into on your own. That is my interest."

"That's it? No other motivation?"

"That's it. No other motivation other than to help you. So you can better care for Reece and have a more stable future for the both of you. Your parents certainly don't seem to have an interest in helping at the moment." A look Ben interpreted as annoyance drew Harker's sculpted eyebrows down.

As if Harker's words and reaction hauled a heavy rucksack off Amelia's shoulders, they lifted. "I know. Tell me about it."

Harker pushed a business card across the bedside tray. "Actually, why don't *you* tell *me* about it? Sometimes it helps to talk."

Amelia's gaze darted to Ben and back. "Right now?"

"How about after I grab my second cup of coffee? Ben has something he wants to talk to you about, which is why he's here with me. I can vouch for his character. Then I'll come back and boot him out so we can have girl chat. Fair?"

Amelia blinked, then her face broke out into a smile. The genuine kind that he'd hoped to be on the receiving end of.

"Your mom faxed the car title." Ben approached Amelia. Her arms snapped across her chest in a stubborn fold.

"You spoke to them?" Her back straightened against the bed.

He shook his head. "Officer Stallings did. What's got your hackles raised?"

"I wanna know why you're helping me. What do you have to gain by this? And don't tell me you don't because otherwise you wouldn't still be coming here." She tilted her chin.

Wow. Blunt as a baseball bat. Good. He liked that. Meant he could be blunt right back and they'd never have to wonder what the other was thinking.

"I want to make sure you and Reece are gonna be okay."

"We'll be fine."

Ben dipped his head at the sleeping girl. "Is her life worth the gamble? Because I can smell your fear a mile away."

Ben leaned so close, Amelia glimpsed almond brown flecks in dark Hershey-chocolate eyes. Their richness reminded her how hungry for a candy bar she was—how long it had been since she'd eaten one. He stared without blinking.

And she could not move, could not look away, as he placed his hands palms down on her table. It creaked as he leaned nearly nose to nose. As he opened his mouth to speak, his breath fanned her cheek. The lilt of whispered words both warmed and warned her heart. "What or who are you running from, Amelia North? I won't rest until I find out."

Failure.

I'm afraid of doing my very best and still failing Reece.

He leaned up slowly, keeping his fingers splayed on her table. "And I won't leave you alone until I know you're not going to go off again and do something unwise and unsafe."

Her jaw dropped. "You have no idea—"

"I have every idea. You could have been in traffic when you passed out Sunday. Or on the interstate careening toward a semi doing sixty. Need I say more?"

Panic and remorse waylaid her at the images his words conjured up. Yet no trace of anger resided in his tone.

The urge to explain herself seized her. She hadn't meant to let it go this far.

Who was he to judge her? He probably had lots of money and no children, and certainly no idea of the kinds of things desperation to meet a child's most basic needs could drive a parent to do.

"There's sense in everything, Amelia. No reason not to let me help you and Reece out."

For three days, he'd shown up voicing this same argument. For three days, she'd rejected his help.

But today, something in her gave way.

No idea how, but the velvet in his voice soothed some deep wound inside.

He's right. She knew to the depths of her being.

No matter what disdain wafted from his dark, impassable eyes, Amelia had a daughter to care for. She couldn't afford to concern herself with anxiety over what Ben thought of her.

Resigned to her fate, Amelia drew in a deep breath and tried not to let the flicker of kindness in his eyes affect the twitch she felt escalating in hers. She'd steel her heart, swallow her pride and she'd be fine.

There had to be a catch.

"You expect nothing in return?"

"Nothing. I simply want you to let me help you. For starters, let me get you some groceries, gas and phone cards."

"What, no cash? Afraid I'll blow it on drugs or alcohol?"

Ben shrugged. "No. I don't think that. Your drug screen came out negative and you didn't smell soused when I found you."

The edge of her hospital bed sank when Ben sat on top of the blanket. "Cops found a Bible in your floorboard, not a bottle of bourbon, so I'd say your only problem is you're too stubborn for your own good." He grinned.

"What do you want, other than to squish my toes?" It took considerable effort, both mental and physical, to tug her feet from beneath the warm weight of his thigh.

He moved to the chair, draping his arm across her side rail in a casual pose. "I want you to use the good sense you've been given and get yourself healthy before you go on the road again. Which reminds me, I dropped by Eagle's Nest."

"How's my car?"

"Critical condition. Mechanic's fast. Making your car a priority."

"How expensive is he?"

"Depends."

"On?"

"Whether he has to order parts and how fast you want the work done. If he expedites it, I'm sure it'll double the price." He rested his chin on his forearm and studied her.

"Think I could access it once I get out?"

He straightened up. "Why? You're not sleeping in it. Too hot. And I can tell you had been. She'll die of heatstroke. The inside of a car can heat to over a hundred degrees in fifteen minutes here. It's summertime. And little kids can't survive that kind of heat."

"I wasn't thinking of sleeping in it. There's something I need to get out of it. I could be discharged any time. Do you have shelters here in Refuge?"

"Yes, but it's comprised mostly of homeless men who are known drug users and it wouldn't be safe. Their security is not tight. Too dangerous. I can hook you up with a place to stay near where I live if the doctor releases you."

He was right about the shelter. She had Reece's safety to think about. But why would this stranger help her? What did he have to gain by it?

As if sensing her questions, he handed her a brochure with what looked like a sprawling Victorian mansion on it. "It's where I'm staying. Refuge Bed and Breakfast. Real nice place. Safe neighborhood. I'll pay for two rooms instead of one. If it makes you feel better about receiving help, you can pay me back when you get on your feet. Don't let the fancy looks of it deter you. It's surprisingly cheap."

Amelia worried the hem of her blanket. She didn't want to need his help. But, truth was, she did.

She didn't have anyone else to depend on.

Wouldn't it be safer to receive help from a stranger instead of parents who'd dangle it over her head and then withhold it anyway? Even after she'd humbled herself to begging for Reece's sake? "Government agencies all declined me because they took into account my parents' income, since we lived with them."

Why she said that aloud, she didn't know. Other than her needing him to know she wasn't a flake. That she had valid reasons for her financial struggles.

Truthfully, she battled feeling scared to death being on her own and caring for another human being who depended on her for life and everything in it.

Amelia swallowed a good portion of pride along with the growing lump in her throat. She'd made hundreds of sound choices the past five years. Unfortunately, one wrong choice preceding that determined the course of her life up to this point.

"I ended up a struggling single mother before I was ready because I wrongly trusted a man with everything I had. I don't know if I can take that kind of risk again."

The moment locked in silence, Amelia held Ben's gaze.

What she saw there were eyes corded to a soul that seemed to reach through with a lifeline and beckon her to believe.

You can trust me, Amelia.

Could she?

Even if she were capable of trust again, was he trustworthy? Was Ben Dillinger a man of integrity who stood by his word? Someone she could take at face value?

Or was he, like Reggie, just out to take advantage of her for his own gain? No one helped another person unless it benefited them. Something motivated this man to act like he cared. What was it?

Her head was filled with questions.

Was he acting? Or did he truly care? If the remote possibility existed he did care, why?

No matter. She *had* to get to that job by next Tuesday.

Chapter Six

"Bad move, Dillinger," Amelia said early the next morning as she slid her queen diagonally two spaces. "Check. Mate."

"No way!" Ben leaned forward, studying the chessboard. "You won again?" Not possible. Except for his teammate, Brockton, no one beat him. Ever. But as Ben searched every angle for possible hope for his king, the board echoed its decree: Check. Mate.

Hands ran overtop his freshly buzzed hair and clamped behind his head, he leaned back and eyed her with healthy respect. "I've only seen one other person win that fast. You blow me away." In more ways than one.

Especially when she smiled with her whole face like that.

Knocks at the door broke the trance that rested over the room. Amelia blinked. Ben scooted back as a doctor entered.

The man, familiar to Ben, approached with an outstretched hand. "I'm Dr. Riviera, an associate of Dr. Callahan."

Amelia shook his hand. "Nice to meet you."

"Pleasure meeting you, too." The doctor looked from Amelia to Ben and smiled. "I'm sure we've met before. You're a friend of Joel and Amber Montgomery's, right?"

"Yeah." Ben nodded, realizing where he'd seen the man

before. Ben turned to Amelia. "Joel's my team leader and friend. He recently married and adopted a son," he explained to her, and faced Riviera again. "You're Bradley's oncologist, right?"

"I am. Little guy's doing fabulous. He'll probably outlive us all." Riviera flipped through Amelia's medical records. "Dr. Callahan is a trauma surgeon and had an unexpected surgical case this morning and asked me to come see you. Your potassium is within normal limits. Everything looks great."

Amelia's legs swung over the bed. "I can leave?"

Riviera chuckled at her rapt movement. "I think it's safe to say you can. I'll write a discharge order. But wait until about ten, which marks twenty-four hours of keeping fluids down. We'll measure and test your output to be certain the dehydration is gone. You look more than ready to go."

"I am." She reached for her socks. "Miss Harker should be back from breakfast with Reece soon. We can catch a noon bus."

"Not today, I hope. Dr. Callahan wants to see you in his office Friday afternoon, at two." His pen waltzed across a prescription pad. He tore the top page off then handed it to her. "Here's an appointment reminder and the address. Need directions?"

Amelia stood, pulling her IV stand close when the line pulled taut. "No. What I need is that appointment moved up so I can catch a bus. I have to be at a job Tuesday morning in another state. I need to prepare." She smiled but Ben didn't miss the quiver in her eye. A tiny wobble remained in her gait, telling Ben she was still mildly weak. Or majorly stressed.

From Riviera's scalpel-sharp gaze, he noticed, too. "I'm afraid that's not possible. Dr. Callahan won't be out of surgery until about one, and our office closes at noon on Thursdays. Tomorrow is booked solid until two. I'll send the nurse in to discontinue your IV if I can get your word you won't try to travel, even by bus, until Dr. Callahan clears you on Friday."

Her shoulders slumped. "Okay."

Face casted in empathy, he nodded before turning to Ben. "Nice to see you again, Airman Dillinger." Head tipped, he left.

Ben nudged a tissue box across her table. He drew near. She angled her face away but her tremulous chin and damp eyes didn't escape his notice.

"Thanks." Her shoulders shrugged then drooped. Like the anvil of her burdens made it difficult to draw breath.

"No problem." Maelstroms of compassion swirled inside Ben. What could he do to lift her? Life repeatedly knocked her down. Yet she remained unbreakably determined to crawl up this hull of hardship and break free of poverty's stranglehold.

Admiration for her rose up. His faith suggested hardship could become a harbor if she got to know God better through it. Unfortunately, he didn't get the idea she felt she could trust God to help. Another reason he wanted to befriend her. For sure, she'd be the object of his present and future prayers.

Help me help her without hindering what You're trying to teach her. Prove You love her and care about what's happening in her life. Be the strong tower she runs to, Safe Harbor.

Ben stepped closer. "Hey listen, I'll take you to your appointment tomorrow if you want."

She lifted her face and studied him.

Maybe humor would make charity easier to receive. He waggled his brows. "Just think, you could be escorted by the cutest chauffeur in Refuge." He splayed fingers on his chest and adopted a French accent. *"Moi."*

That caused her to laugh. She rolled red-rimmed eyes at him. "You're something else."

He grinned, waiting for her to answer.

She nibbled her lip. "Okay, if you're sure it's no trouble." She tucked long, loose curls behind her ear. Her hair boasted a golden-brown luster and shine not present yesterday. Having a thing about ladies with long hair, his fingers itched to touch the silky coils. Her face held more vitality today, too.

When she caught him staring, her head tilted down, causing a thicket of curls to fall over her lazy eye. "I might need to use your phone again to check when the bus leaves Friday evening."

"No trouble on both counts. Though I don't relish the idea of you and Reece riding alone on a bus, not especially after dark." He handed her his phone.

When she took it, her hand brushed his. Tingles traveled up his arm. She froze with an enemy-in-the-grenade-path expression. Evidence she felt it, too. He bit his lip to contain his smile.

The door swished open. "Miss North? I'm here to remove your IV." A woman in teal scrubs appeared through a crack somewhere in the curtain. "We'll see if you can stay hydrated without it."

Another woman trailed in, carrying two breakfast trays. "Thought the little one might be hungry, too. We had an extra tray. I'll leave it for your daughter for when she wakes up."

"Thank you. But she went to breakfast with the social worker." Amelia lifted the lid. Steam wafted up from oatmeal. The smell rumbled Ben's tummy.

It also reminded him he'd promised to take Hutton to Refuge Bed and Breakfast for pancakes and chocolate gravy.

The food-service lady left both trays. "We brought it in, so someone might as well eat it. Otherwise, infection control requires us to pitch the meal." She smiled and scuttled out.

Amelia eyed Ben. "Would you like to eat breakfast with me?"

"I'd like to, but I have other plans."

He hated disappointing her. But he'd promised Hutton his favorite breakfast and a fishing session at Bradley's grandparents' pond outside Refuge. Hutton had seemed excited to have made a friend, and in fact he seemed more comfortable already around Bradley than he did Ben. Maybe this time at the pond would endear Hutton to Refuge. And to Ben.

"Probably wouldn't hurt you to eat both of those." Ben motioned toward the trays.

Her face fell, full of frustration.

"I didn't mean to sound bossy. Or judgmental."

She nodded, but didn't meet his gaze again.

Ben moved toward the door hoping she'd look up. Stupid move, Dillinger. He'd hurt her feelings. Why couldn't he learn to be sensitive and say the right things? He foiled that with Hutton, too. "I'll be back, Amelia."

She never looked up.

Near the exit, he passed Harker. Reece slept soundly in her arms. "Nap time?" Ben said, grinning.

Harker nodded. "Long overdue, too."

His heart melted like butter in the steaming oatmeal at the sight of Reece embraced by slumber yet clutching Bearby like a fuzzy buoy.

"No secret to anyone who knows you how increasingly marriage and family-minded you've grown," Harker observed.

"Seeing how vibrant and happy my newlywed teammates are doesn't help matters."

"How're things with Hutton coming?"

"In a matter of weeks, I'll have charge over him."

"Though you're brothers, because of Hutton's special needs it'll be like taking in an older child, huh?"

"Unless I make great strides earning Hutton's trust, I may let my entire family down." No matter what the cost, he couldn't let that happen. His heritage taught him to respect his elders.

"Might help if you'd spend every spare minute you can with him so he'll feel comfortable living with you when the time comes. Bring him to our Sunday-school class."

"Great idea. You need help carrying her to Amelia's room?"

Harker paused at the nurses' station for a pillow. "No thanks. Proceed. You look like a man on a mission."

Ben smiled. "I am. A mission to prove to my brother he's worthy of time and friendship."

Harker's stern gaze made a direct hit. "Then I'm curious why you haven't mentioned him to Amelia or Amelia to him."

Conviction dropped Ben's stare to the floor. "I know." He met her gaze. "I need to."

"Even if it's not easy?"

"Especially then."

She tilted her head at him.

"Anything worth having is worth sweating over, and nothing that truly matters comes easy."

"See? That wasn't so hard." Nurse Bailey held pressure on the spot where Amelia's IV line used to be.

"Speak for yourself." Amelia glared at the wound.

"Yippee!" Harker whispered from the doorway. "The IV's out?"

"Yes." Amelia moved her sketch pad off the recliner so Miss Harker could lay Reece down. "I get evicted soon."

Nurse Bailey snickered. "Released."

Amelia grinned. "You know you'll miss me."

Bailey's smile straightened. "I really will. You come back through or call and let us know how you're faring. Okay?"

She nodded. Bailey scurried to answer a call light.

"This child can sleep through anything. What a blessing." Miss Harker tucked a blanket over Reece and Bearby.

Blessing.

That sounded like a churchy word. Amelia studied Glorietta Harker. She seemed to be a woman of faith. Is that why she went worlds beyond duty to reach out in kindness to her and Reece?

"Glorietta, you're a far shout from what I've known of people who were close to God. Or maybe those people weren't as close to God as I thought."

"Maybe not as close as they thought, either. And I'm glad you finally decided to call me Glorietta. Progress." She smiled.

Later, Reece wobbled to sitting up in the recliner. She blinked herself awake and looked around.

"Mommy? Where am I?" She rubbed her eyes, slid off the recliner and scampered onto the bed beside her mom.

"Back at the hospital." Amelia rubbed her daughter's bed-head. "I need to run a brush through this."

"Is Reece's brush still in your car?" Glorietta, wrapping up her daily visit with Amelia, asked.

"Yes. In the trunk." A surge of emotion hit Amelia from nowhere. She blinked back tears.

"Well, whatever is wrong?" Glorietta asked.

"It means a lot that you and Ben visit every day. When I was in the hospital on bed rest and pregnant with Reece, no one came."

Glorietta leaned in and hugged Amelia. No words. Just a hug, which spoke volumes.

Amelia battled barely corked emotion she'd bottled up for five years. "So you see how much your visits have meant. My mother snuck into the hospital to see me but I was sleeping. She left the kit. Said it was from Dad to the baby. It had a baby brush and a big kid brush. At least that's what Reece calls it. It would be a hard thing to lose."

"I'll bring it back when I come. Need anything else?"

"No. Ben went to the garage and brought our drawings. That was the only other thing of value there. Well, I don't have anything of value, moneywise. But when a person puts their time and heart into something, that's important."

"That's the true meaning of real value, huh?"

Amelia nodded. "Reece draws to entertain us and to express herself. I have a year's worth of drawings and don't want to lose them, since they're irreplaceably sentimental."

"I'll bet it's wonderful to see her art grow over the years." Glorietta's eyes sparkled with emotion, reminding Amelia what she'd said about having to give up a baby. Her heart tugged.

Maybe she should change the subject. She didn't want to open hard wounds when Glorietta had been so loving and kind.

"Though I can't depend on art as my main source of income, I draw and sell caricatures for decent money. I also draw them as gifts. I made one for you." Amelia thumbed through her pad and tore a page out. "I'm thankful for everything you've done."

Moisture glittered Glorietta's eyes as she studied the caricature of a life-sized Bearby and Reece wrapping a heart-shaped French fry around a laughing Miss Harker.

"My pleasure. We all get stuck in places of need sometimes. It's not fun. It hopefully teaches sensitivity to others in their season of need when we have plenty. Which reminds me, I have something for you, too." She presented a book-shaped package, wrapped in beautiful wrapping paper. "Wait to open it until after I leave." She winked and hugged them goodbye.

After Glorietta left, Amelia tickled Reece. "They're getting ready to let me out. Isn't that great?"

Sudden tears welled in Reece's eyes. She stared at Bearby with an instantly downcast expression.

Having returned to do discharge vitals, the nurse gathered her medical paraphernalia but left two pages of typed sheets. "Everything is within normal limits. Here are some instructions." She started to step out. Panic grabbed Amelia. "Wait. Nurse? May I borrow a Refuge phone book? I might need a cab."

"I'm sorry. Refuge doesn't have a cab service right now."

"City transportation?"

"Afraid not. This is a very small town."

Amelia walked her to the door. "How does the billing cycle work in the hospital from day to day? Is it like hotels where there is a noon checkout?"

"No. Once past midnight, you get charged for the next day."

"So, if we need to, we can stay here up to eleven-fifty-five tonight?"

The nurse looked at her oddly. "Of course. Why, is there no one available to pick you up?"

"I'm not sure."

"Because you don't need to be out walking in this heat."

"I know."

"I'm sure a ride will come through," the nurse said as she walked out.

But Glorietta was on her way out of town. And Ben…she supposed she could call him. But something in her needed to know he'd come back on his own. If she waited until tonight, Reece's bedtime would be messed up. Amelia would give Ben until this afternoon before trying to find a ride to the bed and breakfast. Should she have the nurse lock up his phone in the hospital safe? Or chance catching him at the B and B?

Despising feeling helpless and not being able to decide what to do, Amelia picked up her drawing pad.

Minutes later, sniffling sounded.

Amelia gathered Reece in her arms. "Sweetie? What's wrong?"

"I don't want to leave here." She plucked at Bearby's hair. No wonder he looked mangy these days. Stress always caused Reece to pick at his dwindling fur. In the same way, guilt tore strips from Amelia's conscience. She had to make things better for her daughter, no matter what it meant giving up.

"Honey, it's a hospital. We can't stay here." Amelia adapted a jovial tone. "Besides, there's nothing fun to do." That Reece looked sad and troubled made her feel like a failure. No child should be this forlorn looking, depressed even.

You're not ready to be a mom. You'll fail her like you did us. The audio memory of her father's words stung like a slap in the face of her honest effort.

Amelia twirled Reece's bangs into a side ringlet, moving them out of her eyes. She pulled a butterfly barrette from her purse and secured the hair. Much better. "We get to finish our road trip. Hospitals are sorta boring, don't you think?"

"I don't mean the hospital. I mean I don't want to leave this town. I like it here and they have curly fries as long as your leg and everybody is nice to us and, and Bearby misses Mr. Ben." She unleashed luminous eyes on Amelia. "Why did he leave, Mommy? I thought he liked us."

So *that's* what this was about. She drew Reece close for a hug. "Oh, honey. He'll be back and you'll get to say goodbye to him." But…would he? She hoped he'd return before they discharged her. She also needed to give his gift to him. And she still had his phone. And he'd mentioned the B and B and helping with a room. She'd need it tonight.

Surely he'd be back.

Unless, like Reggie, he was filled with empty promises. Or, like her dad, forgetful of his word, yet never forgetting her mistakes. But Ben was different.

Right?

The wall clock beckoned her gaze. Quarter to ten. Fifteen minutes until her scheduled discharge. Would Ben remember?

If he really was a man of honor, he'd show or else call.

Amelia eyed the clock above the bed.

Ten on the nose.

Ben had said he'd be back. A sudden thought struck her. He didn't owe her a thing.

Believe.

"Let's draw." Amelia pulled her pad out and patted the bed. Reece scrambled up and took the blank paper.

Noon came.

Noon went.

How would she explain this to Reece if Ben didn't return?

I was wrong about him?

For once, she hoped she wasn't. And that little bit of hope scared her more than almost anything.

Twelve-thirty. Time for plan B. Amelia resigned herself to renting a car.

She hated to spend money, but she couldn't subject Reece to walking twenty miles. Not happening. Even if Amanda carried her. Too risky with the heat.

After dressing, Amelia called to check on her car, in hopes the mechanic had worked a mighty miracle with his hillbilly wrench.

She'd have been better off not to call. The parts he'd had to order—backordered. Which meant another week for sure. Time ticked by, taking Amelia's hope of Ben showing with it. The phone alarm she'd set bleeped, signaling time up.

Amelia glared at the wall clock.

One.

Reece tracked her gaze. Tears filled her eyes.

"Mommy, Bearby and me don't think he's coming."

Chapter Seven

I'm sure Mr. Ben has a good reason. Mommy has plan B, baby.

Ben stood outside Amelia's room while the conversation he'd inadvertently walked up on sunk in. He hadn't meant to eavesdrop. But hospital-room acoustics ricocheted voices into the hall. Even though he'd backed away from the door when Reece mentioned his name.

He should have called. But he'd wanted to give Hutton his undivided attention. After breakfast, they'd gone fishing. Then Bradley'd invited Hutton to Cone Zone for pizza and ice cream. And Ben had made another special stop.

Then Joel had called him in for a team briefing, putting them on alert to be sent to a Gulf Coast area in the path of a hurricane. 'Twas the season.

Now, returned to Amelia's room, he'd inadvertently picked up phrases exchanged between Amelia and Reece. He hadn't realized they'd discharge Amelia that early.

Now, he was convinced even more he wasn't imagining this draw to Amelia and Reece. He had to find a way to woo Amelia's trust and keep in touch.

He looked heavenward again. "Make a way. They desperately need security and someone to care about them," he whispered, while raising his hand to knock. "Hello, it's Ben. Everyone decent?"

Shuffling sounded. "Yes. Come in."

Ben rounded the corner and pushed aside the curtain.

Surprise then relief flashed in Amelia's eyes at the sight of him. As though she'd doubted his return. The very thought disturbed him. Her eyes lit on the vase, voluminous with burgundy roses, in his right hand. Confusion skipped across her face before Reece stood on the bed, prohibiting him from seeing her reaction further.

"Mr. Ben! I thought you left us for good!" Reece launched at him like Superman in flight.

He thrust the floral crystal torch vase out a safe distance and caught Reece with his other arm. He grunted on impact and laughed. Little daredevil nearly knocked the wind out of him. "Hey, short stuff."

He placed the expensive arrangement on the table in front of Amelia, who blinked rapidly at them. You'd think the girl had never been given flowers before. Well, maybe she hadn't. Her face reflected cautious hope that they were hers yet rampant unbelief they could be.

Reece grabbed his nose and gave it little pinches. "'Short stuff'? I like when you call me princess better, silly man."

Ben laughed then wiggled his nose at her, mimicking her expression. "Then princess it is."

Reece's fists pressed into her hips and her nose pressed into his. "And why are you late?"

"Because I braved the stores for two damsels." Still armed with Reece, Ben sat in the chair and pulled out a paper sack from the gift center downstairs. He pulled out a jeweled princess tiara and handed it to Reece. "This is for you." He handed her a tiny camouflage jacket. "This is for Bearby. And the flowers are for your mom. Hope she's not allergic."

He peeked at Amelia, who still stared at the vase, then at him. A curiously confused gleam entered her eyes. Like she couldn't comprehend what the flowers were all about.

She brushed fingers along a velvety rose petal. "I'm not allergic, that I know of. I've never received flowers before."

"Not even when you were in the hospital to have Reece?"

She shook her head. "Can I hold them?"

Ben locked gazes with her. "Of course. They're yours. It's okay to embrace what belongs to you, Amelia," he offered softly, hoping she'd get the double meaning that God had so much more in store for her if she'd just stop running and receive instead of letting doubt and fear propel her in the wrong direction.

He felt a song coming on.

Didn't the girl know God grows her flowers after winter? Commands the seed to grow, tasks the sun to make them glimmer?

But, he reminded himself, she hadn't grown up with the kind of family he had. Maybe all she'd ever wakened to was weeds in the grass outside her life's window.

Awaken her with the warmth of your presence and with the melody of the songs you fashion only for her. Like Zephaniah 3:17. Help her envision how you sing and dance over her with delight.

He would send her flowers every single day, if that was what it took to convince the girl she was worth something in someone's eyes.

Cradling both hands on a large bloom, she leaned in as close as she could until her nose disappeared inside one of the flowers. Eyes closed, she inhaled long and deep. Deeper. So deep he was sure she'd inhaled pollen into her lungs.

Yes, Lord. Let her inhale Your presence like that.

He'd never ever seen someone so appreciative of a gift.

"They smell so beautiful. They're gorgeous, and this vase, do I get to keep it?" Her words tumbled out breathless.

He nodded, enjoying the grateful gushing and childlike wonder at what he considered such a small gesture of kindness. But to her, it obviously was enormous.

He laughed because Amelia's joy looked just like Reece's when she'd lunged off the bed, going airborne. Not even pausing to consider that he wouldn't or couldn't catch her. Or that she could be hurt in the process if things didn't turn out as planned. The unquestioning trust and pristine faith of a child.

Restore that to Amelia.

The way she ogled the flowers, obviously she didn't get gifts all that often. If ever.

He aimed to change that. He couldn't think of any woman who needed that as much as Amelia. Crazy to be thinking along these long-term lines this soon. But he couldn't help it. An excitement welled up in him. He liked her. And it had nothing to do with sympathy. He saw deeper than her current life circumstances. Determination. Tenacity. He doubted she could even see it in herself. Regardless, he loved the view.

The nurse entered. "Oh, good. Your ride made it, I see."

Amelia blinked at Ben. "I hadn't asked him yet."

He grinned like a goon in a gin bin. "Like I'd protest the company of two very pretty ladies?"

Reece giggled. Amelia's smile revealed relief.

"Lunch trays came an hour ago. Since I thought you'd be discharged at ten, I didn't order yours. I can call dietary to deliver two if you need," the nurse said to Amelia.

The rolling table squeaked as Ben moved it aside to sit on the bed. "No offense, but I saw fish sandwiches on the menu." His eyes warned Amelia. "They taste like sponges."

The nurse chuckled. "Unfortunately, he's right. But we can order you and Reece trays before you go if you like."

Ben rose. "Nah, they'll grab lunch with me. But thanks."

"Okay, then. I'll get your discharge paperwork." The nurse slipped out.

"Could we have a picnic, Mommy?" Reece asked.

"That's up to Mr. Ben," Amelia said. "He's driving. But whatever we decide, I'd like to treat us." She eyed him. "You fly and I buy?"

He smiled. "Sounds like a plan. I'm game for a picnic." He knew Harker had slipped bills into the Bible Promise Book she'd given Amelia. She'd told Ben to make sure Amelia knew about it. Amelia must have discovered it on her own. He strongly sensed she needed this, to be able to contribute financially.

Amelia shifted in her seat. "I'm curious about something, Ben. I haven't been able to stop thinking about it."

"What's that?"

"When the doctor was here, you mentioned someone named Bradley. I got the idea he's a young boy. Dr. Riviera is an oncologist, right? Does Joel's little boy have cancer?" Sympathy coated her words.

"He had leukemia, but it's been in remission since a successful bone-marrow transplant."

"Must have been frightening for Bradley's parents. I can't imagine going through that."

"Actually, Joel and his wife, Amber, adopted Bradley. Amber was Bradley's teacher. At that time, things didn't look good for Bradley. He'd been abandoned by his birth mother and neglected by his foster mother to the point it endangered his life. So Amber pursued custody. She and Joel married about the time his adoption was finalized."

"I don't understand how a mother could abandon her child. I'm so glad he found another family."

"Bradley's as much a gift to Joel and Amber as they are to him. Kid's an inspiration to everyone he meets. He was so courageous going through what he did. In fact, if courage could cure cancer, that little guy's fight and faith alone would have eradicated it from the earth."

"Mommy, what's cancer?" Reece asked from the corner.

"It's a terrible disease that makes people very sick."

"I know what courage is, Mommy."

"You do?"

"Yep. I found out by watching *Charlotte's Web*. Courage is what the little girl who loved Wilbur was made of. And it's what you're made of, even though your daddy isn't very nice to you sometimes. Grandma even said so."

"She did?" Total shock spread all over Amelia's face. It wasn't half the jolt Ben felt, though, when she turned to him and conveyed a look that touched him across the space separating them.

"Mom has never stood up for me. At least not in my presence," she explained in tones too low for Reece to monitor.

Reece made airplane noises and flew Bearby in circles over her head. "I'm glad Charlotte's three babies stayed with Wilbur. And I'm glad that little boy Bradley's okay now, Mommy. And I'm glad you didn't die in our car crash because I don't have any idea how to fly and farms are stinky."

The gamut of emotions Reece's words provoked made Amelia appear to want to laugh and cry at the same time. Ben resisted the compulsion to reach for her.

Already familiar with the animated version of *Charlotte's Web* from watching it a hundred times with Hutton, Ben knew hundreds of spider babies floated through air to the farm after Charlotte couldn't be with them anymore, but only three babies stayed there with Wilbur the pig.

The nurse reentered, discharged Amelia, then left.

Ben lifted Reece's booster seat, which he'd brought the first day. "I pulled my car up to the front of the hospital. Feel okay to walk through a store to snag picnic stuff?"

Amelia nodded. "I feel gobs better." When she held his gaze for a few mesmerizing moments, he knew she meant more than her health.

"You didn't really think I'd abandon you. Did you?"

Her cheeks flushed. "I wouldn't say *abandon*, really. *Forget* might be a better word." Her eye twitched once. Twice.

Stopped like a fighter jet caught by arresting wires on an aircraft carrier, he faced her. He stepped one foot inside her personal space, with one foot outside in the circle of normal friendship to help usher that precise point across. "Let's clear something up right here and now."

Her eyes flashed apprehension. As if she expected him to initiate a scream fest. To deflect that fear, he raised a gentle hand, wrapping his finger in spirals of lush hair curtaining the eye she tried so hard to hide. In her mind, a flaw. In his, something unique to her that made her all the more special.

She swallowed, but held his gaze.

He twirled her hair between his finger and thumb, longing to lose himself in the feel of it.

Amelia's eye started twitching again.

He slid his gaze to a now-giggling Reece, then back to slowly roam every facet of Amelia's face. "I would never abandon you and Reece…

"And never, ever could I forget you."

Chapter Eight

Amelia had never been so glad to enter a checkout lane. For once, she didn't experience dread that she'd get to the register and not have enough money with people looking on.

She faced Ben. "Had I known Glorietta planted two one-hundred dollar bills under the Provision page, I'd have tried to give it back."

He rolled the cart to the back of the long line. "That's why she had to be sneaky."

But thanks to Glorietta's stealth and kindness, Amelia not only had enough to pay for nonperishable groceries for her and Reece, she could cover today's picnic lunch.

"It feels good to be able to do for another person."

"Hey, Ben."

Amelia turned. A statuesque blonde and three other very beautiful girls eyed her and Ben with curious interest.

"Hey, Brenna." He nodded to the other girls. "Ladies."

To Amelia's surprise, his gaze didn't linger lewdly on them or wander in a wanton manner like Reece's dad's had when they'd been out somewhere and women walked by. In fact, warmth infused Amelia's back as Ben's hand settled there, nudging her forward. She hadn't realized she'd slipped behind him.

Ben smiled tenderly at her, and never moved his arm away. "This is my special friend, Amelia North, and her daughter, Reece."

Special friend.

She was actually somebody's special friend. Someone as wonderful as Ben.

What was a special friend? The concept sounded so foreign. Thankfulness consumed her. Even though Ben was probably just saying that to be nice so she didn't feel awkward, the thoughtful gesture meant more than he could ever know. And how he'd deemed her unforgettable at the hospital. Wow. A guy who actually considered a girl's feelings. They hadn't gone extinct.

Brenna and her friends looked from Ben to Amelia. Though they smiled, Amelia sensed an underlying emotion. One she'd interpret as envy did she not know better. After all, she possessed nothing capable of causing another girl to be jealous. Then why did Brenna's friends' smiles seem forced?

A guy, wearing a Southern Illinois University sweatshirt and who appeared college age like the girls, sauntered up.

Brenna's hand lifted in a gesture of introduction. "Cole, this is Ben Dillinger."

Surprise flooded the student's face. His mouth dropped open and stayed there. Cole's eyes oozed more respect toward Ben than Amelia had ever seen in one man's face for another.

Interesting.

Cole's hand snaked out, grabbing Ben's. "Airman Dillinger. I've heard *so* much about you and your team. You're practically famous. It *rocks* to finally meet one of you. It's so stinking cool that you got stationed at Refuge Air Base." He kept shaking Ben's hand until Ben slipped it from the overzealous grasp.

Cole patted himself frantically as though bugs skittered

over him. Then he swiped off his hat and extended it. "Dude, I mean, sir, can you please, please autograph this for me?"

Autograph? Practically famous?

Amelia tilted her head to study Ben. Who was he, really?

Cole looked starstruck as Ben took the black Sharpie and scribbled his name and something encouraging across the bill, then *Jeremiah 29:11*. A Bible verse? Now she *really* studied Ben.

"Awesome! You—your team, you're American heroes, man, ah, sir." His feet did a nifty little shuffle as he clutched the hat in his hands. "Wait until I tell my friends! They are sooo gonna hate me." He looked close to combusting with excitement.

Ben shook his head and laughed. "If you say so."

"Thanks, man. Thanks a lot for this! My buddies aren't gonna believe it. I wish I had a camera to prove it. Dude, you have no idea how much me and my friends look up to you Ops guys, man—er—sir. Especially those of us looking to go in. We watch the PJ pipeline recruiting disc every time we're at the DZ. I'd give anything to be a cone."

Ben perked up at that. "No need for a camera. Show up at Refuge Drop Zone the second Saturday next month. Ask for me. Unless we get tasked somewhere, we'll all be there. Bring the guys. Let's hang for a few hours. Deal, dude?" He grinned.

Cole's response was to squeal like a prepubescent kid.

"Pick your chin off the floor," Brenna told Cole, whose knees had nearly hit the tiles at Ben's invitation.

She dragged Cole away, eyeing them as she went. "Thanks, Ben. See you at the DZ. Nice to meet you, Reece. Hope to get to know you better, Amelia. I've never seen Ben smile so much. You must be a *very* special friend." She winked.

Similar parting words rippled through Brenna's friends as they departed, waving. Her heart pinched because they seemed the sort of popular girls who'd always overlooked or made fun of her. Or wouldn't associate with Amelia because they obviously didn't run in the same circles. But Brenna's words had seemed sincere.

Heat flushed Amelia's face as the group exited the store. She knew they talked about her because they kept looking back over their shoulders and murmuring. Yet their faces smiled.

Ben bumped her shoulder. "They're not maliciously whispering."

"I've been the victim of enough high school pranks to know you're right." But those were the kind of whispers suggesting they were desperate to figure out what was going on between her and Ben and dying to know who she was. Of course, they wouldn't have batted an eye at her had she not been in Ben's company.

Regardless, for once, Amelia felt like she could hold her head higher. Someone like Ben wasn't ashamed to be seen with someone like her. The longing to live in a small place like Refuge, where everyone seemed intent to help someone in need and show kindness to strangers, snuck up on her from nowhere.

Standing in the long checkout line, Amelia studied Ben. He avoided her direct gaze.

Amelia nudged his elbow with hers. "American hero?"

He shrugged, and unless the fluorescent lights played tricks on her eyes, his ears turned pink. "They're just kids. They don't know any better."

"Ri-ight. Just who and what are you, Ben Dillinger? What are you not telling me?"

The sound of his velvet chuckle filled her ears with contentment. She loved the sound of his voice.

A little too much for her own comfort.

Mounting intrigue won out over her discomfort. An Ops guy? And what on earth was a cone? Wasn't an airman someone in the Air Force? That would make sense. Ben certainly possessed a military bearing, now that she thought about it. And the guy had mentioned Refuge Air Base, though she hadn't seen it on the map. It could be one of those more secretive, unmapped military bases. She grew more intrigued with Ben by the second.

Amelia moved up in the line, now two away from being checked out. "Are you a fighter pilot?"

"Not hardly. With all due respect, I like to jump out of planes. Not fly them. Air combat takes a special breed. I love the sky, don't get me wrong. But I'd rather be attached to a parachute any day than strapped behind F-18 or F-22 controls."

That made it sound as though he'd tried it before.

Next up to check out, Amelia pulled out her wallet and thumbed through bills. Ben unloaded the cart's contents onto the rolling counter.

So he was some sort of military parachutist with medical training. "I've heard of F-15s and F-18s. What's an F-22?"

"Raptor. Most incredible stealth fighter on earth, in my opinion."

The clerk rang up the items and announced the total. For once, anxiety didn't clinch her stomach. Amelia handed over two large bills. "May I have change for the second one?"

"Five twenties be okay?"

"Great." Amelia handed Reece a few dollars and change. "Here's some spending money for you."

Reece pushed bills through the slot of a collection box for a children's cancer hospital, keeping only a quarter for herself.

Amelia's heart melted. "That was nice, sweetie."

"I watched about St. Jude's on the TV with Grandma once. They help kids with cancer and I just want to make sure Bradley has everything he needs."

Amelia hugged Reece.

Gathering sacks containing her purchases, Ben smiled down at them with a tender expression that made her mind go slow and her heart go fast. "You've done good with her, Amelia."

Again his soothing voice rubbed against her like a soft sweater.

"Reece, one of these days we'll introduce you to Bradley," he said.

Her eyes lit up. "Really? Is cancer catching, though?"

He dug out his car keys. "Nope. It's not contagious."

Amelia sneaked a peek at Ben. Him suggesting Reece could meet Bradley hinted at seeing them in the future. She'd hoped he'd want to keep in touch but no way was she gonna make the first move. It wasn't so much that she didn't trust nice guys. She majorly didn't trust her instincts.

Her error in judgment once had nearly cost Reece her life and Amelia the chance of raising her. Hopefully that had sharpened her senses about people.

Sure she struggled now. But things wouldn't always be so. To trust a man again might prove too risky to her and especially Reece, who could grow attached. Better to keep safe boundaries.

Besides that, she never wanted to be in the position again of having to depend on other people for survival. She needed to continue to be independent. She vowed never to depend on a guy or anyone else, ever again. She could only count on herself.

Picket-fence families were fruitless fairy tales, and she couldn't afford to entertain the vanity. Maybe Reece would be more fortunate in the glass-slipper department.

In the parking lot, Ben deposited their bags near his car then scooped tiara-topped Reece up on his shoulders and galloped all over the pavement, making outlandish horse noises with his mouth. Amelia ran to keep up, laughing so much that her stomach ached, her legs grew weak with the sprint and her face hurt from all the laughing.

"You play just like a kid, Ben." *You'll make a great dad*

someday. Tears from nowhere stung her eyes. For Reece not
having a dad that cared about her. And for herself and the loss
of a relationship with her own dad. She busied herself with
buckling Reece in while Ben opened the trunk to stick the
grocery bags in there. His groan pulled her up short, and she
hit her head on the car door molding backing out of the car.

Ben stood at the trunk, eyeing a box in his hand as though
it held the remains of a late, beloved pet.

She approached. "You okay?"

Somewhat dazed, he looked up. "Yeah. I am. This isn't."
He lifted the object to show her.

"Eeww. What was it?" Amelia eyed the glob of chocolate
at the bottom of a melted plastic mold.

"It was a chocolate Garfield. Musta melted in the heat."

"It's still chocolate. I bet it'd still be okay to eat."

He shook his head. "It wasn't for me." He carried it with
him to the driver's side. "I can grab another one. It's just, I'm
bummed I forgot about this one."

She entered the car through the passenger's side. Ben really
was being hard on himself. Since he didn't strike her as the
type to get easily bent, she had to wonder why. What was the
significance about the Garfield?

He stayed silent until they reached Haven Street Park. He
unloaded their lunch on a picnic table beneath a covered
pavilion. Amelia broke Reece's sandwich into small pieces
then opened her kid-sized plastic milk jug. She sat down,
stuffing a carrot stick in her mouth. Heat rushed her face.

Ben's head was bowed and his lips moving.

Reece eyed Ben. "Mommy, why don't we ever pray for our
food?" she asked, after Ben lifted his head.

Now it was Amelia's turn to avoid Ben's curious gaze. "We
just…got out of the habit. You can pray anytime you want."

She fought the fear Reece would discover too soon Amelia
had crossed a line she wasn't sure she could ever come back

from. But if Reece wanted a relationship with God, Amelia applauded it.

"But I want you to pray, too," Reece said between bites.

How could she tell Reece that God probably wouldn't hear her? She couldn't fake a prayer. What if Reece asked her to pray for something important and her faith shattered when it didn't happen? No way could Amelia do that to her daughter.

Unexplained tension mounted. Amelia circled the picnic table in an attempt to evade heat from Ben's precision stare. But it tracked her wherever she walked.

Amelia looked Reece in the eye, knowing she meant every word of what she was about to say. "Believe me, Reece. If *you* pray, God will hear. He wants you to talk to Him, okay?"

"'Kay. But I wish we could pray together sometimes. May I be excused?"

Amelia surveyed Reece's near-empty plate. "Yes."

Reece slid off the bench and scampered to the jungle gym.

Still corralling Amelia with his gaze, Ben patted the seat beside him. "I'll make you a deal. You tell me what your rift with God is, and I'll tell you why that kid wanted my autograph," he said in matter-of-fact tones.

Amelia sat. "I don't have a rift with God." Her teeth sank into her sandwich. She took her time chewing her turkey and his words. She swallowed and studied the seeds dotting her rye bread. "He has a rift with me."

A cough preceded Ben's deep laugh. He fisted his lungs. "Sorry. I know it's not funny to you, Amelia, but I can't imagine God being mad at you over anything." He turned serious. "I think you've got it wrong."

"Not according to my dad." Harsh emotion burned her throat.

"Last I heard, your dad didn't dethrone God. Did he?"

"No, but—"

"No buts about it. I pray you experience His forgiveness

in full, as God intended when He sent the best He had for the worst we did."

She wanted to believe it. She really did. Nothing would make her happier than God not holding her past against her like her parents did. But her parents had been in church longer, so they knew God better. Right?

She sighed. "Thanks for your prayers."

Ben's dark brows rose. "But?"

"But that's all I'm gonna say about that...for now."

Staring intently, he nodded. But not enough to convince her he was giving up that easily. The intrepid guy was like a relentless K-9 sniffing for information.

She smiled and leaned back. "Now, Sir Helps-a-lot, methinks you owe milady an explanation."

His face shuttered. "I've had the opportunity to participate in a televised rescue. That's it. No big deal."

She leaned forward. "No big deal? If you made national news, Ben, that is gigantic. Tell me about the famous rescue."

He grinned. "Which one?"

"There's been more than one?"

He stood, gathered the trash and tossed it in the metal barrel. "If you've heard about it on TV, I've likely been there. But that's all I'm gonna say about that...for now." He smiled in smug challenge as he replicated her words exactly.

"Fair enough." She got it. The only way he was going to share more would be if she did. Smart, smart man. Because no matter who he was, what caliber of hero, she wasn't about to give herself completely away again. And judging by the knowing gleam in his eyes, he knew it. Which meant he possessed secrets he preferred to keep from her, too.

For now.

Chapter Nine

Holding the door open for Amelia and Reece, Ben nodded to the owner of Refuge Bed and Breakfast as she approached his car. "Hey, Miss Evie." He took Reece's hand.

His landlord appeared with a towel-covered baking pan and her usual generous smile. "Why, hello, Ben." She smiled more broadly at Amelia and Reece. "Ben's told me all about you. Welcome to Refuge."

"Thank you." Amelia gathered their belongings from Ben's car.

Miss Evie lifted the pan. "Thought you might be hungry so I made you some coffee gravy pork chops." She peered over her shoulder at Amelia. "Your room's right this way."

Walking along the covered porch, Ben faced Amelia. "I've got urgent business. But I'll call you later." He needed to pick up Hutton and figured Amelia needed rest. "What's her bedtime?" He didn't wanna call too late.

"Eight. But it might be earlier tonight."

Reece let go of Ben's hand and reached for her mom's.

Once Miss Evie opened the door to Amelia's unit, he set their stuff inside, including Reece's car seat, though he didn't expect they'd need it before tomorrow morning. "Thanks, Miss Evie.

I've got to jet. Catch you guys later." Ben waved and stepped off the porch as Miss Evie led Amelia and Reece inside.

At his car, he peered over his shoulder through the open apartment door, hoping to catch one more glimpse of Amelia. She stood in profile behind Reece with hands on her shoulders while Miss Evie set the pan on the counter, visible through the door.

Ben stalled, watching the animation on Amelia's face as she listened to Miss Evie talk.

Then, as if sensing his stare, Amelia's face angled toward the door and her eyes found him. He grinned wide.

Pink tinged her cheeks and she returned his smile, held his gaze a moment longer, enough to deepen the connection, then returned her attention to Miss Evie.

Amazing how one girl's smile could leave his tongue arid, and launch his pulse airborne. After remembering how to start a car, he pulled it onto the road leading to Joel's.

At least the direction he thought Joel lived. Whew! The girl could scramble his brain faster than a missile lock scrambled fighter jet signals.

When Ben arrived at Joel's, Hutton asked if he could finish playing a video game with Bradley before leaving. Ben scooted back into a chair and joined Joel at the soda bar over-looking the game room.

"You met a girl." Joel slid a soda to Ben.

Ben laughed. "What makes you say that?"

"I can tell. I haven't seen your smile that goofy in ages."

Bradley's head peeked above a footstool. "Dad, you ask?"

"Not yet, son. He just got here." Squeaks rankled the bar stool as Joel swiveled it toward Ben. "Bradley wants to know if Hutton can stay the night tomorrow."

A pop echoed as Ben pulled the soda tab. "What's Hutton say?" Carbonation bubbles hissed up his nose as he sipped.

"He seemed excited about it. Said he needed to get your

permission first." Joel lowered his voice when Bradley bumped Hutton's shoulder and nodded back at them. "Said he didn't want to hurt your feelings because you guys planned a video night."

"Actually, we can do a rain check on that if Hutton would rather stay here with Bradley. That might work better for me anyway. Then I can drive Amelia to St. Louis instead of her taking the bus."

"Amelia, that's the girl you found at the mall, right?"

Ben grinned. "Yeah. It's also *the* girl."

"Inn-terr-essting." Joel's eyes narrowed as he dragged the word out. "Anything else?"

"Nope. Nothin' else to tell. I won't lose my head, sir."

Joel's grin grew wolfish. "What about your heart?"

Ben thought about it a moment. Amelia's lovely face graced his mind. Reece's chortling laugh trailed. "Entirely possible."

Game completed, Hutton set the controller aside and untangled his hands from the cord. He pulled himself up with awkward motions and the help of the footstool. Then he conducted his typical side-to-side waddle up to them.

"Hi, Benny." He leaned forward and held out his arms.

Ben hugged him. "Hey, buddy. Have fun today?"

Hutton grinned so big his upside-down-moon-shaped eyes disappeared. "Yeah. Yeah, Benny. I like video games."

"Yeah, Mom and Dad don't have that at their house, do they?" Their parents were more earthy than techie.

"No, Benny. Hutton likes video games. Hutton likes Bradley too. Um, I never stayed over the night at a friend's house before. Mom always worried and said I'm not big enough. But I'm twenty." Hutton's brows pulled together in consternation.

"Don't feel bad, buddy. She hardly let me stay over at friends' houses, either. So, I hear Bradley invited you to spend the night tomorrow night?"

Hutton nodded vigorously. "Yeah. Yeah. But I don't want to hurt your feelings, Benny, or make you mad if you want to watch videos."

"Hutton, it wasn't so much the videos I wanted to watch as much as I wanted to hang out and show you a good time."

"Okay Benny." Hutton swayed side to side and blinked hard.

"But we can always do the video stuff another night, so you can stay with Bradley. How's that sound?"

"Yeah. That sound fun Benny. Fun. Fun. Fun."

"Yay!" Bradley jumped up and down.

Ben eyed Hutton. "You've never stayed the night anywhere besides home before. Well, except for my house. You sure you'll be okay if you wake up in a place you're not used to?"

"Yes, Benny. I be okay. Hutton wants to stay the night with Bradley and play video games all night."

Ben laughed. "Not sure you'll last all night, but if you want to stay tomorrow, I'm fine with it."

"Okay. Okay. Can I play another video game now, Benny?"

"One more before we leave. Be back in a minute, Hutton. Joel and I are gonna go shoot the bull." Ben motioned Joel to another room. A sudden shriek sent both of them into combat mode. Crouched and whirled all in one motion, their hands to their sides, drawing weapons not there.

They straightened, realizing a fire truck hadn't just crashed into the living room with horns blazing. Hutton.

He stood in the corner, near the lamp he'd knocked over on his way to hide behind a table so dainty it wouldn't protect him from a hummingbird. Eyes wide, he wailed in a ratchet-child voice, "You-you have a bull? In-in-in your house?"

Ben swallowed his tongue to keep from laughing. Joel must not have been as successful because his head dipped and stayed there while his body twitched all the way to the hall.

Ben rushed Hutton. "No, buddy. It's a figure of speech.

Not a literal bull, I just meant we're gonna go talk." Ben replaced the lamp.

Breathing hard, Hutton snatched up the lamp, swung it over his shoulder like a baseball bat and craned his thick neck to peer around Ben. "B-B-But you said you was gonna shoot it."

Now Ben felt terrible for nearly laughing. He hadn't realized Hutton was serious. "I don't kill animals. Honest."

"But Joel does." Hutton eyed the elk and deer heads mounting the game room wall. "Did they get in his house too?"

"Uh, no." Beyond that, Ben didn't have a clue what to say.

Joel, now controlled and contrite, approached Hutton. "Oh, wow, Hutton. My apologies, bud. If they bother you, I can take 'em down. I didn't even think about that stuff scaring you."

"No, I—I just don't wanna be here in case it don't die right away. I don't like to watch nothing suffer. And bulls are big. If it got away it'd be mad for getting shot and I don't want it to come in here and get me if you miss."

"Hutton, there is no bull and we're not shooting anything. 'Shooting the bull,' or 'shooting the breeze,' it's a figure of speech. It means we were just gonna go talk for a minute."

But Ben could see by the twisting of emotions evident on Hutton's face, Joel's words only served to confuse him more. He set down Amber's lamp, at least. "It's silly those animals halfway in the wall. Is the rest of them outside?"

Ben shook his head. "No, they're stuffed." No way was he gonna be the one to inform Hutton the animals' heads had been severed. That would have toppled him right over the edge.

Hutton laughed. "Joel likes stuffed animals too? It's funny he makes them stay on the wall."

"Yeah. He likes to display them. Kind of like the trophies you have from Special Olympics." Great. Now all Ben needed was Hutton poking holes in Miss Evie's walls with nails to perch his own stuffed animals on. He knew Hutton thought about it too, because he chewed his tongue as the cogs in his brain turned.

"I skied on the game, Benny. Fast! Wish I can ski again."

"That right? If you want, go ahead and play another, okay?"

"Okay. Okay, Benny." He tottered off, hands clapping.

Ben followed his team leader to the next room. "I feel bad, Joel. Not only did I forget to give him his Garfield, I don't know how to explain things at his level. I forgot how literally Hutton takes everything. It's frustrating to think I don't know my brother at all. Maybe it's best he doesn't live with me. But my parents have already booked their travel plans abroad. Everything I do and say further traumatizes him."

"Nonsense," Joel said. Then he laughed. "But don't feel bad, Dillinger. When I picked him up from the airport, the same thing happened. The intercom announced, 'Will the gentleman in Terminal P who reported missing luggage please return to baggage claim' and it took me two hours to convince Hutton there was no one in the airport with severe bathroom trouble."

Ben chuckled but eyed his brother fondly through the entryway. "I can believe that. He has always hated the thought of anything suffering. He's got the biggest, softest heart on the planet. I don't ever want to break it again."

"You'll figure it out, Dillinger. And what you don't conquer, you'll wing with the ingenuity you do everything else."

His team leader's faith in him made Ben feel increments better. Still, he hoped Hutton would emotionally survive his season with Ben. Besides...

"I'm hoping time spent together will grow the bond Hutton always wanted. I never gave him the time of day. But now, time with Hutton means everything to me. Just like Dad and Mom told me it would."

"Amazing how much smarter our parents become the older we get." Joel laughed. "Now to convince my son of that."

Joel's wife, Amber, poked her head in. "Had dinner, Ben?"

He shook his head.

"Will you and Hutton join us?" Ben knew Amber always

made plenty, since Joel's seven-man Pararescue team often dropped by at odd intervals.

After dinner, Hutton migrated back to the video game. In preparation for tomorrow, Ben provided explicit instructions and pointers to Joel and Amber that his parents passed on to him about ease with Hutton. They reentered the game room.

"You ready, buddy?"

The brothers bid goodbye to the Montgomery family and headed back. Ben tried to fill the miles with chatter, but Hutton stayed reserved around him, as usual.

Once at the B and B, he noticed Amelia's light on in the living area. After getting Hutton settled, Ben went out on the porch and phoned her. He didn't want to go down there in case she was in her pajamas.

She answered on the third ring. "Hello?"

He smiled at the sound of her voice. "Not used to answering someone else's phone, are you?"

Pleasant laughter breezed through the line. "No. I almost didn't answer it, thinking it was for you. Then I remembered you mentioning you planned to call. Is everything okay, Ben?"

"Sure. Why?"

"You left in such a hurry."

"Everything's all right." He loosened his collar against discomfort for not mentioning Hutton. But he wasn't ready to yet. "How's your room?" Mission strategy: Change of subject.

"Wonderful. More like an apartment. Have you eaten dinner? We have pork chops left over."

"I ate at Joel's. Then gorged myself on Amber's Mountain Dew Apple Dumplings." He patted his stomach. "I'm stuffed. But thanks." Ben walked back into his apartment.

"Mountain Dew?"

"Yeah, sounds bad but they're really good. I'll bring some by for you and Reece tomorrow. Hey, I forgot to ask if you guys needed anything before I left earlier." He'd been preoccupied with thoughts of Hutton. "I noticed yesterday at Mayberry Market you bought breakfast and lunch stuff. Need milk or anything?"

"I might borrow some. Reece will eat oatmeal without it, but prefers it with." Amelia laughed. "But I got the really important things for oatmeal."

"What's that?" Ben treasured the sound of her laughter. Wished he could keep her on the phone all night.

"Sugar."

He laughed and started to say he was glad she was eating that, then stopped himself. Might hurt her feelings. He didn't need to tell her what she already knew. It would put some much-needed weight on her.

"So, tomorrow. What's the plan?" he asked.

"Hold on, Reece is stirring. I'll call you back."

"Okay, bye."

Speaking of plans, he needed one too. He could drop Hutton off at Joel's on his way to the gym after his morning run. No, that wouldn't work. Ben usually got up at four to run his miles, do cardio and pump iron until seven every day, nearly without fail. The rigors of his job demanded it. He also supplemented the workouts with sports activity and strenuous training events with his team.

Hutton usually didn't wake up until eight. This was gonna be a problem. Unless Hutton could stay asleep while Ben ran. He might have to switch workouts to the evening until Hutton and he could work out a schedule. And until Hutton wasn't going to wake up fearful at being alone in a new place. His phone rang.

"Hey. Sorry about that. Reece needed a drink. Anyway, about a plan. Would you care to leave early before carting me to the doctor's so I can buy bus tickets? I'll also need to run by Eagle's Nest to get things from my car and let the mechanic know I'll return for it later."

"Sounds great." He'd just have to figure out what to do with Hutton. Things would be much easier if Amelia knew about him. But that couldn't happen until he got better at handling Hutton. He didn't want pretty Amelia to see his total ineptness in dealing with a person with disabilities. Especially humiliating was that this person was his own flesh and blood.

Who he should probably go check on, since no sounds had come out of Hutton's room in several minutes. "Listen, I gotta run, but I'll see you tomorrow. I'll bring milk over in the morning unless you need some tonight."

"Tomorrow's fine. 'Night, Ben."

Ben hung up missing her voice. He knocked on Hutton's door. No answer. He started to walk away when muffled sobs sounded from within. Blasted with compassion for his brother, Ben grabbed the door handle then paused. Hutton, though like a child, was in fact an adult and deserved to be treated like one.

Ben knocked again. "Hutton? Hey, buddy, you okay?"

Sniveling sounded. "Yeah, Benny. I okay. Everything okay."

But the raw, desperate element to Hutton's voice said otherwise. Ben knocked again. "Mind if I come in?"

"No, Benny. I don't want you to come in."

"I wanna be sure you're okay." *Please talk to me, buddy. Please. Let me into your world.*

"I be okay, Benny."

"You know, Hutton, I have rough days sometimes, too."

"You do?"

"Yup. And sometimes I wish I had someone to talk to."

"Oh. I didn't know. Am I making you have a bad day, Benny?" The distress in Hutton's voice escalated. Ben couldn't take it. He pushed open the door and rushed to his brother's side.

Hutton sat in the middle of the bed, with covers bunched up around him all the way to his close-set eyes and low-set ears.

Ben halted.

Hutton also had every single item in the entire room stacked mile-high in the bed with him. Clothes. Stuffed animals. Phone. Lamp. Alarm clock. Mirror. Wall pictures. Everything, piled around him. Looked like a volcano shaped lump with Hutton's tears the eruption. The sight could have been comical had Hutton not looked so surprised at Ben barging in.

Approaching the bed, Ben cleared a place and sat in the spot. "Hey, buddy. What's going on?"

Hutton nudged the comforter down slightly. Far enough Ben could see his eyes blinking as fast as automatic gunfire and his mouth chewing like Psych, his teammate's cat, devouring his beloved tuna.

"I don't want to tell you."

"Anything I can do to make it better?"

Rocking, Hutton darted his gaze all over the room. "Yeah, Benny. Yeah. You can. I—I'm scared of what's under the bed."

Okay, so *sometimes* he needed to treat Hutton like a child. Ben remembered now how Hutton had always been afraid of monsters in the closet and under the bed. But Ben wished he could remember what his mom and dad used to do about it. "What will help you not to be afraid?"

"To put the bed all the way down. That's what would help."

"Be happy to. Can you hop up? That way I can get the mattress off." Hutton scrambled from the bed, dragging half the contents with him. Not until Hutton evacuated the bed did Ben realize the closet contents covered the bed, too.

Ben glanced at the closet. Completely empty. Even the hangers littered the bed. No idea why Hutton nested stuff beneath and around himself like that. Some protective or defense mechanism, no doubt.

"I sorry about the room a mess, Benny. I clean it for you."

"Don't sweat it, buddy. I'm not worried about the room,

okay?" Bed cleared, Ben pulled off the mattress and leaned it against the wall. Then he retrieved a screwdriver from the tool kit Hutton had gotten from the closet. "I just feel bad I didn't know you were scared. Next time, I hope you'll tell me so I can help you not be scared anymore."

"Okay, Benny. I just don't want to be a bother."

"You're not. I enjoy you being here."

Even if the entire room, including curtains and the rod holding them, and every single item in the closet, including the light cover got stacked in the middle of the bed. Ben wanted to laugh. But didn't dare, for fear of hurting Hutton's feelings.

He wondered if Hutton had ever pulled this stacking, nesting and hoarding of items at home. If so, his mom owed him big time for neglecting to warn him.

"Okay, all set." Ben took the bed frame apart and moved it into the living room. Partly so the mattress could sit flat on the floor, and partly so Hutton wouldn't still be able to fear something lurking under it. But mostly to tell his brother without words that he'd go to any length to make him feel welcome and comfortable, and the transition easier.

"Tanks, Benny. Tanks." Hutton blinked furiously while Ben remade the bed. "I help you." He plopped down and did. And Ben let him, though it took twice as long.

"You want the safe things put back in your bed?"

Usually a man obsessed with extreme order and discipline who hated clutter, Ben felt waves of grace against compulsion to clean the disorderly room and set everything in its place. Hutton's feelings were more important than Ben's neat-freak standards.

"Yes, Benny. But I have to be able to see everything. Sometimes things move if they're not together. If I can't watch it all at once, they spread out."

Huh? "Okay." No clue what that meant. But okay.

Ben piled soft items on one corner of the mattress. Then clumped items Hutton could get poked with, cut on, or otherwise strangled in, such as the lamp cord should he tangle up in it during sleep, over in the corner of the room in plain sight.

"There ya go. Let me know if you need anything else. Make yourself at home, okay? If you get frightened again, come get me or holler. It won't disturb or bug me. Okay?"

Hutton blinked. "Okay, Benny. Thanks for being nice to me."

That statement shouldn't have hurt, but it did. And for the life of Ben, he didn't completely know why. But pain seared his chest at the thought of how many times he *wasn't* nice to Hutton. And how him being nice to his brother, in Hutton's eyes, should be the expected, rather than the unexpected.

Growing up, he'd messed up. Plain and simple.

Heal the damage.

No matter how long or what it took, Ben determined Hutton would one day come to see that Ben being nice was the rule rather than the exception.

Which meant if he wanted into Hutton's world, then Ben needed to do more to let Hutton into his.

Which meant revealing Reece and Amelia, and their deepening feelings despite the fact that they'd known each other only a short time.

Ben flicked on the Garfield night-light he'd gotten Hutton and pulled the door to where he thought Hutton liked it.

"Night buddy. I love you." *And I hope I can get better at showing you how much.*

Feeling another song coming on, Ben grabbed his guitar and headed for his place on the porch. "Tune in," as Joel termed connecting with God.

Perched on the rail, Ben pulled the acoustic in his lap. Eyes open, he bowed his heart but lifted his face to where glimmering stars filled Refuge's Air Force-blue sky. Strums poured from his fingers along familiar paths over the strings.

Words streamed out, exclusive worship to the God he knew could right every wrong thing. Even if the thing was Ben's own heart, and the fear lying within.

"No matter how many times I fail, You never see me as a failure. No matter how many times I fall, You won't give up on me at all. In mercy You hold me to the standards You decree, lovingly mold me from what I am into who I'm meant to be…"

Just as Amelia drifted off, emollient music lifted her mood and her head from the pillow.

For the second time tonight, she found herself mentally investigating. The first time was hours ago in the living room, when Ben's car pulled back in. She'd watched for him. Waited. Hoping to talk after Reece fell asleep. She'd felt like a spy when his car returned with two heads instead of one. And now, she couldn't stop wondering who the other person was.

Still hearing the calming music coming from outside, Amelia rolled over, inched forward on her knees and leaned over the antique headboard. Parting the curtains, she strained to see past shadows diffused over the yard by moonlight.

Was it the radio? A person? Sounded like it drifted from the back of the Victorian. Some units had balconies that faced hiking trails flanking the sides and back of the building.

The music wasn't loud. In fact, she almost thought she had imagined it until she strained her ears and heard an ethereal melody wafting from another unit. An acoustic guitar. Agile strumming.

Not disturbing. Dulcet. Soothing. She snuggled back beneath the sound and her covers, resting in whatever was making her feel at peace for the first time in a long time. Delicate. Just like a lullaby. Soothing…

"Mommy, it's morning time. Wake up, sleepy head."

Bright light assaulted Amelia's eyes when she opened them. The sight and sound of Reece jolted her to a sitting position. She never overslept. Never. Nor did she not rise before Reece. The thought of her roaming around unwatched made Amelia's heart pound. Acid rushed up her throat. How long—? She eyed the clock. Only six. Her pulse slowed.

"Hey. When did you wake up?" She hugged Reece.

"Just now. Bearby and me are hungry and thirsty. But we have a tummy ache."

Oh, no. No. No. No. Not the flu.

"I hope you're not getting what Mommy had. Here, lay down in my bed. I'll bring Sprite."

"Is that what helped your tummy?"

"Yup." That was a Ben term if she'd ever heard one. The guy was beginning to rub off on her.

"Want to try a cracker, too?"

Yawning, Reece nodded. Sometimes Reece complained of ailments when she wanted an excuse to crawl into Amelia's bed. Hopefully that was the case here.

The last thing they needed was for Reece to get sick in the middle of all this.

Please, please don't be getting sick. But even as she wished it, she recognized Reece's glazed eyes and flushed skin. Did she even have medication on-hand for fevers? Amelia plunged fingers in her hair. What would she do? Instinctively she knew: call Ben. He would help without expecting something in return right? Her heart begged him to be the man of honor who would.

Chapter Ten

"What's the bowl for?" Ben asked when she got in the car, after they'd checked her out of the B and B.

"She woke with a tummy ache. Though I think she just wanted a reason to sleep with me since she woke up in a strange place, I didn't want to take any chances with your car upholstery."

Ben grinned. He started to tell her he'd ended up with someone in his bed last night, too.

Hutton had emerged sometime between two and three in the morning, asking to make a pallet on Ben's floor. Then, fear of what lurked beneath the bed had Hutton sleeping on Ben's bed. Otherwise he would have taken a second bed apart. Maybe he should anyway, just in case Hutton coming to his room became a habit.

The words lodged in his throat. He wanted to tell Amelia about Hutton.

He couldn't.

Not yet. Given time, he would, though. Because he couldn't very well keep someone that important from his brother nor keep someone as important as his brother from her.

Ben hoped Hutton would do okay staying at Joel's today

and tonight. He had had to get Hutton up two hours early in order to get his workout in. And Hutton hadn't slept well to begin with. Getting Hutton up and out of the bed this morning was like trying to single-handedly budge a B-52 off a runway.

Ben had cut his workout in half for the sake of eating pancakes with Hutton at the Bed and Breakfast. He admittedly went early with the sole intent of avoiding Amelia should she walk in. He'd even walked past her unit to recon the sleep situation, be sure the lights were still off and no sign existed of anyone stirring. Guilt tossed a grenade at him.

Help me push past this. No matter how uncomfortable or unpleasant for me. Hutton deserves to be known.

Ben knew he meant it. That didn't mean telling her was gonna be easy. But when did he ever take the easy road?

Apparently, right now.

When they pulled into Refuge's bus station, Reece was asleep, the lopsided tiara still affixed in her hair. She'd worn the thing nonstop.

"Kind of early for her nap, isn't it?" Ben placed a hand along her forehead, then met Amelia's gaze. "She's feverish. Got any kids' fever reducer?"

"Yeah. I'll get a cool cloth, too." On her way inside to the water fountain to moisten a washcloth she kept in her purse, she thought it sweet that Ben had grown accustomed to Reece's rhythms and schedule. *Don't read too much into it.*

Returning outside, Amelia brushed damp hair from Reece's eyes. Her cheeks looked flushed. Amelia dug in her bag and found the medicine while Ben set aside the tiara and woke Reece.

"Hey, princess. Can you take some medicine for me?" Ben put the pink tablet on her tongue. "Go ahead and chew that up."

"Mmmm. Smells like bubble gum," she mumbled, eyes glassy.

Nothing scared Amelia more than Reece getting sick. Amelia suddenly wished her mom were there. What if Reece got deathly ill? Would she know what to do? Her heart lurched at the thought.

Reece's hands fumbled for her head. "My crown!"

"Right here." Ben handed it over.

Reece clutched it close. "If I take it off I might not be a princess anymore and if I'm not a princess then I might not get a daddy because princesses always have daddies." Her eyes slid open and looked right at him. "Mr. Ben, I wish you were my daddy. You're nice and you remind me of a king and we could call our land Kindness Kingdom."

Widening, Amelia's eyes swerved to Ben. "I'm sorry. She's talking out of her head. Delirious."

"It's okay. Fevers do that some—"

Reece bolted up. "Mommy, I don't feel so good. I need the bathroom quick."

After sprinting inside the bus depot past wide-eyed patrons—Reece barely making it in time—Amelia, fighting tears, sat on a bench and clung to her listless daughter.

Kneeling, Ben rested his warm hand on her shoulder. "Don't get worked up. We'll handle this, okay?"

"I took her for a flu shot."

"They don't cover every type."

She nodded. They returned inside to the ticket line. Near the counter, Reece's head lifted. "I gotta go again."

"I better take her before she has an accident." Amelia stepped out of line.

Afterward, Amelia returned to the back of the line. With Reece's next tummy pain, Ben ran Reece to the bathroom, visible from the line.

He waited by the door, listening for Reece since Amelia

was next up at the counter. "I need to purchase two tickets to St. Louis for departure after two today."

"Next Saint Loo bus leaves at ten p.m. All others are filled to capacity."

"Can I be put on a waiting list in case someone doesn't show for an earlier bus?"

"They's already a waiting list a mile long. That your daughter?"

Amelia turned. Ben held Reece in the middle of the room, her head rested against his shoulder.

"Yes." The way the woman eyed Reece incinerated Amelia's hope of getting on the bus.

"Mo-ommeeee!" A horrible wretch and splat sound cut off her cry. Ben never flinched except to move toward the door since the bathroom was now occupied.

Amelia ran with the bowl. Too late. "I'm sorry," she said to the wide-eyed ticket clerk. "Do you have paper towels?"

The bugged-out clerk tossed her a roll. "Don't 'spect me to come over there 'n help, or you'll be cleaning up after two." She shoved her shirt over her mouth as Ben rushed Reece outside.

Amelia dashed after them but called, "Be right back to pay for two tickets."

"For you and the child?"

Amelia paused at the door when Ben waved her back. Obviously he had things under control. Kneeling to mop up the mess, Amelia nodded to the clerk with a sense of impending doom.

"Nuh-uh. We can't let a child that ill on a bus with all those other people. No way, no how," she said through her shirt.

Amelia knew it was futile to argue. Senseless, too. Being a mom herself, barring an emergency, she'd be ticked if another parent brought an infectious child onboard a crowded bus.

The clerk shuddered and picked up the phone. "Bring a mop."

Amelia felt nauseous herself. Not so much the smell, but the situation. Could things get any worse?

She immediately wished to snatch back her thoughts. Things could *always* get worse. Unspeakably worse. How could she worry about her job when Reece could end up in the hospital? Kids could die from the flu, right?

Amelia fought paralyzing fear, the way she did every time Reece fell ill. Then Ben's calming words floated back. *Don't get yourself worked up. We'll handle this.*

For once, she felt she had someone to lean on during a hard time. That brought profound relief.

Which was pathetically short-lived.

Leaning on Ben meant the risk of growing dependent on him. And that could prove the riskiest thing of all.

"I called the doctor's office. They said they'll see her when you come in," Ben said after returning from a store across the street. He joined Amelia, seated on the bus stop curb holding a cloth on Reece's forehead.

"Oh, good. Thank you." His shirt was different. "Did she throw up on you?"

He grinned. "A little."

"I'm sorry, Ben."

He shrugged. "I've had worse. I'm a paramedic. Body fluids don't faze me. You didn't buy a bus ticket, did you?"

"No. They wouldn't let me."

"Good. I was leery of you riding the bus alone. Even during the day."

"Actually the next bus available to St. Louis is ten p.m."

"Then I definitely don't want you on it. If we drive there after the appointment, we'll still beat the bus. St Louis is only two hours from Refuge. Let me take you."

Since he had medical training, that made Amelia feel a thousand levels of relief. "I hate to keep inconveniencing you, Ben, but I don't see that I have other options."

"Hey, it's not your fault. Don't feel bad. If I didn't want to do it, I wouldn't have offered. Okay?"

She nodded.

"The three things you need to learn about me, Amelia, are, I say what I mean, I mean what I say and I do what I say."

Three things you need to learn about me...

That almost made it sound like he desired to keep in touch. The very thought fluttered her heart with romantic hope.

Stop. Things would never work. For reasons she could never reconcile, or bring herself to tell him.

"What's that?" Reece mumbled.

"Flu artillery." Ben lifted the bulging sack.

"How much do I owe you?" Amelia asked.

"Nada. It's free sample Friday," Ben answered. Armed with two pharmacy bags for Reece, they left the doctor's office after getting travel clearance for Saturday.

Reece talked more in the last twenty minutes, since getting the shot to hold flu symptoms at bay, than she had all day. That and Ben's presence lifted the weight of fear off Amelia. It did little to alleviate her growing anxiety about her job, though. Dr. Callahan had strongly advised against traveling today.

When Ben said he could still drive Amelia tomorrow, he'd hesitated, telling her he'd already had other plans.

The last thing she wanted to be was a burden to Ben. He'd been so kind and now felt obligated to take them. But he'd insisted when she'd protested that she could rent a car.

"You sure Miss Evie doesn't mind us staying another night?"

"She said to stay at the Bed and Breakfast as long as you like. Forever, if you want."

"She said that?" Strange. Even stranger was how intently Ben studied her when he'd shared the words *forever, if you want.*

Why?

"Ben, I can't accept that," Amelia said in the B and B parking lot Saturday morning.

Rattling sounded as Ben filled the cooler he'd just given her with ice. "Sure you can. Besides, I have another one." He shoved Pedialyte Popsicles down in the ice along with other items, then set the cooler in the backseat.

He helped her prop pillows around Reece and her seat belt. Working side by side with him, their hands brushing together. The close proximity caused things inside her to awaken.

This togetherness, the teamwork between them, opened up longing in her that was best left undisturbed. She couldn't get used to this. Couldn't set herself up to depend on him, because dependence on others always led to disappointment.

"I'm thankful for all you've done, Ben."

"No sweat." His grin turned her inside out.

After running by the garage and transferring the rest of their stuff to Ben's car, they started on the road for Missouri.

She dreaded getting the garage bill and now the double doctor bill, but at least Reece was feeling better. And Dr. Callahan hadn't charged her for the medicine.

"May I use your phone to call Nissa to inform her when we'll get there? She told me to come whenever, but I hate to drop in unannounced. I'm not as spontaneous as she is."

"Of course." Ben handed her his phone. Amelia called and left a message for Nissa to call her back.

"That's strange." Amelia eyed Ben's phone. Clouds of dread accumulated in her chest.

Ben eyed her. "What's that?"

"Not sure. There was a message on Nissa's answering machine directed at me, saying she knew I'd call and that she had exciting news."

"You don't have a good feeling about it?"

"Intuitively, no. Hopefully it's just because I know Nissa's bipolar and isn't great about taking her medicine. She sometimes makes rash, outlandish decisions and she's fairly flighty to begin with."

Ben nodded. "So, maybe we should come up with a plan B, in case living with your cousin ends up not working out."

We? "I can't comprehend that notion, Ben. She can't do that to me. I have no plan B. Period."

Amelia didn't have a good feeling about this. Not at all. But what on earth could Nissa's surprise be?

"You *what?*" Amelia said when Nissa called back minutes later, nearly dropping Ben's phone as her arms numbed. "Oh, Nissa, please tell me you're kidding."

Giggling came across the line. "Nope. Aren't you happy for me?" Amelia's cousin asked in a singsong voice.

"How long have you known this guy? Because when I talked to you last month, you weren't seeing anybody. Now you're marrying him? *Marrying* him, Nissa? This week!"

"Not marrying exactly. Eloping." More giggles. "But don't worry. I can still watch Reece when I get back in three weeks. He's taking me to an island!"

"What?" Amelia groaned and put her face in her hands. "Three weeks? How am I supposed to find child care, effective immediately, for three weeks? I start my new job Tuesday. Oh, Nissa, how can you possibly think of eloping with a guy you hooked up with two weeks ago? Are you crazy?"

"You know I'm not. I thought you'd be happy for me. Remember we always dreamed about finding the perfect one? Well, I have."

"I thought that about Reece's dad, too. Look how that

turned out. Nissa, please wait. Wait at least six months before jumping into marriage. Please."

"But he already bought me the ring. And it's a rock. He's loaded, Amelia, and he wants to spend it all on me. We've been together every day and night since we met. So I know him and he knows me."

"What's he do for a living?"

"Oh, er, one job is he plays in a local band."

"What kind?"

"Um, pubs. Bars. Mostly strip clubs. Okay, look, I know it sounds bad, but at least he has a job. And lots of money."

"Where does he get it all?"

"Uh, he says he's in sales."

"Oh, I'm sure he is. Did you ask him what kind?"

"No, that's not important."

"Not import...God have mercy." And she meant it. Amelia tilted her head back. "What's his middle name?"

A heavy pause. "Um, it starts with a P. I think. Oh, Amelia, you're way too logical. For once, you should throw caution to the wind. Oops, forgot." Giggling. "You did that once. Otherwise Reece wouldn't be here."

"Thanks for the reminder of my indiscretion."

More silence. Heavier this time, which let Amelia know she hadn't heard wrong about Nissa being with the guy every day—and night. "Nissa, please pray about this. I know we don't often talk about God or faith, but please, consult Him before making any rash decisions. Promise me?"

"I promise. But, oh, he's a dream!"

Heart-heavy, Amelia hung up. The dreamy lilt to Nissa's voice dropped rocks of bewilderment in her gut. Dread settled like sludge. How would she find child care for Reece in a matter of hours if Nissa fell through?

How?

She refused to put Reece in anyone's care without screening them first. Not only that, Reece might still have the flu and be contagious. And she only had a few hundred dollars to her name. No credit. No checking account. No savings. Nothing. Which meant day care was out of the question unless they let her pay later. Fat chance. She needed this job, but things weren't looking good.

Something deep and raw and desperate broke inside her. "For once, God, please. Give me a break."

Ben's heart went out to Amelia. Obviously that phone call didn't go well. Silently praying for unflinching trust and at the risk she'd flee, he reached a hand across the car anyway and placed it on Amelia's.

"Please help Amelia see Your hand in her life. And shine truth through to her cousin." *And please assuage this acute distrust Amelia has of men. At least of me. I so badly want to get through to her, even if it does nothing to benefit me.*

Ben strongly sensed Amelia wasn't meant to be in St. Louis. But because a small possibility existed that she was, he thought that because he wanted her in Refuge, he couldn't voice it again.

"Show Your goodness and heart toward her, Amen."

Though Amelia didn't verbally agree with his prayer, tears dripped onto her hands, which trembled during Ben's prayer. He knew because she left it in his grasp.

Now, please help her leave her life in Yours.

Relief hit him that she prayed at all and that she'd encouraged her cousin to do the same. That meant she had a small trust in God. Maybe her weary, ragged faith was starting to turn around and run back home.

Progress. Go, God, go!

"What's going on?" Ben asked after a few minutes, knowing from earlier tears she'd vehemently hidden from Reece, that she'd have difficulty speaking moments after the call.

"She—she, oh, I can hardly bring myself to say it. She's making a big mistake, Ben. I know she's going to regret it."

"Does this affect you and Reece staying there?"

"Nissa says it won't, but it will. Big time. She's eloping this week. And by the sound of background racket on the phone, she's moved her boyfriend—and his entire band—into the apartment."

Ben's head swerved around. "What?"

"Yeah. And I know for a fact a guy she's been dating got her to experiment with drugs recently, because she called me when she was out of it."

"Think it's the same guy?"

"Kills me to think so. I think I know what he looks like from Nissa's MySpace page. So we'll find out when we get there if it's the same guy."

Ben hoped it wasn't. But an uneasy feeling told him it was.

He placed a hand on Amelia's shoulder. "Hey, look. If it's as bad as it sounds, we'll handle it. I won't leave you on your own, okay?"

"Okay" came from her mouth while her gently trusting eyes blinked back jaded tears that begged him to mean it.

Chapter Eleven

"It's him." Amelia wavered on the steps outside the slashed-up screen door she'd just knocked on. She eyed a framed photograph sitting on a bar stool. It depicted Nissa sprawled across some guy's lap. Amelia's face lost color. Ben braced a sustaining arm around her waist.

Through the screen, he eyed the apartment, which resembled a beer-battered frat house. Risqué pinups covered several walls. He immediately shielded Reece's eyes by picking her up, turning her around and holding her head tight to his chest, angling away from the pictures.

Ben assessed the carnage in a room that vibrated loud music. A battered drum set filled the kitchen, leaving no room to move around. Old food, ashtrays and whiskey bottles littered every surface. Drug paraphernalia trashed the top of a guitar amp.

No way was Ben letting Reece and Amelia stay here. Hopefully Amelia would conclude that herself.

A palefaced male rolled off the stained couch. A hiss sounded as he pressed his cigarette into a beer can and stumbled toward them. "Yo. Whussup?" The guy opened the door and brushed a leering gaze up and down Amelia.

Ben stepped forward. "Nissa here?"

He scratched his head. "That Dino's chick?"

"Where is she?" Ben asked, facing the guy.

"With Dino to get some smokes." The guy stumbled into a bedroom, looking highly annoyed that they'd interrupted the misery of his hangover.

Amelia waved a hand over her nose, shook her head and motioned Ben back outside.

"I smelled it, too. Not your imagination," he said, referring to both the reefer fog and old vomit. Ben secured Reece in the car and approached Amelia.

She paced across the porch. "I can't let Reece be exposed to this."

"Hold on." Ben cranked the engine, turned on the air. He asked Reece to draw him a special picture and closed the car door to dim conversation.

Amelia's eyebrows crinkled into a frown and her eye twitched. "We can't live here. Can't even stay five minutes."

"I agree." Ben moved close then stopped, wanting to hold her but holding back, afraid he would crash through the thin ice of her fragile trust.

She paced back and forth across crumbling sidewalk then over mile-high grass and weeds. The yard looked like a small forest.

"I have to look for an apartment, pronto." She turned and sped toward his car then stopped abruptly, as if just now remembering she didn't have her own car here.

Her countenance took a crestfallen dive. He surged forward. "Amelia, don't worry. I'll take you." Hopefully Hutton would be okay at Joel's longer. He'd done all right last night. Ben hoped it held. When Ben slipped away from Amelia one of several times to check on Hutton, Joel said Hutton could stay as long as Ben needed. He put sustaining hands on her shoulders.

She stiffened under his touch. "I can't ask you to do that. You already said you needed to get back to Refuge."

He did, to get Hutton, but hopefully Hutton would understand if Ben were late. "I can change my plans. However, I can't, *won't,* leave you and Reece here alone. This area isn't safe. You have no business walking around here. There aren't potential jobs close by that I saw." He didn't remove his hands from her.

"I know," she whispered, looking more distraught by the second. He gently massaged her shoulders. Taut muscles relaxed under his fingers as did her stance. Finally, slightly, she leaned into him. *Progress. Thank you.*

"Look, I can change my plans today and this evening." *Please help Hutton understand.* Ben felt so torn. But he'd have lots of time with his brother later, in the ensuing weeks when Hutton moved to Refuge. He'd make it up to him.

Tears dangled from her lashes as she probed deep in his eyes. "Ben, I'm so sorry about all this."

"No big deal." *Please let that be so.* Hopefully Hutton wouldn't have a meltdown. But Ben could not abandon Amelia and Reece. Being a pararescueman had trained him to do triage, and that meant assisting the one in the greatest amount of danger first.

He wished there were two of him right about now. His heart beckoned him to his brother, but his creed called him to Amelia and Reece. A sense of human decency and his personal code of ethics wouldn't let him leave them here to fend for themselves.

It is my duty as a pararescueman to save life and aid the injured. I will be prepared at all times to perform my assigned duties quickly and efficiently, placing these duties before personal desires and comforts. These things I do, "That others may live."

His pararescue creed meant setting his own feelings

aside. Hutton was safe at least. He couldn't say the same for Amelia and Reece. Split by his obligations, Ben knew what he had to do.

With reluctance, he released her shoulders. "Let's grab a paper and look for housing close to your job. Just not in this part of town."

Her hands wrung. "I hate to do this to you, but okay. I'll need to call my boss. Obviously I won't be able to start this week. Hopefully he'll be understanding. Even if we were fortunate enough to find a safe place to live this evening, I'd need more time to secure child care."

"Maybe he'll let you bring Reece to work with you for a few days until you find decent housing and safe child care."

Fear accosted her features. "I'll ask. Let's wait here a bit to see if Nissa comes back. I'm going to try to talk sense into her or knock her silly."

Ben smiled, knowing Amelia kidded. At least he hoped so. It'd been a long time since he'd broken up a catfight. He gestured toward his phone. "Call your boss."

She nodded, stared at the phone, started to dial then hesitated. Wide, vulnerable eyes cited his. "Pray?"

Trapped in her gaze, Ben nodded. "I am."

Amelia hadn't gotten two sentences into explaining her dilemma when bursts of yelling and vulgar words interrupted.

She held back the dead phone. "He hung up on me." She redialed. "Sir, please try to be reasonable…"

More screaming and cursing blasted from the phone.

How he'd like to get hold of that guy for speaking to a lady with those words and that tone.

Ben caught verbal remarks accusing Amelia of being undependable. Insinuations she was as big a flake as her cousin and he should've know better than to hire Nissa's family.

Amelia's spine stiffened. At a moment of silence, her eyes closed as she put her mouth to the phone. "Sir, please listen a minute. I am desperate. I really need that—" Her lovely face fell. She slowly closed the phone. Convulsive swallows claimed her throat. "I've been fired before I ever even started."

Good. Because he was about to grab the phone and resign her himself, then go cauterize the creep.

"I think it's for the best. I feel God's protecting you."

The startled, uncertain look on her face told him she couldn't comprehend that possibility. *Help her know You.*

Ben shut Amelia's door, then strode to the driver's seat. As he pulled out, another car skidded to a halt in the driveway.

"That's Nissa." Amelia jerked the handle. Ben stopped the car. Exiting, Amelia raced purposefully to Nissa.

Ben looked back at Reece. Asleep. Bearby in one hand, colored pencil in the other. The flu and the meds must be making her doze. Reaching over the seat, Ben slipped the pencil from her fingers and set it a safe distance.

He faced the window. Obviously a heated exchange was going down between Amelia and Nissa. Not liking the venomous looks Nissa's boyfriend threw Amelia's way, Ben stepped from his vehicle.

The punk took one look at Ben, scuttled backward and stuffed himself into Nissa's tin-can car. Could have been comical had it been under better circumstances.

"If you can't see plainly why Reece and I cannot live here, Nissa, I am very concerned about you."

Nissa flipped purplish red hair over her shoulder. "I'm sorry I ruined your plans."

"Never mind that. You *cannot* marry this guy."

Nissa's arms folded. "Yes, I can."

"Not and keep from ruining aspects of your faith and life."

"You're a fine one to talk about faith, Miss Sunday School dropout."

"I didn't reject that church. They rejected me and you know it. They judged and rejected you, too, for going Goth, even though I tried to tell them it's only a manner of style and that you were still the same person on the inside."

"Well, you're rejecting my fiancé."

"No. I'm doing what's prudent to keep my daughter safe. When you figure out what that means, or when your life crumbles around you, call me."

Nissa's eyes averted, then returned.

Amelia jabbed a finger at Nissa's brooding fiancé. "And, if the latter happens before the first, I'll help you pick up the pieces like you helped me when I let a guy as lame as that leave my life in a lurch."

"You don't know that's gonna happen. How can you say something so mean, and curse my future before it starts?"

"How can you not see how dangerous it would be for me to bring my daughter into a drug house?"

Nissa's eyes widened. "You don't know it's a drug house."

"Then why are the bongs, burnt spoons and capless needles lying around, which could stick a child if she picked it up?"

Nissa darted looks at the ground. "Sorry. I didn't know they'd left those things out."

Amelia turned to go. "My point exactly. Love's flying you First Class blind."

Nissa clutched handfuls of her shirt. "I swear the drugs aren't mine. Please don't narc to the cops."

Webbed in her cousin's black-nailed grip, Amelia halted but didn't turn around. "I don't want you to go to jail. I want you to get away from this guy and this hard-core partying life-style before it hurts you."

"I can't. He loves me."

Amelia turned. "You can find a better guy to love you."

Nissa shrugged. "You say yourself all guys are jerks."

"Well, I was wrong." Amelia glanced at Ben. "Way wrong."

"I'm happy. Okay? Can't you be happy for me?"

Placid, Amelia shook her head. "Absolutely not. I love you too much not to tell you the truth. Look, I need to go."

Nissa took tentative steps toward Amelia. "I'll see you at work. Maybe we could talk over lunch?"

"No on both counts. I lost the job. Ben's taking me to look for another one, and someplace to live." Amelia hugged Nissa and jogged to the car. She swiped tears once they cleared the driveway. "Seems all I do is cry these days. I'm not usually this wimpy."

"You're not wimpy. You care about Nissa and hate to see her making grave choices." So did he.

Amelia nodded and seemed devoid of words a moment. "Thank you, Ben. For everything. I'm overwhelmed really. I don't even know what to say for all you've done."

Just say you'll consider my idea if things don't work out here.

Six hours after purchasing a local paper, scouring every ad and visiting dozens of establishments, Amelia leaned against Ben's car in a discouraged slump. "No one's hiring without a college degree. Minimum-wage employers won't work around Reece's school schedule."

"And there weren't any affordable apartments near the ones that did." Ben knew his words added to her defeat, but he didn't want her contemplating trying to live on minimum wage as a single mom in the city. Many moms did, but he'd feel safer with Amelia closer. But was that for his benefit, or hers?

Ben didn't want to put undue influence on Amelia, but it was past dinnertime and Reece was beyond tired and cranky. She needed a good rest.

He folded the paper closed. "Tell you what. Let's stop the search for now. We'll relax at a restaurant and talk about options."

Defeat crumpled her face. "I don't see that I have options. But Reece is hungry. The doctor said to try Jell-O for dinner."

"And you need to eat, too."

Something flared in her eyes at the words.

"I didn't mean it like that. I'm not trying to control your life. I'm simply trying to give you hope and help."

"I'm beginning to think I'm a helpless, hopeless case."

"It's never hopeless and you're far from helpless. Don't think along those lines."

"But life hasn't shown me anything else."

"Not yet. Life has a lot left in store for you, Amelia Grace North. And you have a lot left to offer life and the people in it."

Her eyes grew hazy with suspicion. "Let's go eat. I think you're delirious from hunger."

"Tell you what. Everything's closing. Reece needs to recoup. You could use some rest, too," Ben said hours after dinner, as they left another job that yielded zilch.

"I can't. Have to keep looking." Sheer desperation drove her now.

"We'll get two hotel rooms in St. Louis tonight. Then resume the hunt tomorrow." He'd arrange for someone to cover leading worship for him at church tomorrow morning.

After Ben let Amelia and Reece have a chance to get settled, he knocked on the door that adjoined their rooms.

"Hey." Amelia held open the door while Ben passed by.

He set the leftover containers in her fridge.

"Mommy, can I watch cartoons?"

"If you'll eat another popsicle." She peeled open a frozen purple Pedialyte stick and held it out to her daughter.

Reece pulled a face. "But they taste yuck."

"No popsicle. No TV." Amelia headed back to the freezer.

"'Kay, fine. I'll eat it." Reece took the popsicle.

Ben was impressed at Amelia's stick-to-it-iveness and ability to keep a sick child hydrated. She'd been creative with every aspect of Reece's illness and treatment.

Ben remembered seeing the chessboard they'd played at

the hospital in the lawn bag when they'd transferred stuff to the vented plastic bins Ben gave her. According to Reece, Amelia was teaching her how to play the game. "Wanna play chess?" he asked. The concentration might take Amelia's mind temporarily off things enough to help her get a good night's rest.

She paused before answering. "Sure."

"You hesitated. Something wrong?"

"Not really. It's just, my dad hand-whittled the pieces and taught me how to play. Mean as he's been, I miss those times with him." Seeing tears glitter her eyes, Ben started to go to her. But she mumbled, "I'll get it." She snatched his keys off the table and headed for the door.

Figuring she needed to collect herself, he kept his distance but watched over her from the window. They'd found a parking spot in front of the room.

"Mommy, you shouldn't gloat," Reece said later.

"What makes you think I'm gloating? Not like I bragged about beating him for the third time." She smirked.

"Well, you aren't gloating with your words, but you are with your body," Reece said.

Amelia batted her eyelids dramatically, feigning innocence. "Me? Whatever gave you that idea?"

"Your face. Because it's twinkling bright and you look like a big ol' lightning bug with its butt stuck on backwards." Reece turned her attention back to cartoons.

"Reece Mercy North, don't say that *B* word. Use the other one."

"Okay, Mommy. Bottom-bottom-bottom-bottom," she sang, as she climbed off the bed and skipped to the bathroom.

Ben snickered, then cut it short when he became the prime target of Amelia's ballistic Mommy Look.

"She must be feeling better." Holding back a grin, he helped her return the game pieces to their starting positions.

When her hand brushed his in passing, he was accosted with the urge to hold it. "So, her middle name is Mercy?"

"Yeah. After God's mercy in letting her live when she almost didn't," Amelia whispered, as the toilet flushed.

"So, you *do* believe in God?"

"I believe in Him. I just don't think He believes in me."

How badly he wanted her to know that wasn't true.

Before he could speak, Reece bounded from the bathroom and washed her hands at the sink. More like splashed in the water.

"Thought you said you were chess champion in college." Face alight with humor, Amelia returned pieces to the box.

"I was. Good thing we didn't attend the same one."

Her smile faded. "I never went to college."

"Hey…" He tipped up her chin with his finger and stared in her eyes. "You still can. You're very intelligent."

"Thank you." Thick sincerity transfixed her eyes, breaking the threshold of his control. He reached across the checkered board and wove his fingers through hers. And she let him.

All he could think as he studied their entwined fingers was how the brown and white intermingled squares of the chessboard suddenly seemed symbolic of the two of them.

He gently squeezed her hand, still linked in his. She gave an answering squeeze.

And for the life of him, any recall of the human language fled his brain.

In fact for all he knew he could be drooling all over his chin and couldn't care less. Her smile sent him to paradise. The feel of her hand in his, and the trust it meant was forming, sent his heart and hope soaring to outer space.

Chapter Twelve

"Another fruitless day of searching." Amelia's hands trembled as she buckled her seat belt the next evening.

Ben cradled her hands in his. "Come back with me to Refuge, Amelia. At least temporarily. I phoned Miss Evie. She'll waive your rent until you get a job."

"School starts in a few weeks. I have to find a place to settle. I can't add to Reece's insecurity by moving her mid-school-year."

"Refuge lives up to its name. I know two local teachers who'd love to welcome Reece. Try it for a year. You can find a job in Refuge. I have friends who could hire you, or I could."

She looked at him sharply. "I appreciate your kindness. I know you don't mean to be anything other than noble by your offer. But I need to be able to support myself." The tenuous emotion in her eyes melted his heart like Hutton's chocolate Garfield.

"I need to know I can take care of my daughter. Because my parents have me nearly convinced that I can't." Her voice dissolved on the last word.

"I understand."

"I'd like to come to Refuge. But I need to secure a job on

my own. So promise me you won't help, or talk to anyone on my behalf unless I ask you to."

The conviction in her voice and deep plea in her eyes pierced his heart. She really did need to believe in herself as a mother. To know she could take care of Reece without depending on others to bail her out. To help her too much could impede the burgeoning confidence that would sustain her for life.

"I respect that. I won't help you find a job unless you ask. But feel free to if it comes down to it, okay?"

Eyeing Reece, probably to be sure she remained too consumed with mazes to overhear, Amelia leaned in. "Believe me, Ben, I'm thankful. But, I need to know I can make it on my own. At least in the job department."

"Okay. I won't interfere. Promise."

"Then I guess we're Refuge-bound."

Ben grinned at Amelia, then Reece. "You want to tell her?"

"Hey, Reece's Pieces. Ben thinks Mommy might be able to find a job in Refuge. What would you think about that?"

She bounced in her seat and clapped. "Yay! I don't like it here. There are so many buildings running around all the time."

Amelia laughed. "As much as we'd driven around today and yesterday, it probably looked to Reece like buildings were running past the car. We've always lived in a small town. It's what she's used to."

"What about you?" Ben asked.

"I prefer small-town living, too."

He smiled. "Refuge fits the description. Shall we venture back?" He needed to check on Hutton. Last time he called, Joel said Hutton was having difficulty, but wouldn't go into it. Probably didn't want Ben to rush home.

An hour from Refuge, Reece, previously asleep, bolted upright screaming. Ben's shoulders clenched at the sound.

Amelia jerked awake. "Sweetie, what is it?"

"Bearby! Mama! I forgot him!"

Ben pulled over and searched the car. No Bearby.

Ben phoned places they'd stopped.

Moments later, Ben clicked shut his phone. "He's safe, Reece. A clerk found him. She'll hold him until we get back there."

"Ben, that's two hours out of your way—for a tattered toy."

"He's Reece's security right now." Amelia nodded. They started back.

Ben's phone chimed. He eyed caller ID. Joel. A thud hit Ben's gut. "Yo," Ben said.

"Hey, bro. How far out are you?"

"I was about an hour from Refuge."

"Was?"

"Yeah, we, ah, had complications. We're going back for something valuable left at a gas station. What's up?" He didn't want to ask if Hutton was all right, because Amelia might ask who he was.

"Hutton's having a high-speed come-apart. Any suggestions on what I should do?"

"What's the problem?"

Joel's hesitation set barbells of dread on Ben's shoulders.

"He thinks you've abandoned him. Amber and I have tried to console and convince him it's not true but his anxiety escalated. I waited to call you."

"What's he doing now?" Never mind what Amelia thought. Hutton was hurting.

"Pacing. Crying inconsolably. Mumbling crazy stuff."

"Such as?"

"Says you don't like him."

Ben wanted to laugh and throttle himself at the same time. "Joel, I love him."

"Everyone knows that, Dillinger."

Everyone except Hutton.

The one who needed to know it most.

"Can you put him on the phone?"

"Hang on." Joel called for Hutton. Ben's insides clenched at the wailing. Ben felt ripped in half.

Judging by the heightened awareness grazing Amelia's wide eyes, she could hear Hutton. Ben hated for her to hear how awkward he was with Hutton, but he loved his brother more.

"Hey, buddy. It's Ben. You okay?"

"Why you leave, Benny?" Hutton groaned.

"I'm helping a friend. Thought you'd have more fun there."

"You don't like me." Sniffling.

"Not true. I love you. We'll spend all day tomorrow together, okay?"

"No, Benny," he bawled.

"I'm sorry. I'll be there in three hours, okay?"

"Benny, I want home to Mom's."

"If that's still what you want when I get there, I'll make sure it happens."

Ben knew Hutton's condition enough to know when he got this worked up, he couldn't be reasoned with. "Can you put Joel back on the phone? Hello? Hutton?"

Rustling sounded, then, "Hello?"

"Amber? Yeah, I'm sorry about this."

"It's not your fault, Ben. Bradley invited him to stay."

"But if I were there, he may have been okay."

"Hard to say. I wonder if it's more him missing your mom."

"Think that could be it?"

"Partly."

What Amber didn't say told Ben what he didn't want to know. Most of the reason for Hutton's emotional collapse was because Ben wasn't there.

"Be there as soon as I can."

"Drive safely. We'll handle it until then."

Ben hung up feeling terrible. The way Amelia looked said she felt terrible, too. But Reece would be devastated if they didn't get Bearby and there was no way to mail him because the clerk was leaving.

"Ben, if you need to go back—"

"It's fine." He didn't mean to cut her off. But, the sound of Hutton's cries scraped against him. He had to make Hutton more of a priority. Had to.

It haunted Amelia to wonder who was on the phone.

Did Ben have an older child?

Had it not been for Ben helping her, the person wouldn't be upset.

She felt terrible for accepting his help. Her problems were corroding everything around her, just like her parents said. Anxiety accosted. Regret ravaged.

Ben was the last person she wanted to poison with her difficulties. "I'm sorry, Ben."

"No reason to be," he said. But his words went without heart, and his thoughts soared somewhere else entirely.

Yes, she had every reason to be sorry. Story of her life.

The way to remedy this was to put herself in a position where Ben didn't feel obligated to help.

Chapter Thirteen

After retrieving Bearby, they finally arrived in Refuge. Ben set a hand on Amelia's shoulder, rousing her from sleep. "Hey, we're home."

Home. Now, why had he said that?

Thankfully she'd still been groggy enough that he didn't think she noticed. Amelia sat up, ran a hand through sleep-mussed hair and blinked awake.

"Wait here with Reece. I'll get your key. Miss Evie put it in my unit when she knew to expect you."

Ben hurried for the key. After settling Reece in her bed for Amelia, Ben said a quick good-night and left. Hated to run off, but he needed to get to Hutton. He eyed his watch. Just past midnight.

He phoned Joel that he was on his way. Thankfully traffic was sparse this time of night.

Blocks from Joel's, eerie blue lights swooned his interior. Foot yanked off the gas, he eyed the speedometer. "Great."

"Officer Stallings," Ben said moments later, when the lawman sauntered to the window.

"Airman Dillinger. I certainly hope you're rushing to a national emergency at those speeds."

Ben felt himself blush as he dug out his wallet. "Unfortunately, sir, no national emergency. Unless you get Hutton's side of the story."

"You headed to Joel's to pick him up?"

Ben eyed Stallings. "Yeah. How'd you know?" No secrets in a small town.

"I was called by neighbors earlier for a—disturbance."

Foreboding knocked Ben's stomach in a loop. "Didn't happen to involve my brother, did it?"

"Put your license away. Professional courtesy. I'm not ticketing you. But you need to slow it down for me, okay?"

"Thanks, sir. I will. Appreciate the grace." Ben didn't miss that Stallings completely ignored his question. "Mind giving me a rundown of what happened with Hutton?"

"Old fellow who lives left of Montgomery's told the 911 operator he heard a zoo animal loose in the neighborhood."

"Hutton ran through the street wailing again?"

"Apparently. You're a good brother for wanting to take care of him, Ben. I imagine it can't be easy. See you later."

"Gee, I hope not. No offense."

Stallings' laughter trailed to his cruiser.

Ben headed to Joel's.

Once there, Ben's heart cringed at Hutton's profile in the window. Sad eyes hugged the desolate street. Fretting teeth chewed an enlarged tongue. When Ben approached, the door opened.

Amber stepped aside. "Hey, Ben."

"You look tired. Go on to bed. I'll talk to Hutton."

Amber cast a sleepy smile and sympathetic looks their way before retreating to her room. Joel rose from the couch near the window where Hutton paced.

Ben approached cautiously. "Hey, buddy. Ready to go home now?"

Hutton turned, murmuring and blinking and avoiding eye

contact. He shuffled over and shook Joel's hand. "Tanks for putting up with me. I know I was bad."

"No, Hutton. You weren't bad. You're just getting used to things changing is all." Joel turned him to face Ben.

"I ready to go now, Benny. Home to Mom's."

Ben's heart sank. He'd meant the B and B when he'd said "home" but apparently Hutton lodged in his mind "home to Chicago."

Once in the car and nearly to the B and B, Ben cleared his throat. "I'm really sorry I upset you. I was kinda hoping you'd stay the night with me. We could hang out tomorrow."

Hutton's head swiveled back and forth and he chewed his tongue. "No Benny. You promise I go home. To Mom's. I know you have friends more important than me but that's okay. I know I'm not like everybody else. Why you don't like to be around me is I'm different. I understand. Lotsa people feel that way."

But I'm not lotsa people. I'm your brother.

But Ben had treated him like he was different growing up; he had wished his brother was normal and had told him so. That his imbecile words had assisted in shaping Hutton's poor view of himself cut Ben to the core.

For the first time since early childhood, and his first rescue effort turned recovery, Ben actually felt like crying. The sting of tears grew swift. Emotion and remorse burned his throat like sulfuric acid. Pressure mounted behind his eyes.

He swallowed three times before words would come. "Buddy, I'm—I'm different now. I know I treated you badly growing up. But, Hutton, I love you and I'll try to do better at showing it. I wish I knew how to convince you that I *do* care about you."

"You could take me to Mom. That's what would make me know a little," Hutton said nearly too low for Ben to hear. Hutton's words deflated by the end of the sentence to the point

Ben knew Hutton didn't really believe Ben would drive him to Chicago tonight. Ben was dead-dog-tired and Chicago was six hours north. But if that's what it took to earn Hutton's trust, he'd do it. Hutton was worth losing sleep over.

"Though I'm disappointed not to get to spend more time with you tomorrow, I understand and am happy to take you to Mom's tonight if that's what you want. I'll need to stop by my apartment real quick to get your things first, though, okay?"

"Okay. Okay. Tanks, Benny. I sorry to be a nuisance."

Again, emotion ambushed Ben. "You're not a nuisance. You're my brother and I'd do anything in the world for you, buddy."

Please believe that.

Hutton wouldn't understand Ben's need to get a good night's sleep before making the six-hour drive there and another six hours back. Not like Ben could sleep over at his mom's and drive home tomorrow, either, because he had a mandatory training and meeting at noon he couldn't miss. In fact, even if he drove straight to Chicago and back, he'd be pushing to make it on time.

He phoned his mom and explained the situation.

"Ben, there's no sense in you driving twelve straight hours. Your dad and I will meet you and Hutton in Decatur, Illinois. That's three hours for both of us one way."

"Thanks, Ma. I appreciate it."

Ben had hoped Hutton would change his mind and stay. Not for convenience's sake, but for time-spent sake. But when he hung up and found Hutton waiting by the door with gloves donned and a winter coat zipped up to his nose in the middle of summer, he knew it was a no-go. Hutton was ready for Chicago.

Regardless if it was seventy degrees there, it was subzero in this apartment. Hutton had grown stone-cold quiet, setting a chill of ice over the room that Ben felt powerless to chip through and incapable of warming.

In helping one person, he'd hurt another.

God, I don't know how but I know you can. Please redeem this situation.

Liquid bliss slid down Amelia's throat as she swallowed her last sip of warm amaretto tea. She set the dainty teacup she'd found in the cabinet in the sink. Then she rinsed it out and turned it upside down on a towel.

Where had Ben gone in such a hurry? Was something wrong? Someone taken ill in his family? She couldn't help but worry. And why hadn't he shared the struggle so evident on his face?

"I wish Ben felt like he could talk to me," she said to Bearby, on the chair by their sketch pads, then groaned. "I've really lost it. I've resorted to talking to inanimate objects."

She checked on Reece. Sound asleep. She tucked Bearby beside her, resisted the absurd urge to tell him good-night, then returned to the living room. She dead-bolted the door. An outside lamppost cast antique yellow light through her front room window. Two streams of brighter light roved across the gravel and beamed at the wraparound porch rail.

Leaned in, Amelia peered through the gauzy sage curtain. That looked like Ben's sporty red sedan returning. She wasn't sure why she was so curious about Ben and his goings-on.

She pulled the drawstring on the blind to let it down. Footsteps sounded up the steps and along the boardwalk in front of her unit, which sat close to the top of the steps. The footsteps veered left. Probably Ben, going to his apartment. But his car was still running. She twirled the blind twist, causing the slats to open enough to allow a peek.

She really ought not stare at his agile, fluid stride as he jogged. She closed the blind slats, slower this time. Again, she caught sight of someone else in the car. Certainly not a child. Because of the dim light and the fact that the wraparound porch roofing covered the car—and the person in it—in shadows, Amelia couldn't make out anything except the shape of an oblique adult head and a set of broad, stoopy shoulders.

She lowered the blinds for real, completely covering the window. She shouldn't be nosy and wondering.

Amelia put her hand to her stomach. She'd nibbled an apple with her tea earlier. She felt hungry but her stomach was bungee-jumping over the job situation and Nissa's crazy behavior. It'd be all she could do to keep that apple down. No way could she muster the guts to eat one of those rich-looking rolls Miss Evie had left on the counter of the furnished unit, along with a Welcome note. She'd save them for tomorrow. Maybe even invite Ben.

Speaking of whom…Amelia migrated to the window as the car pulled out. No, she shouldn't stoop to wonder, but she couldn't cork the questions spewing through her mind.

Who was in the car with Ben? Where were they going at two in the morning? And why?

Amelia shook off the questions and her shoes and headed for her only pair of pajamas.

Emotion swept over her when she pulled them out. Dad bought them for her the Christmas before she'd gotten pregnant with Reece. How she missed better days with her dad.

If things were ever going to be as they were, she could never be with Ben.

She shouldn't be concerning herself with aspects of Ben Dillinger's life whatsoever. After all, hadn't her near brush with death and the near loss of her child at the hands of her enraged ex-boyfriend taught her to be more cautious?

She exerted mental effort to otherwise occupy her mind. Her thoughts cavorted to what Ben said earlier. When he suggested that the loss of her job could be God protecting her, what could he have possibly meant by that? Like Glorietta, was Ben's faith the reason behind his reaching out?

Maybe he didn't have a secret motive. But why would God want to protect her? Wouldn't He still be mad at her for messing up her life in high school like her parents and old Sunday school teacher said?

Maybe she'd been listening to the wrong voices all along.

Upon arriving in Decatur, concern hit Ben, seeing his mom alone in the car. He woke Hutton. "Hey, buddy. We're at the truck stop. Mom's here to take you the rest of the way home, okay?"

Hutton rubbed his eyes and blinked through the windshield. When he caught sight of his mother, he disentangled from the seatbelt and scampered from the car in a lopsided gait to her.

Ben held a small amount of hope that Hutton's outburst and panic attack at Joel's was set off mostly by missing Mom. How would Hutton ever cope once he moved in with Ben for that year? He just needed to have Hutton come more often.

"Where's Dad?" Ben asked his mom.

"He wasn't feeling well."

Ben didn't like the hesitation in her voice.

She helped Hutton buckle. "Hold on," she said to Ben, flicking glances at Hutton. Ben knew she couldn't say more with him in earshot.

His mother hugged him. "We'll talk tomorrow. Call me."

He figured she'd fill him in then. Ben went around the car. He leaned in, hugging as best he could with Hutton being buckled.

Hutton tensed but patted Ben's shoulders. "Tanks, Benny for bring me to Mom."

"You're welcome." He knelt. "Hey, you think you might want to come back next weekend?"

"No, Benny, I don't want to come back." He stared forward.

Standing, Ben breathed hard against the pressure of disappointment and regret that he'd let his brother down again.

Then Hutton blinked up at Ben. "But, if you want me to, I can come next weekend after that. I have a birthday party to go to this weekend." A smile twinkled in Hutton's eyes.

"I'd love you to come next weekend. Unless my team gets sent to a rescue somewhere, I'll see you in two weeks, okay?"

Hutton nodded and chewed his tongue the way he often did when nervous or unsure in a social setting. Ben figured Hutton was scared to believe him. After all, Ben hadn't often given Hutton a reason to trust his word.

That was about to change.

God have mercy on anything that tried to prohibit it.

Chapter Fourteen

Haggard, Ben pulled into the B and B in the wee morning hours. Debated whether to expend energy to go inside and catch a catnap or stay in his car and snooze. Opting to drag himself in, Ben set his alarm to screech in two hours. Sleep. A fleeting, overrated luxury. The sun was already hovering above the horizon.

He pulled his shades, glad to see Amelia had done the same. Maybe he'd ask them out to breakfast in the morning before his team meeting. Then he'd call Hutton. See how he was doing.

He should check on his dad now, though. He dialed. His mom picked up.

"How's Hutton?"

"Sleeping."

"How was he when I left?"

"Better. Hopefully just got homesick. Give him time, Ben. And give yourself time...and grace. Okay?"

"How's Dad?"

"I'm concerned. He didn't look good. And you know how he never wants me to drive alone, much less six hours at night."

"He musta felt bad. He never even liked you walking to the end of the driveway in daylight to get the paper by yourself."

She laughed. "True. I wish he'd felt well enough to come. You could have been a better judge, medically."

"Any other symptoms?"

"He complained of pain in his neck radiating to his jaw. And yesterday, he napped all day. This morning, he's back on the golf course, though."

Ben knew his dad's history of high cholesterol and high blood pressure. "Still, he needs to see a doctor pronto."

"I begged him to seek medical attention."

"He won't?"

"Not unless it gets worse."

Worse could put him in a grave. "Mom, urge him to go see a doctor."

"I doubt he'll go, Ben. I'll take him to the ER if his symptoms return."

"No, don't attempt to drive him. Call 911 and wait for an ambulance."

"Now you're scaring me, Benjamin."

"Heart disease is nothing to sneeze at, Mom. If that's what this is, he doesn't need to take any chances. Most people having a heart attack deny it to themselves. It's better for him to go to the hospital a hundred times when he doesn't need to than not go the one time he does."

"I'll try. But you know how stubborn he can be."

"I also know how dead he can be if this is heart-related. Tell him what he always told me growing up regarding choices. There's a difference between stubborn and stupid."

"It's probably just heartburn. But I'll do my best to get him to go to the doctor. So, any progress on the girl front?"

"Oh, sure, Mom. Change the subject."

She laughed. "I really want to know."

He thought of Amelia.

"So do I. Fact is I met a girl I like and we're becoming

better friends. I should probably jet. I need to grab some winks before taking her to breakfast." He yawned.

"Oh! Do tell me more?"

"When there's more to tell, I will."

"It's just, I want to be a grandma. I can't wait to hold one of your fuzzy-headed babies in my arms."

"Believe me, Ma. No one wants to hold a baby I made more than me. The girl I like, she already has one child from a previous relationship. But you know I'm a Christian now, and want the wedding ring to come before the teething ring."

"Will her old relationship be a problem if things progress?"

"No way. Guy's out of their life for good."

"I want to hear more about this special girl, Benjamin."

He laughed. "Oh, almost forgot…I might have found Hutton a potential job."

"Yeah? What's that?"

"Dishwasher at the B and B where I'm staying. They have a Help Wanted sign on the dining hall door. I inquired about it with the manager. Told him about Hutton and mentioned him working in your bakery."

"Did he sound interested?"

"Yeah. Said they might have to modify his duties, but would have no reservations hiring someone with a disability."

"Did you put an application in for him?"

"Yeah. She's gonna leave the sign up a few more weeks, then start interviews."

"How many employees are they hiring?"

"Only one."

"Have quite a few applied?"

"Not really. So he has a decent shot at the job. I told him about it, thinking that would endear him to Refuge."

"Did he sound excited?"

"Very. He's already practicing for his interview."

"I hope he doesn't get disappointed."

"Me, too." Ben yawned. "Okay, Mom, I'm off."

Ben hung up worried about his dad. Hopefully Mom was right. This was just heartburn. And hopefully, he hadn't gotten Hutton's hopes up about the job for nothing.

Hopefully.

"Mommy, someone's here!" Reece called from the living room.

Amelia shut off the hair dryer provided in the bathroom. She moved into the living room. "Thought I heard a knock." She peeked out the curtains. Her heart did a little flip at the sight of Ben waiting at her door.

Giving her still-damp hair several pats to tame down flyaways, Amelia turned the dead bolt and opened the door.

Ben smiled sheepishly. "Hey."

"Hey. Come on in." Amelia stepped aside. "I heard you pull back in a couple hours ago."

Mustn't have fazed him. Not only did he not acknowledge the statement, his expression remained neutral as he stepped over the threshold. So much for fishing. How could the man look so chipper after so little sleep?

"Coffee?"

He turned a chair around and straddled it. "You already have some made?"

"No, but Miss Evie must have stocked cabinets before we got here because there are filters and an unopened coffee canister."

"Sounds like Miss Evie. Don't fuss with the coffee. I wanted to take you and Reece to breakfast here at the B and B."

"They have omelets?"

"Dozen different kinds. All of them to die for."

"Eggs cooked in bacon grease?" She arched a brow.

He arched back. "If you ask."

Amelia walked toward the first bedroom. "Reece, where'd you go? Ben's here."

She emerged. Amelia and Ben laughed. She already had on her princess tiara and the rhinestone movie-star sunglasses he'd bought her. Strings trailed her shoes when she walked.

"Heads up, princess. Don't trip."

"Can you help me tie them?" She plopped at Ben's feet and extended her legs.

"Sure." Ben knelt and took the shoestrings in his hand. "How are you today?"

"Fine. And I cannot possibility tie my own shoes, ya know."

Ben chuckled, probably at her misuse of the word. "That right?"

Reece nodded. "Yup. Because princesses don't have to tie their own shoes if they don't want to."

Amelia elevated her voice. "Uh, excuse me, little princess. Queen Diva decrees you must learn to tie your shoes."

"Your mother's right. If you don't practice, you'll never get it down," Ben said to Reece.

Sitting to put her socks on, Amelia faced Ben. "She's used to shoes with Velcro. I admit I'm not adept with teaching how to tie shoes. Plus I'm left-handed and she's not."

"I noticed that about you." Ben looked up and absorbed Amelia's gaze long enough for her cheeks to start boiling.

"I—I'll just get my purse." She stood, scurried into her room. Then remembered. She smacked her forehead and laughed.

Her purse wasn't on the dresser but in the front closet by the door. Stalling, she sat on her bed and caught sight of herself in the mirror. Wished she had some makeup to put on.

Makeup had been among the first nonessentials to go when things got tough financially. Amelia remembered a time when she wouldn't dare leave the house without lipstick or blush.

Tiptoeing to the bathroom, she scrunched curls in her hair and unplugged the hair dryer. She reentered the living room and slid past Ben, hoping he wouldn't notice her pulling her purse from the closet.

Strap slung over her shoulder, she turned. Frozen a moment in time, her eyes and heart caught in a wondrous web of watching Ben interact with Reece. A flash of her own dad teaching her to tie shoes at Reece's age backed Amelia into a bar stool. She sat.

Ben's large hands guided Reece's small ones in crossing two strings and curving one over the other and looping it through the hole. "Now, pull this tight and the bunny's mouth closes."

Reece giggled as their conjoined hands tugged strings taut.

Ben pressed Reece's finger over the tiny knot, preventing strings from loosening. "Next, hold your finger over the button nose. Then make a lop-ear with this big loop. Then make the second bunny ear and bend it so the bunny runs through the burrow hole. The other chases it around and pull tight."

With slightly uncoordinated movements, Reece followed his instructions until a disheveled bow formed. "I did it, Mommy!" Reece surged to her feet and pranced over. Her lifted shoe proudly displayed a delightfully crooked bow that matched Ben's grin as he met and captured Amelia's gaze over Reece's head.

"You did!" Amelia agreed with her daughter.

Why did it twist and loop her insides out just like that bow to have him look at her that way? Not to mention how his interaction with Reece resurrected Amelia's dreams for her daughter to have a dad who cared. She wanted it for Reece even more than she wanted it for herself.

Just shy of fawning over Ben, she broke the gaze but knew he didn't. Heat from it dried her throat. Not sensual, but one that bored as if searching for something.

What?

Confirmation of a connection?

Evidence of attraction?

Invitation for progression?

All of the above.

Amelia's mind raced to regain where they were before the serendipitous exchange.

She rumpled the top of Reece's hair and bent to study her shoestring bow. "It's perfect!" she fibbed. "Are we ready to go? Mommy is actually hungry this morning."

Ben opened his mouth then shut it. Amelia laughed.

"What?"

"I could tell you started to say something then stopped."

His only answer was a grin.

"Smart man. Had you brought up my food faux pas again, I might have had to leave your body for the trail buzzards."

He moved past her.

She enjoyed the scent of his woodsy, manly cologne. More than she should for someone who'd supposedly harbored caution from the wind.

Reece dived at him. "Thank you, Mr. Ben, for teaching me how to tie my shoes." She squeezed his knees.

"No problem, princess. Where's Bearby?"

"Right here." Reece turned a half circle and wiggled her backpack. Bearby's nose peeked above the opening.

Ben motioned toward the door. "All-righty then. Let's *hasta* lapasta."

Reece giggled. "*La vista,* silly. Mr. Ben, why do your eyes look like posh trophies?"

"Apostrophes," Amelia amended, cheeks burning. "He's Asian, sweetie."

"Part Asian," Ben corrected. "My mother's Taiwanese and my father's Caucasian."

They walked around the building and entered the dining hall.

"Mommy, I miss Shasta." Reece's smile waned.

Ben looked at Amelia as they entered the buffet line.

She drew a breath. "My parents have a dog. He's part Husky. He used to be mine. Ours." She cleared the lump from her throat. She could barely afford food for her daughter. It would have been utterly irrational to keep the dog.

"Reece was so upset when I told her we'd have to give him away, so my parents took him in." Amelia laughed. "My dad hates dogs, and Shasta jumps in Dad's lap every chance he gets." She blinked back tears and distracted herself by filling her and Reece's plates. "We moved back in with them when things got hard. But then Dad and I clashed even worse. I couldn't afford to bring the dog."

"Even though things are strained with your parents, you miss them, don't you?" Ben said as they settled into a booth.

She'd been doing great holding her emotions at bay until those words left Ben's lips, and the softness with which he spoke. She finally figured out why she equated his voice with velvet. Words came out plush and thick with the most considerate layer of kindness she'd ever encountered in another human voice.

Realizing Ben still waited for an answer, she drew a sustaining breath. "Yes. Because, though they're not perfect, they're mine. They're all I have." Her voice strained. She eyed the drink menu. Didn't see a word. All she could see in that moment was what she'd lost. What one wrong choice had cost.

She missed her dog. She missed her mom. She even missed her cantankerous dad.

At least she still had Reece. And she meant to keep it so. If Ben had been placed in her life for no other reason than to teach her that her parents were the ones making wrong choices, it was worth it. Still, she hoped it could mean more.

"I wish you could come meet my puppy, Ben. But Grandpa would run you clean out of the yard," Reece said, after the hostess filled their drink orders.

Ben's eyebrows lifted. Amelia's face flamed. "Reece!" Amelia shook her head sternly. "Not polite."

Amelia wanted to melt into the woodwork. She also wanted to go clobber some sense into her dad. It was no secret to Amelia that he was prejudiced against Asians and so staunchly against interracial relationships that he'd threatened all her life that if she got into one he'd disown her.

Sipping, Ben studied her above his glass. She felt he deserved an explanation.

"My father can be cruel to people who are different."

"Meaning he's racist?"

"I wouldn't say that," Amelia said.

"Then what *would* you say?" Kindness never left Ben's face or tone. He leaned forward.

Amelia drew a slow breath and stared into Ben's eyes. "No one else in my family agrees with my dad, nor do we share his opinion. Ever since he came back from Vietnam, my mother says he's disliked people of Asian descent."

Ben's expression didn't fluctuate. Amelia expected him to get defensive or angry. But he nodded evenly like he understood.

How? When she didn't understand herself how he could feel that way? Maybe the war traumatized him somehow. Amelia didn't know. But she hoped God would work it out. God. She had been thinking about Him more and more.

To her surprise Ben's face broke out into a witty grin. "Guess that means you'll have a hard time taking me home to meet the parents, huh?"

Amelia's throat constricted because it just now dawned on her. She'd never be able to take Ben to meet her parents'. Ever. And if Ben was insinuating he wanted a relationship with her, she may indeed have to choose between Ben or her parents. Because if things got serious with Ben, things would seriously implode with her dad.

"What are his views on interracial relationships?"

Gulp. "Not good."

"Ouch." Ben studied her. "That could be a problem." His gaze intensified.

"Excuse me. I—I need to visit the restroom." She fled there, wondering what on earth he meant by that.

He couldn't possibly mean the two of them. Could he?

And if he meant what she thought, then she had every reason to reel over the repercussions. If Ben was in the picture romantically, there'd be no father-daughter restoration. Period.

Ben had a point. Not until this moment did she consider the future conflict that would await them if their friendship continued to blossom into something deeper. A part of her still couldn't wrap her mind around Ben being interested in her. Yet another part could hardly deny it. After all, she knew she'd make a good wife someday. She just didn't know if a decent guy would ever give her the chance.

Maybe one was.

The very possibility made her breathless with delirium.

Hard to imagine how such a deep bond had formed in so little time. But they'd been nearly inseparable since her car wreck. And here she was giving Nissa advice. Yet Ben was worlds apart from Nissa's fiancé.

If Ben fell for Amelia while seeing her at her worst, then he was definitely keeper material. She certainly wasn't brave enough to bring up the subject first.

As she returned from the restroom, a sign on the French doors caught her eye.

Kitchen Help Wanted.

Kitchen help. If she got the job, she wouldn't have to drive or spend gas money. That sounded perfect! Excitement welled up in her like she hadn't experienced since before leaving North Carolina. She rushed to the counter. Hope soared.

"May I have an employment application?"

"Sure." The man handed her a form. "Questions?"

"What kind of kitchen help do you need?"

"Dishwasher. The one we have leaves for college in the fall."

Thank goodness they didn't need a cook. Amelia wasn't stellar in the culinary department. "Do school buses run by here?"

"Yes, matter of fact they do." The man handed her an envelope addressed to the Bed and Breakfast. "If you're unable to return it in person this week, mail it back in the envelope. We'll phone you for an interview next month if interested."

Next month! That was too long. Maybe they'd move it up.

"Thank you." Amelia slipped the packet inside her purse and headed back to the table.

"Ben, would you mind if Reece and I rode with you to town? I'd like to check on my car then put in applications."

"Sure. I have an hour before I need to be at the Drop Zone. We can snag a local paper. I'll show you around town before dropping you off."

"Mind if I give them your cell number until I get a phone?"

"Sure. In fact, keep the phone until you get your own."

"Thank you. The garage is in the middle of the business district, right?"

He nodded and wiped his mouth. "It sits on the main road that runs through Refuge, which is aptly named Verbose Street because people gather at shops and cafés all up and down it to talk. Everything's within walking distance. Police station sits across the street and lots of people commute by foot around town. It sits miles from the shady area of town. You and Reece should be safe."

"I hope the car's ready soon, so I can tell potential employers I'll have no trouble with transportation to work," Amelia said, as Ben pulled up to Eagle's Nest after showing them around town.

"Gus Johnson works fast. After my mandatory meetings, I'll find you and we'll grab dinner. So be thinking about where you and Reece want to eat." Ben opened the door for them.

"I'd like to try those curly fries as long as your leg."

"Then back to the B and B it is. See you later." He drove off.

Water bottles and a tiara in tow, Amelia and Reece walked around Refuge for hours. Amelia kept track on paper, but lost mental count of how many jobs she applied for. Her mind drifted back to the Bed and Breakfast position. Of all the places she'd applied, that would be her dream job. But since when did she ever get her first choice?

Pray, then trust and believe. Amelia could almost hear Glorietta's favorite five words as if she were right here whispering them in her ear.

Pray, then trust and believe.

Okay, fine. Here goes.

Amelia knelt beside Reece. "You want to pray with Mommy about a job?"

Reece nodded. Amelia took hold of her hand. "God, it's been too long since we've talked. I am thankful for everything you've done." *Like when you protected me from losing Reece after the assault.* "As you probably know, I'm really in need of a job. And, we'd really like to live in Refuge." *That B and B position seems so perfect. And-and I wondered if I could have it.* "Amen."

There. She prayed. "Oh, I forgot, please help me to trust and believe. Amen."

"Mommy, you forgot to say 'in Jesus' name'!"

Amelia smiled. "I left the most important part out, huh? Wanna say it with me?"

Reece nodded. "Please give Mommy a job so Shasta can come live with us again. Bearby misses him even though Shasta chewed his ears off and Mommy had to sew on new ones. In Jesus' name."

Amelia blinked back tears and quelled laughter. "In Jesus' name," she whispered. "Amen."

Exhausted of heat and possibilities, she headed to Eagle's Nest to check on her car and wait for Ben. This time, unlike that day at the hospital, she knew in her heart he'd show.

But would God come through for her, too?

Chapter Fifteen

"**I** mighta been wrong."

Rattle noises clanked from Amelia's car when Gus Johnson, the mechanic, cranked the starter. She'd hoped to be able to drive it today, since the body work was done.

She trailed him to the front. "What do you mean?"

"She's worse than I thought. Motorwise, anyhow."

"How bad?" She stared beneath the open hood into a confounding maze of coils, tubes, metal and rubber.

"I'm afraid she's on her last leg. I'm doin' all I can to fix her but truth is, she needs a new engine. I've used as many donated parts as I can. So I won't have to charge you except for labor, which won't be nothing since my clock fell off the wall and busted my addin' machine."

"Donated parts?"

"Yes'm. Folks been coming by all week, dropping off new and used parts, in hopes I can use them on your car." He pointed to a small mountain of parts accumulated in the corner.

"That pile is big enough one could don a pair of dented bumpers and ski down it, huh?"

"Yeah. Or a car hood and sled down it. Who told people?"

"Can't tell. Sworn to secrecy."

Had to be Ben. Or maybe Miss Evie. Then again, could have been Glorietta. Or Nurse Bailey, or Officer Stallings. Or even a tag team of Doctors Callahan and Riviera. According to Miss Evie, they'd all been calling to check on her well-being this week, which she'd spent applying for jobs and getting acquainted with Refuge…and Ben. Everyone seemed concerned for her and Reece's well-being…except her own parents.

Amelia wanted to cry. "Does anyone in Refuge not know about my fender bender? The entire town has a kindness conspiracy. Including you. There's no way I'm not paying for the repairs."

A toothless grin answered her. "This community, we're an Acts Chapter Two kinda town. On the matter of payment, my office could use a good cleanin'. For havin' a little one, your car's about as pristine as I've ever seen. Plus, I know those caricatures you drawed me took a chunk of your time. Everybody's been asking about them. I saw you drawed Miss Evie one too."

She'd drawn one for Glorietta and the ambulance crew who came to her aid, and also the police officers who'd helped her. "It's my way of showing thanks."

"Well, let me know how much you want for 'em. Because everbody that walks by here asks. You got business cards?"

"No. But they can call Ben's number for a quote. And I'd love to clean your office. What all can I do?"

"Whatever you got time for. Mainly, carpets could use a good vacuumin' and windows a shine. Supplies are in the closet by the bathroom." He stooped back under her hood.

"That's it?"

He adjusted his oil-covered cap. "If you still have git-up-n-go after tacklin' that, feel free to straighten my desk. Organization isn't my strong suit, and I'm pert-near tired of scooping papers around to find my phone when she rings. Think you can handle all that?"

"And more. You have a filing system in place?"

He grinned. "Can't say as I do. But you look like you're rarin' and ready to go. So I gotta feelin' I'm about to acquire the aforementioned filing system."

"Can Bearby and I help, Mommy?"

"I'll find something you can help with. Let's get started."

"Just watch the little one around the oil and stuff. Hate for her to eat it or get covered up like a dipstick."

"I won't let her or the oil out of my sight."

"You're a right good mama."

His words riveted her to the spot and crashed waves of emotion over her. "Thank you. You have no idea how much I needed to hear that."

"Maybe I do." He stood silent a moment. "I lost my daughter to a car wreck under two years ago. My wife just a year ago to cancer. She never stopped grievin' our daughter." He swiped a hand over his face. "I'd give anything to be able to tell both of them one more time what good mamas they were. Least they're together again now. And I've got my grandkids. Twins."

"Wow. Your daughter carried double-deckers, huh?"

"Yeah." He chuckled and pulled out a demolished wallet. "She got me this wallet when she was seven. Don't reckon I'll ever part with it."

"I don't blame you."

Unfolding it, he pulled out pictures of two toddlers. "They hafta have a nanny because their daddy's military. In fact, that enamored airman fella who drops you off here—"

"Enamored?"

"Yeah, Benjamin. The one who's been a courtin' you—"

"Courting?"

"You got oil in your ears or something? Boy can't take his eyes off you. Anyway, his team leader was recruited by my son-in-law, Aaron Petrowski, when Joel was young. From here originally. Returned a couple years back. Married a local teacher. Petrowski's my claim to fame. He's brass, see? Pulled military strings to get the PJs set up in Refuge. Aaron was a PJ too. Them boys are the unsung heroes of the Air Force. And most of 'em like it that way. Ain't the types to hype themselves up in the public eye, but you can bet your bottom dollar they're some of the most superbly trained operatives in the world."

He pulled out another picture from his chest pocket. "This is their mama." The picture was as worn as the wallet, telling Amelia he pulled it out an awful lot.

"I'm so sorry for your losses. Do you have pictures of your late wife?"

His eyes brightened. He waved a hand around him. "All these? Are her. Some of her and me and the family, that was before—" He took a hard swallow. He stuffed the boys' pictures back in his wallet. Then studied his daughter's photo once more before tucking it back where it belonged…close to his heart. "But hey, I'm quite sure you got better things to do than listen to an old man jabber."

She shook her head. "No. I'm quite sure I don't." In fact, there was nothing she wanted to do more than lend empathetic ears to words that desperately needed to be said. She slid an upside-down bucket over and sat. And listened. And he talked. And talked. And talked.

She caught glimpses of a life changed forever in the blink of an eye. Then he stumbled over the sentence that stunned her when he told her his daughter and he had had a falling-out and hadn't spoken for weeks before she died. His words of regret rocked her to the core.

Only in her case, it wasn't too late to reconcile.

Then he talked about how Ben's team rallied around him and Petrowski in the aftermath of grief.

And now she was even more enthralled with Ben.

And with possibilities she never dreamed possible.

Reece had grown antsy, so she needed a diversion. "I've

got a few hours to kill. Looks like you could use quite a hand around here. I think your phone rings more than the Refuge operator's. I could answer it for you a couple days a week." That would also enable her to be a regular sounding board.

His frosted brows rose. "How much'd that cost me?"

"Nothing. I'd do it for free. Donate my time since you're working so hard on my car." By the looks of the place, she doubted he could afford to pay her.

"Why sure. I'll never turn down help. In fact, come on. Let me show you the office."

She and Reece followed him into a cluttered storage room.

Scratch that. This *was* the office.

Oh. My.

"As you can see, the biggest wreck of all's in here." He chuckled, so her shock must have shown.

He scratched stubble on his chin. "Notepad's on the desk which is…somewhere. If you can find a pen in that mess I'll know there's hope. My business partner up and flew the coop on me. He took care of all this racket. I took care of the cars. I'm no good at organization."

"But I'll bet you can make a dinged-up car sing."

That made his eyes sparkle. "Yes'm. I can. Refuge has a wildlife preserve in it. Many businesses stick with the theme. When you answer the phone, you say, 'Eagle's Nest.'"

"Will do."

He turned to go but stopped at the door and faced her. "I'd be right proud if you were my daughter. Offering to pay your own way when you don't have to. That's mighty kind. You were raised right. Not too many like you around nowadays."

Tears pricked Amelia's eyes. She turned away from Gus, who her heart had endearingly adopted as her mechanic, and hid her face from Reece before she burst into tears.

No, her father wasn't proud of her. Not in the least. He'd ridicule her for even being in an establishment such as this.

Two hours later, Amelia had neat piles of messages for the mechanic, separated in stacks. To Do. To Call. To Ask. She'd cleaned the office top to bottom and filed every paper in sight. Disinfected the bathroom, floors, scrubbed walls and every conceivable surface with supplies she'd found in the closet. She'd even cleaned that. Decluttered then organized it. Then found hardware to finish putting up utility shelves someone had started but never finished.

Reece was handing her one more screw to drill into the wall when a throaty sound from behind made her pivot on the ladder.

Ben leaned against the doorframe, hands pocketed, watching. Her cheeks flamed even more than they were from working amid heat in this office. Aware she was covered in sweat and nine kinds of grime, she swiped a hand across her forehead.

By the multiplication of his grin, she must have smeared the grease instead of removed it. "I—I planned on washing up in the sink, but wanted to get this shelf hung first." How long had Ben been standing there? How did he sneak up on a person without being detected like that?

He pushed off from the wall and sauntered toward her. "Didn't know you were so mechanically inclined."

"I'm not, really." She waved a vague hand at the shelf, trying to get his bold and unabashed attention off her and onto something else. "This is pretty basic stuff."

He peered around the immaculate room. "Basic? I haven't seen the place look this good since Gus's brother died."

"Oh! My goodness. When he said his partner flew the coop, I didn't realize that's what he meant."

"Yeah, Gus downplays a lot. Like someone else I know. You'll never cease to amaze me, Amelia." Coming closer, he stepped up the ladder until they stood nose to nose.

"M-may I ask what you're doing?" Amelia asked in a shaky voice when he just stood there.

"Standing on a ladder getting ready to ask a girl slathered in grease to date me. And hoping like crazy she'll say yes."

Reece giggled in the background.

"Date?" she squeaked.

"I want to get to know you better. That's usually why people date." He grinned.

Her heart raced her thoughts, which never quite caught up.

"I—I want to get to know you better too. I—I like you. A lot." *Please say you like me too, Ben. Please, please say it.*

He studied her intently for a moment while she thought her lungs, heart and hope might burst from holding their breath.

Then that slow grin she'd grown so fond of spread across his face like Miss Evie's sweet apple butter on homemade bread.

"I like you, too, Amelia." He stepped even closer. "A lot."

Time suspended. His breath hovered over her cheek, forehead, and her eyes then lingered there. Warming her the way the mysterious music did coming from behind the Bed and Breakfast.

The singing and guitar strumming that lulled her to sleep every night. She'd grown to suspect it was Ben, just because her amateur sleuthing had clued her in that the music started after he either left her and Reece's unit, or when he pulled in from wherever he went on the evenings he didn't spend with them.

The look on Ben's face right now had a mesmerizing effect. For the first time in a long time, she felt vibrant and alive.

"Is Mr. Ben gonna kiss you, Mommy? Because it seems like he wants to. That's the way movie people act right before they smooch."

Ben's grin widened and mischief entered his eyes.

Speech evaded Amelia. Because in truth, she couldn't deny having dreamed what kissing Ben would be like.

The ladder step creaked as Ben shifted his weight, putting

his back to Reece. "But since I'm incurably honest, I have to admit I came here to give you a hand. Not a kiss."

Genuine disappointment crept through her.

Until his gaze ignited in earnest and seared a slow path down her face, danced over her lips and strolled back up again. "But the latter isn't such a bad idea, either."

Amelia let loose the breath trapped in her lungs.

Reece jumped up and down. "Kiss her! Kiss her! Kiss her! Even Bearby says you should!"

Heat flashed to Amelia's face and she tried to peer around Ben to unleash The Mommy Look. But he shifted again, effectively blocking her. If it were possible, he leaned closer, leaving only inches between them. He raised his arms above, on either side of her head, bracing them on the top of the ladder and angled his face down.

He inched in and brushed a gentle kiss on the brow bone just left of one eye. As feathery as the contact was, her skin felt branded.

He'd kissed her eye, he'd kissed her eye, he'd kissed her eye. Oh. Kay. He'd only kissed her eye. She peeked. He stared. And his kinetic expression boomed thunder-loud and lightning-clear. She didn't need words to read the message that burned like lasers in his eyes.

Had Reece not been in the room, he would have kissed her lips instead. And thoroughly.

She'd never in her life had a guy look at her like—like— well, frankly, like she was steak and he was starving.

She felt cherished and irresistible. Attractive, even.

He slipped the tools and hardware she'd forgotten she was holding from her numb hands. Then helped her finish suspending the shelf. Her brain buzzed.

He'd kissed her, he'd kissed her, he'd kissed her.

Her mind couldn't stop shouting it out. Even if it had only been on her eye.

He stepped off the ladder leaving her to hyperventilate.

"Hey, if you go on a date, who will watch me?" Reece asked.

He knelt. "I hoped you would hang out with us this evening too. We could watch *Charlotte's Web*. Figured I'd order burgers and curly fries to go from the B and B while your mom cleans up."

Amelia laughed. "Do I smell that bad?"

He stood, reaching to help her off the ladder. When her feet found solid surface, he didn't exactly let her go right away. He leaned close again. "You smell like hard work. Grit and determination. You smell a lot like courage and a little like motor oil and I love every drop."

She started to tilt her face away but his gentle hand stopped her. "Don't hide. Just for the record, when I see you, I don't see imperfection. I see beauty."

She wanted to snort. "In this case, I think blindness rather than beauty is in the eye of the beholder."

"You're wrong. And I'm on a mission to prove it to you."

Chapter Sixteen

❧

"Mommy, this is so good!" Reece said weeks later as she scooped enchilada pie onto her spoon and slid it into her mouth.

"Isn't it?"

Celia Munez, the wife of one of Ben's teammate, Manny, had brought food by this evening, welcoming Amelia to Refuge. Last week, Joel's wife, Amber, had brought Mountain Dew Apple Dumplings and a welcome basket. Amelia had begun to feel at home here, yet she still yearned for her family, dysfunctional as they were.

"I wish Mr. Ben was here to eat with us."

"Me, too."

"Why isn't he?"

Like Amelia, Reece had grown used to Ben's near constant presence. Amelia pondered how to answer. She and Ben were past the point of friendship, yet there were still aspects of his life he wouldn't divulge. Like where he went every nonworking Saturday after spending Friday evenings with her and Reece.

He said he wanted to date her. She didn't want to date other people. But what about Ben? Was that where he went? On dates with other girls?

How could she measure up to other girls in Ben's eyes?

Any guy who looked like Ben had to have hordes of girls after him wherever he went.

The thought made her queasy. She needed to think about something else. She pivoted to face the kitchen.

The crystal vase Ben had bought her in the hospital sat boldly on the counter. The burgundy blooms remained in full force, because Ben replaced them weekly.

The sight of them helped to combat the lies. She'd choose to believe in Ben's sincerity. And fidelity.

"Reece, you want to go for a walk after dinner?"

"Yeah. I miss our walks, Mommy. I wish Grandma was here to go with us."

Amelia swallowed past the lump. Reece, Amelia and Amelia's mom would take strolls around the North Carolina neighborhood and along the beach every weekday evening after dinner. Amelia brushed Reece's hair out of her eyes. "I wish she was, too."

Reece slid off the chair. Clops sounded as her shoes hit the floor. "Let me get Bearby."

"Okay. You do that and wash your hands and face while I put this food away."

She could freeze it. There was enough for another meal. Miss Evie had left another bag of fruit also, as she had the day Amelia had moved in, to welcome Amelia as a tenant. She covered the pan with foil she found in a drawer and put it in the fridge.

Miss Evie must have stocked everything the day they arrived because the dates on all the canned goods were for years away and everything in the cabinets was unopened.

"They're right. Refuge lives up to its name."

The only trouble spot was that none of the gazillion applications she'd turned in had produced results yet.

The ones that had asked her for interviews were leery of hiring her without dependable transportation. Soon as Gus fixed one thing, something else broke. He'd suggested she sell her car for parts, but what she really wanted was to stick dynamite in the tailpipe and be done with it. The transmission was toast and the engine shot. In short, the car was totaled. She'd be better off to put the money into a newer one.

Problem was, to buy even a used car, she had to have income. To have a car, she'd need a loan. She couldn't get a loan without credit. And she couldn't get credit without a job. And she couldn't get a job without a car. And she couldn't get a car without money.

Her life was a maddening catch-22.

Amelia hoped she'd get the kitchen dishwashing job at Refuge Bed and Breakfast. That would be her salvation. Then she could save enough to get another car. And she still wanted to pay Gus for his work, even though it hadn't resulted in her car being fixed. She knew it wasn't because he hadn't tried. He was more than competent.

She didn't want to mention the potential job at the B and B to anyone because she didn't want to jinx it. Every other potential job she'd mentioned to Ben or Glorietta had fizzled.

There was a day-care center right down the road, and school buses ran by the B and B. She'd need to enroll Reece in school somewhere soon. So she had to find a job in Refuge before she decided whether they were going to be able to live here.

Amelia hated to hope for the job only to be disappointed, but she really, really, really hoped the job could be hers.

"I might have found a job for Hutton," Ben said between heavily loaded barbell lifts, as Joel spotted him at the gym Joel built on his property.

"Yeah?" Joel suspended his palms under the weight bar.

"Yeah, he's one of thirty applicants who got picked for a preliminary interview at the B and B."

"He did okay washing dishes for your mom at the bakery, right?"

"He did great at it. He also dusted powdered sugar on every surface in the kitchen besides the donuts, including himself. But he always cleaned everything up. Excluding himself. Most people who saw him leave the bakery thought he was an albino."

Joel laughed.

"But other than that, he handled the duties well."

"Sounds like the job would be perfect for him."

"That's what I thought, too. And since he'll be living here with me, he can walk around the front of the building to work. So transportation won't be a problem." Ben pushed the bar up again for his next set of reps.

"How's your dad? What'd the doctor say?" Joel helped Ben replace the bar on the last lift of the set.

A heavy sigh. "He never went."

"You're kidding. He still that extraterrestrial shade of gray you mentioned?"

"No, last Saturday when I went to visit, his skin was pinker. I pressed his arm and his capillary refill was about three seconds." Ben started another set of reps.

"So just a little delayed."

"Yeah, not bad. Except I noticed at times his bottom lips looked streaked blue. Like veins."

"But no true cyanosis?"

"Not that I could tell." Ben blew breaths out between the words. "Maybe Dad's right and it's just the arthritis in his neck from gawking at Mom all these years."

Joel laughed then grew serious. "Hopefully."

Ben stood and swiped sweat off the weight bench. They switched places on the machine. Ben positioned himself behind Joel's head to spot him.

Joel tried to lift the weight and strained. He sat up and eyed the barbells. "You moved up in weight I see."

Ben grinned. "I have good incentive."

Lying back, Joel laughed. "The girl."

Ben nodded, spreading his legs to better spot Joel as he lifted his first set.

Joel replaced the bar in the metal slots. "How's that going?"

"Stuff with the girl?"

"Yeah." Huffs puffed from Joel as he lifted his next set.

"The four of us have a date tonight."

"Four?"

"Yeah. Me, Amelia, her daughter Reece, and Bearby."

"Bearby?"

"Little stuffed animal that her seven-year-old is attached to at the heart."

Joel laughed. "Bradley has one of those. Little paratrooper toy Amber and I gave him when we first met and he was sick. So, how serious is this?"

"Serious enough for me to notice jewelry stores around town that I never knew existed before. And I stay up half the night thinking about her and the days spent with her."

"Whoa."

"Yeah, and I know the first question you're going to ask. And yes, she is a Christian. Sort of."

"Sort of? That doesn't make me feel good, Dillinger. So anyway, what's the big dig on this girl you're losing sleep over?"

"It's not just her. I'm juggling stuff with Hutton, too. And you saw for yourself how that's going."

"Yeah, yeah. Back to the kind-of-Christian girl. Spill." Joel squirted water in his mouth then swiped his chin.

"I look up to you, Joel. Not only as our leader and phenomenal airman. I admire you as a friend and trust you as a spiritual leader. Any of us would follow you into a lake of fire and back. Plus, you've been married longest."

"I take it you want advice?"

Ben nodded and pressed the weights harder. "She's a good girl. Got pregnant in high school by a violent jock who used her then deserted her. She made me understand under no uncertain terms if I even hint at trying to seduce her, she'd walk and never look back."

"What's her relationship with God like?"

"Arbitrary. She's not obstinate toward Him. Raised in church. Her earthly father won't forgive her mistake and her mother won't take up for her."

"Poor kid."

"You have no idea. Which reminds me, her dad's also prejudiced against Asians and warned her all her life if she ever entered an interracial relationship he'd disown her."

"That's gonna be tough on you guys as a couple."

"Yeah, and Mom says the closer we get to a permanent future together, the tougher the strain. Being in a mixed marriage herself, she'd know. But she wouldn't trade being married to Dad for anything."

"Marriage. That where this is heading?"

"I want it to. She has trust issues, for obvious reasons."

"Probably doesn't help that her father is how he is."

"But it's not like she and him are on talking terms now."

"I see."

"Anyway, I suspect she thinks she's used up her ration of grace and there is no more mercy or forgiveness available, since she knew God then turned her back for that short time."

"You said she was raised in church. What kind?"

"I get the feeling it's legalistic. Small congregation but they shunned her when she got pregnant."

"She resistant to church now?"

"Not sure. I confess I haven't asked her because she's trying hard to prove to herself she's a capable mother. People in authority over her haven't exactly spoken encouraging words to her throughout her life."

"Tough break."

"Yeah, so anyway, I thought if I invited her to church too soon, she might take that as me thinking she's tainted or not good enough or something. So, I'm trying to be tactical about inviting her."

Joel swigged from his water bottle. "If anyone can move the treacherous mountain of a prejudiced heart, God can. Entrust the outcome of this to Him, Dillinger. Hard as it may be, pray for this girl's dad."

"Thanks. I have been. Guess I just needed reassurance I'm on the right track."

"I feel you are." Joel wiped sweat from his forehead.

Doing the same, Ben stood. "I should go. She might need a ride to town and I need a shower. I'm bringing her to Manny's birthday party. So warn the guys that if they tease or drill her for information, I'm sabotaging chutes."

Joel laughed. "I hope you're kidding, Dillinger. But I'll warn them. However, you know how they can be. Whether they listen off the field is out of my control."

"You can threaten to make them pay through other means."

"Such as?"

"Subjecting anyone who disobeys your no-teasing-the-shy-girl orders to a rucksack run in their skivvies around Refuge. And I get to choose what goes in the rucksacks."

Joel laughed and clapped a hand on Ben's shoulder. "I'm glad you're kidding, but the very idea you've plotted your revenge in this sort of detail concerns me about your sanity."

"Sir, I *am* crazy. Crazy about her. She's just really shy and self-conscious because of her lazy eye. I don't want the guys scaring her off. You know how they can be."

"Yeah, and until you met this girl, you used to join them.

In fact, if memory serves, you're the one who gave Evie the idea to name a street after Amber and her Mustang mishap."

Ben straddled the arm curl bench. "Who told?"

A smirk covered Joel's grin. "I know all, hear all and see all. And I can see that you've got it bad for this girl."

"Concerned?"

Joel studied Ben a few seconds then shook his head. "Nah. Glad. I trust your judgment, Dillinger. Can't wait to meet her."

"I'd appreciate feedback once you do. Privately, of course."

Towel flipped around his neck, Joel laughed. "I'll fill out a full spec report. In the meantime, keep me posted. I'm praying for stuff between you and Hutton, too. See you at the party. Hutton be there?"

"Uh, no sir. That's the other thing. I haven't exactly told Amelia about Hutton."

Joel nailed him with a harsh look. "You're gonna need to man up and deal with that one, you know."

"I know. I'm trying."

Maybe if he bended a little on extending trust, she would, too. But that meant they both had to stretch in the vulnerability department. Ben didn't know if he was willing or able to be quite that limber yet.

"Likely someone will bring up Hutton at dinner Friday. Amelia would start figuring some of it out on her own." Just, hopefully, not the part about how utterly inept Ben was in dealing with Hutton.

"With her being exposed to your sometimes disorderly, outspoken teammates, and you facing the Hutton revelation, Manny's party will be an important test for each of you."

"And certainly an important turning point for our relationship, should we have a future in store." Ben knew the recent ladder maneuver had been bold, but he couldn't help it. Chalk it up to recon for Amelia's feelings. He wanted to know if she was interested in him as more than a friend.

"Definitely." Joel transferred to the free weights, leaving Ben alone with his thoughts. Ben lowered himself onto the leg-press machine and let Amelia take over his mind.

Sure, she had some faith issues to work out first, and he knew he couldn't be unequally yoked. But he had a feeling that once she truly got to know God and experience His unconditional love and acceptance, she'd surrender her tender heart for good. Hopefully Ben's kindness reflected God's heart toward her.

And as far as the other big obstacle—her dad having racial hang-ups—he'd figure that out as they went along. Hopefully the odds weren't insurmountable.

If anyone can make a way, You can. I rest my trust in You.

Chapter Seventeen

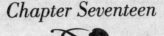

His DZ duties concluded, Ben drove to the garage to pick up Amelia and Reece, who were becoming regular as wrenches at Eagle's Nest. Amelia worked on her drawings between phone calls and filing.

Like clockwork, the foursome, including Bearby, piled in Ben's car as they had for weeks. Ben smiled. Amelia had stopped apologizing for inconveniencing him. Progress. Growth.

"A princess movie! Yay!" Reece held the DVD Ben rented for their Friday video night.

"Animation okay?" Ben asked Amelia as rubber met the road.

She nodded and picked a cloud-covered pamphlet off the seat. The front said *Refuge DZ*. Multicolored parachutes dotted it like candy in the sky. "Ben, what's the DZ?"

"It's a skydiving facility term. *DZ*, or *Drop Zone*, is the area skydivers are supposed to land." Ben laughed.

"What's funny?"

"When Refuge revamped addresses to zone for a 911 system, they let Joel, who now owns Refuge DZ, rename the streets around the facility. My teammate Manny crashed through a grove of trees between the building and the Drop Zone. Joel named the road near where he crashed Pena's Landing."

"Ouch. I take it he's okay now?"

Ben nodded.

Amelia flipped through the pamphlet. "Must be a town thing. Because Miss Evie mentioned naming Mustang Lane after a woman who crashed her car into the B and B."

"Yup. That would be Joel's wife, Amber. She offered to watch my—" he nearly said "brother when I have to leave on mission" but remembered he hadn't told Amelia "—stuff when I have to travel for work," he finished. Stuff? He'd reduced his brother to "stuff" now?

Pathetic, Dillinger. He just needed a tad more time to figure things out with Hutton.

Problem was, the day that they'd agreed for Hutton to come live with Ben was closing in faster than a ruthless enemy soldier.

He needed to come up with the courage to tell her before then, or trust would become a casualty.

Ben's phone rang, as it had been several times a day. Ben knew from Gus that people continually ordered Amelia's caricatures. He'd been seeing them everywhere around town.

People loved seeing themselves depicted as exaggerated cartoons that featured them in spoofy poses in their jobs. Her talent amazed him. Maybe she'd do one of his team once she met them.

Amelia closed the phone after her conversation. She looked back at Reece. "That was Glorietta. She leads a group of girls your age, like Girl Scouts, only it's based out of her church. The group is called GIGs and it stands for Girlfriends In God. She's wondering if you want to go to meetings with her?"

"Yay! Yes. Can Bearby go?"

"Well, er—he's not really a girl." The look on her face provoked Ben to laughter. He could tell she argued with herself about why she was even conversing about this when the bear wasn't real.

"Maybe Bearby could be the GIG mascot," Ben said, laughing.

"I know! I'll let you Bearby-sit him, Mr. Ben. In case the other girls don't carry stuffed animals."

Now it was Amelia's turn to laugh. "I think that's a grand idea. Anyway, GIGs meet Tuesday evenings, but tonight they're having a sleepover at Miss Evie's church."

Which was Ben's church. Only he hadn't thought to tell Amelia. Yet another secret.

"I wanna go, but I told Mr. Ben we'd watch movies." Reece eyed him.

"We'll watch the princess show another time if you want to do the GIG thing."

"You sure, Mr. Ben? I wouldn't want you to get lonely."

"I won't. Your mom and Bearby will keep me company." He smiled at Amelia. Their first date alone without Reece. Maybe they'd open up more. He didn't want to talk about certain aspects of his job around Reece, anyway. He sensed Amelia had perceived that.

"Glorietta's meeting us at Haven Street Park when she gets off. We have time to run by the B and B, pack Reece's overnight bag then play at the park until she gets there."

Once there, they raced each other across the grass to the swirly slide. After they took several spirals each down it, Ben motioned toward the swings. "Come on. I'll push you guys."

Reece stuffed Bearby into a plastic baby swing next to them then sat in the rubber-strip swing beside Amelia.

Ben positioned himself in the grass behind the swings. He took a running start and pushed Amelia so high her feet cleared his head. He ran beneath the swing then around back. He didn't push Reece high. He got a rhythm going so they were all three, including Bearby, airborne in different positions at once.

Glorietta arrived and Amelia handed her Reece's backpack.

"Here are her clean clothes and pajamas." Amelia hugged Reece. Then Reece hugged Ben before snatching Bearby out of the swing and skipping with Glorietta to her car.

Ben grinned. "You still wanna watch the princess flick?"

"No. I'd like not to watch animation if I can help it." She laughed.

"We could explore the hiking trails behind the B and B," Ben said on arrival.

Amelia took the hand Ben extended and they ascended the steep hill behind the B and B later.

"Can you describe what you do during a rescue?"

"Nope." He grinned. "But I can show you." He swooped her up and slung her over his shoulders, then ran full tilt in a sweat-producing sprint up steep, treacherous terrain and rocky trails.

She squealed at first then relaxed to the point of laughing. He kept running. She kept laughing. Thirty minutes later, he set her down near the trail that led to the waterfall.

"How did you ever build up endurance to do that?"

"In my training, which is as constant as breathing."

"Is that where you go on Saturdays?"

Ouch. "Yowza. You should consider a career in interrogation." He chuckled and braced hands on his knees. "Yup, training is where I go. Some of the time."

She eyed him, but didn't press. They hiked at a rapid clip up the remainder of the trail. They got close enough to the waterfall that mist sprayed their faces.

Catching her breath, Amelia sat on a flat rock and pulled off her shoes and socks. Her toes stretched out and glistened as water misted her feet. "What are some of the rescues you've done that I might have heard about?"

She wasn't giving up for anything. She was nothing if not tenacious. He needed to give a little. She deserved that.

He sat beside her on the rock, enjoying a rainbow visible in the wall of water. "Helped in Asia after the tsunami.

Rescued climbers from Oregon's Mount Hood. That's always fun. I've been to Everest and into the deep Atlantic. I've recovered astronauts after water landings. Every nook and cranny of the world, I've been there. Glaciers. Every sea. Most national disasters you hear about on TV, and some you won't hear about, I've likely been there. Floods. Earthquakes. Tornadoes. Terrorist attacks. I've dropped behind enemy lines to rescue downed Allied pilots. Also helped rescue Katrina victims after the hurricane that devastated New Orleans and the Gulf coast."

"Wow. I'm in awe, Ben. Speaking of which, it's under way." She shivered.

"What?"

"Hurricane season. My parents live in the danger zone."

"Ahh. Hopefully they won't be too bad this year."

She laughed. "My parents? Or the hurricanes?"

He leaned in, letting the mist cool him off. "Is there much difference?"

"Not really. They are decent people. It's just, they had high hopes for me. I'm hoping distance will strengthen our relationship." She pulled her socks and shoes back on.

"So, once your dad finds out I'm part Asian, how's that gonna work?"

She opened her mouth to speak, then clamped it shut and looked away. Dismay widened her eyes, telling him what she couldn't bring herself to say.

When Dad finds out, it's not going to work.

He stood, pulling her up with him. He drew her into his arms in a loose embrace. "I am not sure how this'll pan out. But I am sure that I can't stand the thought of you and Reece not remaining in my life. Somehow."

Amelia gulped. "Well, it's not like Dad and I are even talking right now."

"I can't imagine a man not wanting anything to do with his

daughter and granddaughter forever. He'll eventually come around." He released her and led them, hand in hand, back down the trail. Darkness would descend soon.

"I hope you're right."

A disturbing thought detonated inside Ben's brain.

If her dad came back around, would Amelia shun Ben for the sake of her father, and for Reece knowing her grandparents?

Ben sensed a hard decision on Amelia's horizon.

Chapter Eighteen

"I'll bet Amber's embarrassed to drive down the road," Amelia said the following Tuesday, as Ben drove them along Mustang Lane to the B and B after dropping Reece off at Glorietta's for GIGs.

"Miss Evie asked her permission. Amber has a great sense of humor. I think she felt honored."

"Your friends sound fun-loving and nice, Ben."

"They are. Hey, I'd love them to meet you. In fact, one of my teammates is having a birthday party Friday night at the local Mexican restaurant. I'd love it if you went with me. Bradley'll be there so Reece can meet him. There's also someone else I want you to meet the weekend after. Someone very important to me."

There. He said it. Now he was bound by his word to introduce her to Hutton.

They exited the car and walked up the B and B steps. "Sure we wouldn't be intruding on the party?"

"No way. I'm the one planning it."

"You're a good friend to people, Ben."

"And you're deserving of good friends, Amelia."

"Friends. Now that's something I can use."

"You'll make plenty this weekend." Ben motioned toward a bench swing on the wraparound porch. "Joel told me his wife and Manny's have been dropping by your place."

"Yeah. I really like Celia and Amber. I envy their friendship. I had that with Nissa before she met this creep. Did you put them up to coming here?"

"Nope. They decided all on their own." He grinned. "They want to get to know you. They're curious."

"Why?"

"Because my team, we're like family. They know how important you're becoming to me."

"You saying I have to pass inspection?"

"You already have. Now they're just hanging around because they like you. And because they know I like you but can't always be here if you need something. So they cover for me of their own volition."

"It's been a long time since I've had something to look forward to. I'm excited about getting to know them better this weekend. And meeting the rest of your team and learning more about what you do."

Ben smiled. "I'm sure Celia and Amber will fill you in."

Amelia's stomach was a bundle of nerves Friday. Ben would be here any minute to pick up her and Reece. She rearranged refrigerator contents for the umpteenth time. Townspeople had been coming by to drop off food, welcoming them to Refuge.

Amelia would feel terrible if she and Reece didn't end up getting to stay. But so far, not one of the dozens of applications she'd turned in had resulted in a job. Even Ben said it was strange. Each day that her phone—Ben's phone, actually—didn't ring with a job, her panic escalated. Thankfully, orders for her caricatures were keeping them afloat.

She remembered Ben's offer to find her a job. She hoped

it didn't come to that. In her mind, not securing a job herself meant failing Reece. People couldn't bail her out forever.

The doorbell chimed. Reece ran toward it then stopped. "Oops. Forgot. I'm not supposed to answer phones or doors."

"It's great you remembered the rules. It's probably Ben, but it's always better to be safe." Amelia eyed the wall clock on her way to the door. If it was Ben, he was early.

Amelia peered outside. "Oh, it's Miss Evie." She unlocked the door and swung it wide.

Miss Evie stepped inside, holding papers. "Hello, Amelia. I came to let you know I reviewed your application for the kitchen position. You made the final cut for interviews. I whittled my choice down to five applicants."

Thumping started in Amelia's chest. "I didn't realize you were in charge of hiring."

"Yes, I pretty much run everything here. But I'm getting up in years, and I look to start handing over the reins more. I can't stay but a minute. Just wanted to know if you can come for another interview the first of next month."

That was four weeks. School started in five. Amelia really needed more time than a cramped week to figure out whether to sign Reece up for school here. But this was the first sign of a job. "Sure. But if you have a slot open sooner, I'll gladly take it."

The woman chortled. "No, four weeks it is. Which reminds me, you didn't list references. That's why I stopped by."

Her hands wrung. "Truth is, I've only had one other job. An insurance office, but the owner passed away and they closed it."

"Don't fret this, Amelia. But even if you have a previous teacher, or a relative who can vouch for your character, it would improve your chances for the job."

Maybe her mom would give a reference. But that would mean calling. And risk getting yelled at by Dad. But truth was, she missed her parents, especially her mom. This would give her an excuse to call.

She walked Miss Evie to the door. "I'll get names and numbers to you in the next few days."

"Sounds good. We'll talk later." Miss Evie left as Ben, decked out in a black T-shirt and green camouflage pants tucked into combat boots, jogged up the steps.

He pulled off a maroon beret and walked into her living room like it was commonplace. "I know I'm here before we agreed to meet. But I finished drowning people early."

"Drowning?"

"Yeah. Underwater training with PJ recruits. We weight them down with lead, then hold them underwater for near fatal lengths of time and inflict harassment until they pass out."

Her neck craned. "Underwater?"

"Yup. We only had to haul two students out and revive 'em today, though. So it was a good day." He grinned.

"Are you serious?"

"See why I keep aspects of my job from you?"

"I'll say. Be right back. I'm going to change."

"Hopefully not your mind, now that you know what I do."

She shot him a cheeky grin that thrilled him as much as a HALO jump. "Not on your life."

Reece skipped over. "You wanna play tea party with me, Ben?"

"For a minute." Hopefully none of his teammates strolled by. His ego would need a hoist extraction.

Reece led him to a miniature table embellished with a girlie tea set. "Hey, you think you'd ever wanna marry my mom?"

"Why do you ask?" He sat next to Bearby, who occupied the tiniest chair he'd ever seen.

"Dunno. You got weird eyes. She's got weird eyes. You could have babies with weird eyes."

Ben laughed and held the tiny cup she handed him.

"And give me a hundred brothers and sisters."

Ben's laughter died in his throat. "You want siblings?"

"Lots and lots. And I want Shasta back to live with us."

"What would you think if I did want to marry your mom and be your stepdad?"

"I think you'd always be nice to us and you'd never yell or leave us and I think you could give me brothers and sisters." She poured invisible tea into his dainty cup. "Especially sisters to play tea party with me."

He pretended to sip. "Maybe I could start with getting Shasta back."

She stirred something invisible into Bearby's cup. "I heard siblings fight over things a lot. Mom said cousin Nissa is like a sister and sometimes they argued growing up. Grandma said she told them the one who got the toy first could have it first. That was the rule."

"That right?"

"Yup. So I don't care how many brothers and sisters you bring from the baby place as long as they remember that I'm the one who found you first." She wrapped her arms around his neck and squeezed. "I love you, Mr. Ben."

Overcome with fierce, protective emotion, Ben set his cup down and hugged her back. "Love you too, princess." He pulled back with his arms still braced on hers. "So why don't you stop calling me Mr. Ben and just say Ben?"

"But Mommy says that's not good manners."

He leaned in. "Can I tell you a secret?"

She nodded.

"I don't think your mom will mind if you just call me Ben. Besides, that might help her think about marrying me so I can help her bring you all those brothers and sisters you want."

She covered her mouth and giggled like she held the world's biggest secret.

Then Ben realized this was perfect for a practice moment of truth. "You know, I've got a brother."

"You do?" She refilled Ben's and Bearby's teacups.

"Yup. He has special needs so he lives with our parents. But soon, he's coming to live with me for a year."

"Does he have cancer like Bradley?"

"Nope. He was born with a birth defect called Mosaic Down Syndrome."

"Mosaic. Sounds like something my mom paints. Something very neat and colorful and makes ya feel good to look at."

"Well, that really describes my brother. Would you like to meet him next weekend?"

"Yeah!"

Amelia reentered the room. "Who are we meeting?"

Here it was. The real moment of truth. Ben held Amanda's gaze. "My special needs brother."

Her steps paused. She nodded slowly and resumed.

"My mom's bringing him next weekend. To live with me." Rising, he moved closer, out of earshot of Reece and Bearby. "Look, I know I should have told you about him before."

"I'm sure you had good reasons why you didn't."

"Thanks, but in fact I've been a coward about it. I don't want you to think I didn't tell you because I'm ashamed of him. I'm ashamed of me. I'm not the best at talking or relating to him on his level. But I'm learning."

"I'm sure you are. I'm also sure you are not a coward. Can I make a suggestion, Ben?"

"I'm all ears." And all mush, the way she stared at him with smiles beaming out her eyes like that.

"Just be what you're best at."

"What's that?"

"His friend, Ben. You're a good friend to people. The best I've seen. If you treat your brother like you treat everyone else, things will work out."

Why hadn't he thought of that before?

"There's no way you could know this, but that's all Hutton— that's his name—all he wanted growing up. For me to treat him like everyone else. Be his friend. I'm ashamed to admit I was ashamed of him then."

"It's clear you care about him now. If you want to win him over, just be yourself."

"So, I've been myself around you. Did it work?"

"What?"

"To win you over?"

"From the first moment I met you."

Chapter Nineteen

"Dude, she's a stunner," teammate Brockton Drake said to Ben at Manny's party. They'd reserved the entire Mexican restaurant.

"Dead on." Vince ogled Amelia as Amber whisked her away.

Ben thumped Vince on the forehead. "Eyes off."

Nolan laughed.

Vince faced Nolan. "If you weren't still hung up on an old love, you'd be checking her out, too."

Nolan shrugged and sipped his soda.

Chance Garrison leaned in. "She got a twin sister?"

"No. Don't be crude around her or I'll deck all of you."

Vince laughed. "Like to see you try."

Manny jabbed Ben's pectoral muscles. "I don't know, Reardon. I think he could take us. He's hitting the gym pretty hard these days."

Brockton massaged Ben's shoulders. "To impress the girl."

Celia's son, Javier, peeled off a straw wrapper and snickered.

"Dude, it doesn't bother you that she has a kid?" Javier's friend Enrique asked Ben.

Vince smirked. "That's probably why he's chasing her, because she comes equipped. Anyone who knows Ben knows how bad he wants to father a kid."

"Any moron with working parts can father a kid, bozo." Javier made a weird face at Vince. He looked at Ben. "But it takes a man with working faith and guts and heart to be a dad. I've been fortunate enough to have had two good ones in my life, dude. For sure, that chick and that little girl would be lucky to have you around."

"Thanks, Javier. That means a lot."

Vince blew his straw wrapper at Ben and Manny. "I see how it is. You're Daddy First Class and I'm Major Moron."

Javier punched Vince. "Chill, I didn't mean it like that."

"Shh. Here she comes," Ben warned.

"Hey." Amelia scooted into the booth next to Ben a minute later.

Celia came over. "Well, if it isn't Skinny Mouse."

Ben's brows rose.

"She calls me and Reece Skinny and Minnie Mouse." Amelia laughed. "Then chases me around with large quantities of fudge."

Celia pushed a plate of nachos toward Amelia. "Yo, Skinny. Amber tells me you think you look plain."

Amelia blushed. "I—I…"

Manny gave Celia a look then skipped his gaze to Amelia. "Don't say 'plain' in her presence. She'll have your face covered in gook before you can blink."

Amelia laughed. "I prefer to wear makeup, when I can afford it, actually. Um, excuse me? Why is she looking at me like a vulture circling something dead?" Amelia asked Amber, since Celia mumbled things in Spanish.

"I'm pretty sure you're her next victim."

"Of?"

"One of her famous makeovers."

Amelia patted her split-ended hair and the cheeks of her pale face and laughed. "I don't mind being a guinea pig if that means I get free makeup."

"That's it." Celia dragged her up, snagging Amber's arm on the way to the restroom.

"You might want to rescue her from Celia's clutches," Manny said.

"She looks like she's having a good time," Joel said.

"Yeah. Besides, I'd kind of like to see her all dolled up."

In the bathroom, Celia circled Amelia. "We've also got to get you some clothes that fit. You're so skinny!"

"Celia!" Amber jabbed Celia in the ribs.

Celia's arms flailed in the air. "Well! Look at the girl. She looks practically anorexic." Celia swooped in, clutched Amelia's shoulders in her fingernails and got nose to nose. "Are you anorexic? Come on, what gives? Why are you thin enough to give people paper cuts when you turn sideways, huh? 'Fess up."

"I'm not anorexic. I had the flu and I admit I hadn't been eating right for a few months."

"A few months? The flu doesn't go on for months. And just how many stripes do you have on your pajamas, huh? One?"

Amelia laughed because Celia sounded serious. "I've lost weight recently but I was small to begin with. I have a high metabolism and my mother is thin also. It runs in our genes."

Celia's nose squished up. "Well, I must admit I really despise you for that."

"She's kidding." Amber put a hand on Amelia's.

"I figured." Amelia smiled. She loved these women and longed for their kind of friendship. That they automatically pulled her into their closely knit circle meant oodles.

"I'm not entirely kidding. Look, Amber. Here's the scoop. Stock up on chocolate because I can't have two good friends looking thinner than me."

Two good friends? Celia already considered Amelia a friend? Tears pricked her eyes. She blinked them back.

Amber laughed. "You're not that big, Celia."

"Who says I'm big? I never said anything about being big. I'm not…big. I'm just…a mite hippy."

"Manny says you're curvaceous." Amber held Amelia's hair back while Celia attacked her face with a mascara brush from her huge bag.

"Don't worry, Skinny Mouse. This makeup's never been used. I keep samples with me. It's yours to keep."

"Thank you." Tears welled.

"Don't blink! Or cry!"

Amelia laughed. "Yes, ma'am. I see how you and Manny are so right for each other. He's so laid-back, he's horizontal. And you're, well, a fireball."

Amber handed Celia the lipstick. "Yes, but believe me, it took a miracle for Manny to convince Celia to marry him."

"A miracle."

That's precisely what Amelia and Ben would need if things ever progressed past the realm of friendship. What was she saying? It already had. And soon as her dad got wind of it, their already strained relationship would snap.

A big choice was swirling to shore.

Ben blinked. Then again, nearly not believing his eyes.

"Down, boy." Nolan laughed.

Ben sat, not even realizing he'd stood.

"Celia, stop force-feeding her. That's so rude," Amber was saying as the women returned from whatever groups of women convening in restrooms did. Amber and Amelia ventured toward the game tables where Reece and Bradley were involved in air hockey.

By the looks of Amelia, Celia'd unloaded her makeup bag. Wait. Celia was bugging Amelia about food. Now Ben did stand. So did Manny. They dragged Celia off.

"Celia, don't harass the girl," Manny warned.

"Oh, hush. The moment she stops being able to use a Cheerio for a hula hoop, I'll stop bugging her about food."

Ben eyed Amelia as he talked with Amber. Her face looked fuller, healthier. The hollows in her cheekbones were less pronounced. And, well, she boasted a little more curve all the way around. Not that he'd noticed. Okay, maybe a little. His face heated. Ben had never been embarrassed about noticing women's shapes before, but then again, he'd also never respected a woman as much as Amelia. "She's gained since I met her."

"Yeah? Well, not enough. Here I'll prove it." Celia stood on a chair, waved her arms madly and yelled across the room, "Yo, North! Turn sideways and stick out your tongue."

Amelia must have gotten used to Celia's strange ways because she only gave her a mildly odd look before obeying.

Celia's hand jabbed out. "See? The girl looks exactly like a zipper."

Ben laughed. "You're something else, Celia. Just do me a favor and don't bug her about food. It's a sensitive subject."

"Ah, and the truth comes out. You do care about her, don't you? Come on, 'fess up."

"No way. Anything I tell you will get back to her."

"You take the fun out of everything."

"For you. Not for me." If Amelia was going to find out his romantic feelings, it was going to come from his mouth, and not from Celia's. Speaking of which… "Did you attack her with lipstick?"

"You noticed, huh?"

He saw how much fuller her lips looked. Her eyelashes stood out and so did her eyes. He couldn't stop looking at her.

"Yeah. I noticed." Ben grinned because he couldn't stop it. Couldn't stop the giddy way she made him feel when she aimed her eyes at him. "I never met a girl who could smile with her eyes more than she smiles with her mouth." But Amelia did. And he'd noticed she didn't cover her lazy eye as often. She must be feeling more comfortable and confident around him.

Ben smiled. Amelia lifted her face as if sensing his stare across the room. She smiled back. Something fluttered inside his chest.

He tilted his head at her, realizing what this compelling surge of emotion and longing was.

"Whoa, amigo! You love her," Celia whispered.

Ben nodded, holding his girl with his gaze. "Very much."

Chapter Twenty

"I like her because she got funny eyes like me," Hutton said the following weekend at Cone Zone.

"Your eyes aren't funny, Hutton. They're uniquely yours. But I'm glad you liked Amelia." Ben had introduced them the previous night. Hutton and Reece had hit it off big time.

"I know God gave me my eyes, Benny. And at least I can see. Some people are blind. Did you know that, Benny?"

"I did. Sad, isn't it?"

Benny nodded his head then blinked fast.

"He also gave you a good heart, Hutton. And I hope you see with your eyes and with your heart how much I admire you."

"I mire you too, Benny. Always have. Even when—" Hutton chewed his tongue, effectively cutting off his words.

Ben reached over and took his brother's hand, and didn't care how it looked. "Even when I was mean to you?"

Hutton stared at the table then nodded. "Yeah, Benny. Yeah. But you've always been my hero."

"Yeah? Well, seems we have more in common than we realized, because you're my hero, too."

Hutton's face squished up in a grin. Ben pushed the dessert

menu in front of him. "Another thing we have in common is milkshakes. So pick which one you want."

Hutton snorted laughter and pointed to a large chocolate shake domed with whipped cream.

Hutton had opened up to Ben more this week than he had in years.

"I really enjoy hanging out with you, Hutton."

Hutton grinned. "Me too. When did you say I go to my job interview, Benny?"

"In a week." Ben gave Hutton the same answer he had all day. He supposed Hutton repeatedly asked out of nervousness.

"Would it help if we practice the questions they might ask you?"

"Yeah. Benny. I want this job more than anything besides having you as a brother. And a friend. That's the most thing I ever wanted, Benny. I always wished you would be my friend."

"I'm sorry I wasn't a better friend growing up."

"But we can be best friends now. If you want." Hutton chewed his tongue and scratched his head.

"I definitely do want that. I'm honored you do. So, are you excited about your interview?"

"Yeah, Benny. But kinda scared too."

"That's natural."

"Do even normal people feel this way before a job?"

Interview. He hoped Hutton understood it wasn't totally in the bag yet. He needed to prepare him, in case he didn't get chosen. After all, there were five applicants, but only one position. "I'm sure the other applicants are as nervous as you."

"Are they getting interviews next Thursday too, like me?"

"Yep. Miss Evie's son said she's doing all of them on the same day." Ben hadn't mentioned Hutton to Miss Evie because he wanted Hutton to be able to get the job on his own.

"I'll take you there and wait outside the door." If Hutton

faltered, he'd venture into the room for moral support. But he wanted Hutton to see he'd gotten the job on his own credentials.

"I understand if they want to give somebody else the job besides me. Especially somebody normal. I might be very sad if I don't get the job. But I'll understand."

"Hutton, don't think negatively. If the job is meant to be yours, God will make sure you have it."

"Yeah Benny. God will work this out how He wants. I just hope he wants to work it out how I want it so that I can have the job."

"He knows how bad you want a job. He'll do what's best. Honest."

"God knows how bad you want this, Amelia. Stop fretting." Glorietta followed Amelia into the bathroom Thursday morning of her scheduled interview.

Amelia patted makeup beneath her eyes. "I barely slept a wink last night. Thanks for agreeing to watch Reece today."

"No problem. I'd better head out, but know I'm praying for you. Also know that God has your best interests at heart, no matter what happens, okay?"

She nodded and brushed a hand down herself. "Okay. And, thank you for bringing this business suit by."

Glorietta hugged her. "You look very professional in it. It looks much nicer than those boxy clothes you've been wearing. I'll bet if Ben sees you today, he's likely to have a coronary at how this hugs your figure."

Amelia blushed. "I've always worn my clothes four sizes too big. Ever since Reece was born."

"I see your caricatures all around town. They're becoming quite popular. The rave of Refuge, in fact. Word on the street is, tourists have even started asking about them."

"I still need another job so I can start paying Miss Evie rent."

"She's not hurting for money, hon. Her husband left her

with a huge life insurance policy. That man took care of her before he died, and afterward by planning ahead."

"I think Gus kinda likes her. He gets nervous when he drops me off at the B and B sometimes when Ben's gone on trainings. It's cute to watch the two of them."

"That's another one who has money."

"Gus?"

"Yeah. You wouldn't know it by the way he keeps his garage, but he got a multimillion dollar settlement out of the corporation that knowingly served booze to the minors who smashed into his daughter and took her life. But he can't bring himself to spend the money. Says it won't bring his daughter back. So he's waiting to find a community project to donate it to." She eyed her watch.

"It's time?" Amelia's breath fell short. Interviews made her so nervous. Especially this one, since she'd invested hope.

"Me and Reece are gonna go to Cone Zone and have a good time, and you're gonna go blow Miss Evie's socks off during your interview."

"Pray for me, Glorietta?"

"Rest assured. Call me soon as you know something. She happen to say when that'd be?"

"Said she'd decide today. I'm fourth to be interviewed. There is one other person after me. So wish me luck."

"You don't need luck. You've got God on your side."

"Have a seat, Amelia." Miss Evie waved to a chair across from a gleaming mahogany desk. The warm colors in the room set Amelia at ease. Except her stomach, which suddenly twisted up.

Miss Evie pulled out a folder with her name on it. Amelia glimpsed at the other folders to the right of Miss Evie. Folders much thicker with papers than hers.

No.

No.

Was written in red on each tab. Beside those two folders was another with *Maybe* on the tab. A red Sharpie lay on top of the stack. Another folder rested to Miss Evie's left, and there was no red mark on it. That must be the appointment after hers.

Which meant the job was between Amelia and two other persons. Hope soared.

Until her eyes lit on the name.

Hutton Dillinger? Hutton? Ben's brother applied for the job? Her heart sank. This was the job Hutton had talked about so excitedly to Reece?

Miss Evie finished flipping through the pages. "Not many references here."

"I—I know."

Miss Evie ran her finger down Amelia's skill list.

Her very. Short. Skill list.

She set the folder on the desk, then removed her glasses. She folded her hands on the desk and smiled in a sympathetic manner. "I don't conduct interviews like most people, Amelia. I don't much care about your credentials. I want you to tell me about you. And before you get more nervous than you already are, know I'm more apt to base my hiring decision on whether I think a person can be taught, regardless of experience."

Miss Evie closed the résumé folder. "So, without further ado, tell me about you. Never mind about your experience. What are your hobbies, your interests? What's your family like? People's personalities come out when they talk about their passions. Tell me about your drawings. When did you know you wanted to do that?"

"From the time I can remember…"

After several moments, Amelia realized she'd been rambling. But Miss Evie was smiling.

Until she put her glasses back on. "You don't have many references here. Only one I could reach in fact was your mom."

Amelia nodded and lowered her head.

"Among other things we discussed, she assured me you have the drive to learn, which is important to me in an employee. And I happened by the garage yesterday to get my oil changed. I nearly walked right back out of Gus's office, thinking I'd gone into the wrong building. I hardly recognized it. He told me you're the one who cleaned and organized it."

Amelia nodded. Tried to focus on what Miss Evie was saying, but her eyes kept veering back toward Hutton's folder. How disappointed he'd be if he didn't get the job. Thankfulness hit her though that her mother had said good things about her. But, if Amelia got the job, that meant Hutton wouldn't.

I don't understand why You pit us against each other like this. There's only one job and two of us. I need to feed my daughter and Hutton needs to feel a vital part of society.

She tuned back in to Miss Evie.

"Gus then showed me how you created a filing system for him and organized his office. I'm impressed with your work ethic, people skills and efficiency. He said he got lots of positive feedback the two hours a day that you answer his phone. Word on the street is you are helpful, friendly, polite and professional."

She was about to get the job. She could tell by Miss Evie's excited chatter. Her heart soared and sank at the same time.

Until Miss Evie drew a breath and sighed. "I'd hire you for the dishwasher position for that alone, Amelia, but…"

But she needed a job!

"I'm afraid you're overqualified. You're worth more than minimum wage."

"B-but please. I'm willing to work for minimum wage. I understand."

Miss Evie held a hand up. "Before you get upset, I'm not finished. Hear me out. I was saying that I think you're overqualified for the dishwashing position."

"Can I say something? I didn't know Ben's brother had applied for the same job. I think the position belongs to him."

"I agree. He needs to be made to feel like an active member of society and that's one way he could contribute. So, out of the three of you, I'm leaning equally toward you and him. But mostly toward you."

"I can't do this to Hutton. Or to Ben. I'm sorry, Miss Evie for wasting your time today. I'm retracting my application."

"I think that's prudent. And honorable of you, considering the dire straits you're in."

"I understand." And truly she did. She couldn't be angry with Ben for looking out for his brother and putting him first. Though she really needed that job, she'd humble herself and concede it for Hutton. What would she do now? She could barely afford a fifty-cent paper to look for job listings.

"I'd really appreciate it if you wouldn't tell Ben that I conceded the job to Hutton. Ben has been so kind, I don't want to make him feel bad."

Nodding, Miss Evie plucked on her bifocals and turned to a credenza to rifle through papers.

Amelia assumed that meant she was dismissed. She stood, fighting tears, but longed to be polite without her voice quavering. Her possibilities in Refuge were exhausted. She'd have to look elsewhere for a job. The thought of leaving Refuge made her throat ache.

"Thank you. I appreciate your time."

Startled, Miss Evie looked up. "Well, Amelia, where are you going? Please sit down. Our interview is far from over."

Amelia sat, confusion weighing her down. She wouldn't take Hutton's job. She wouldn't. And she had to get out of here before she embarrassed herself by bursting into tears. Then everyone would know how weak and scared she really was.

Pray, then trust and believe.

Ugh. Glorietta's stupid words coming back to stalk her again.

Pray, then trust and believe.

I did that. And it didn't work.

Pray. Then trust. And believe.

Understanding suddenly dawned

Pray and trust didn't always go together. Trust was tougher when what you believed for didn't come true.

I believed but it didn't happen. But this time, I'm gonna choose to trust You anyhow.

And what on earth was the woman doing, pilfering through her own drawers?

Miss Evie continued to rifle through papers a moment more before tugging a file out. "Aha. Here it is." She turned back to face Amelia. "I was saying, however, I do have something else you may be interested in. Take a look at this." She tugged papers from the file and handed them to Amelia.

Amelia's eyes scanned the header. She further she read, the more confused she became.

"But, this is a list of duties for a salaried management position here at the bed-and-breakfast." A position that paid three times what the dishwasher position did. "I'm sorry, I don't understand." She looked up.

Miss Evie grinned over her bifocals, hands folded on the desk in front of her. "Don't you, Amelia? Because I think you'd be perfect for the job. You're sharp. What you don't know, I'll teach you."

"But Miss Evie, what if I'm not qualified?"

"How will we know unless you try? You could set up a caricature station in the kitchen if you like. Tourists would love them. That'd be extra money. Many of these duties you could delegate out to employees. Also, the budget there is off. The salary is about twelve thousand more a year."

"Twelve thou—" Amelia coughed, emotion having closed her throat. With Refuge's cost of living, she could nearly exist on that alone. Could this moment be possible? Tears sprang to her eyes. Was she dreaming?

Miss Evie lifted her brows. "Well? What do you think?"

Amelia surged to her feet. "I think you're plumb crazy—and wonderful for giving me this chance." Amelia couldn't hold back the tears and she lunged around the desk and hugged Miss Evie's neck. She squeezed and squeezed and just couldn't let the woman go. "And I think I'll love working for you, and with Hutton. Thank you. Thank you. Thank you."

Laughing, Miss Evie dabbed Amelia's tears. "Well, this is a first. I've never had an interviewee get me in a headlock. It's quite nice. I think we'll work well together."

"What do I need to do? How should I dress? When can I start?"

Miss Evie held up a graceful hand. "Hold on to your horses. Here's my suggestion. You'll need to register Reece for school. Why don't you spend the day doing that? I can give you a stipend to live on until your probation period is up in thirty days."

Amelia smiled. "What is it with this town and their overwhelming generosity?"

"Refuge is like that. Most of it, anyway. We have a few trouble spots, but all in all, we're praying for it to be just what the name says."

Praying.

No wonder.

Maybe the woman's faith was why she was doing all this. That would be the only reason Amelia could think of that a person would give without expecting anything in return. Though she held her own faith struggles, she wanted to raise Reece in church.

"Where you go to church, is it Christian?"

"Yes. Refuge Community Church. Would you like to visit?"

"If I could sit by you. I'm nervous to walk in by myself."

"We'll ride and sit together. Pick you up at nine. They

have a wonderful kids' program. Reece will love it. I have a feeling you will, too. You'll recognize some faces there."

Amelia wondered who. She also wondered why she didn't have reservations about going to this church. She knew why. Leaned forward, she hugged Miss Evie again. "Thank you. Before meeting true Christians like you and Ben, Manny, Celia, Amber and Joel—"

"And Gus." She patted her hair.

Amelia grinned. "And Gus, I never believed people extended goodness without agenda." She eyed the wall clock. "Time for Glorietta to return with Reece. I'd better scoot."

Miss Evie smiled and opened the door. "Sounds good. Hutton's interview is in ten minutes. That'll give me time to grab some coffee."

Amelia rounded the corner of the B and B and was run over by a haze of fur. "Ooomph!" She sat up and blocked her face from wet slurps. "Hey!" She peeked. Then stood. "Shasta?" The dog barked and spun in circles, wagging its entire behind. "Shasta?"

"Hello, Amelia."

Tears sprang to her eyes and she whirled around. "Mom?"

A wary-eyed woman approached cautiously. "H-hi."

"Mom?"

Seeing tears streaking down her mother's face, Amelia dashed off the wraparound porch and wrapped arms around her.

After several moments of sniffling and murmuring and holding tight, both women pulled back.

"What are you doing here?" Amelia whispered.

Her mom tugged more tissues loose and handed half to Amelia. She then looped her arm through Amelia's. "Let's go for a walk. And I'll tell ya."

After leaving Glorietta a note explaining where she was, Amelia led her mom down one of the trails behind the B and B. "You don't know how bad I missed our walks."

"Not half as bad as I've missed you and Reece." She drew a breath. "Which is why I'm here."

"I noticed you brought suitcases. Lots of suitcases."

"You left without some of your things. And one of the suitcases is mine." She met Amelia's gaze. "I left your father."

Amelia gasped. "Mom! Why?"

She reached down and scooped up a pinecone, then met Amelia's gaze again. "Because I can't live without having a relationship with you and my grandbaby. Not even for your father." She tossed the cone at a tree. Hard. "Your very stubborn father."

Amelia laughed. "I heard you said I'm courageous. Is that true?"

Her mom nodded. "Very. You have more courage than I do. I should have stood up to him years ago." Tears flooded her eyes again. "I'm sorry, Amelia. I've so much to be sorry for."

Amelia put an arm around her waist. "Let's not be sorry. Let's just start over."

"Gramma!" Reece squealed on the way back when they came into view.

Glorietta stood, grinning. "You made it, I see."

Amelia's mom nodded.

"You knew she was coming?" Amelia said to Glorietta.

"I knew she'd called asking to find you. So did Miss Evie."

"How long had you been planning this, Mom?"

"Since the day I figured out your dad wasn't going to humble himself and call you. But he's been moping around the house like Shasta in a thunderstorm."

"Maybe you leaving will help him try."

"Doesn't matter. No matter what he decides, I want a chance to be the mom you've deserved all your life and never got. And, I know you'll need someone to watch Reece. I'm glad to help. Miss Evie offered me a place to stay. But I was hoping I could stay with you and Reece. At least for a few

weeks. I missed you dreadfully and worried about you something awful."

"Hi Meal-ya! I got a job!" Hutton ran toward her.

"You did? Hutton, that's great!" Amelia hedged.

Ben eyed her.

Amelia put her arm around her mom. "Ben, this is my
mother."

He nodded, leaned forward and shook her hand. "Nice to
meet you." He smiled in his kind-mannered way. "What
brings you to these parts?"

"My baby and grandbaby. I decided I can't live without them."

Ben smiled. "I know just what you mean."

Amelia's mom's eyebrows rose and a knowing gleam
entered her eyes. "Is that so?"

Ben nodded and lingered a thankful gaze over Reece and
Amelia and the half miracle happening here now. "Absolutely." He took Amelia's hand and met Amelia's mom's gaze.
"So, I hope you're okay with that because it would mean a
lot to Amelia to have your blessing for our relationship."

"If you're half the man that Glorietta claims you are, I'm
more than okay with it." She picked up Reece and eyed Hutton.
"I heard you like *Charlotte's Web* as much as Reece does. I
happen to have the DVD in my suitcase. Shall we watch it so
your mom and Ben can sneak off on a romantic date?"

Glorietta and Evie grinned. Amelia blushed. Hutton and
Reece giggled.

Ben, grinning the most, moved like a rocket from a launch-
pad. "I'll show you how to work the DVD player."

"I can't believe we're taking a stuffed bear on a date." Ben
eyed the stuffed toy that Glorietta had insisted could chap-
erone them.

Amelia laughed. "I can."

"Not much of a date, playing chess at the B and B, is it?"

"I like it here. Besides, I know you don't want to stray too far away from Hutton in case he gets nervous without you."

"You picked up on that, huh?"

She nodded. "I also picked up on how much he looks up to you, Ben." Her voice betrayed her by going whispery and breathless. "He admires you, as does anyone who's ever met you."

He set his guitar aside and pulled her into his arms. The way he gazed deep at her made her feel like the most beautiful woman on earth.

He smiled. "You're nervous. Aren't you?"

"A-a little. Not that I don't trust you. I'm just unsure in this kind of situation."

"I hope you're not unsure about how I feel about you."

He set Bearby on the rail they leaned against.

She started to dip her head but his finger on her chin prevented it.

"You know how I'm always telling you to trust and believe, even when there's no proof?"

She nodded, drifting into him as he pulled her closer.

"Well, this time, I'm going to prove it to you instead."

Ben lifted her chin higher, and placed a tender, chaste kiss on her mouth. Tentatively, he brushed his lips against hers. She didn't pull away, but she didn't respond, either. "Is this okay, Amelia?"

She nodded and swallowed. "Except, absurd as it sounds, that stupid bear is watching."

Ben laughed, reached over and tipped Bearby forward so his nose and eyes rested on the banister rail instead of facing them. Amelia's laugh caused one of his.

"That's much better," she said.

"So is this." He lifted her chin once more and kissed her, this time like he meant it. Trying to infuse her with confidence and knowing that she was attractive and the kind of girl any guy would be proud to have.

* * *

"I wanna know which one of you is giving the other guitar lessons, and which one's giving the kissing lessons." Amelia's mom smiled over the paper a month later as Amelia joined her for late-night tea after returning from Ben's balcony.

Amelia laughed. And stalled answering the question by going in to check on Reece. She was in bed, sound asleep, armed with Bearby. Hutton, adjusting well to living with Ben over the last few weeks since his parents had left to travel, had spent the evenings here playing games, watching videos and talking about his dishwashing job with vigor.

Sitting across from her mom, Amelia tucked her feet beneath her. "You know?"

Smile intact, Amelia's mom sipped her tea. "Of course. Where do you think you and Reece inherited your sleuthing and insatiable curiosity? Do you care about him?"

"More than that. I think I love him."

Her mom smiled. "He seems very honorable."

"Does it bother you that he's part Asian?"

"Of course not."

"It's going to bother Dad."

"Everything bothers your dad. He's a grumpy old curmudgeon." She eyed her phone. "Who won't stop calling me. But until he calls you and issues a sincere apology, I'm ignoring him. And yes, he has the number. He's probably living off cold corn from cans. Stubborn man."

"But you love him."

"Sometimes I wonder why, but yes. I do."

A pounding on the door brought both of them to their feet.

Before Amelia could fully open the door, Ben rushed in. "Pack a bag. Both of you. Glorietta's keeping Reece and Shasta. She's on her way."

"Ben, what's wrong?" Amelia's heart pounded at the serious look on his face as he sat her mom down.

"The hurricane shifted. It grazed your hometown pretty good. Petrowski arranged for a military craft to take us. We need to leave immediately."

Amelia's mom covered her forehead with her trembling hand. "Our home. Your dad—" Tears choked off her words. Amelia pulled her close. "Whatever happens, we'll get through it. I'll grab our stuff."

She nodded then faced Ben.

"Your dad's neighborhood wasn't hardest hit. But it was hit. There are no domestic flights into the area, but we have our own ride if you think you can handle riding in a military chopper."

She nodded. "What about Hutton?"

"He'll have to come with me. I can't risk leaving him."

Soon they piled into Manny's truck. A dozen men dressed in military garb and parachute harnesses occupied the truck bed.

"Who are they?" Amelia's mom asked.

"Petrowski tasked a few of our recruits and part of my team to help rescue anyone stranded from floods."

Manny drove with Hutton beside him. Ben rode shotgun and Amelia and her mother were in the backseat of Manny's extended cab.

Amelia recognized Manny's son, Javier, and his friend Enrique in the crowd. She also recognized Vince Reardon and Nolan Briggs, from Ben's PJ team. She didn't recognize the others.

Amelia's mom held her cell phone to her ear minutes later. "I can't reach your father."

"With a disaster of this magnitude all the phone lines and cell signals will be jammed. Just because you can't reach him doesn't mean he's not okay."

"But it doesn't mean he is, either." Amelia chewed her lip.

Amelia suddenly worried if her father were really okay, he probably wouldn't be the moment he saw her together with Ben. How would she handle that?

* * *

"You're pretty good with a hammer. Why don't you build yourself some sense and get your sorry boots off my roof." Amelia's father glowered as he towered over Ben.

Ben slapped another shingle down on the fresh plywood. "Your wife's home and all its contents will be ruined. Quit being so stubborn and accept the help, for her sake at least."

The man's fists clenched. "I don't need help from the likes of you."

Upon arriving, they'd discovered the North home's roof had been ripped off by wind, despite hurricane ties in the trussing. But at least her dad had survived and the rest of the structure stood sound.

It wouldn't for long with all this rain. After rescuing people trapped by flooding, his teammates and recruits had helped secure things with tarps and industrial plastic, then helped lay new plywood. But it would only be a matter of time until the rain slipped through the seams and ruined everything beyond repair.

They were fighting against time.

And Amelia's father was fighting against Ben.

Ben wanted to laugh as he looked around at his recruits and his team, pitching in around the property, cleaning up debris. They were a multiethnic group, and Ben was sure it was driving Amelia's dad beyond crazy to have the entire United Nations helping on his property. Ben fought a grin.

"What? You got nothin' to say?" the man said.

Hammer down, Ben drove the nail all the way in with one slam. "When I think of a sentence severe enough for you, I'll say it."

The man stood and squared off with Ben. "Why don't you get off this roof before you get pushed off."

"I'm a man of my word. I said I'm not leaving until it's repaired." Calm, Ben stood to get another pack of shingles.

The man clanged his hammer down and followed. "I oughta knock you off right here and now."

"You knock me off, you better knock me hard enough to knock me out. Because nothing short of a coma is keeping me off this roof."

"You sleepin' with my daughter?"

"No, sir. We're waiting until we get married."

"You asked her?"

"Nope."

"Why in tarnation not?"

"Haven't asked you yet."

"Well, well. What's the world coming to."

Ben started pounding the next layer of shingles in. The wind picked up, lifting one end of the shingle with it. He looked around for something to set on the end of the shingle so he could maintain positioning. Otherwise the roof would leak in the long run. This was taking twice as long due to winds. And storm-raging adversity from Amelia's dad.

"What, you ain't gonna defend yourself?"

"Not to you. No point."

"Just why is that?"

"Because all you wanna do is argue and intimidate me. And it's not going to work. I don't know what those people did to you in Nam, but I'm not them. I serve my country same as you did. I'd bleed to death for freedom. And you're certainly not going to deter me from wanting to marry Amelia and be a dad to Reece. And I won't stand for you yelling at Amelia."

"I might not be able to stop you from marrying her. But I can withhold my blessing and make your lives as miserable as a leech-infested rice paddy." He stormed off the roof.

Ben clenched his jaw against frustration. He'd never met a more stubborn, irrational man. Ben laughed. "I see where Amelia gets her tenacity."

The man half-turned as he started to climb off the roof.

Ben didn't miss the half smile the statement evoked that the man tried to bite back.

Progress. Albeit amoebic, Ben would take anything at this point. Ben swiped sweat from his brow and looked around the roof. Still a ton of work to be done. He'd work all night if he had to. He took a swig of water and screwed the cap back on as he surveyed the ground.

Amelia's mom and dad were talking. Heatedly. Amelia stood back a ways, face stern, arms folded. Hutton approached the man. Ben stood, preparing to defend his brother. But, for once, Amelia's dad's face softened as Hutton spoke. Ben knelt back down. "Wish I had my gun."

Nolan laughed.

"Nail gun. For the roof, Briggs. Not the man."

"For what it's worth, I'm proud of you, Dillinger. Guy's a jerk and you're keeping your cool in the face of ugly prejudice," Manny said.

Vince had taken Javier, Enrique, and most of the PJ recruits to other houses hit worse in the neighborhood. A handful of them stayed here to help with the North home.

Moments later, the three PJs heard a rhythmic clopping, as a hovercraft came into sight.

"That's Joel." Ben stood with his teammates.

Manny's military phone rang. He answered it. Seconds into the conversation, his dark face paled. He glanced at Ben and walked to the other side of the roof, hidden by the pitch.

Nolan eyed the hovercraft, then Manny. "Something's up."

"Yeah." And Ben didn't have a good feeling. Not at all.

"Dillinger." Manny surfaced from the other side of the roof and waved Ben over. The look on his face set Ben on alert.

Nolan moved close when Manny put his hand on Ben's shoulder. "I'm afraid I have bad news, bud. Your mom called." Emotion filled Manny's eyes. "Your dad…" Voice thickened, Manny shook his head.

Ben's legs went weak. Face in his hands, he sat.

Manny whispered something to Nolan and they both knelt, hands on Ben's back and shoulders. "I'm sorry, bud. He died very suddenly. Your mom's on standby for the next flight from Paris."

Ben surged to his feet. Swallowed against nausea. "But… He can't be gone. Him and mom, they didn't get to—"

But they had. For three weeks, thanks to Ben taking Hutton early. Speaking of which…

Ben whirled and paced. "How'm I gonna tell my brother?" Ben sat and picked up a hammer.

Nolan reached for the hammer. "Ben, Joel brought the chopper back for you and Hutton. You need to go be with your mom now. We can finish this roof."

A group ascended the roof. The sight of his entire team choked him up. Joel, Chance Garrison, Brockton Drake, all armed with nail guns and expressions of sympathy. Vince trailed behind with the recruits.

Amelia's dad peeked his head over the roof. He approached Ben, who knelt, pounding in nails. "Your superiors told Amelia about your dad. Then she told me." He dropped to his knees beside Ben. "Sorry for your loss."

Ben nodded.

"Me saying this doesn't mean I'm okay with your relationship with Amelia. But you don't have to stay and fix my roof, son."

Ben pounded another nail. "I told you I'd stay. And I told you I'm a man of my word." Plus, he needed a minute to figure out how to break news to Hutton about their dad. Did Hutton even understand the concept of death? How much had his mom told him?

"Dillinger, I can have the pilot fly you and Hutton back. Your mom's meeting you in Refuge. She's going to need you to be there. We can finish the roof for you," Joel said.

"Mom won't be back in the country for another twelve hours. We can get back in four. That means I have eight hours to get this roof done." Fighting tears, Ben pressed the nail gun into the edge of the shingle.

Pop. Pop. Pop.

His dad was gone.

Just, gone.

Pop. Pop. Pop.

Ben fought a crumbling dam of tears. And lost. They dripped. On his hands. Shingles. Nail gun.

Memories of helping his dad with the roof of the house they'd build together after the first one burned. Drips turned to steady streams. Big splotches spattered the shingles.

And everyone just stood there staring. He wished he could be alone. Hating the tears, he pressed the trigger.

Nothing.

He turned it over and opened the chamber.

Empty, just like his heart right now. Just like his mom's dreams with his dad. Vanished in a breath that could still be there had his dad gone to the doctor.

He pulled the ring that held the nails.

Dad's gone.

Gone.

Ben suddenly deplored the word. Hated it with everything in him.

Hope.

Heaven.

He'd see his dad again. So would Hutton. That's what Ben would say. Focus on the hope.

How?

"Heart attack?" Ben asked Joel, now beside him working.

Joel nodded. "Appeared to be."

Ben clenched his jaw and jammed another ring of nails into the machine.

Pop. Pop. Pop.

Frustration grew when the wind folded back the shingle. Ben fought the urge to slam it down and pressed it down instead.

More tears. Another gust. The shingle flipped up again.

Dropped to his knees beside Ben again, Amelia's dad moved forward and held it down. "Now look who's being stubborn." He scowled. "Maybe you and Amelia'd make a good pair after all."

Ben wanted to laugh. He'd said it with a scowl.

But at least he'd said it.

Chapter Twenty-One

"Ben is acting weird today." Amelia scooted over so Amber and Celia could sit next to her at church. "Granted, his father's funeral was just two months ago, but still. He's avoided me all morning."

Celia smirked and Amber cleared her throat with a cough that didn't seem real.

Amelia eyed them carefully. Suspicion mounted. "You two are acting strange, as well. You're all wiggly and stuff."

Her two friends simply sat straighter and smiled as if they held a secret. Ben stepped out from a side door and onto the church stage with his guitar. Where was the rest of the worship team? And why was Ben looking at her so seriously?

He approached the microphone. "Hi, everyone. Worship will start shortly. But first, I'd like to ask Amelia to come up."

Her mouth dried and her palms moistened. She looked at Celia and Amber for any clue as to what this was. Celia's grin and Amber's sparkling eyes told her it might be what she'd dreamed of since she was little. Arms numb and heart pounding from all the eyes on her, Amelia made her way to the stage.

Ben started strumming a tune she didn't recognize. All the while, never taking his eyes off of her. Now on stage with him,

Ben motioned her to the stool across from his. He strummed. He smiled. He never removed his eyes. A hush fell over the auditorium. The pastor brought Reece from her classroom to sit in the front row.

Still strumming, Ben put words to his soul-stirring song.

"From the moment I first saw you, I knew it was meant to be. Baby, I can't fathom life had God not brought you to me. So now I pledge my love forever and I'm asking you to be. My one and only, only one I love, my only love." Removing the strap, Ben set aside the guitar, and then knelt.

Amelia's hand flew to her mouth but Ben peeled her fingers from her face and held toward them a heart-shaped diamond. "Amelia, I've loved you from day one. I can no longer imagine life without you and Reece. Will you give me the honor of being your husband and a father to your beautiful daughter?"

The stool nearly toppled when Amelia surged from it and threw her arms around Ben's neck. "Yes! I will be your wife. And I love you, too." Cheers roared as the congregation stood and applauded. Reece ran onstage. Ben pulled her into a hug. An all-consuming hug Amelia knew meant he pledged his commitment to lead their family lovingly in the ways of God.

"Think he'll show?" Celia asked Amelia and Ben, seated around the reception table with their friends. Ben's mom, Amber, Celia, Miss Evie, Glorietta and Amelia's mom had decorated Refuge Community Center for her and Ben's engagement party, two months after Ben's dad's funeral.

Ben clasped Amelia's hand. "He was sent an invitation."

"Two invitations," Amelia's mom said.

"Three," Miss Harker added.

"Four." Miss Evie patted her hair.

"Five." Gus slid into a chair beside Evie.

Amelia eyed the empty doorway, then the wall clock. Ten minutes after the hour her engagement party was to have started. "Doesn't look like it. If he intends to be somewhere, Dad usually isn't late."

"Not unless I had to make a special stop for a special girl."

Amelia whirled. So did Ben.

Her dad approached with Manny. "Found him headed to the wrong building."

Amelia's dad extended the vase of flowers to Reece and motioned her close. He whispered something in her ear and then plucked a burgundy rose from the middle of the bouquet. He passed it to Reece, who covered her mouth and giggled before walking over to Amelia.

Hand outstretched, Reece presented the rose. "This is from me because you're a-a—" She dashed back to her grandpa and whispered, "What was I s'posed to say again?"

He whispered something in her ear and Reece raced back to Amelia. "Because you're a one of a kind mama and you've bloomed into something beautiful over the years."

"And I don't just mean on the outside." Her father stepped forward and extended the other eleven flowers. "Be right back."

He went out the side door, taking Nolan Briggs with him as he went. They started carting in boxes. All filled with flowers.

Amelia lost count when she got close to a thousand.

Her dad stood in front of her and knelt to one knee. "I know I don't deserve it. But I'm asking if you'll consider being my daughter again."

"I've never seen a dad propose to a kid," Bradley said.

"I'm proposing a change. I want a chance to be the kind of dad you always deserved, Amelia. You're a good mom. And I know you'll be a good wife. So, will you give me the honor of letting me walk you down that aisle?"

Flowers in both hands, she knelt and hugged her father for the first time in years. "Yes. I forgive you." She leaned back and laughed. "But I have a few questions."

"You always did." He chuckled.

"Why so many flowers?"

He winked at Ben. "I have it on good faith from a man I've come to respect that you like burgundy roses. These are to make up for all the times I should have known that and didn't. Besides, I can't let him steal your whole heart. I'm hoping there's still room left for me."

She hugged him again. "What changed your mind?"

"Not my mind. My heart. Ben did. And—" he pointed to Hutton "—that feller right over there. The day you boys trespassed on my property to fix my roof without permission." He chuckled. "For which I'm now grateful. And Hutton had a talk with me."

"Hutton? What did he say?" Ben asked.

"Right after I threatened to toss you off the roof, he told me he thought I was mean. He asked me why I had pictures of Jesus up on my walls when I didn't love like Him." He laughed. "He went on to tell me that he didn't know how I could tell everybody I was a Christian because he'd looked and looked and looked all day and couldn't see Jesus living anywhere in my heart."

Hutton grinned, clearly pleased with himself.

"I also snuck into the funeral. You all didn't see me because I came late, left early and got the heck out of dodge. I didn't want to bring more pain on the family. But when I saw Hutton pat his daddy's cold hand and tell him he'd be happy to know that him and Ben were best friends now, just like his dad always said would happen, something broke in me." He swallowed.

Ben swallowed, too. Amelia grasped his hand.

Amelia's dad cleared his throat. "I realized I wasn't promised another breath. That I was ugly on the inside and it don't matter what a person looks like outwardly. I grew ashamed of myself and of the prejudices I'd held, and asked God to help me let it go. I also wanted to save my marriage."

Amelia's mom stood by him and put her hand to his back.

Amelia's dad looked at Ben. "Don't know how this woman put up with the likes of me for so many years. All I ask is that you make things better for my daughter and Reece than I did for my wife and Amelia. You give me your word on that, and we're good."

"On my honor, sir. I will."

"I know you will. I believe it. I also believe you need to know I'd be honored to be your father-in-law."

Hutton tapped Amelia's dad on the shoulder. "Um, would you be my father-in-law too? Because I don't have a dad anymore. He went to heaven."

The man's eyes filled with tears and he hugged Hutton. "Buddy, you can call me whatever you want. Just as long as you call me when you need someone to talk to about missing your daddy."

They went off and talked. Ben faced Amelia and grasped her hands. Warmth filled her heart and hope wasn't far behind it.

"Let's pray, Mommy. Together!"

"I don't know what to say," Amelia whispered. "Other than to thank You, God for giving me a newly made family by changing Dad's heart, and for leading me to Refuge." She closed her eyes and squeezed Ben's hand.

Taking Reece's hand and keeping Amelia's in his other, Ben nodded to Hutton, bowed his head and squeezed back. "And for giving me such a smart brother and this ready-made family."

* * * * *

Dear Reader,

I came to know God as an adult partly as a result of His people showing kindness to me. They loved me as I was, even though I wasn't like them. They didn't expect me to act like a Christian, because I wasn't. Yet I knew there was something different about them. That they hung out with me and genuinely cared about me, even when I didn't share their beliefs, made me want to know the God they served. In the same way, Amelia was drawn back to God by the kindness of Ben and other Christians in Refuge. They determined to love her and help her without expecting anything in return. Yet, they did pray for her to come into a right relationship with God. Because of spiritual abuse, Amelia had a distorted view of God; she saw Him through a clogged filter of His flawed people. I don't know your church background, and I don't know how you view God. But I do know that God knows you intimately and has seen every day of your life. He feels our struggles. I pray that you have a place where you can worship with a body of believers in Jesus. A place that feels like home. A place that feels like family. I love hearing from readers. I invite you to e-mail me at Cheryl@CherylWyatt.com or write me at P.O. Box 2955, Carbondale, IL 62902-2955.

Blessings on you and yours,

Cheryl Wyatt

QUESTIONS FOR DISCUSSION

1. Ben's brother Hutton has Mosaic Down Syndrome. Through the story, Ben didn't often have confidence in his ability to do or say the right thing because he was afraid of hurting Hutton's feelings. Do you ever struggle with this when relating to someone with a disability? How do you wish you could respond?

2. Amelia falls on tough times in the book. Have you ever been in a situation in your life where you've had to rely on total strangers for help? How did you respond? Do you think you would have responded differently, or much the same as Amelia did, in choosing to trust Ben and his friends?

3. Amelia packed up everything she had and moved to another state with her daughter because she had high hopes for a job. Then things fell through. Have you ever suffered a disappointment such as this? Do you work with a difficult boss? If so, how do you cope?

4. Ben fell in love with Amelia and it didn't bother him that she was a single mother. Have you ever been in a single-parent home? If so, what are the struggles you had that you wished people would have been more aware of? If not, do you think you'd feel more comfortable asking your family for help, or your local church? Why or why not?

5. Ben is a man of his word. He was determined to help Amelia's dad even when the man was mean. Have you ever been in a situation where you felt obligated to do something for someone because you gave your word,

only to find the task was more challenging than you imagined? If so, how did you manage to push through?

6. Amelia had been shunned by the church for being an unwed mother. She found it hard to plug back in but she finally did. What was it that drew her to Refuge Community Church? How do you think your church would respond to an unwed parent visiting? How would you respond?

7. When Amelia learns that Ben is a Christian, she realizes that his relationship with God was the driving force behind his helping her. Of course he was attracted to her, but for the most part, his motives weren't self-serving. Have you ever met a person who you suspected to be a Christian because of acts of kindness they did? Did you find out later they were?

8. In *Ready-Made Family*, the bed and breakfast owner gives Hutton a job. Did this aspect of the book touch you? Why or why not?

9. Amelia can't believe her good fortune when this hunky airman not only voiced interest in her, but in her daughter. At what point in the story did you recognize that Ben wasn't going to give up on Amelia? Do you have someone like that in your life?

10. Amelia left her parents' house because of harsh words. Do you agree it was wise of her to set out on her own with a daughter to care for? Do you think she did the right thing for herself and for Reece?

11. Amelia's dad was bound by prejudice. Ben's kindness combated that, and God used it to soften the man's heart,

especially when he saw Ben's determination to help repair the storm-damaged roof despite getting word that his own father had died. If you were Ben in that situation, how do you think you would have responded?

12. Amelia lands a wonderful job that she doesn't feel she deserves or is qualified for. Has there been someone in authority who has had more belief in you than you had in yourself? What do you think motivated the bed and breakfast owner to take a chance on Amelia? Do you feel this was risky or wise on the business owner's part, and why?

13. Refuge is a community that lives up to its name. Throughout the book, Amelia picks up on a conspiracy of kindness. Would you like to live in a small town like this, where people reach out and help one another? Or would you feel your privacy was invaded and want everyone to mind their own business? Why so?

Turn the page for a sneak peek of
Shirlee McCoy's suspense-filled story,
THE DEFENDER'S DUTY
On sale in May 2009
from Steeple Hill Love Inspired® Suspense.

After weeks in intensive care, police officer Jude
Sinclair is finally recovering from the hit-and-run
accident that nearly cost him his life. But was it an
accident after all? Jude has his doubts—which get
stronger when he spots a familiar black car outside his
house: the same kind that accelerated before running
him down two months ago. Whoever wants him dead
hasn't given up, and anyone close to Jude is in danger.
Especially Lacey Carmichael, the stubborn, beautiful
home-care aide who refuses to leave his side, even if it
means following him into danger....

"We don't have time for an argument," Jude said. "Take a look outside. What do you see?"

Lacey looked and shrugged. "The parking lot."

"Can you see your car?"

"Sure. It's parked under the streetlight. Why?"

"See the car to its left?"

"Yeah. It's a black sedan." Her heart skipped a beat as she said the words, and she leaned closer to the glass. "You don't think that's the same car you saw at the house tonight, do you?"

"I don't know, but I'm going to find out."

Lacey scooped up the grilled-cheese sandwich and shoved it into the carryout bag. "Let's go."

He eyed her for a moment, his jaw set, his gaze hot. "*We're* not going anywhere. You are staying here. I am going to talk to the driver of that car."

"I think we've been down this road before and I'm pretty sure we both know where it leads."

"It leads to you getting fired. Stay put until I get back, or forget about having a place of your own for a month." He stood and limped away, not even giving Lacey a second glance as he crossed the room and headed into the diner's kitchen area.

Probably heading for a back door.

Lacey gave him a one-minute head start and then followed, the hair on the back of her neck standing on end and issuing a warning she couldn't ignore. Danger. It was somewhere close by again, and there was no way she was going to let Jude walk into it alone. If he fired her, so be it. As a matter of fact, if he fired her, it might be for the best. Jude wasn't the kind of client she was used to working for. Sure, there'd been other young men, but none of them had seemed quite as vital or alive as Jude. He didn't seem to need her, and Lacey didn't want to be where she wasn't needed. On the other hand, she'd felt absolutely certain moving to Lynchburg was what God wanted her to do.

"So, which is it, Lord? Right or wrong?" She whispered the words as she slipped into the diner's hot kitchen. A cook glared at her, but she ignored him. Until she knew for sure why God had brought her to Lynchburg, Lacey could only do what she'd been paid to do—make sure Jude was okay.

With that in mind, she crossed the room, heading for the exit and the client that she was sure was going to be a lot more trouble than she'd anticipated when she'd accepted the job.

Jude eased around the corner of the restaurant, the dark alleyway offering him perfect cover as he peered into the parking lot. The car he'd spotted through the window of the restaurant was still parked beside Lacey's. Black. Four door. Honda. It matched the one that had pulled up in front of his house, and the one that had run him down in New York.

He needed to get closer.

A soft sound came from behind him. A rustle of fabric. A sigh of breath. Spring rain and wildflowers carried on the cold night air. Lacey.

Of course.

"I told you that you were going to be fired if you didn't stay where you were."

"Do you know how many times someone has threatened to fire me?"

"Based on what I've seen so far, a lot."

"Some of my clients fire me ten or twenty times a day."

"Then I guess I've got a ways to go." Jude reached back and grabbed her hand, pulling her up beside him.

"Is the car still there?"

"Yeah."

"Let me see." She squeezed in closer, her hair brushing his chin as she jockeyed for a better position.

Jude pulled her up short. Her wrist was warm beneath his hand. For a moment he was back in the restaurant, Lacey's creamy skin peeking out from under her dark sweater, white scars crisscrossing the tender flesh. She'd shoved her sleeve down too quickly for him to get a good look, but the glimpse he'd gotten was enough. There was a lot more to Lacey than met the eye. A lot she hid behind a quick smile and a quicker wit. She'd been hurt before, and he wouldn't let it happen again. No way was he going to drag her into danger. Not now. Not tomorrow. Not ever. As soon as they got back to the house, he was going to do exactly what he'd threatened—fire her.

"It's not the car." She said it with such authority, Jude stepped from the shadows and took a closer look.

"Why do you say that?"

"The one back at the house had tinted glass. Really dark. With this one, you can see in the back window. Looks like there is a couple sitting in the front seat. Unless you've got two people after you, I don't think that's the same car."

She was right.

Of course she was.

Jude could see inside the car, see the couple in the front seats. If he'd been thinking with his head instead of acting on the anger that had been simmering in his gut for months, he would have seen those things long before now. "You'd make a good detective, Lacey."

"You think so? Maybe I should make a career change. Give up home-care aide for something more dangerous and exciting." She laughed as she pulled away from his hold and stepped out into the parking lot, but there was tension in her shoulders and in the air. As if she sensed the danger that had been stalking Jude, felt it as clearly as Jude did.

"I'm not sure being a detective is as dangerous or as exciting as people think. Most days it's a lot of running into brick walls. Backing up, trying a new direction." He spoke as he led Lacey across the parking lot, his body still humming with adrenaline.

"That sounds like life to me. Running into brick walls, backing up and trying new directions."

"True, but in my job the brick walls happen every other day. In life, they're usually not as frequent." He waited while she got into her car, then closed the door, glancing in the black sedan as he walked past. An elderly woman smiled and waved at him, and Jude waved back, still irritated with himself for the mistake he'd made.

Now that he was closer, it was obvious the two cars he'd seen weren't the same. The one at his place had been sleeker and a little more sporty. Which proved that when a person wanted to see something badly enough, he did.

"That wasn't much of a meal for you. Sorry to cut things short for a false alarm." He glanced at Lacey as he got into the Mustang, and was surprised that her hand was shaking as she shoved the key into the ignition.

He put a hand on her forearm. "Are you okay?"

"Fine."

"For someone who is fine, your hands sure are shaking hard."

"How about we chalk it up to fatigue?"

"How about you admit you were scared?"

"Were? I still am." She started the car, and Jude let his hand fall away from her arm.

"You don't have to be. We're safe. For now."

"It's the 'for now' part that's got me worried. Who's trying to kill you, Jude? Why?"

"If I had the answers to those questions, we wouldn't be sitting here talking about it."

"You don't even have a suspect?"

"Lacey, I've got a dozen suspects. More. Every wife who's ever watched me cart her husband off to jail. Every son who's ever seen me put handcuffs on his dad. Every family member or friend who's sat through a murder trial and watched his loved one get convicted because of the evidence I put together."

"Have you made a list?"

"I've made a hundred lists. None of them have done me any good. Until the person responsible comes calling again, I've got no evidence, no clues and no way to link anyone to the hit and run."

"Maybe he won't come calling again. Maybe the hit and run was an accident, and maybe the sedan we saw outside your house was just someone who got lost and ended up in the wrong place." She sounded like she really wanted to believe it. He should let her. That's what he'd done with his family. Let them believe the hit and run was a fluke thing that had happened and was over. He'd done it to keep them safe. He'd do the opposite to keep Lacey from getting hurt.

* * * * *

*Will Jude manage to scare Lacey away, or will he learn
that the best way to keep her safe is to keep her close…
for as long as they both shall live? To find out, read
THE DEFENDER'S DUTY by Shirlee McCoy
Available May 2009
from Love Inspired Suspense*

REQUEST YOUR FREE BOOKS!

2 FREE INSPIRATIONAL NOVELS
PLUS 2
FREE
MYSTERY GIFTS

Love Inspired.

YES! Please send me 2 FREE Love Inspired® novels and my 2 FREE mystery gifts (gifts are worth about $10). After receiving them, if I don't wish to receive any more books, I can return the shipping statement marked "cancel". If I don't cancel, I will receive 4 brand-new novels every month and be billed just $4.24 per book in the U.S. or $4.74 per book in Canada, plus 25¢ shipping and handling per book and applicable taxes, if any*. That's a savings of over 20% off the cover price! I understand that accepting the 2 free books and gifts places me under no obligation to buy anything. I can always return a shipment and cancel at any time. Even if I never buy another book, the two free books and gifts are mine to keep forever.

113 IDN ERXA   313 IDN ERWX

Name _____ (PLEASE PRINT)

Address _____ Apt. # _____

City _____ State/Prov. _____ Zip/Postal Code _____

Signature (if under 18, a parent or guardian must sign)

Order online at www.LoveInspiredBooks.com

Or mail to Steeple Hill Reader Service:
IN U.S.A.: P.O. Box 1867, Buffalo, NY 14240-1867
IN CANADA: P.O. Box 609, Fort Erie, Ontario L2A 5X3

Not valid to current subscribers of Love Inspired books.

Want to try two free books from another series?
Call 1-800-873-8635 or visit www.morefreebooks.com

* Terms and prices subject to change without notice. N.Y. residents add applicable sales tax. Canadian residents will be charged applicable provincial taxes and GST. Offer not valid in Quebec. This offer is limited to one order per household. All orders subject to approval. Credit or debit balances in a customer's account(s) may be offset by any other outstanding balance owed by or to the customer. Please allow 4 to 6 weeks for delivery. Offer available while quantities last.

Your Privacy: Steeple Hill Books is committed to protecting your privacy. Our Privacy Policy is available online at www.SteepleHill.com or upon request from the Reader Service. From time to time we make our lists of customers available to reputable third parties who may have a product or service of interest to you. If you would prefer we not share your name and address, please check here. ☐

LIREG08R

Love Inspired

TITLES AVAILABLE NEXT MONTH

Available April 28, 2009

BLIND-DATE BRIDE by Jillian Hart
The McKaslin Clan
It's police officer Max Decker's lucky day when he and
Brianna McKaslin both get stood up by their blind dates in
the same restaurant! Max isn't ready to give his heart to anyone,
especially someone as vulnerable as Brianna. But when he realizes
she's as sweet as the cakes she bakes, he's not sure he'll ever be able
to let her go.

THE BABY BOND by Linda Goodnight
Firefighter Nic Carano loves being a bachelor, until a rescued
baby leads him to the woman of his dreams. Suddenly a mother,
Cassidy Willis is grateful for all the help Nic and his family have
offered with her infant nephew, but she isn't sure she can give her
heart to someone whose life is always in danger. It's up to Nic
to show her the bond between them and her baby could be the
forever kind.

TIDES OF HOPE by Irene Hannon
Lighthouse Lane
Everyone in Nantucket may be smitten with Coast Guard
Lieutenant Craig Cole, but single mom Kate MacDonald can't
stand him, even if he has captured the heart of her little girl.
Kate doesn't want to like him—she certainly doesn't want to *love*
him—but Craig's quiet honor might win her heart after all.

THE COWBOY NEXT DOOR by Brenda Minton
Jay Blackhorse is not about to let a city girl like Lacey Gould get
under his skin. But that won't stop the cowboy cop from offering
her and her baby niece all the help he can. When a dark secret from
Lacey's past returns, will his help be enough? And who will help
Jay once he realizes he's fallen for the city girl next door?